LEAVING CLARE

ALSO BY GERALDINE O'NEILL

Tara's Destiny

Tara Flynn

Tara's Fortune

The Grace Girls

A Different Kind of Dream

PUBLISHED BY POOLBEG

*L*EAVING
*C*LARE

Geraldine O'Neill

POOLBEG

Published 2010
by Poolbeg Press Ltd
123 Grange Hill, Baldoyle
Dublin 13, Ireland
E-mail: poolbeg@poolbeg.com

© Geraldine O'Neill 2009

The moral right of the author has been asserted.

Typesetting, layout, design © Poolbeg Press Ltd.

1 3 5 7 9 10 8 6 4 2

A catalogue record for this book is available from the British Library.

ISBN 978-1-84223-381-8

Typeset by Patricia Hope in Palatino 10.3/14
Printed by
Litografia Rosés, S.A., Spain

www.poolbeg.com

NOTE ON THE AUTHOR

Geraldine O'Neill was born in Lanarkshire, Scotland, and now lives in County Offaly in Ireland. She is married to Michael Brosnahan and has two grown-up children, Christopher and Clare.

ACKNOWLEDGEMENTS

Thanks to Paula Campbell and all the staff at Poolbeg for their valued support and encouragement. A special mention to my editor, Gaye Shortland, for her work and dedication in reducing the manuscript, without losing the essence of the story or her sense of humour!

Warm thanks to Mandy, James and all the staff at Watson-Little for their constant support of my writing.

I am indebted to my mother-in-law, Mary Hynes (Brosnahan) for her patience with my research about the dance halls, fashions and lifestyle in Ireland in the fifties. Whilst Kilnagree and my characters are all fictitious, authentic details about the time and area help make them feel real.

Thanks to the many people who encourage my writing: the O'Neill and Brosnahan families, and people in Stockport, Ireland and Scotland. I must also mention my good friends Page and Eric in Annapolis.

I wish Brother Baiste good luck with his continuing travels, and I look forward to his long descriptive e-mails from different corners of the world.

To all the pupils in Daingean National School, many of whom show great talent in writing. I promised two of my pupils that they would see their names in my book so hello to Corey Galvin and Michael Matthews!

A warm welcome to our lovely twin nephews, Cormac and Lorcan O'Neill, and Michael O'Hara and Isabelle Brosnahan.

A final thanks to my readers here and abroad who continually lift my spirits by asking when the next book is due.

As always, loving thanks to Mike and Chris and Clare.

With love to

Michael and Alison Murphy

*friends through the good
and not so good times*

Change is the law of life.
And those who look only to the past or present
Are certain to miss the future.

JOHN F KENNEDY

Chapter 1

April 1958

County Clare, Ireland

Rose Barry woke at half-past eight to a blue sky more suited to August than April, and the smell of bacon and sausages wafting through the small cottage that she shared with her parents and grandmother Martha, her seventeen-year-old brother Paul and her two younger sisters Eileen and Veronica.

One of her first thoughts was whether Michael and Ruairí Murphy would call in at Slattery's pub that afternoon. Most of the local girls had an eye for them but working part-time in the only pub-cum-shop in the area gave the dark-haired, eighteen-year-old Rose a distinct advantage. Well, if they didn't come in during the afternoon for their usual Saturday game of cards, they would definitely be there later on. The two lads spent most weekend nights in Slattery's, joining in with the music sessions – Michael on the fiddle and Ruairí on the accordion.

Rose smiled at the thought of the day ahead and threw the bedcovers back.

Martha Barry had been up and about a good hour or more before Rose stirred. Dressed in her customary cross-over, flowery apron, she had lit the stubborn old Stanley range and then set about cooking breakfast for the whole family as she routinely did at the weekends. Rose's mother, Kathleen – a dark-haired, good-looking woman who was an older version of her daughter – had left the house around eight o'clock as usual. She worked in the local Guards' Barracks, doing all the cooking and washing and general looking-after of the Guards.

"You should have taken a bit of a lie-in for yourself," Rose told her grandmother as she sat down at the white-painted kitchen table. The comment was only perfunctory, as it would have been a sad Saturday if she had no cooked breakfast made for her.

"Ah sure, a young girleen like you needs a decent bite when you have a good walk ahead of you and then be on your feet all day at work." Martha put the plate of bacon, sausage and black and white pudding in front of her grand-daughter, then affectionately tousled her thick, straight hair. "You can make a start on that. I have a bit of fried soda bread and an egg still cooking in the pan for you."

Then she went back to the range where she would stay contentedly for most of the morning until all the family had been fed.

The twenty-minute walk down to Slattery's bar at the quayside was all the more pleasant since it was such a lovely sunny morning, and Rose called out or stopped to chat to various neighbours who lived in the whitewashed cottages along the way. On a fine morning there were always people around the houses, bringing in turf or emptying ashes or going in and out tending to the cattle.

Rose's Saturday shift started off on a high note when

she arrived at the pub to find that the landlord and his wife were all dressed up and ready to head out for a day in Galway. Mary Slattery was bustling around in her good red coat between the bar and shop, her black court shoes tapping on the old stone floor, while Joe was huffing and puffing about being made to wear a suit and kept running his finger inside the neck of his starched white shirt.

"Will you leave your shirt alone, for God's sake!" Mary hissed as she went to the till in the shop with a bag full of copper which would be needed for change.

Joe looked at Rose, rolled his eyes to the ceiling and sighed loudly.

Mary put her hands on her hips and gave him a long look. "Get yerself out to that car and get it warmed up," she told him, "and don't be acting the eejit with me this morning!"

Joe shook his head and smiled. "You're easy riled, Mary Slattery, you're easy riled."

Mary banged the small sack of coins down on the bar counter and then turned to look at Rose with a resigned look on her face. "What would you do with an *amadán* like that?"

Rose just smiled. She listened carefully as Mary Slattery ran through a list of instructions for the day.

"Now remember, no tick in the bar – *under any circumstances* – for Noel Pearson, and no tick in the shop for the Mullens and the Foleys." She tutted loudly. "I could kill that Joe for startin' that racket off – letting them pay when they like! They think we're running a charity here!"

Rose nodded her head understandingly, although she

had already been told by the landlord to give a loaf and a few potatoes to the two aforementioned families any time they were in need. But always to make sure his wife wasn't around.

Mary picked her handbag up. "I know you're a sensible girl, Rose, and I can trust you to manage things on your own like you did when we went to the wedding. And if I'm satisfied, there might be a little bit extra in your pay this evening."

With a final glance about the premises, she went to join her husband.

Rose stood at the door of the pub watching as the landlord's car disappeared off along the coast road, then she went back inside, delighted to have the place to herself for the day.

It was rare that Rose had anywhere to herself. It was very hard to be alone in the Barrys' house. Especially in the colder weather when everyone congregated in the kitchen seeking the warmth and comfort of the old range. Occasionally on a warm summer day, Rose would go into the bedroom she shared with her grandmother and younger sisters, to lie on her bed and enjoy a few minutes of cool solitude. But it never lasted. After a while the younger ones would come looking for her, and if she chased them out her mother would appear shortly afterwards to check that she was all right.

Rose never quite found the words to explain her need for a bit of peace and quiet, to have some time to herself just to think. It always came out sounding a bit strange and broody.

"As long as you're all right," her mother would say.

"As long as there's not something wrong . . . something you don't want to tell us."

And so it was easier for Rose to keep smiling and pleasant and join in with the general hustle and bustle of the house.

As she entered her teenage years and was allowed a bit more freedom, Rose found that walking down to the shop or post office on her own allowed her to have the space and the peace that she couldn't find at home. The mile or so there and back – feeling the fresh sea breeze running through her hair and the warmth of the sun on her face – gave her exactly what she needed. There were times when she walked really quickly to allow herself a short break later along the strand. Rose loved that. She could lose herself in the sound of the waves and among the small sea-pools in the rocks on the shoreline.

As she closed the door of the empty pub behind her, Rose decided that the chores could wait. Instead she slowly wandered around the bar, pausing at one of the four windows to gaze across the street to the small post office and the grey stony hills of The Burren which stretched out far beyond.

Nothing stirred apart from a few cattle in the field opposite.

Drifting to the back of the pub, she looked out over the shimmering, bluish-green water of Galway Bay where local fishermen eked out a seasonal living.

Then the bell from the small shop rang out, shattering the absolute silence and heralding the first of the morning's customers.

Rose had completed most of the tasks on the

landlady's list by the time Ruairí and Michael Murphy arrived in the bar. She was delighted to see them but her pleasant, casual manner gave no indication that she held them in any greater affection than the other local lads.

After she served them, Rose gave half her attention to the glasses she was rinsing and drying and the rest to the two fair-haired brothers as they played cards at the table by the window.

Time passed as she pottered about behind the bar. It was lovely to be able to do things at her own pace without having to keep watching out for Mary Slattery. She glanced over at the two brothers again and Ruairí, the younger, caught her eye. She immediately felt herself blush. They were both good-looking lads but it was Michael she preferred.

Ruairí held up his almost empty glass, the white frothy Guinness dregs sliding to the bottom. "We'll have another two pints when you're ready, Rose!"

The shop bell sounded.

"I'll be back in two ticks," Rose said, putting her drying cloth down on the counter.

She went through the door behind the bar and stepped down into the little shop.

Two thin, pale faces looked up at her – Patrick and Ella Foley. Around ten or eleven years of age, they were somewhere in the middle of a squad of nearly a dozen children. Like the other members of the family, they were inadequately dressed and to Rose's mind they looked too skinny and underfed.

"A stone of spuds, Rose," Patrick said, heaving an old battered shopping bag up on the counter. The handles of the bag had broken and were reinforced with pieces of twine.

Rose weighed out the stone of potatoes for them and piled more on top, just as Joe would have done if his wife wasn't in the vicinity to witness it. Then she reached under the counter to the tray of currant buns and gave them two of the staler ones, left over from the day before.

"Don't tell a soul I gave you them," she ordered, "or Mrs Slattery will take my life."

As soon as they were finished eating, the two children lifted the heavy bag between them again and Rose held the door and stood watching as they started the good mile's walk back home with their awkward load.

Rose was just putting the head on the pints of Guinness when the bar door swung open and a large group of lads came through, loudly discussing the match they were all heading for. Rose felt her cheeks immediately flame up, uncomfortably aware of being the only female in the place – and because she would have to serve them all herself. The fact that her younger brother Paul was in the middle of them didn't help. She would have the worry of him trying to sneak a glass or two of Guinness when he wasn't eighteen and risking the wrath of her father if he found out. As usual, he gave her the briefest salute of acknowledgement before disappearing into a corner with the noisy crowd.

She carried the pints over to the Murphys, earning two big smiles from them. When she came back she was inundated with orders from the other group and time flew as she drew pints and poured lemonade.

Eventually there were only three lads left leaning on

the bar. She flushed as she realised one of them was Liam O'Connor.

"Rose Barry! The finest lookin' girl in Kilnagree!" he announced, his hands drumming lightly on the counter. "*'The Darlin' Girl from Clare'*!"

Liam O'Connor was the tallest and most athletic-looking of all the lads in the parish and was hugely admired for his skills on the hurling field, being the only one of them to have reached the level to play in the county team. He worked hard and he played hard. Like many of the local lads, he kept two jobs going, working on the small family farm with his elderly father and helping his brother out with deliveries in his greengrocer's shop in Gort. He also did bits and pieces of woodwork and often helped his neighbours out with complicated repairs on furniture and windows.

Rose took a deep breath. "Now, lads," she said, affecting a casual manner she didn't at all feel, "what can I get ye?" She lifted the bar cloth and started to polish a glass she had already dried and polished earlier.

"I wouldn't mind a kiss," Liam went on, winking at the other two, "but I suppose, since it's the middle of the afternoon, I'll just have to make do with a pint of stout."

Rose gave an embarrassed smile and shook her head. "It doesn't matter what time of the day it is," she retorted lightly. "It's only drinks I'm serving."

One of the other lads clapped him on the back. "By Jaysus, O'Connor, you're the boyo when it comes to the women!"

Rose turned away now and, as she stood on her tip-toes to reach up to the shelf for the three glasses, she felt suddenly conscious of her skirt moving up higher on her legs and the flush on her cheeks grew deeper.

"If you want to take a seat, lads, I'll bring the drinks over to you when they're ready," she told them, anxious to remove herself from the spotlight of their stares. Especially Liam O'Connor's stare. The close attention he gave Rose always made her feel slightly unnerved.

"Go on, you two," Liam told his companions with a nod of his dark curly head. "I'll be across in a minute."

The two lads moved away from the bar now, used to taking the lead from him.

Liam paid and Rose started to pull the pints.

"It's a fine day," she said, keeping her eyes well away from Liam's face. She nodded towards the windows at the back. "I see there's a few fishing boats out now, taking advantage of the good weather . . ."

"Rose . . ." Liam said, leaning across the bar towards her, his voice softer and his manner suddenly serious, "I hope I didn't offend you earlier . . . about the kiss? I was only coddin' – a bit of oul' banter with the lads. I would hate you to think badly of me."

Rose rolled her eyes to the brown, smoke-stained ceiling. "Ah, sure I'm well used to it, working in here! I don't pay any attention to half of what's said."

He nodded his head slowly, his face still serious. "I was wondering . . . will you go with me into Galway this evenin' to see an oul' film? I have the loan of my brother's van for the night . . ."

Rose took a deep breath, her mind working rapidly on an excuse as she lifted the first pint onto the bar. With any of the other lads she would have just laughed and fobbed them off but she knew it wouldn't work with Liam. He was a couple of years older than the others and she knew his loudness was only a front for the other lads and that behind it he could be serious enough.

"I'm working again tonight," she told him in a low voice, turning away to top up the second pint.

"How about tomorrow night then? Or a night through the week?"

"I think my mother needs me at home . . ." She gave a little shrug, then bent her head so that her dark straight hair formed a curtain, shielding her from his stare. "And I don't think my father would be keen on me going to Galway in a van with a lad on my own."

Liam paused for a moment, his tanned brow furrowed in thought. Then he nodded his head. "Ah, sure, fair enough . . ."

Rose lifted the second pint onto the bar now, careful to keep her hand steady so as not to spill it. She didn't know what else to say to him so she stayed silent. She knew there was no point in giving him any hope because, even if she wanted to go out with him, there was no way her father would allow it.

When she'd started working in the pub, her father had warned her about the way some of the men treated women in pubs, especially when they had a few drinks on them.

"I know what I'm talking about, Rose," he told her. "I've heard the filth that comes out of their mouths after they've drunk more than their share, and I'm not having any daughter of mine putting up with the likes of that."

"Now, Stephen," her mother said, "you know well

that Joe and Mary Slattery wouldn't allow that to happen to Rose. They keep a close eye on everything that goes on in the bar and they'll make sure she always has someone sensible to see her home."

"I'm only warning her," he said quietly. He turned back to Rose. "Just make sure that you don't go making too free with any of them. There's no decent man that needs to be intoxicated to ask a woman out and, besides, you have time enough for all of that nonsense. You're only working in the place to make a few shillings, so make it plain to any of the young lads that spend half their week in Slattery's that you have no interest in any of them." He paused. "There's time enough for you to meet the right type of fellow who'll treat you decently and be able to look after you."

But, despite those strong words, she felt that her father approved of the two Murphy boys and that when the time was right he might even allow her to go out to a dance with them or to a concert. Even though he hadn't voiced anything of the sort, she had heard him say that the Murphys weren't just musically talented, they also had brains or they wouldn't have got the good jobs they both had in Gort.

But she knew he wouldn't allow the likes of Liam O'Connor anywhere near his family. And, actually, her father's strictness was a good excuse to get out of this particular situation. For all he was good-looking and confident – and for all that most of the other girls had an eye for him – Liam O'Connor just wasn't her type. He might be good on the playing field and a hard worker, but she was looking for more than that in a man.

"You'll be at the dance down in the hall next weekend?" Liam asked, as she put the third pint on the bar.

"Yes," she said, nodding her head.

"Well, keep me a dance, so," he said, his gaze still fixed on her.

"I will," she said, with a smile that didn't quite reach her eyes.

The shop bell gave a loud ring now, giving her the perfect excuse to end the conversation.

A short while later a small coach pulled in at the side of the pub. About eighteen lads came pouring out of it and they all made straight for the bar. They were supporters of the opposing team from a neighbouring village and they greeted the local lads they knew with a shout or a wave. A crowd this size arriving unannounced would have put pressure on the pub staff any Saturday afternoon but with Joe gone Rose felt overwhelmed – and more than a little self-conscious – as the crowd of lads tried to catch her attention and laughingly jostled with each other as they waited to get served.

Eventually Rose had served their first round of drinks and set about sorting out empty glasses before they returned in ones and twos for refills. Thankfully, the shop had been quiet but of course it didn't last. A small but steady stream of customers to the shop kept her busy going back and forth between there and the bar for the next hour or so.

At one point she was just returning to the bar when she saw Michael Murphy standing there waiting to be served and her heart skipped a beat.

"Last round," he told her light-heartedly, glancing up

at the clock. "We'll all be gone after this for the match and you'll get a bit of peace."

"Sure, it makes no difference to me," she replied in a cheery tone. "The busier it is, the quicker the time flies." Rose looked up at the clock now and realised that she should have called drinking-up time nearly five minutes ago. "Is it the same?" she asked him, feeling a little flustered as she rang the bell under the counter.

"It is," he said, indicating the two empty glasses he'd put on the bar.

Rose was conscious of him watching now as she pulled the two pints of Guinness.

"Have you heard from that cousin of yours lately?" he asked. "The one from Offaly – Hannah, isn't it?"

Rose suddenly stiffened at the mention of her cousin's name. The last time she'd been down for a holiday in Clare, last October, the dainty, blonde Hannah had made a hit with all the lads – but this was the first time that Michael Murphy had shown any particular interest in her. Hannah had obviously made a big impression on him. The thought gave Rose a tight feeling in her stomach.

"She keeps in touch regularly," she said, trying to sound normal. "I got a letter from her last week."

"And how's she doing? She was talking about going over to England or up to Dublin at some point, wasn't she? Did she go yet?"

"Oh, that's Hannah for you," Rose said, raising her eyebrows to the ceiling. "She's always planning to go somewhere and do something – but she's never left home yet. And there was no mention about her going anywhere in the letter." She put the two pint glasses to the side now, waiting for the froth to settle before filling them up to the brim. "That's as far as she gets, talking about it."

A small frown appeared on Michael Murphy's face. "It's a mighty big step – going away from home. But sometimes it's the only way forward." He leaned his elbows on the bar now, a thoughtful look on his face.

"Will you be playing at the dance next week?" Rose asked. Chatting about the music was an easier, more subtle way of finding out if the two brothers would be there.

"They have a three-piece band booked from Ballyvaughan," he said, nodding his head, "but we usually end up playing a few tunes one way or the other. I usually have the oul' fiddle along with me just in case."

Rose felt her heart lift. There hadn't been a dance in the local hall since Christmas. This coming weekend would be the first one of the year and thankfully there was no sign of Hannah travelling down for it. Rose had been careful not to mention it in any of her recent letters and Hannah hadn't enquired if there was a dance coming up – so all was safe on that front.

"I believe your cousin can play the piano," Michael said now. "She was telling me she's been going for lessons since she started school. She must be a well-accomplished player after all those years."

Rose felt a stab of irritation now and hoped that it didn't show on her face, because Michael Murphy might interpret it as jealousy – and it certainly wasn't. It was sheer annoyance at the fact that Hannah complained non-stop about her mother making her go for music lessons, moaning about having to practise every night at home, and yet, when she had been sitting all cosy with the musicians at the last dance, she had made out that she was absolutely passionate about her music just to get their attention.

"I've not heard her playing for a few years," Rose said casually, "but, like you say, she must be good if she's been practising all that time."

"I'd love to hear her playing. We must get her out to the hotel in Kinvara that has a piano some evening and let her play a few tunes for us all."

Rose nodded her head. "That's a good idea. It would make a bit of a change from here."

After he left the bar, Rose had a heavy feeling in her chest. The sort of feeling she got when she heard bad news. Why did Hannah have to spoil everything?

There was a time when they were younger when she had really liked her cousin – but that had changed. It was hard to like somebody when you couldn't trust them. Hannah had shown herself to be a liar on a number of occasions. She had no hesitation in making a story up on the spur of the moment to get herself out of an awkward situation. And she had involved Rose on a couple of occasions without even warning her about what she was going to say.

Rose tried to get on with her work now and not let the fact that Michael Murphy had enquired after Hannah annoy her. As she briskly dried the glasses to a fine polish, she comforted herself with the knowledge that Hannah wouldn't be coming to the next dance in any case.

Rose couldn't put her finger on what she actually liked about Michael, because he was – and always had been – a fairly deep and quiet type. Of course the fact that he worked in a bank – which made him a cut above the other local lads – was certainly a factor. But an even bigger attraction was the fact that he could play almost any tune on the fiddle. Even the older men grudgingly admitted that he was the best player they'd ever had in the area. He was the best fiddle player for miles.

But it was more than that. There was something about Michael Murphy's eyes – a strange, almost sad quality – that made her want to put her arms around him.

A short while later the few older men at the fire were finishing off the last mouthful of their whiskies for closing time and the younger lads finishing the dregs of their pints when the shop door went again.

Trained to the sound, Rose turned automatically and was moving down the step when she saw the petite but striking figure glide inside, clad in her customary waxed green hat and coat. There were only a few people Rose dreaded serving in Slattery's bar or shop – and this was one of them.

The fifty-odd-year-old widowed Leonora Bentley lived up in Dublin and she drove down to Kilnagree in her white Mercedes every so often to visit her daughter Diana. A schoolteacher in Gort, Diana was married to the local veterinary surgeon and they lived in the oldest and largest house in the village, overlooking Galway Bay. There had been a bit of talk when they first moved to Kilnagree, as the Bentleys were Protestant, but Diana had taken 'instructions' in the Catholic faith before they got married and was now a practising Catholic herself.

When Leonora paid her daughter and son-in-law a visit, she would always be seen first thing in the morning striding along the circular coast route that took her from the big white house along the edge of the sea and then onto the small main road that led to Kinvara and back around to the house again. After dinner in the evenings she took the exact same route again – a good brisk walk which covered approximately three miles.

Dressed in her long Barbour coat and hat, Leonora Bentley greeted everyone with an abrupt "Good morning" or "Good evening", depending on the time of day. She never broke the rhythm in her stride to wait for a return greeting, but carried straight on as though heading for an urgent appointment.

On the odd occasions that she came walking down to the post office, she sometimes looked into the shop for a loaf of fresh bread or some fresh scones or cakes. But she could go six months between one visit and the next.

If her straight-backed, elegant figure was seen going into the post office, Mary Slattery was notified immediately and she would take up residence behind the shop counter, all prepared should Mrs Bentley deign to come in. Joe would be ushered into the bar just in case he did or said anything in front of the sophisticated Dublin lady that might just show them up. Rose would also be kept in the background, unless she was needed to serve another customer to allow Mrs Slattery to devote all her care and attention to the lady.

But Mary Slattery obviously had not heard that Leonora Bentley was in Kilnagree on this particular occasion, as she had left no instructions with her young charge as to how she should approach or serve such an important customer.

Rose took a deep breath and went forward into the shop. "Hello, Mrs Bentley," she said in what she hoped was a cheery but polite voice. "What can I get you?"

"Nothing for the moment." The older woman's voice was unusually low and had a slight tremor in it but the usual strident edge was still there. "You can attend to your business . . . I just need a few moments' peace and quiet . . . *please*."

She moved backwards now until her legs touched the wooden bench under the window, then she sat down. She made a sudden 'oohing' sort of noise and pressed the palm of her hand up against her temple, inadvertently cocking her wide-brimmed green hat to the side.

Rose watched in alarmed silence, until Mrs Bentley looked up and caught her eye.

"Are you okay?" the young girl asked.

Leonora Bentley closed her eyes, then nodded her head. "It's probably a migraine. It came on very suddenly. I thought I would make it back to the house, but the pain is very intense . . ." She waved her hand towards the bar. "If you could get me a drink of water, I think I have some tablets in my pocket that will help."

The hurling supporters were all starting to leave the bar now as Rose came rushing through to pour a glass of water.

Liam O'Connor was heading towards the door when he saw her and made a quick detour over to the bar.

"You're sure you can't persuade your parents to let you out tonight?" he said.

Rose moved her head to look over his shoulder as Ruairí and Michael Murphy headed for the door, both giving her a casual salute as they went. She could barely conceal her irritation with Liam O'Connor for making her miss having a word with them before they went. "No," she said in a decisive tone. "I've told you already, I've got things to do at home."

Liam turned to see what she was looking at and his eyes narrowed when he realised it was the two brothers. He looked back at Rose and gave a small shrug. "I'll see you again, so . . ."

Rose went back through to the shop and saw that Leonora Bentley had her hat off and was holding her head in both her hands. Even in such a pose she looked elegant and her thick ash-blonde bobbed hair had hardly moved out of place.

"I have the water for you," Rose said in a voice loud enough to be heard but not too loud for her customer's painful head.

Very gingerly and with only one eye open, Leonora stretched her hand out for the glass. "Thank you, my dear," she said in a weary but grateful voice.

Rose moved back behind the counter. "If you need anything else?"

There was a few moments' silence as the woman put the pills in her mouth, took a gulp of water and then threw her head back to help swallow them down.

"A brandy," Mrs Bentley suddenly said, her usual commanding tone back in her voice. "And I think you'd better make it a large one."

Rose hesitated. The bar was officially closed now until five o'clock and she had been reminded by both the landlord and his wife to stick strictly to those hours. She quickly asked herself what either of them would do, if they were in this situation.

Two minutes later Rose came back out into the shop holding a glass with a good measure of Hennessy's brandy in one hand and a small jug of water in the other. "I'm not sure how much water you want in it . . ."

"The same amount of water as brandy will be fine."

"Is the pain in your head easing yet?" Rose carefully poured water into the brandy.

"Very slightly . . . but it's affecting my eyes as well."

Rose took the empty water tumbler from Leonora Bentley's outstretched hand and gave her the brandy glass. "If you sit for a while and give the tablets and the brandy a chance to work . . ."

"That's exactly what I intend to do."

Rose looked out of the window now and saw two local women approaching the shop. Instinctively she knew Mrs Bentley would not want to be viewed in such a position. If it were her own mother or grandmother they would be mortified to be seen ill in a public place.

"Mrs Bentley, I see some customers coming across to the shop . . ."

"Oh, good heavens!" she groaned and made to stand up, looking suddenly flustered.

"Maybe you'd like to sit in the bar for a few minutes?" Rose suggested. "There's no one in there and there's a nice fire on."

"Perfect."

She straightened her back, took a deep breath and then made her rather unsteady way behind the counter and into the bar.

As she passed by, Rose was struck for the first time by how small and slender the Dublin woman actually was. She couldn't have been more than a few inches over five feet, but there was something about her manner and attitude that gave the impression of a taller, formidable type of woman. She was very different to the other females in Kilnagree. She dressed differently, spoke differently and acted quite differently.

In many ways – particularly when she was dressed in her severe winter outfits – she seemed older than women of her own age. But when summer came, in her cream linen trousers and straw hat or flowery dresses and dark sunglasses, she suddenly seemed much younger – almost girlish.

And Rose and her mother and granny weren't the only ones to comment on this – she had overheard two of the men in the bar talking about Leonora Bentley when they'd had a few drinks, and their coarse comments left her in no doubt that she was still an attractive woman.

As she bustled about organising the bread and vegetables the two women had asked for, Rose glanced every now and again into the bar, but she couldn't see any sign of Mrs Bentley by the table at the fire.

When she went back into the bar the place was strangely dark. At first she thought there was no one there but when she looked more closely she saw a stretched-out form on the long bench by the window. It dawned on Rose that she had obviously reached up and closed the curtains to keep out the light.

Rose tip-toed over to the bench. She could hear the

gentle sound of Leonora Bentley's snoring. The tablets and the alcohol had obviously done the trick.

Very quietly, Rose worked around the sleeping figure, lifting glasses and ashtrays across to the bar where she left them in a neat pile to wash later, lest the noise of the rickety old tap wake Leonora up.

She then went silently around the tables with a damp cloth and a polishing rag to clean and shine to the standard that Mary Slattery would expect when she returned.

She wandered back into the shop and tidied around there for a few minutes and was standing with her arms folded looking out of the window when she saw her mother's neat figure coming out of the post office and making towards the shop. Kathleen Barry often walked down to post things for the Guards or letters for herself or her mother-in-law. Rose moved quickly to open the door as gently as she could and then held it open to keep the bell mute. As her mother approached the shop, Rose pressed her finger to her lips to warn her to be quiet.

"What's wrong?" Kathleen whispered, her brow deeply furrowed.

"Mrs Bentley – Diana Tracey's mother – is asleep in the bar!"

"What?" Kathleen's face was a picture of utter shock.

"She has a bad migraine headache," Rose whispered. "She nearly collapsed when she came in so I gave her a drink and she took some tablets for it."

Kathleen leaned on the counter and stretched up on her toes to try to see into the bar.

"She's lying on the old bench at the window," said Rose. She motioned to her mother to move further down the counter so they couldn't be heard talking, just in case Mrs Bentley woke up. "She had a brandy as well – she said that sometimes helps."

"A *brandy*?" Her mother's face was truly aghast now. "A brandy at this time of the day? Good God! And her one of the Quality! Who would believe it?"

Rose shrugged. "She must be used to taking it for the headaches."

"She'll have a bigger headache waking up after drinking that at this hour of the day!" Kathleen shook her head in a bemused fashion. She had very limited experience of alcohol – the odd sherry at Christmas or funerals – and it always went straight to her head. "Of course, she's a Protestant," she said now. "They have their own strange ways . . ."

Rose didn't say that the brandy had actually been a large one, as she knew her mother would only disapprove further and might well gossip about it to her father or, even worse, the Guards down at the barracks. Since working in the pub, she had come to realise that her parents had a very puritanical attitude to drink.

Kathleen shook her head again and turned her attention to her daughter. "Anyway, one of the reasons I called in was to tell you that I got a letter from your Auntie Sheila yesterday. I meant to tell you last night but I clean forgot."

"And what did she have to say?" Rose asked, lifting the small soft brush from under the counter to wipe away a few stray crumbs from an empty cake tray.

"She said that Hannah is definitely coming down for the dance next weekend – won't that be nice for you?"

Rose suddenly froze, the brushing of the crumbs forgotten. "But how does she know about the dance?" Her dark, arched eyebrows were knitted together in annoyance. "I never told her about it."

"Oh, I mentioned it to Sheila a few weeks ago in one of my letters," Kathleen said airily, "and I told her to tell Hannah about it, since she enjoyed the last dance so much." She smiled at her daughter now. "I thought it would be company for you and your father won't mind you going if she's there with you. He can hardly stop you going if Hannah has come all the way down from Offaly and everyone else is walking down to it." She looked at the expression on Rose's face now. "Is there something wrong? Do you not want Hannah to come down for the dance? Have you had a row or something?"

Rose forced herself to smile. "No, no . . . it's just that I thought Hannah was saving up to move to Dublin or London. I didn't think she'd have the money to come down."

"Oh, there's no fear of Hannah going anywhere! She has it too comfortable at home with only herself there, now the boys have gone. And anyway, Sheila says she still has her birthday money saved from January and she's keeping it for the coach fare down. She said that Hannah was writing to tell you what coach she will be arriving on next Wednesday or Thursday. I suppose you'll get the letter Monday."

"That's grand," Rose said, trying to sound enthusiastic. She pinned a smile on her face now. It was obviously all arranged. Hannah would be there at the dance making big eyes at Michael Murphy and all the other lads – and there wasn't a single thing that she could do about it.

Chapter 2

When Rose went back into the bar, Leonora Bentley was awake and sitting up straight on the bench.

"Thank you so much for being so kind and helpful," she said. "I'm feeling better now. I think I should be able to walk back to the house."

"It was no trouble," Rose told her, surprised that she felt quite relaxed with the older woman. Everyone she knew was very wary of her and the younger ones dodged out of her way if they saw her coming. Rose suddenly saw her as an unusual but not unlikeable woman who was different from anyone she had ever met. In fact there was something about her now that she found intriguing. "I could close the shop for ten minutes and walk back with you, if you like."

"Not at all," Leonora said, standing up now. "The pain and the pressure in my eyes have eased off and I feel tons better." She walked towards the door, then turned back, "I didn't ask your name . . ."

"It's Rose – Rose Barry."

"That's a lovely name . . ." She paused. "And is this bar your full-time work, Rose?"

"No. There isn't enough work for that. I only work weekends and the odd evening."

"What do you do the rest of the time?"

"I help out at home," Rose said, suddenly feeling awkward and self-conscious – as though she was being interrogated. "My mother works full-time in the Guards' Barracks and I help to look after my little brothers and sisters and my grandmother."

"And have you no other ambitions for yourself?" Mrs Bentley asked, a softer tone in her voice. "You seem a clever enough girl – isn't there any sort of work or profession you would like to go into?"

There was an awkward silence.

Rose shrugged, feeling her face start to burn up now. "I've never really thought . . . I couldn't stay on too long at school. My granny was sick at the time and my mother had to go out to work, so I was needed at home."

The woman nodded her head. "Things won't always be the way they are now, Rose," she told her. A faraway look came into her eyes. "Everything changes . . . *life* changes."

* * *

Mary Slattery was first through the pub door just before four o'clock, her eyes darting here and there to check that everything had been done as she had requested.

"Good girl," she told Rose. "You have the tables and the bar shining. Did you have many in?"

"The usual football supporters and a crowd of lads in a minibus," Rose reported, "and they stayed for a good hour or more."

"And drank plenty, I hope?" Joe said, winking at her.

"They did."

"Anything strange or unusual?" Mary said, taking her hat off.

The gesture suddenly reminded Rose. "Mrs Bentley," she said, her eyes opening wide. "She nearly collapsed in the shop with a bad migraine headache. I had to let her lie down on the bench in the bar."

"What?" Mary said, her voice high with shock. She looked over at the bench with its faded grubby cushions. "You say she had to lie down in here?"

Rose nodded, her face flushing now from the feeling that she had done the wrong thing. "She was sitting in the bench in the shop and there were people coming in and she didn't want to be seen."

Mary gave a weary sigh. If she'd thought for a minute that somebody like Leonora Bentley would come in, she would have at least washed the cushions – if not replaced them with decent ones. "Well, I suppose there was nothing else you could do . . . she must have been very bad to need to lie down."

"She could hardly see but luckily enough she had tablets with her that help, so she took them and then had a little lie down."

"And was she all right then?" Joe asked, loosening his tie and the top button on his starched shirt now that he could. "Was she well enough to walk home?"

"Oh, she was," Rose reassured him. "But the only thing is," she said, reaching down under the bar, "she left this behind in the shop." She placed Leonora Bentley's hat on top of the counter.

Mary reached over and lifted it up. Then she turned it around in her hands, studying it carefully. "I'd say this hat doesn't owe her anything," she said, looking distinctly unimpressed. "She must have had it for years." She looked inside the hat now to examine the label. "*Barbour*," she read. "Never heard of it. It must be an English label."

"I could drop the hat into Traceys' on my way home," Rose offered.

Mary looked over at Joe. "I could take it round myself," she said.

Joe thought for a few moments. "It might be less awkward if Rose takes it – she was the one that dealt with her this afternoon."

Mary pursed her lips together, thinking that it would be nice to have an excuse to call at Traceys' and maybe be invited in. But although the spirit was willing, the flesh was definitely weak – her feet were sore after traipsing around Galway all afternoon in her high heels and she was desperate for a cup of tea.

"Ah, you go on," she said to Rose. "She might be anxious thinkin' that she dropped the oul' hat along the beach or somewhere like that." She sucked in her breath. "She probably won't be the type to go throwing her money around on buying new hats – the ones with the money keep things for years." Mary suddenly felt better about the cushions in the pub. If Leonora Bentley was the landlady, she probably wouldn't go splashing money out on fancy furnishings either.

Rose checked that there was nothing else to be done in the pub then set off for a couple of hours' break at home before returning for the evening shift at seven o'clock.

She walked quickly up along the main road, then turned down the narrower road that led towards the seashore and Traceys' rambling, two-storey, white-painted house. Although she had walked past it many, many times Rose had never ventured up its small stony path. Apart from seeing the Traceys at Mass on a Sunday, she never came across them. The local families who had farms and animals were the ones who would know them on account of James Tracey being a vet.

Diana Tracey answered the door. She was taller and bigger-boned than her mother, and her mid-brown hair was tied back in a ponytail. She wore a quizzical frown on her face. "Yes?" she said, looking Rose up and down.

Rose produced the hat from her bag by way of explanation. "Your mother left this in the shop this afternoon," she said, holding it out.

"Oh . . . yes," Diana Tracey nodded her head now, understanding the situation. She took the hat. "I believe she had a bit of a headache and had to sit down."

Rose immediately knew that Leonora Bentley had not told her daughter the full extent of her migraine attack. "Is she feeling better?" she enquired.

"Yes, she said the worst of it had passed by the time she got home. She's having a lie down before dinner." She looked down at the green waxed hat. "Thank you so much for bringing this around . . . and for being so helpful to my mother earlier on."

"It was no trouble," Rose told her, turning away from the door. Then she halted. "If you would just say that I hope she feels much better soon."

"Of course. I'll tell her the minute she gets up."

Rose headed off down the path again, suddenly conscious of the darkening sky – and even more conscious of Diana Tracey's eyes watching her as she went.

Chapter 3

The following Tuesday afternoon, Rose was sitting at the kitchen table opposite her grandmother, helping her to prepare the meat and vegetables for the evening meal. At one time Martha Barry would have had the washing out and blowing on the line by nine o'clock and the carrots, turnips and parsnips peeled and cubed by mid-morning. But that was before arthritis had set in, stiffening her hands and slowing her step. She still managed to do most things that she had always done, but it was now at a much gentler pace. Rose now did all the heavy work around the house like bringing in the turf and washing and wringing out and ironing the bigger items, while her grandmother did the smaller jobs.

Martha was wearing her cross-over style apron and Rose a pink flowery one that tied around her waist. They worked together pleasantly and easily, the radio on in the background, until Rose's younger sisters arrived in from school – then everything moved at a noisier, quicker pace.

It was around two o'clock when the car pulled up outside the white-washed cottage. Rose was in the back garden, checking whether the sheets on the washing line were dry enough to bring in, when she heard the unusual noise of an engine. She walked around the side of the cottage and was startled when she saw Leonora Bentley emerging from the cream Mercedes. Rose immediately started to untie the strings of her apron, embarrassed to be seen in her working clothes. She quickly whipped it off and crumpled it up into a tight little ball in her hand.

"I hope you don't mind me calling," Leonora said, smiling warmly at the girl.

It struck Rose how much the smile changed the older woman's face and made her seem a warmer, more approachable person.

"I wanted to thank you properly for being so nice and helpful last Saturday afternoon." Leonora came to stand in front of the old stone wall which had been painted white to match the house.

Rose held the apron behind her back. "Sure, there was no need . . . I did very little," she said, feeling her face flush. The confidence she'd felt with the woman back in the pub was a far distant memory. She wondered what Leonora Bentley would be thinking of the plain cottage that she and her family lived in, and whether she would be comparing it to her daughter's imposing house.

Rose was unsure whether to invite the woman into the house or not. Her mind flew to the kitchen cupboard as she tried to remember whether they had any coffee. There was every chance that Mrs Bentley would prefer coffee to tea. They had American visitors over for the afternoon last summer and Rose's mother had been mortified when one of them asked for coffee and she had to tell them she didn't have any. She had meant to keep a bottle of coffee in the cupboard from then on in case a similar situation occurred.

Rose's hand tightened on the apron at the thought of having to invite this woman into the cottage.

"I won't keep you back from your work, I can see you're busy," Leonora said, as though reading her mind. "I just wanted to give you a little gift."

Rose's brow furrowed. *A gift?* This was the last thing she expected. What on earth would a woman like Mrs Bentley be doing buying a present for her?

Leonora turned back to the car and came out with a carrier bag with the distinctive Moons emblem on it – the biggest, most expensive department store in Galway. The sort of shop that Rose and her mother would be terrified to even look into.

She handed it to Rose, saying in her more familiar strident tone, "Now, I have some other things in the car for you. I'm sure you won't be offended – but Diana was sorting out some things that were too small for her – or gifts she'd been given that weren't suitable – and I asked her if I could have them."

Rose's face started to burn up with embarrassment.

Leonora went to the car and came back with two bigger carrier bags, filled to the brim with clothes. "No one needs to know where they've come from," she went on. "They've never been worn around here and Diana won't say a word."

"Oh, I couldn't take them! It's far too much – I really did nothing, I only got you a glass of water."

Leonora placed the bag on the wall beside the other

one. "Nonsense! You were very practical and sensible and, more importantly, you were kind. You deserve a small reward for that." She took a deep breath and it seemed to Rose that she suddenly seemed to grow a couple of inches. "Now, if anyone asks, you can say a relative gave them to you or whatever you like." She put her hand out and patted Rose's. "And don't feel in the slightest bit embarrassed about taking clothes that someone else has worn. They're excellent quality and have hardly been used, and it would be an absolute crime to throw them out." She leaned forward, her blonde head almost touching Rose's. "When I was your age I often wore clothes that were given to me, and I was glad of them."

Rose looked at her in amazement. She just couldn't imagine her ever wearing anyone else's cast-offs.

"They were better than anything I could have afforded at the time," Leonora went on. She raised her carefully shaped eyebrows. "Don't go thinking that I was always in the position to afford new clothes – I most certainly wasn't. I often had to rely on the kindness of my wealthier cousins in London and America to send me their hand-me-downs which were certainly not in the almost-new condition of the clothes I'm giving you."

Rose realised that it would be churlish to refuse to take the things from her. And it would have been a very stupid thing to do. The warm, summery weather was coming soon and this year she needed to replace all her lighter clothes as she had both grown taller and filled out, especially in the bust and hips. Last summer she'd had to give away a few of her own outfits because she couldn't do up the buttons or zips, and she had been conscious of how tight the dresses and blouses she'd managed to squeeze into had been by the end of the summer. If she was lucky, she might be able to afford to replace a few items but her choice this summer would be severely limited. She had no idea what was in the bulging bags but there had to be something that would fit her amongst all these clothes.

"Thank you," she said simply. "It's very kind of you and I really appreciate it."

Leonora suddenly halted for a moment, staring closely at the young girl – almost scrutinising her. "You know you're a very striking-looking girl, don't you?" Her words were a question, not a statement.

Rose blushed and then started to laugh. "I'm not too sure about that!"

"Well, you *should* be sure. We need to be very aware of our assets in this life. Especially females. You need to know exactly what you're worth. It's very easy to sell yourself short in many areas." She put her head to the side, her green eyes narrowed. "You are both beautiful and clever. Diana knows your old teacher from school and she told her that you were one of the cleverest girls she had ever taught. And, from the little I know of you, you also have a very pleasant nature. A rare enough combination." She smiled now. "I expect you don't get told that very often down here, do you?"

Rose shook her head, mortally embarrassed now. She was beginning to think that Leonora Bentley wasn't quite right in the head – or was at the very least eccentric. *Nobody* talked like that in Kilnagree. And she couldn't imagine her old schoolteacher Miss Lavery telling anyone how clever she had been. At school if anyone had said anything along those lines, you knew they were only having a jeer and a bit of a laugh. And at home any signs of vanity would soon be knocked out of you. "If you look in that mirror for much longer," her father would say, half-joking and wholly in earnest, "you're going to break it. And don't forget what Benjamin Franklin once said – 'Pride that dines on vanity sups on contempt'!"

The Barry family were quite unlikely ever to forget what Benjamin Franklin said, as their father trotted out that particular quote at regular intervals. As a curious young child, Rose had once asked him what it meant. Her father had got down on his haunches beside her and said: "It means that people who think themselves lovely are laughed at by everyone else."

Leonora Bentley had hit the nail on the head. There was definitely no room for self-praise or any kind of vanity in the Barry household.

"Well, no doubt you'll be given plenty of compliments about your looks at some point in the future," Leonora said, her voice almost a sigh, "and let us hope it's from the right man." She smiled now but there was a faraway look in her eyes. "But you're as well to hear the truth from a stranger like me who has nothing to gain, so you don't sell yourself short." A light breeze lifted a strand of her bobbed blonde hair across to the wrong side of her head and she moved her hand now to settle it back in place. "You have to value yourself first before other people will value you. And it's better to listen to good advice rather than have to learn that lesson the hard way."

It suddenly dawned on Rose that a lot of what

Leonora Bentley had just said was related to her own life experiences. They were things she'd obviously learned the hard way. Rose's mind was full of questions that she'd like to ask the older woman. Questions that she'd never dare ask her mother. Questions that she knew Leonora Bentley would have no trouble answering.

Leonora turned back towards the car now. "I'm heading back up to Dublin in the morning but I'll pop into the shop to see you next time I'm back in Kilnagree."

"I'll look forward to it," Rose said and surprised herself by actually meaning it.

* * *

Later that afternoon, Rose carefully laid out all her new clothes on the two double beds in the room she shared with her grandmother and younger sisters.

"Oh, Rose . . . they're beautiful!" her mother gasped.

At the bottom of the bed there also lay three handbags – an everyday leather shoulder bag, a white leather clutch bag and a dark-beaded evening bag with a chain handle.

Rose lifted a pink and black flowery blouse. She held it up to her. "Isn't this gorgeous? I'll be able to wear it to the dance on Saturday night with the black straight skirt." Her eyes lit up. "Believe it or not, every single thing fits perfectly."

Kathleen's eyes lit up with amusement. "You won't be able to dance too well in that skirt – you'd be better off with a pleated skirt or one of the dresses."

Rose started to giggle now. "You're right! I'd be a fine sight trying to do *The Siege of Ennis* in that!" She paused for a moment, then lifted a pale pink, short-sleeved jumper from the bed. "Most of the things would be too tight for you, but I think this would fit you, Mammy. It's nice and stretchy, and the colour would suit you as well."

"Not at all," Kathleen said, shaking her head. "The clothes were given to *you* and it would look very bad if I was seen wearing them outside. Sure, I could bump into Diana Tracey at Mass or anything and she might recognise it."

"Take it," Rose insisted. "It would look lovely on you for special occasions at work and the Traceys aren't likely to be around there. Don't you have somebody very important coming to the barracks next week?"

Kathleen raised her eyes to the heavens. "Oh, there's some bigwig coming down from the Dáil next Friday and I have to cook the dinner and everything for them."

"Well, you'll want to look nice for that, won't you?" Rose said, putting the jumper into her mother's hands. "You could wear it with your nice pearls."

Kathleen hesitated. "Well, I suppose there's no harm in trying it on."

Rose picked up a black and white flowered dress in a boat-neck style with a big broad belt. "I think that little black hat is supposed to match this one," she said. "It's in the same material. It's a lovely outfit for a special occasion, isn't it?"

Kathleen nodded her head. "You have enough dresses and blouses there to last you for the next two or three summers." She looked at the Moons carrier bag. "And what was the present she bought you?"

"*Two* presents," Rose told her. "You're not going to

believe it!" She lifted the bag very carefully from the bed as though it was a piece of china. She had taken the two gifts out a dozen times already to examine them, then each time she had put them back into the carrier bag. Every time she came back to it, she had the same feeling of disbelief and delight. She opened the bag once again, and brought out the first item. A bottle of *Chanel No. 5* perfume.

"Oh, my God!" Kathleen gasped. "I'm sure I've seen that scent advertised in magazines – it must have cost her a small fortune!"

Rose bit her lip and nodded her head slowly. She had also seen pictures advertising the perfume and had seen it in a display in Moons window on one of her rare visits to Galway. But she had never imagined that she would ever own a bottle of such an expensive, famous perfume.

But then – she had never imagined that she would meet someone like Leonora Bentley.

"You can borrow the handbags and the perfume any time you want," Rose generously offered. "In fact, you can have the perfume to sit out on your dressing-table. It would look lovely sitting on the little lace cloth."

Kathleen opened her mouth to disagree but then it dawned on her that there was nowhere to display anything in her daughter's bedroom apart from the window ledge. The two beds and two small wardrobes took up every spare inch in the bedroom.

"You can leave it on my dressing-table if you want," she said, "and you'll always know where it is."

Rose reached into the bag now and brought out the second gift – a lilac chiffon blouse with short, delicately puffed sleeves and a tie-bow at the neck. "Isn't it beautiful?" she said, her voice slightly breathless. "And it's my favourite colour."

Kathleen sat down on the side of the bed, shaking her head. "It's like Christmas," she said, gesturing towards the pile of clothes. "Who would have believed it?" She looked up at her daughter. "Do you realise just how lucky you are? Nobody has ever done anything like that for me." She gave a little shrug. "But then, I've never known anyone with the money to do that kind of thing."

"I still don't know why she did it," Rose said, smiling excitedly now, "but I'm going to enjoy every single minute of wearing both the perfume *and* the lovely clothes."

After her mother left the room, Rose lifted up a blue dress that was splashed all over with brilliant red poppies. She held it up to herself and then walked over to the mirror. It had a full, flared skirt and looked perfect with her straight, shiny black hair. Rose instantly decided that she would wear it to the dance next Saturday night. None of the other girls would have anything remotely like the style of this dress.

A surge of delight ran through her. No matter what her cousin wore, it would pale in comparison to this gorgeous dress.

Rose smiled to herself, knowing that for once she would definitely outshine Hannah.

Chapter 4

Hannah Martin looked out at the dull grey sky and the fine rain that had been falling relentlessly all day. But she was only vaguely aware of it. Weather and ordinary boring things like that had little effect when her head was full of plans for the forthcoming weekend.

Especially when the plans involved getting away from home for a while. Away from her mother's constant disapproval and mournful prayers. Away from the boring routine of school and studying and piano-playing.

Hannah wanted to enjoy herself – and just thinking about going down to a dance in Kilnagree sent a huge surge of excitement through her. She closed her eyes and hugged her arms around herself.

She had a few hours alone in the white two-storey house where she lived with her parents and two older brothers – John and Kevin – when they were home from university. This afternoon her mother had gone cycling into Tullamore hospital on the other side of the town to visit an elderly neighbour and then she was going to stop off on her way home to pick up some shopping. Hannah had to stay in the house in case anyone called to buy eggs or in case her father took a break from tending the sheep and cows for a cup of tea.

The house was only a half a mile out from the town and Hannah usually took the chance to escape from it any time she could. But on dreary days like this she didn't mind being at home and she quite looked forward to people coming up to the house for eggs because she never knew who might appear.

Hannah had already planned the outfits she would take down for her week's holiday at her Aunt Kathleen's. It wasn't difficult. Anything she had was far better than anything her cousin Rose or any of her friends in the little village would be wearing. The girls in Kilnagree were very old-fashioned and boring in their dress. They would never think to put a bright ribbon in their hair or to add a nice brooch to a dress – all the little details that Hannah enjoyed working out. Just the thought of the impending trip was enough to lift her spirits. And although it was miserable enough today, the weather was generally getting nicer and she could look forward to wearing her lighter dresses and skirts and blouses.

It was one of the few good things about her mother. Sheila Martin insisted that they both had new outfits for Christmas and Easter for Mass. And they always made a special trip to Dublin for them.

"We don't want to bump into any oul' Tom or Jenny wearing the same things as us," her mother would say. "So if we go up to Clery's at least anyone who buys the same outfits will be of a decent class."

It was one of the few bright occasions in Hannah's life

when she and her mother caught the train up to Dublin to pick their seasonal outfits. Her mother was always smiling because, she told Hannah, it was always important to keep up appearances as you never knew who you might run into. And Sheila Martin was usually in a good mood because she enjoyed the rare occasions she got to spend her husband's money.

Now, Hannah glanced across the parlour to the old brown piano she should be practising on and then over at the boring desk she should be writing her letter to Rose on. The sheets of fine Basildon Bond lay scattered on the table, alongside the pen and bottle of black ink. Her mother had gone mad this morning when she discovered that Hannah still hadn't finished writing the note to her cousin to say exactly when she would be arriving for the weekend.

"They'll need to make arrangements to meet you at the bus! It's only polite to let them know in time!" Sheila Martin had said, her dark-brown eyes blazing. "Do you want them all to think that you're nothing but an oul' ignoramus from the bogs?"

Hannah had stared silently at her mother.

But Sheila had caught the defiant look in her daughter's eye.

Her hand had shot out and caught her curly blonde-haired daughter on the side of her head. The blow had sent Hannah reeling and given her a ringing noise in her ear that lasted for a good ten minutes.

"And don't dare ask what you got it for!" Sheila had warned, her eyes narrowing dangerously now. "How many times have I told you about that look?"

Hannah had lowered her head into her hands, having discovered it to be the best reaction to outbursts like these. Staring ahead and pretending it hadn't happened only infuriated her mother further – as did turning her head to the side.

"Never mind all the dramatics," Sheila had said, poking her daughter in the shoulder. "Get back over to that desk and get that letter finished and in the post today. It would look fine now if you arrive before the letter!"

It actually amazed Hannah that her mother let her go down to Kilnagree at all on her own. There was a time when they all used to go on family holidays to the tiny village, then a few years ago Sheila had all but stopped visiting her sister. Hannah didn't know whether her mother was willing to let her go because she enjoyed getting rid of her for the week or because she felt that Hannah's visits made up for her not going. Nor did she care. She was just grateful to have the trips to look forward to and the time away from home.

She wandered away from the window now and out through the hallway to the big, high-ceilinged kitchen to make herself a cup of comforting cocoa and search out something to eat. She opened cupboards and containers and eventually decided on two slices of white soda bread thickly spread with honey as the sweet taste would go with the hot chocolate drink.

Then Hannah did a thing she would never have dared do had her mother been home – she brought the mug and plate out to the parlour and sat them down on the green-leather-topped desk. Then she ran upstairs to her bedroom and went straight to her bed. She knelt down on the cold linoleum floor, lifted a corner of her mattress and slid out a copy of a woman's magazine that she had hidden away.

In return for sending her copies of the Irish local paper, Sheila Martin's cousin in London occasionally sent over half a dozen magazines, which Hannah was not allowed to touch. Sheila kept the magazines in the tall mahogany wardrobe in her bedroom and, when she was finished with them, threw them in the fire or in the bin. Hannah had rescued the odd one from the bin any time she got the chance and had gathered a few of them and hidden them under her mattress, along with money she had picked up here and there and any other items that she didn't want her mother to know about.

She came back into the parlour now and settled herself down in front of the fire with her cocoa and bread and her magazine. She would be safe for the next half an hour or so, and then she would make herself finish off that damned letter and walk up the town to post it before her mother came back from the hospital.

* * *

Hannah had been back from the post office about a quarter of an hour when she heard a noise outside in the yard. It was probably her mother or her father. She flew across the parlour, sat down at the piano and proceeded to bang away at the opening bars of 'Danny Boy'.

When she heard the rap at the door, she realised it was most probably someone looking for eggs.

She opened the front door of the farmhouse to an impeccably dressed, sandy-haired man in his early thirties.

"Good afternoon, Miss Martin," he said, stepping in the door.

"What are you doing here?" Hannah gasped. She moved so that her back was pressed against the wall.

"Calling for a dozen eggs," he laughed. "What else?" He closed the door behind him and then he stood opposite her. "I met your mother in town a few minutes ago and she told me to come on up and collect the eggs that Ursula asked for." He looked straight into her eyes, then leaned over and touched a long curl of her blonde hair. "I offered her a lift back in the car but she said she still had a few shops to go to, including a prescription at the chemist's . . ." he paused deliberately, "that wouldn't be ready for another half an hour or so."

"She has the bike anyway," Hannah said, looking at him through lowered eyelashes.

His eyes moved up to the ceiling, calculating. "That will add another ten or fifteen minutes on . . . which gives us plenty of time."

"Plenty of time for what?" Hannah said, her blue eyes wide and innocent.

Then before she could say another word, he had moved towards her, pulled her almost roughly into his arms and pressed his lips hard down on hers. And it was then that Hannah gave up any kind of pretence, gave up the little game she liked to play with him, wound her arms around his neck and responded to his kisses with more expertise than many women twice her age.

"Into the kitchen," he whispered hoarsely. "We'll hear anyone coming in and I'll have time to do myself up quickly."

"I'll put the eggs out on the table so it'll look like I was sorting them out for you," she said in a low sort of giggle. "There's a big basket of washed eggs by the sink. My mother made me do them this morning."

"I'm glad to hear that somebody is keeping a tight rein on you . . ."

Hannah gave an overdramatic sigh. "Don't talk to me about her! That woman is the biggest tyrant God ever put breath into!"

They went into the kitchen now and Hannah rushed over, gathered up two handfuls of the eggs and set them down carefully in the middle of the table.

"Come on," he said, reaching out to catch her hand and pull her close to him. "We're only wasting time . . ."

"You're surely desperate," she said, raising her eyebrows and smiling. "Have you missed me?"

"Of course I have," he told her, his fingers reaching for the buttons on her soft woollen dress. "I always miss you!"

Hannah put her arms around his neck now and ran her fingers through his hair. She could feel his hands move down her back, over her hips and down towards the hem of her dress. Then his hands moved upwards, bringing the dress up around her waist. He held her like that – taking a step backwards to take in the sight of her flesh-coloured stockings and plain white cotton knickers.

"I would have worn the fancier ones if I'd known you were dropping in," she whispered in his ear. She had two pairs of lace knickers – one red, one black – carefully hidden alongside all her other little secrets.

"Take them off," he urged, his fingers finding the elastic at the waist.

x

46

The noise of the front door opening brought the escalating passion to an abrupt halt.

"Oh, God, it'll be my father," Hannah said, raising her eyebrows and giving a resigned little sigh.

"Aw . . . feck it!" he breathed. "He's got some sense of timing." He moved away from her now, quickly adjusting his trousers and jacket.

As her father's heavy working boots tramped along the stone-flagged hallway, Hannah calmly smoothed down her dress and her hair, and then went over to the cupboard in the big old pine dresser to find a carton for the eggs.

"Was it a dozen you said?" she asked casually as her father came in.

"How-ya, Simon?" Bill Martin hailed the visitor, coming across to shake hands. He was dressed for the wet weather in his heavy working raincoat and cap.

"Grand, grand, and yourself?"

"Ah, sure no point in complaining and who would be listening?" Hannah's father said, taking his damp cap off and setting it down on the table. He pulled a chair out and sat down in it. "Sit yourself down there, Simon." He gestured towards a neighbouring chair and Simon sat down.

Hannah carried on putting the dozen eggs into the cardboard container, then went over to put the kettle on to make her father a cup of tea.

"I'm just picking up a few eggs for Ursula," Simon said, motioning towards the egg box.

"How are they all down at the bank? Still raking in plenty of oul' money?"

Simon Connelly laughed. The kind of affable laugh he

kept for his customers. "Ah, now, you're all glad of us when you need us!"

"Have you time for a cup of tea, Simon?" Hannah said, looking over her shoulder.

Simon held her eyes for a few moments, then he checked his watch. "Ah, sure I wouldn't want to be holding your father back . . ."

"You won't be holding me back at all," Bill Martin said, "because I'm not stopping. I only came in for a roll of rough twine I left in the drawer there." He stood up now, holding his hand to his stiff back as he walked over to the dresser. "It's not worth my while getting comfortable – I'll be finished for the evening in another hour or so."

"Are you sure you won't have a cup of tea, Daddy?" said Hannah.

He lifted the roll of string out of the drawer and put it into his deep coat pocket. "No, I'd rather get the job finished out in the barn." He thumbed back to their guest. "Give poor oul' Simon a cup of tea – those bank clerks need to keep their brains well watered."

All three laughed, then Bill left the kitchen.

A minute later they heard the front door closing behind him.

Smiling, Hannah moved back to the table. Simon checked his watch again, then he pulled Hannah down onto his knee. "This will have to be the quickest one ever . . . I shouldn't be here at all . . . but after watching your tight little backside going backwards and forwards . . ."

Hannah giggled and squirmed about in his lap, knowing the effect it would have on him. Within a minute they were standing against the kitchen door, Hannah's dress pulled high around her hips, and Simon Connelly's mouth fastened down hard on hers as his hands roamed around her breasts and up and down her thighs.

The first time it had happened, Hannah was amazed by the intensity of his kisses, which were like nothing she had ever known before. She discovered that there was a world of difference in being kissed by a man – as opposed to a boy. But the biggest discovery had been the rush of passion that swept through her – totally consuming her. Feelings that she never even knew her own body was capable of.

It seemed ages ago now but, when she looked back on it, it was only last Christmas night. Just over three months ago. And it had changed her life forever. Turned it upside down. The stolen kisses at Christmas had turned into stolen hours back at Simon's house when she was baby-sitting. Simon would leave his wife back in the local hotel or at a table in a restaurant while he drove off quickly – ostensibly to see someone about a bit of private business – and spent half an hour with Hannah while his children were sleeping upstairs.

And the kisses and caresses had recently turned into a full sexual affair – something that Hannah had been entirely ignorant of until her entanglement with the older, sophisticated man.

And then there were the little trips in the car at night when Hannah was supposed to be at the library, or when he would meet her straight from school. On other occasions they would drive out into the woods at Charleville Castle with Hannah slouched down low in the front seat in case anyone saw and recognised her.

And although she knew it was wrong, Hannah felt the risk was worth it.

Simon made her feel like the most beautiful girl in the

world and he laughed at all the silly little things she said and did. He thought everything about her was wonderful. In Simon's arms she felt clever and desirable and that made up for all the wrong bits in her life. He made up for the way she was treated at home by her mother and at school by her teachers who thought she was stupid.

Her mother had this great notion that Hannah was going to train to be a music teacher and get a job in the local secondary school. But Hannah already knew she would never get the marks to get into music school. The teachers had told both her and her parents that Hannah simply didn't have the brains for it – but Sheila Martin was convinced that all her immature daughter needed was a lot more piano practice and an extra year staying back at school.

Hannah was now the oldest girl in the school and she was no nearer passing her Leaving Certificate this year than she had been last year. But at least she wouldn't have to worry about it until the end of the summer when the results came out. She would think of something by then. She would work something out.

Both Hannah and Simon knew that if they were caught together it would cause a huge furore and scandal in Tullamore town. The fact that Simon Connelly was a married man with a family would be bad enough, but the fact that he was an upstanding pillar of the community and the church who worked in the local bank made it even worse.

But the worst thing of all was the fact he was Hannah Martin's uncle.

Chapter 5

Leonora Bentley turned the cream Mercedes in through the high, black, wrought-iron gates and then continued up the long driveway towards the imposing country house she had lived in since she was a young, married woman. As usual, she had mixed feelings about returning home to Glenmore House.

Somewhere along the journeys back from visiting Diana in County Clare or her son Jonathan in London, Leonora always felt she had lost another little piece of herself. There was a part she left behind with them.

It was even harder to think of her elder son, Edward – an architect – who had gone to live in America two years ago. She hadn't seen him since. There was a possibility he was coming home for a visit at Christmas but at this stage she daren't even think of it. She would wait until he had bought his ticket before she allowed herself to start looking forward to it. Before she allowed herself to start making plans for the busy, lively house that she would have once again.

It wasn't as though Leonora was completely lonely and couldn't fill her time. It was more a case of not having the company she wanted – and most of the time that was her children. But having them back around her was the impossible dream. It was trying to turn the clock back. Trying to hold back the tide. Being a pragmatic sort of woman, she knew that it was against the natural order of things.

And though both Jonathan and Diana had offered that she come and live with them – or at least stay for extended periods of time – she knew it wasn't the right thing either. It was much too soon. She wasn't old enough to throw herself on them yet. Although there were days when she felt much older, she had just turned fifty-six and she was still more than reasonably fit for her age. She couldn't bear to think of the time when she wouldn't be able to look after herself or Glenmore House. She couldn't see that far ahead and she didn't want to.

She had left Kilnagree after breakfast to ensure that she got home in the early part of the afternoon. It was a lovely day and she had enjoyed most of the drive back up to her home on the perimeter of Lucan, a town some ten miles or so from Dublin. When she recognised that her spirits were starting to flag a little, she had bolstered herself up by thinking of all the things she would be busy with over the spring and summer. She had the gardens to occupy her during the bright sunny days and her newly discovered artwork, her books and her daily walks to fill the remaining time. And of course she could always travel to visit family and friends when she felt that she needed a total diversion from home. There was no need to sit and brood.

The habit of making lists of the enjoyable things in her life was one of the positive things that Andrew had given to her – his remedy for the ups and downs of life which had been the mainstay of his professional life as one of the most eminent Clinical Psychologists in Dublin and the mainstay of the Bentley household.

Throughout their marriage Andrew had remained upbeat and cheery in the face of most difficult situations. He had found out early on that reading, walking and gardening with his wife, and playing golf with his friends diverted him from the worst aspects of life. Of course that had changed later after the bomb dropped in their lives. The silent, lethal, secret bomb.

Neither the garden nor the long walks in the Wicklow hills had helped either of them escape from that. But ironically Andrew's philosophy on life had equipped Leonora so that she was eventually able to deal with the fall-out of it all. Even when he was beyond affecting the situation and certainly beyond helping his wife, his logical, common-sense suggestions had helped her survive the darkest hours in her life. And years later they still helped her to get through the daylight hours.

The nights were a different matter but Leonora had developed other ways to get her through them.

As she made her way up the gravelled driveway through the secluded three acres of gardens and grounds, she glanced on either side to see if she could detect any differences from when she had left the previous week. The fat pink buds on the half dozen or so Cherry Blossom trees could be seen quite clearly, and the bare towering weeping willow on a small hill had feathery gold branches as the new leaves and catkins forced their way through. The clumps of early-flowering big yellow daffodils that were blooming when she left were now starting to die off, and the smaller, white-headed varieties were taking their turn on the centre stage of the lawn.

The sight of them lifted her heart and suddenly made it easier to return to a house where the staff outnumbered the family.

* * *

As soon as she heard the car on the gravel path, the sparrow-like Mrs O'Shea came up the stairs from the kitchen and into the portrait-lined hallway to greet her employer. She wore her daily uniform of a white pinafore over a plain black dress, and her grey hair was swept back in a tidy bun. The small matching white cap which she kept on a window-ledge in the kitchen was only donned when there were visitors in the house.

"Welcome, welcome home!" she called as Leonora emerged from the Mercedes. She stood under the stone archway of the door, her arms folded across her flat chest.

"Thank you, Mrs O'Shea," Leonora said, giving her a grateful smile.

"Did you have a reasonable journey back up from Galway?" the housekeeper enquired, her Glasgow accent still strong after forty years in Dublin.

"I did," Leonora said, lifting her handbag and coat from the back seat, before going to open the boot of the car.

"It's a fine enough day, although there's still a bit of a nip in the air," the Scotswoman went on. "I got two good lines of washing out this morning – and they're all back inside and dried and ironed already."

"Well done . . ." Leonora said in a faint voice, her

mind automatically switching off when it came to mundane domestic matters such as laundry.

Mrs O'Shea was well aware that her audience wasn't an appreciative one but it didn't deter her. "Oh, it does my heart good to see a line of fresh washing blowing in the breeze. There's nothing like it. I love to stand back and watch the sheets and the towels flapping up and down . . ." She was almost enraptured now as she remembered her morning's work but as she rambled on – more or less talking to herself – she realised that Leonora was rifling around in the boot. "Now don't be struggling with a case or anything like that – Tommy is around the back of the house somewhere and he'll lift it out for you. Don't be trying to lift it yourself."

Tommy Murray was a local man who came in a few days a week to help Leonora with the bigger jobs in the garden.

"I hear you," Leonora said, raising her eyebrows. "I'm just getting a small bag that's easy enough to carry." She lifted out a brown bag and then slammed the car boot shut. She straightened up and suddenly felt a dull ache in the lower part of her back, and as she walked towards the imposing Palladian-style entrance of Glenmore House she noticed that her legs were also aching from the long drive.

"Are you sore after the journey up?" Mrs O'Shea missed nothing. She had worked as housekeeper and cook for Andrew and Leonora Bentley since they got married, and she knew her employers as well as if they were her own family. In truth, in many ways they were her family, because all her relatives were across the sea in Scotland and she had been widowed five years after moving to Ireland. She had then rented a small cottage in the nearby village and cycled to work until Andrew died when Leonora suggested that she move into a couple of the unused rooms on the top floor. And so far the arrangement had worked out perfectly well for them both.

"I'm getting old," said Leonora. She smiled wearily and shook her head. "I'm getting stiff and old, Lizzie."

"Get away wi' you!" Mrs O'Shea said, waving her hand in the air. "You've hardly changed in the last twenty years. You could give women half your age a good run for their money with your lovely hair and your fashionable style!"

"I don't feel it today. You're a good bit older than me and I bet you could move quicker than me at this minute."

"You'll feel different tomorrow," the housekeeper reassured her. "Being cooped up in a car and bent over a driving wheel for hours would make anybody feel the very same."

They went inside the house and Leonora was assailed by the welcoming, comforting scent of strong coffee and home baking.

"Oh, something smells lovely!" she said.

"Go on into the drawing-room," Mrs O'Shea said, indicating the first doorway off the hall. "Tommy has kept a nice fire on for you, so it will be lovely and warm." She halted, then a little smile came on her lips. "Would you like one of your special coffees?"

Leonora closed her eyes and nodded. "I would love one."

"It'll do you the power of good – and I'll bring you up a bit of freshly baked brown bread and salmon to keep you going until dinner tonight." She started towards the door in her efficient manner.

"Lizzie . . ." Leonora said, holding out the bag she had carried in. "There's a few things in there for you that Diana sent and a new cardigan that I bought for you."

Mrs O'Shea whirled around. "Now, what did you go doing that for?" she asked, her voice sounding cross.

"If you must know," Leonora said, lifting her eyebrows, "I noticed that the one you keep for Mass had a frayed cuff."

"You'd no need to be bringing me back anything at all!" She ground her lips together, then made a hissing sound from between her teeth. "You're a terrible woman doing that!" Then, shaking her head and muttering to herself she took the bag.

"And make yourself an Irish coffee when you're making mine," said Leonora. "Then you can tell me all that's been happening while I've been away."

Mrs O'Shea's face brightened. She enjoyed both the drink and the chat with her employer on the rare occasions that it happened. "You had a phone call from that funny artist woman you go to. She said there was some kind of a charity exhibition on in Dublin next week and she was putting one of your drawings in for it."

Leonora's eyebrows shot up. "Really?" A little tinge of excitement ran through her at the thought. She could guess which one of the paintings Terry Cassidy had selected – an oil still life of an old tin jug with snowdrops spilling out of it. It was one she had painted a few months ago when the garden was just coming back to life.

"She said she wouldn't price it too high since it was

the first time any of your drawings would be on show," the housekeeper said.

Leonora stopped herself from smiling at the description of her artwork – *drawing* – for she knew well that the Scotswoman didn't approve of her wasting her time on such a trivial pursuit. And in a way Leonora could see her point. Up until now she herself felt she had only been dabbling and playing around with art in an almost childish fashion.

"You also had a visitor," Mrs O'Shea went on, "who left you a wee present. I'll tell you all about that in a wee while. I'll wait until we're good and settled . . ."

"Oh? Who was it?"

But Mrs O'Shea was gone.

Leonora went over to stand by the white marble fireplace with the ornate French mirror and mantel. She rubbed her hands together and held them out to the glowing coals.

Warmed up now, she sat in the deep floral armchair near the hearth. Within a few minutes, she could feel the muscles in her back start to relax. Mrs O'Shea had placed a blue and cream vase filled with white tulips on the small table next to Leonora's chair, where she kept her reading glasses and the book or magazine she was currently engrossed in. The housekeeper had also left a small pile of mail there.

Leonora glanced at the unopened envelopes. There was no handwritten mail or anything that looked remotely urgent or interesting. She leaned her head on the back of her chair and closed her eyes for a few moments.

Leonora was home now and, although there was still

a small loneliness about her for her children, she was beginning to feel a sense of comfort and belonging in her own surroundings. It was something she never took for granted – living in this old, gracious, period house with its rolling lawns and beautiful gardens.

She remembered how she had felt the first time that Andrew had brought her to Glenmore House all those years ago. They had been courting about six months and she hadn't been quite sure where their romance was leading at that stage. He had mentioned beforehand that the house was fairly big and, from the bits and pieces that he told her about it, Leonora had conjured up an image of a Georgian-style family home that was slightly larger than the very nice five-bedroomed townhouse in Ballsbridge that she grew up in. But it had been a typical Andrew understatement, for his family home was like no other she had ever visited and when his black Rover had pulled up outside Glenmore House, she had been stunned. But the young and extremely confident Leonora had simply taken a deep breath and walked into the old country manor house as though she had been doing it all her life.

"I feel a bit like an auctioneer who's trying to sell a place," Andrew joked as he told her how old the house was and a bit about the history of it.

"It must have been wonderful growing up in a house like this."

Andrew had wrinkled his brow in thought. "Most of the time it was . . . but we had had our ups and downs. People are only human, I suppose."

Little did Leonora know, as they went to meet his parents, that one day she would be the sole owner of this stately pile, that she would live a life filled with a husband and three children, running here and there to school, horse and sports events, and become a lynchpin of the local social and charity scene.

And she could never have foreseen that after twenty-five years of a bustling, productive routine she would find herself completely alone with little to organise and worry about – apart from the minutiae of domestic life that Lizzie O'Shea tried her best to involve her in.

As she heard her housekeeper's feet coming along the hallway, Leonora vaguely wondered about the visitor she had mentioned, and whether it might be someone from the local Church of Ireland or perhaps one of her old university friends. But then again, knowing Lizzie, it would probably be just one of the neighbouring farmers calling in about some trivial matter. What her housekeeper would find interesting was not always what Leonora would consider worthy of any note.

Mrs O'Shea elbowed the door open, then came in carrying a silver tray filled with salmon and cucumber open sandwiches, slices of brown treacle cake – an old Scottish recipe – and home-made shortbread fingers. In the middle of the tray stood two large wine glasses filled with sweet black coffee and Irish whiskey, topped with thick double cream.

The first time she had been asked to make the Irish coffees for a church fundraiser, the housekeeper had been aghast that anyone could drink such a peculiar mixture. The whiskey she could understand all right – but the coffee mixed with it, never! In fact, she never really understood what people saw in coffee at all. She much preferred a nice cup of tea – plain and ordinary. But life with Leonora Bentley had gradually brought her round to many things. And after a while she was tempted to try the black and cream hot drink and had developed a taste for it. Any time she was asked to make Irish coffees for Mrs Bentley or her guests, she always made enough for an extra one for herself. And like everything else, it didn't escape her employer's notice.

Leonora ate two pieces of the brown bread and salmon and a tiny piece of fruitcake while Mrs O'Shea filled her in on all the news.

"Put me out of my misery," Leonora eventually said, as both women sat back in the fireside armchairs enjoying their drinks. "Who called at the house while I was away?"

Mrs O'Shea raised her eyebrows and smiled. "An old friend of yours . . . one you haven't seen this long time."

"Who?" Leonora demanded.

The housekeeper paused for a moment for effect. "Daniel Levy."

Leonora's stomach suddenly tightened. "*Daniel Levy!*" she repeated in a low, surprised voice.

"He brought you a lovely bouquet of flowers that I put in the dining-room," Mrs O'Shea informed her. She nodded towards the small vase of tulips and added, "He brought those ones for me, but I thought we could both enjoy them if I put them in here. I made him a nice cup of tea and he had a slice of fruitcake and he sat in the kitchen chatting away to me. Oh, he's a lovely man!" The housekeeper's face lit up like a young girl discussing a boy with her friends. "He's one of those people who can just make himself at home anywhere."

Leonora didn't need to be told any of this. She knew exactly what Daniel was like and how well he related to people from all walks of life. Like Andrew, it was his vocation. Daniel was a consultant psychiatrist who travelled between two Midlands hospitals – Mullingar and Portlaoise. He occasionally worked teaching students at one of the Dublin hospitals, and this had brought him into contact with Leonora's husband and the two men had become firm friends.

Mrs O'Shea nodded towards the window. "He even had a wee walk into the garden to see what you've been up to outside. He's a keen gardener too."

Leonora took a deep breath. "And did he say what he wanted?"

The housekeeper shrugged. "He said that he was up in Dublin for a meeting at one of the big hospitals and that he had a few hours to spare and decided to call out to see how you were."

"Very nice of him," Leonora said, although her words belied her true feelings about her visitor.

"I told him you would be more than disappointed to have missed him but he said that he would be up in Dublin again over the next few weeks."

Leonora nodded. Lizzie knew lots of things that went on in this house but she had no idea as to the nature of the relationship between her employer and Daniel Levy.

Leonora would find reasons to be out often this week.

Daniel Levy was the last person she wanted to see.

The previous Christmas she had made it plain that she had no interest in him and she was sure she had hit the message home fairly hard. She had been sure that he wouldn't come back to Glenmore House.

But she had obviously been very much mistaken.

Chapter 6

On the Wednesday afternoon before the dance, Rose was down at the local Guards' Barracks helping her mother. She washed, dried and put the lunchtime crockery away, then went out to the washing line and brought in the laundry. Afterwards she manoeuvred the legs of the heavy old ironing board into place and leaned her weight on it, to check that it was indeed secure. Satisfied, she lifted the electric iron from the floor and plugged it into the socket on the skirting-board, wishing, as usual, that they had such a handy way of ironing at home.

Back at the cottage she had all the trouble of putting an old blanket on the kitchen table and heating the flat iron up on the fire. Heavy things like sheets and trousers and shirts were grand enough, but using the flat iron on the more delicate things was always a bit hit and a miss. And if she was starching collars or white pillow-cases, quite often the bottom of the iron would overheat and the starch would turn brown, leaving streaky burnt marks that were the devil to remove.

While the electric iron heated up, Rose went back into the laundry room and came back out carrying a basket overflowing with the Guards' shirts and underwear and hankies. She placed it on the floor by the ironing board and then went over to the sink to lift the bowl of starch she had made up ten minutes earlier.

To break herself into the task, she started on the smaller items first and within a short time she had a dozen stiff white squares of hankies piled up alongside a pile of cotton vests and underpants on the kitchen table. When she got into the swing of it – especially with the electric iron – it was one of the jobs she actually enjoyed. There was something very satisfying about pressing down the iron on the freshly dried cotton, making flat and regimented the crumpled heaps of material.

Rose was just starting on the second blue shirt when the back door of the kitchen opened and her mother came in with a wooden crate full of carrots and turnips, spring cabbage and potatoes.

"Oh, that's grand!" Kathleen said, looking over at the neatly ironed items. "I was afraid I wouldn't get time to get through that lot." She dumped the vegetable box down on the draining-board at the sink, then sat down at the table.

"Sure, I don't mind giving you a hand now and again," said Rose.

She put the iron down on the board now and went over to close the door that led out into the hallway. Then she came back to stand at the corner of the table.

"I was wondering if I could press a couple of things of my own for the weekend," she said in a low and slightly hesitant voice. "You let me do it at Easter."

Kathleen sucked her breath in through her teeth. "Now, you know I don't like to be doing things like that too often . . . it could put me in an awkward spot. Sergeant Doherty is on this afternoon and you know he has an eye like a hawk for anything out of the ordinary."

The other Guards were very different – especially Guard McGuire who was easy-going and great to have a bit of craic with. Even Rose got on with him. Any time she or the younger girls called down to the barracks when he was on duty, he gave them any minerals, cakes or chocolate biscuits that were going. Sergeant Doherty was a very different matter. He did everything by the book and he would no doubt raise his bushy eyebrows if he caught sight of a lady's garment on the ironing board.

"I don't mean to make things awkward for you," Rose said, pulling a little anguished face, "but I ruined the bit of lace on the cuff of my blouse last week using the old iron at home. I had to end up taking the lace off the two cuffs and it doesn't look the same at all."

Kathleen let out a little hiss of annoyance. "Oh, what have you got with you?" she asked, the irritation clear in her voice. "I hope you haven't brought a load of stuff because you'll only get me in trouble if you have."

Rose's face flushed, realising she had caught her mother on one of her bad days. Most of the time she was easy-going enough but when she felt under pressure at work she got a bit awkward.

"My good blouse," she said, "and two dresses . . . I wanted to have them all nice and pressed to wear for the weekend." Hannah was due to arrive on the evening coach from Galway the next day and Rose planned on meeting her wearing one of her new outfits.

Kathleen rolled her eyes to the ceiling. But Rose was a good girl and she rarely took liberties. "Go on," she told her daughter, "you'd better get them done now before Sergeant Doherty appears back."

An hour later, Rose had cleared all the ironing for the Guards and was on her way back up to the cottage with her own things carefully pressed and folded and back in her fancy Moons bag. She was stepping along, humming to herself, when she became aware of a noise behind her.

She turned around and was confronted by a bicycle skidding to a halt only a few feet away from her.

"Paul! You great *amadán*!" Rose exclaimed to her younger brother. "You nearly gave me the fright of my life!"

"I caught you! I caught you!" he laughed, delighted with himself. He stood now, leaning his forearms on the handlebars, his long legs splayed either side of the bike.

"Do you want to hop on the back and I'll bring you up home?"

Rose shook her head. "No, I'm grand. I'll enjoy the walk back up since it's such a nice day."

He motioned towards the bag of newly pressed clothes. "Give me that and I'll carry it on the bike for you."

"You will not! They're my best clothes and they'd be a fine state by the time you'd get them home on the bike."

Paul pulled a face and laughed. "I'll walk along with you, so," he told her, dismounting from his bike. Even though he was two years younger, he stood a good head taller than Rose already, with the same dark hair and deep brown eyes as his sister. "Are you all set for the dance on Friday night?"

Rose raised her eyebrows and shrugged, affecting disinterest in the event.

Paul nudged her elbow with his and said, "Come on, you love an oul' dance! When the boys see you and Hannah in all your finery, there'll be a mighty stampede to get to the two of you!"

The mention of her cousin's name sent a little wave of irritation through Rose but she hid it. The only one she revealed her true feelings about Hannah to was her grandmother. Although Martha was old and her sight and hearing were less than perfect, she was more aware of what was going on than people realised. In fact, it was Martha who had quietly alerted Rose to her cousin's very fleeting acquaintance with the truth.

"Are you looking forward to Hannah coming down?" said Paul. "She's some gas character, isn't she?"

"I suppose she is," Rose said vaguely, snapping a small twig off a yellow gorse bush that was growing at the side of the ditch.

"Every one of the lads has been asking after her," Paul went on, his eyes shining. "I'm suddenly the centre of attention every time there's a dance on. Even the girls ask after her – they're always asking me questions about when she's coming down and will she be coming to the dance and all that kind of thing." He looked at Rose and grinned. "Although I have a feeling they're more jealous of her than anything."

Rose frowned. "And why would they all be jealous of Hannah?"

"Don't be an eejit!" Paul said incredulously, looking at his sister as though she were mad. "Her looks, of course – all the lads think she's gorgeous – they think she has a look of Marilyn Monroe"

Rose's stomach muscles tightened as though she had just been punched. "And do *you* think she's gorgeous?" she asked in a low voice. "Do you think she looks like Marilyn Monroe?"

Paul's face suddenly became serious. "Aw, Rose . . . you can't expect me to answer a question like that – sure Hannah's our cousin. I don't see her the way the other lads do."

"By the sounds of it, you're the only one who doesn't fancy her," Rose said, raising her eyebrows and forcing a smile on her face. "I suppose the rest of us will just have to make do with her leftovers then, since she can only dance with one at a time."

Paul gave her a sidelong look. "Ah, you're only looking for compliments now! You know well that they all have an eye for you, too. Sure, the lads for miles around are always asking about you. You must know they like you from the way they chat to you down in the bar. And of course Liam O'Connor is absolutely mad about you and doesn't take any care to hide it. I think he has the other boys afraid to go near you." The idea that this might be true horrified Rose. "Why do you think that?" she asked.

"Oh, I don't mean that seriously. Sure they're afraid to go near you anyway because of our father. He's so strict and oul'-fashioned compared to a lot of the other fathers around."

"But I'm nearly nineteen – he can't keep us tied to the

house forever," said Rose with more confidence than she felt.

"That's one of the reasons that I'm delighted Hannah's coming," said Paul. "He's always easier when we have visitors and he likes Hannah. She always manages to talk her way around him and knows the right thing to say to get her own way." He shrugged. "I suppose we're that bit more wary around him because we know what he's like when he's in a bad mood."

"Hannah thinks she can get around anybody."

"Well, I'm happy enough if it means we can get out for the night instead of being kept back to do a dozen extra decades of the Rosary."

Then a voice called out from the cottage they had just passed.

"It's Johnny Morrison," Paul said. "He'll want to know who's playing in the match on Saturday. You go on and I'll catch up with you in a few minutes."

Rose gave Johnny a wave and walked on, her good mood of earlier now evaporated. She really wished that Paul had left her in peace to walk back to the house, enjoying the sunshine and the cool sea breeze. She'd even managed to put Hannah's imminent arrival to the back of her mind and had been imagining the reaction she would get when Michael Murphy saw her wearing the new flowery dress that she had more or less decided to wear.

She looked down at the Moons carrier bag and suddenly felt tears pricking at the back of her eyes. She felt foolish for being so excited about the dance and about wearing her fancy new outfits. She felt foolish for thinking that Friday might be the night when she'd catch Michael Murphy's eye. After listening to Paul going on about their cousin, she knew she didn't stand a chance beside her.

It didn't matter what she wore, everyone would only have eyes for the blonde-haired, blue-eyed Hannah who looked like Marilyn Monroe.

Chapter 7

"Have you everything packed and ready?" Sheila Martin asked as she took her coat from the hook on the back of the kitchen door.

"I have," Hannah said quickly. "I finished ironing my things this morning and I have everything all packed now.

Sheila's eyes narrowed as she looked at the plain skirt and jumper that her daughter was wearing. "You're not going dressed like that, are you?"

"No," Hannah said, shaking her blonde head vigorously. "I have a good skirt and blouse laid out upstairs." Her mother always insisted on her looking her best, especially when she was going down to her Auntie Kathleen's. Her mother's attitude bothered and embarrassed her. It was as if some sort of point was being made – that the Martin family never dropped their standards even if they were visiting relatives who were much plainer and less well off than them. And although Sheila wore basic clothes around the farmhouse, when it came to any other occasion she was always dressed in her best and insisted that her daughter was too. Hannah was acutely conscious of other women and girls giving sidelong glances to each other as though saying, 'Who do they think they are?' It always made her feel awkward and she knew that her mother's attitude must grate on their relatives.

"I've got the sausages and rashers and black and white pudding wrapped up in greaseproof paper, like you told me." She touched a hand to one of the rollers in her hair to check if it was dry and set yet. She had got up early this morning to have a bath and shampoo her blonde hair, as the bathing facilities down in her Aunt Kathleen's weren't as straightforward as those she had at home and she needed to have her hair just right for the dance the following day.

"I've got the perfume I bought for Rose packed in the case and the earrings for Auntie Kathleen, the chocolates and sherry you gave me for Granny Barry, and the presents for the younger ones."

"And did your father give you the bottle of whiskey for your Uncle Stephen?" asked Sheila.

Hannah nodded vigorously. "It's already in my case. I wrapped it inside a thick cardigan to keep it safe."

Sheila Martin's lips formed into a tight, straight line. "Well, make sure you don't keep Simon waiting when he comes to collect you," she warned, a note of irritation in her voice. "It's his dinner break at the bank and Ursula was good enough to ask him to drop you off at the station."

"I won't keep him waiting," Hannah reassured her. "Like I told you, I've everything packed."

There was a pause as Sheila's eyes darted around the kitchen, checking that Hannah had washed and dried the dishes they had used earlier and that she had brushed and mopped the kitchen floor and the stone flags out in the hall.

"I've already told Ursula I have an appointment at the doctor's, so I won't be here when you're leaving," Sheila said, "and I've explained that your father can't leave that sick cow he was up half the night with to drive you. He's waiting for the vet to call out at some point in the afternoon."

"I'll be ready," Hannah promised, unpinning one of the rollers from the back of her head now. "I've just to put my suit on, comb my hair out and I'll be all set." She ran her fingers through the loose curl now, smiling with satisfaction that it was dry and going the way it should be.

Sheila gave a loud sigh and her eyes narrowed. "Hair, hair, hair!" she said in a low, barely controlled hiss of a voice. "That's all you ever think about in that stupid head of yours – it's no wonder that you can't even pass your school exams. You're too busy preening and admiring yourself."

Hannah's face drained. She had done everything this morning she could think of to keep on the good side of her mother. She had tried to anticipate the things that would rile her and avoid them.

Sheila poked her daughter on her arm – hard enough to bruise her. "It's sheer vanity, and you know what they say in the bible about *that*. One of these days I'll take a pair of scissors to that damned hair and I'll cut it all off! I swear to God I'll do it!"

Hannah swallowed hard, feeling a rage building up inside her against the injustice that her mother regularly meted out to her. "I'm only trying to look tidy before going down to Clare – you always tell me I should look my best." she said, in a deliberately low, placatory voice. "They only have that oul' tin bath and you have to boil the water up for it."

Sheila's face suddenly stiffened. "Are you daring to *argue* with me?" she whispered. "Because if you are, you know what you'll get."

"But I'm not arguing –"

"Don't you dare!"

Hannah's blue eyes closed and her arm instinctively came up in front of her face to ward off the blow she anticipated. She waited a few seconds but thankfully it never came. She brought her arms back down to her sides. "I'm sorry, Mammy," she said in a low, shaky voice. "I was only trying to explain . . . I didn't mean to say anything to annoy you."

"Well, see that you don't."

As soon as the front door closed behind her mother, Hannah's head sank into her hands. Thank God I'm going away, she thought. Thank God I'll have a week away from this.

A short while later she went upstairs to her bedroom. After taking off her older clothes, she stepped into the straight wine skirt she had laid out on the bottom of the bed, and then she took the puff-sleeved white chiffon blouse off its hanger and put it on. She fastened it up to the second button. There was no need to have it any lower for the time being – it was easy to undo a couple of more buttons if the occasion called for it. She fastened a wide black belt around her tiny waist, which matched her black sling-back shoes.

Then she went over to kneel by the corner of her bed, lift up the mattress and remove the women's magazines she had hidden there. She put them in the zipped compartment of her case. She would take them down to Clare to show Rose and the other girls. She smiled to herself because she knew they would be very impressed with them, particularly the problem pages. It was the sort of thing that would make them look up to her. Then she took the brown envelope she had hidden under the mattress with eleven pounds and fifteen shillings in it. Her mother knew she had saved a few pounds from her birthday and Christmas, but she knew nothing about the other money she had been hiding which included contributions from her Uncle Simon.

Finally she reached far under the mattress and took out the paper bag that held her two pairs of lace knickers and a black lace bra. She quickly put that into the zipped bit of the case as well. She couldn't leave anything that could be found that might indicate signs of growing up, becoming independent and having different views from her mother. There was no point in taking chances.

If her mother was to find out about her personal bits and pieces – especially the lace knickers – there would be no containing her anger. And if she ever found out about her affair with her Auntie Ursula's husband, God knows what would happen. Probably the very worst. It would make it impossible for her to continue living at home. And no matter what her father and brothers might do to intervene, she knew that her mother would never forgive or forget.

Hannah couldn't wait to move away from home. But the time wasn't right. She had neither the means nor the money. It would have to be planned carefully and at the moment she wasn't in the position to do it.

But she would do it. And before long.

* * *

Hannah held the block of black mascara under the dripping tap and let exactly two drops fall onto it, then she rubbed the water into the mascara until it formed a paste which she could brush onto her eyelashes. Then she stood on her tip-toes to look in the small shaving mirror above the kitchen sink. After she had applied several coats, Hannah carefully outlined her mouth with pearly pink lipstick and fluffed up her blonde curls. It was a new hairstyle – one she had copied from a magazine that showed you how you could look like Marilyn Monroe.

Hannah leaned in close to the mirror and made a pouting, kissing gesture – the sort of thing that a sexy film star would do. Then she licked the tip of her finger and slicked it over her eyebrows to make sure they were in place. She stood back and observed herself, half-closing her eyes first and then opening them wide.

A tingle of excitement ran through her. Today was going to be a great day. It was the start of a whole week away from home – a whole week away from her mother and her bad temper – a whole week of doing more or less what she liked.

There was also the possibility of meeting new people, which Hannah loved. Especially new men and boys. Strangers gave her the chance to be anything she wanted. She could tell them anything and they wouldn't be any the wiser.

In any case, she always felt far more popular down in the small fishing village. Everyone seemed to like her there and if any of the girls were a bit quiet or cool with her, she knew it was only because she had nicer clothes and knew how to make the best of her looks. That – and the fact that the local lads always made a beeline for her. But Hannah couldn't help that – it wasn't her fault that the boys reacted to her that way. The main thing was that she and Rose had always got on very well and as long as that continued everything would be grand.

As it was best to keep on the right side of her cousin she had bought her a small blue bottle of *Soir de Paris* from the chemist's shop in Tullamore. She knew that Rose didn't have the money to spare for luxury things like that and she knew that the gift would help to ensure that she would always have a place to escape to from home if things got really bad.

She was just checking her hair again in the mirror when she heard the car arriving. She rushed to the door to greet Simon and was more than slightly taken aback when she saw the tall, thin shape of her aunt emerging from the passenger side of the car. Then, the back door opened and her young cousin Philip came out, a hanky held to the side of his face.

"Are you all ready?" Ursula said to her niece, an impatient look on her pinched white face. "We have to get Philip into the dentist's – the poor little soul is killed with a pain in his tooth." She looked across to the barn and outhouses. "Is your father around? I want a quick word with him about Mammy."

"He's in the shed with one of the cows," Hannah

said, pointing across the farmyard. "He's waiting on the vet – he's been up half the night with it."

Ursula lifted her eyes heavenwards and pursed her lips tightly together. "Men are always busy when you need them," she muttered, in a voice loud enough for her niece to hear. She took Philip by the hand and they headed off in the direction of the farm buildings.

When there was no sign of Simon getting out of the car and coming to help her with the case as she expected, she went back down the hallway to get it herself. When she appeared back on the doorstep, Simon eventually got out. When she got a glimpse of his face, Hannah immediately knew that something was up and her heart sank.

At the beginning of their romance, Simon had always been laughing and joking but she had noticed recently that he wasn't the happy-go-lucky fellow all the time and it was one of the reasons she didn't mind having a week away without him.

"Ursula's like a feckin' briar this afternoon," he said, going around to open the boot. "I wish I'd stayed in town. The minute I walked in the door she started ranting and raving about her mother and I'd say she's giving out hell about it now to your father."

"What's wrong?" Hannah asked, a fluttery, nervous feeling coming into her chest. She was used to her mother causing atmospheres at home and she could usually predict how the ensuing arguments would go but she wasn't too sure how to react to her aunt's obvious bad mood. Ursula Connolly was usually quiet and fairly even-tempered – along the same lines as Hannah's father. Hannah had no way of gauging what to do and say that would help to placate her –

or indeed whether she would be best to stay quiet and say nothing at all. And by the look on Simon's face as he lifted her case into the boot, it looked as though he didn't have much of a clue how to handle his wife himself.

"It seems your Granny Martin is looking to come and live with either ourselves or your mother and father," he told her. He felt in his pocket now for his packet of cigarettes and his lighter.

Hannah's heart gave an excited little leap at the unexpected good news. "Do you think she might move in with us?" she asked, trying not to sound too delighted. This would be the answer to all her prayers. Her mother would be so busy looking after the old woman that she wouldn't have time to be hounding her.

Also, her mother liked to keep appearances up when there were other people around and she certainly wouldn't want anyone hearing the sort of rages she was capable of getting into. She even kept the worst of them from Hannah's father because he was basically a peaceful man and hated any disturbances at home. The two lads were the same and they just got out of the way if their mother started and didn't come back down home from university for a few weeks to let her cool off. And their attitude obviously had the desired effect for it was rare these days that she got into a temper when they came home. For some reason, the only one she gave full vent to her rages in front of was Hannah.

All in all, Hannah instinctively felt that having her grandmother living with them would divert a lot of the attention away from herself.

"Nora says she can't stick living out there with Finbar and that wife of his much longer." Simon shook his head and gave a long, low whistle. "That's going to set the cat amongst the pigeons and no doubt about it." He lit his cigarette now and took a long, deep drag on it.

Hannah's Uncle Finbar had been a confirmed bachelor for years and ran the family farm a couple of miles outside Tullamore. He and his widowed mother had jogged along together just fine until last year, when he had turned up one evening with a serious, stocky woman called Angela – and then had stunned everybody by announcing that they were engaged. Apparently he had met her through some farming organisation Christmas 'do' and had been seeing her regularly ever since, under the guise of going to meetings or to church services.

The wedding had taken place six months ago and Angela had moved in as the new mistress of the house. Within days she had taken over cooking the breakfast and the midday meal for her husband and the other farm workers, and Nora had suddenly felt herself redundant. The older woman had done her best to rub along with the younger one but it had became more and more apparent that she was regarded as nothing but an encumbrance to the newly-weds.

Hannah came around to lean on the car beside Simon. She noticed that he hadn't offered her a puff on the cigarette as he often did when they were alone but that wasn't surprising in the light of his mood and the fact that her father and aunt were in close proximity.

She leaned closer to him and touched her fingers to his hand. "I thought you were coming to pick me up on your own," she said in a low voice. "I wasn't expecting Ursula and Philip to come along with you . . ."

Simon raised his eyebrows. "You were lucky I got down here to collect you at all. I've had the most feckin' awful morning at work and then just as I was leaving Ursula phoned and I had to rush home and pick her and Philip up for the dentist's." He shook his head. "Then, when I was trying to eat my bite, she was going on and on about her mother and that wife of Finbar's. I tell you, Hannah, at this moment in time I could just run away from it all."

Hannah's face creased up. "You don't mean from me as well, do you?"

Simon gave a sidelong grin. "No, I don't mean from you. I'm going to miss you when you're away."

"Well," Hannah whispered, "they say that absence makes the heart grow fonder . . ."

Voices sounded from the entrance of the barn now and then Bill Martin and his sister and nephew emerged into the sunlight. They walked across the yard towards the car.

"I've just explained the situation to Bill," Ursula told her husband. Her voice was calmer and more relaxed than earlier.

"Sure, it'll all sort itself out," Bill said. "We won't see the old lady stuck . . . we'll work something out." He glanced over at Hannah. "Is that you all ready to go now?"

"I am. The case is in the boot of the car."

Simon glanced at his watch. "We'd better be heading into town now or we'll miss the train."

Bill started towards the house, his gait slightly quicker than his usual slow, steady plod. "Give me one minute while you're getting into the car. I just want to get something from the kitchen." He emerged a few minutes later as Simon was turning the car about and when it stopped he came over to knock with a thick knuckle on the back window. Hannah wound the window down and he leaned in and threw a few silver coins in Philip's lap. He winked at the boy and said, "That might help to cure the toothache!" Then he thrust a screwed-up five-pound note into Hannah's hand. "Treat yourself while you're away," he told her in a low voice, "and say nothing to your mother."

"Thanks, Daddy," Hannah said, giving his hand a quick squeeze. She was so taken aback at the money. Her father had already given her extra pocket money at the weekend for going away. Had he forgotten about it?

For a split second Hannah felt like jumping out of the car, wrapping her arms around her father's neck and giving him a big kiss. But she didn't because she knew her father would probably be mortified in front of his sister and her husband. Hugs and kisses were rare in the Martin family and any sign of public affection was regarded by Sheila Martin as being embarrassing and attention-seeking.

But however strange it was to her mother, Hannah Martin felt the need to be held and hugged and kissed. Since she was a little girl she often imagined she came from a family who wrapped their arms around each other when they were happy and she wished she had a mother who held her in her arms and dried away her tears.

But recently Hannah had discovered that there were ways and means of getting all the hugs and kisses that she needed. But it wasn't from her mother and her immediate family that she now looked for it.

It was from men like Simon Connolly.

Chapter 8

Leonora walked over to an ancient but sturdy bench which was perched on a small hill in one of the gardens to the right-hand side of Glenmore House. The bench gave her a view of the Victorian wrought-iron conservatory, the freshly cut lawn and several flower beds. She could also see two bird tables and a number of nesting boxes. Andrew had been particularly fond of watching and identifying birds, and recently Leonora had found herself staring out of the window or sitting quietly on this particular bench in the same way as her husband had done.

Signs that old age is approaching, Leonora, she wryly told herself on those occasions, because for many years she had associated activities like bird-watching and gardening with two elderly maiden aunts who had been obsessed with both activities. She would shrug to herself, for she was well aware that her busy, social life had changed even before Andrew's death and her activities were more home-based and solitary.

She sat down on the old bench with a grateful sigh. She had worked hard this morning, completely clearing a flower bed that she had planted three years ago which hadn't quite worked out as she had imagined. The crimson and purple rhododendron bushes that stood close to the old stone wall at the back of the bed had struggled against the limey soil and had grown woody and scrawny and were eventually able to produce nothing more than a few weak blooms. And the pink and blue hydrangea bushes – which had started out as vibrantly colourful potted plants – had shrivelled in the soil and were reluctant to yield any more than small, curled-up leaves and a couple of miserable, faded flowers.

This morning the sickly rhododendron and hydrangea bushes had been carefully dug out by Tommy Murray and had been wheelbarrowed away to the larger of the two greenhouses. There, Tommy hoped to rescue them before it was too late by planting them in large wooden tubs filled with a different soil which was more suited to their needs. Then Leonora – dressed in her gardening trousers, rubber Wellington boots and Aran sweater covered with a green canvas apron – had spent two hours clearing weeds from the bed and finally raking the broken soil.

Sitting up in bed the previous night with a gardening book and a tumbler of hot whiskey, she had planned the whole flower bed in her mind. She had pictured the new flowering bushes and shrubs that she would plant against the back wall, the rows of fragrant lavender that would form the borders, and the smaller shrubs and flowers for the main body.

Leonora sat on the bench now, surveying her morning's work – the clean-raked bed that was like a fresh page waiting to be written on. The thought of bringing new life and colour to it gave her a little tingle of excitement which in turn gave way to a sudden, inexplicable surge of emotion. As she sat blinking back the huge hot tears, she realised that she had a great deal to thank her garden for.

Growing flowers and herbs and a few basic salad vegetables had been a source of strength to her during the worst time of her life. The soil and earth had sustained her.

And the mindless, routine tasks of watering and pruning and deadheading roses had given her life a rhythm and a purpose.

Quite a change for Leonora Bentley, who had been at the very core of all the social functions in this part of the world, who had a full diary of her own activities every weekend and several week-nights, apart from being involved in her children's activities. But she knew exactly when she had started to withdraw from many of her social engagements and she knew exactly *why*.

For a number of years, Leonora had been quite happy jogging along with the parties, the theatre outings and the fundraisers until a certain two ladies had joined the group – two fashionable, socially conscious, younger women. Soon afterwards, Leonora had become increasingly aware of the subtle competition amongst the females to organise the most extravagant dinner party, to have the most expensive wines and the most exotic menus. And when it came to the charity golf tournaments or fund-raising balls, the pressure to have the patronage of higher profile supporters became immense.

The discussion amongst the ladies in the circle began to focus on ways of snaring the wealthier of Dublin's society and Leonora suspected it was more to do with raising the profile of certain members than making money for the charities involved.

When she tentatively mentioned her feelings to one or two of the older crowd, she was surprised at their response.

"It's good to have new blood in our circle," one of the ladies had said. "And it means we can take a back seat and just follow along."

"I agree with you entirely," another one of the group confided in Leonora, "but saying anything openly to those particular ladies might harm John's business dealings . . . so I'll probably just have to grin and bear it."

Leonora had of course discussed the situation with Andrew, and he had shrugged and said he entirely agreed. He had always been happy to go along with whatever Leonora wanted but he had often commented on the shallowness of some of the social circle and was more content sitting at home in the evenings with a good book and a glass of whiskey. He had pointed out that it was Leonora who had enjoyed all the group activity and he would be quite happy for them to take things easier and spend more time at home.

Leonora carried on with the group but after a while she found that the organising and hosting of evenings at Glenmore House had become a stress and a strain as opposed to a pleasure. All the old easiness had gone and she found herself being quizzed as to where she had purchased her outfit for the evening, where she and Andrew were planning to holiday that summer and what florist had supplied her flowers. And when she found Mrs O'Shea being interrogated in the kitchen about the origins of the wild salmon she had cooked, Leonora decided enough was enough.

She pulled back from the regular functions, using a variety of excuses not to attend. With both Diana and Edward at university during the week, she explained to the women in her circle that her children's weekends at home were more precious now and came before any other social commitments. Then fate gave her a very real excuse to be absent when her sister Isabel in Edinburgh took ill. Leonora flew back and forth to Scotland over a period of months until she was satisfied that Isabel had recovered.

At first there were lots of phone calls checking on her absences but gradually they fizzled out. Leonora made sure she still contributed to any charity events, buying tickets even though she did not plan to attend. And she and Andrew attended the Christmas functions if they were around and the occasional dinner dance when she knew exactly who would be seated next to them at the table.

Gradually their lives moved into a different, slower gear.

It had turned out to be a blessing that she wasn't involved in the big social whirl when things suddenly went very wrong in her married life. She would have hated to face people every day, smiling and pretending, and all the while hiding the hurt and pain she felt at being betrayed.

Leonora felt a tightness come into her chest now as the old, dark memories came flooding back into her mind. She stood up from the bench, straightened her spine and her legs, and then slowly moved down the slope towards the house. She slowed up at the newly emerging peony rose bushes outside the conservatory to check how far the foliage had come on. She looked forward to the few weeks in early summer when they would be in bloom. She would cut a dozen or so stalks and display the pink and white flowers in two tall glass vases on the round rosewood table in the entrance hall.

The vases were dear to her heart as Jonathan, Diana and Edward had pooled their pocket money together to buy them one Mother's Day when they were children. Although she had countless crystal and china vases, she preferred the shape of the cheap glass vases and felt they were the only ones that did the peony roses justice.

Leonora walked around to the back porch which led straight into the main kitchen. It was a handy place which she used as a gardening room. It was bright and cheery with white-painted shelves filled with pots of scarlet geraniums and Busy Lizzies, and there was a tall cupboard in the corner which housed her gardening tools and clothing.

She had just taken off her Wellingtons and was standing in her stocking feet when she heard her housekeeper's shrill Scottish voice calling for her. It was a habit that Leonora had tried to stamp out many years ago, insisting that Mrs O'Shea come looking for whoever she wanted rather than stand by the phone screeching for people. For a number of years it had worked, but recently the housekeeper had reverted back to using her voice as opposed to her legs. Leonora reckoned it had more to do with the Scotswoman's arthritis than laziness and at times she found herself responding rather than pushing the point on every occasion.

"Coming!" she called back. She quickly lifted down her indoor shoes from the shelf and stuck her feet into them.

Mrs O'Shea came to greet her at the porch door, her

white maid's cap in one hand and two hair-clips in the other. "You've a visitor waiting for you in the drawing-room," she said, turning back into the kitchen.

Leonora's heart stopped. "It's not Daniel Levy again?" she asked in a low voice. She had managed to avoid him on his last two visits and she didn't want to be caught by him now.

"Not at all. It's that odd lady with the wild red hair that does the paintings."

"Terry Cassidy?" Leonora's voice was high with surprise. Terry Cassidy taught the art classes she attended on a Monday morning.

Mrs O'Shea went over to the mirror above the sink to check as she pinned her maid's stiff white hat on her greying hair. "I'll bring a pot of tea and some scones in – I dare say it's too early for a drink?"

Leonora looked up at the clock. It was going on for half past twelve. She hesitated for a moment. "Tea will be fine," she decided. It was much too early for a sherry or a whiskey and besides she didn't know how the art teacher stood with regards to alcohol.

Leonora recognised the artist's signature spicy perfume as she walked along the hallway. Terry Cassidy was wandering around the drawing-room examining the paintings and the family photographs. Not much taller than Leonora but more generously proportioned, she was dressed this afternoon in a colourful ensemble of wide purple trousers with a purple and black silk coat more suited to a night at the opera. She wore a long purple scarf which trailed almost to the floor. Her red hennaed hair was swept up into a French pleat and held in place by a wooden clasp.

"What a wonderful room!" she exclaimed, holding her hands up expansively. "In fact, what a wonderful *house*! I often wondered how this old building would look inside. It's surprisingly homely and comfortable for such a big rambling place – and you have some lovely artistic touches in the way you display things." Her accent was indeterminate – a bit of Irish thrown in with what she herself described as a 'cosmopolitan mix' when she was questioned about its origins.

"Thank you," Leonora said.

"Although," Terry said, giving a little theatrical sigh, "I have to confess it's just a tad too dark in here and in the hallway for my own liking. I would have to open it up somehow and let the sunshine in – and perhaps paint the walls white or yellow."

"Do you think so?" Leonora replied, amused at her guest's bluntness. Terry often caught her by surprise by the things she said. She was an unusual woman by Dublin standards – in her forties and single, fiercely independent and unflinching in her opinions. And yet Leonora detected a gentleness and a vulnerability beneath her Bohemian exterior.

In the two years that Leonora had been attending Terry's weekly art class, this was the first time that they had spent any time on their own. Leonora found it both strange and interesting to be on her own with the quirky art teacher.

There was a bit of a noise outside in the hallway and then Mrs O'Shea came in carrying the tea things. She put the tray down on the low table in front of the fireplace and started to unload the cups and plates and silver teapot. The two women went over to the armchairs on either side of the table, Terry Cassidy unwrapping her long scarf from her neck as she sat down and throwing it over the back of her chair.

The housekeeper lifted the teapot and moved towards the cup and saucer in front of their guest.

Terry's hand flew to cover the top of the cup. "Oh – how very silly of me! I should have said before now that I don't actually drink tea."

"I should have checked," Leonora said apologetically. "Is coffee okay, or maybe a cold drink?"

Mrs O'Shea pursed her lips together as she awaited their guest's decision.

"Coffee please," Terry Cassidy said, turning to look the formidable housekeeper straight in the eye. "That's if it's not too much trouble for you."

"It's no trouble at all," the Scotswoman said in the sing-song voice Leonora knew she used when she was irritated and, putting the silver teapot down with a thud, exited the room.

"Leonora, I'll get straight to the point of my visit," Terry said then. "Do you remember the charity art exhibition that I entered your jug and snowdrop painting for?"

"Yes. Indeed I do."

"Well, you not only sold your little painting – you've had a commission for *two* more. Another one identical to the one sold and something along the same lines and in the same colours, to hang as a pair."

Leonora's mouth opened in shock. "Who? Who bought them?"

Terry shrugged. "A woman from Donegal bought the actual painting, and then a man came along afterwards and, when he discovered it was sold, asked if he could commission another two."

"*Commission*?" Leonora repeated, shaking her head in bemusement. "I can't believe it. I can't believe anyone would pay money for that simple little painting."

"Ah, but they're not quite so simple, Leonora," Terry said, smiling. "You definitely put your own little twist on it and you paid to have it nicely framed which improved it no end."

A huge smile suddenly appeared on Leonora Bentley's face – a smile which lit up her green eyes and instantly took several years off her. "I'm delighted," she said, joining her hands together. "I'm *absolutely delighted*. It's the loveliest news I've had in a long time. And I'm so grateful to you for insisting that I enter the painting and for taking the trouble to come and tell me about the exhibition."

"It's my pleasure, dear, and talent must always be promoted!"

Mrs O'Shea returned carrying a pot of coffee. The artist thanked her profusely and the housekeeper went off looking mollified that the extra trouble had at least been acknowledged.

The two women chatted over their buttered scones and Leonora arranged to come down to the art studio for a full day the following week in order to work on the paintings.

"Are you sure it won't be any trouble?" she asked. "I know it's a day when you don't have any classes. Won't I be intruding on your personal time?"

"Not at all! If you only work on the paintings during the class time it will take weeks. Besides, it will be lovely to have your company while I'm doing my own work."

When Mrs O'Shea came through a while later to remove the tea things, a thought suddenly struck Leonora. She glanced at the clock that stood on the marble fireplace. It was getting on for two o'clock. She turned to the artist, who was now winding her purple scarf around her neck in preparation to leave. "Will you have a drink to celebrate my unexpected success? A sherry or a whiskey – or whatever you would like."

There was a brief moment's hesitation, then Terry took her scarf back off again. "I'd love a gin and tonic if you have it."

"I'll join you with that," Leonora said delightedly. "I always find it a rather refreshing drink at this time of the day." She got up from her chair and went towards the mahogany sideboard. "I'll sort the drinks, Mrs O'Shea, if you wouldn't mind bringing through some ice and lemon."

They had their second drink wandering around the garden, as the chilly morning had gradually turned into a pleasantly warm afternoon.

"I can see where you get your artistic inspiration from," Terry said, pausing to admire an archway that was entirely covered with dark green clematis leaves, which would soon be festooned with pink flowers. "It's wonderful that you can combine your gardening and art."

"I suppose it is," Leonora said thoughtfully. "I've never really made that connection before. I've just painted the things I'm drawn to."

"Do you find it very lonely out here?" Terry suddenly asked. "It's such a very big house for so few people."

Leonora caught her breath. This was the question that she dreaded most. "I'm used to it. Of course it is very big but I couldn't imagine living anywhere else."

There was a brief pause.

"You can be lonely in a small space too," said Terry, raising her eyebrows. "I think I'd go mad if I didn't have my painting. I don't know how I could possibly fill all those long winter nights." She suddenly laughed. "And all the long *spring* and *summer* and *autumn* nights. My work fills every little void in my life."

Leonora looked at her now. She did not want to appear in any way intrusive but curiosity got the better of her. "Don't you have any family nearby?"

"I have a brother in Kildare and a sister in Donny-brook." She took a sip of her gin and tonic. "We don't see each other that often – high days and holidays. They're very different from me, or rather," she gave a wry little smile, "*I'm* very different from them. They're not a bit interested in art or anything like that. We're from farming stock and they've followed the family tradition while I've veered off on a rather different course. In actual fact I've veered off on a number of different courses . . ."

"You've travelled?" Leonora said. The breeze whipped a strand of her ash-blonde hair and she reached to tuck it behind one ear.

"Oh, yes." Terry nodded vigorously. "And I still do when I can afford it. I have friends in all sorts of places and I love to visit them."

"I wish Andrew and I had travelled more extensively when we were younger," Leonora confessed. "When I look at my art books now and think of all the wonderful places that inspired those paintings – we should have visited France and Italy at least . . ."

"Of course it was a man who started my *real* travels off," Terry mused. Her eyes had a distant look in them now. "It often is, isn't it? I was only in my twenties, just out of Art College. He was older, sophisticated and worldly wise, the usual story . . . and separated from his wife." She sighed and gave a little shrug. "Or so he told me."

Leonora looked at Terry, hoping she would elaborate further. There was a time when a story like this might have shocked her, but not now. She had too many lonely days and nights listening to Mrs O'Shea rattling on about how washing windows with vinegar in water then polishing with scrunched-up newspaper was the best way to clean them, or about a new cake recipe she had heard on the radio.

Leonora led her visitor to a bench in a sunny spot. It crossed her mind that they made a strange-looking pair – Terry in her black and purple ensemble contrasting sharply with her own rough gardening clothes. The thought made her smile to herself.

She listened intently while Terry described her years spent studying art in Paris and sharing a rambling old apartment with five other students in the city.

"I came back to Ireland – back to my parents' farm in Kildare. I worked part-time for a while teaching art in schools but I was always looking for a way out again and that's exactly what Ned Corrigan offered me. He had a travel business and he often went abroad to check places out and I was more than happy to accompany him."

"How did your parents react?" Leonora was intrigued now at how people could live their lives in such different ways. Then, for a brief moment, her mind flitted to Rose Barry in Kilnagree and she thought how the provincial girl's life was the very opposite to that which the younger Terry had lived. She wondered if Rose would live and die in the small fishing village without seeing anything more of the world – or even Ireland.

"Well, of course my parents knew nothing about him being a man who was separated from his wife," Terry continued. "I couldn't possibly have explained all that. I told them I was working for his travel company – which in a way I was – and they didn't know any different. Of course, as the years have gone by, I feel guilty about having deceived them but you see life very differently when you're younger. You live for the moment and don't stop to think of the possible consequences it might have for you and for those who love you." She gave a little sigh. "Looking back, I was very lucky. I had a few narrow escapes but nothing drastic happened. Well, nothing *too* drastic."

Leonora felt a small pang of alarm now as she thought of her own three children. Had they fobbed her and Andrew off with made-up stories, when they were in fact off somewhere else doing God-knows-what? And had they ever been in trouble and not told them? Even now? What if Edward was struggling all alone in America with nobody close to confide in and help? She visited Jonathan, his wife and children in London and spoke to them often on the phone. And of course she had regular calls and visits to Diana and James in Kilnagree. But Edward was a worry to her. The thought of him drifting away until he became a polite stranger was devastating to her, and, if she wasn't reassured about the state of their relationship over the next few months, she planned to jump on a plane to America and find out how things were for herself.

In the meantime, she comforted herself with the knowledge that both Jonathan and Diana had promised to keep up regular written and phone contact with him.

Leonora wished she had someone to discuss Edward with properly but she wouldn't feel comfortable talking about him to her own sisters or any of Andrew's family. When she thought about it, Leonora had never talked *really* personally with anyone but Andrew. He had known her views on simply everything in life – from her political and religious views to her smallest worries about their children. There was nothing she hadn't shared with him and there had been no problem that she hadn't sought his advice about. He had been her husband and her closest friend. To have lost that precious intimacy through death would have been devastating. To have lost it through carelessness was more painful than anything she could ever have imagined.

Terry suddenly became aware of the silence. "Are you shocked?" she said, her voice slightly hesitant.

"No, no . . ." Leonora said. "I'm not shocked about *you* . . ."

The artist looked at her quizzically.

"Oh . . . I suppose it's just touched a raw nerve, being a mother myself." Leonora took another sip of her drink, conscious of sounding censorious. "It makes me feel I should perhaps check things out more thoroughly."

Terry touched Leonora's hand. "Your children are all grown-up and flown the nest," she said gently. "They are more than capable of managing their own lives. And if it's of any comfort to you, I don't regret any of the adventures I had – good or bad. I've learned from them and grown. And I certainly don't blame my parents for not knowing what I was up to – how could I?"

"Really? In retrospect, don't you feel they were too lax allowing you to gallivant off all over the place?"

Terry shook her head. "Not at all. That's what being young is all about. It's the time when we should explore the world and, through doing that, explore ourselves. We can't do that if our parents are constantly watching our every move."

"I think I was brought up rather carefully and kept close to home and consequently, I've brought my own children up in a similar way. I couldn't imagine any of them going off to Europe on their own when they were eighteen. I would have worried about them constantly."

"Horses for courses. The world would be a very boring place if we were all the same."

"I do hope you're not offended." Leonora's tone was concerned.

"Not in the least," the artist laughed. "I would never have survived this long back in Ireland if I took offence every time people had a different view of things from mine. And besides, even though I don't have any children of my own, I do see your point entirely."

They talked on and some time later a light shower of rain drove them back indoors.

"The time!" Terry Cassidy said, looking up at the kitchen clock. It was almost four. "I must go."

"Have you an appointment?"

"No, but I've been here taking up your time for much too long."

"Why don't you stay and have something to eat with

me? We could have an early dinner since we haven't had a proper lunch. That's if you don't mind something very simple and quick like lamb chops and potatoes? Mrs O'Shea is a very good cook."

Terry hesitated for a few moments. "That sounds perfect and it would save me having to rustle something up when I go back home. If you're sure it's not too much trouble?"

Leonora settled her guest by the fire in the drawing-room with a pre-dinner sherry and a bowl of cashew nuts to keep her going, then she went off in search of Mrs O'Shea. As she climbed the panelled staircase lined with old framed hunting-prints, she was aware of having a sense of lightness about her that she had not felt for a long time. A sense of pleasure from being in Terry Cassidy's invigorating company.

Of course the couple of gin and tonics had helped to add a little glow to the afternoon but it was more the conversation and the glimpses into another world that the artist had given her.

At the second turn of the stairs, an archway gave onto a little corridor that led towards the back of the house and to the housekeeper's rooms.

There was a fresh smell of the beeswax polish that the fastidious Scotswoman favoured, mixed with the lavender water that she used for ironing, and as she strode along, Leonora found the basic scents comforting and familiar. As she stopped to tap on the door, she could hear Lizzie's radio quite clearly. She waited a few moments for an answer and, when there was none, she knocked again – more firmly this time. Eventually, she heard footsteps on the other side of the door and then it opened wide, revealing a room filled with comfortable old-fashioned Victorian furniture, lightened with chintz curtains and well-starched lace cloths on the tables and backs of chairs. From the slightly vacant look on the housekeeper's face, it was obvious she had been having an afternoon nap.

"Oh, I'm sorry for disturbing you, Mrs O'Shea," Leonora said apologetically, "but I wondered if we might have dinner early this evening?"

"Is something happening?" the housekeeper asked in a croaky, sleepy voice. "Have you to go out?"

"No, no. It's just that Terry and I got caught up in conversation and I've just noticed the time and realised I haven't given the poor woman anything since the scones at lunch-time. I thought we might have those lamb chops with some plain boiled potatoes and whatever vegetables you have."

Mrs O'Shea's brow furrowed in annoyance. "You mean you've asked that woman to stay on for a meal after being here for half the day already?" Her Scottish tone was clipped and abrupt, the way it always was when she disapproved of something.

"Yes, I have asked her. There isn't a problem with cooking for one more, is there?" Leonora's own manner had now cooled considerably and was more than a match for her housekeeper's. "I checked earlier and we have enough chops for all four of us if Tommy is eating here. And if you're at all worried about the amounts, you can put a few sausages on as well just to be sure."

The housekeeper nodded her head. "Whatever you say yourself. I'll be downstairs in a few minutes."

"There's no need to rush," Leonora said, her voice softer now. "Take your time and come down when you're ready. We're having a sherry with some nuts to keep us going in the meantime."

As she made her way back down the stairs, Leonora wondered why Mrs O'Shea had to be so awkward at times. She had such strong opinions on certain people and certain things and she had made it perfectly plain that she didn't approve at all of Terry Cassidy. Of course it would be something absolutely trivial like the way the artist dressed or coloured her hair that had made the housekeeper decide that she wasn't the sort of person who should be welcomed into Glenmore House.

* * *

It was half past six when Leonora, now dressed in charcoal-coloured slacks and a pale grey cashmere sweater with a double row of pearls that had belonged to her mother, drove Terry Cassidy down the long driveway of Glenmore House.

"I've had a wonderful afternoon," Terry told her as they drove through the tall, iron gates. "And all the more appreciated for being unplanned."

"I enjoyed it very much, too. If I'm truthful, I felt a touch flat coming back after my visit to Diana – it often takes me up to a week to shake the feeling off."

"Talking about exhibitions, you know there's an Impressionist exhibition coming to Dublin next month?"

"No. I hadn't heard about it."

"You would absolutely love it – in fact I think it calls for a class day out in early summer. I'm going to mention it to the ladies at the next art class and we'll get a group organised. We can visit the art gallery, have lunch and a wander around the shops afterwards."

"That sounds like a lovely plan."

A few minutes later the cream Mercedes pulled up outside the artist's cottage, which was down a small lane close to the town.

"You've been so kind," Terry told her, winding her troublesome purple scarf around her neck. "But I really should have walked – it might have helped to reduce some of the padding around my hips."

"It was no trouble – and thankfully that glass of wine with our meal didn't affect my driving too much. I always feel rather guilty getting behind the wheel when I've had alcohol . . ."

"You drove perfectly, absolutely perfectly."

Terry negotiated her way out of the car with some difficulty as her silk outfit kept sliding on the leather seats. After three attempts she made it and then stood leaning on the car door for a few moments as she adjusted her coat and her scarf.

"I'll see you at the studio next week," she said then.

Leonora raised her eyebrows. "I'll have to put some thought into the second painting. I'm not quite sure what would work with the jug and snowdrops . . ."

"Sleep on it and the muse will strike. You'll find plenty of inspiration both inside and outside of the house." She paused. "Have you ever thought of turning one of your empty rooms into a studio?"

Leonora stared at the flamboyantly dressed woman as though she were mad. "An *artist's* studio?"

"Why not? You have plenty of space for it and it would allow you to paint when the whim takes you."

"At my age?" Leonora's voice was high and incredulous. "Taking art classes is one thing – making an artist's studio is quite another."

"Lots of famous women have done great things in their later years. It's a wonderful time to reinvent yourself." Then, a small gust of wind caught the purple scarf and sent it flying up and over her face. "I must go and feed my cat."

Leonora carefully turned the car and set off back in the direction she had come.

As she drove along, she started to laugh. Turn a room in Glenmore House into an artist's studio? What on earth would the children think of it? She had vaguely mentioned to them that she was attending a class but, feeling slightly foolish, she hadn't elaborated and she had never shown them any of her work. What would Andrew have said?

And then the laughter stopped.

She knew perfectly well what Andrew would have said. He would have agreed with Terry Cassidy. He would have told her to do whatever made her happy.

In spite of what had happened, she knew that he had always wanted her to be happy.

Chapter 9

Stephen Barry stuck his head into the kitchen, his half-read *Irish Independent* by his side. He had been up early planting potato seeds at a local farm this morning and had come home for a few hours' break before returning to help with lambing later in the evening.

"Are you watching the time for the coach?" he said, looking directly at his daughter.

"We've a good half an hour or more," Rose said. "I'm just going to peel the spuds for the dinner so that it's all ready for Mammy coming in."

"I wouldn't leave it too late – it could come in early and Hannah would be left standing out there at the crossroads. You know that oul' Behan fella is always watchin' out for whoever comes and goes on the coaches – he would be out like a shot if he saw her standing there on her own."

"Go on, Rose," her grandmother said, getting up from her chair by the fire. She moved slowly, her bones always stiff after sitting for a while. "I'll sort the spuds."

Guilt washed over Rose now as she looked at the old woman. "Ah, that's not fair, Granny! Sure you did all the carrots and parsnips and the meat. It's not fair to leave you doing it all on your own."

"Go on," her grandmother said, smiling warmly at her. "Get yourself ready to meet Hannah." She went over to the sink and started to fill the basin with water.

"You're not walking down on your own?" said Stephen.

"Paul says he'll walk down with me."

"That's grand," he said, satisfied. He went back to the small sitting room to finish reading his newspaper.

Rose was grateful that Paul was going down with her because she knew none of her friends would have been too keen on spending any more time than was necessary with Hannah. Even her best friend, Cathy Brennan, had been reluctant when she'd asked her to come over to her house and then walk down to the coach.

"I'll see her at the dance and at Mass on Sunday," Cathy had said, "and that's more than enough for me. She'll only get my goat up going on about all the lads and where she buys her clothes and everything." She'd paused. "She's not very keen on me and I'm sure she deliberately tries to get between you and me. She's always making out that she knows secrets about you that I don't know."

Rose had rolled her eyes to the ceiling. "Sure, what secrets have I got? You know everything there is to know about me."

The fact that the other girls she saw regularly said very little about Hannah and never asked after her when she went home, told Rose all she needed to know. And then there was her grandmother's attitude. She had never been mad on Hannah although she never let it show in front of anyone but Rose.

"She's one of those girls who is more at home in the company of men than she is with other women," Martha Barry had said recently.

And if Paul's attitude was anything to go by, her grandmother was right.

"I'll carry the case for Hannah," he said now. "Knowing her, she'll have it filled to bursting with all her fancy clothes."

Rose felt a stab of annoyance. She went to the sack of potatoes by the sink, lifted several handfuls out and put them into the basin for her grandmother.

"Hannah will be hard pushed to keep up with Rose's finery this weekend," Martha Barry commented, beginning to scrub the potatoes.

"The lads in Kilnagree will have to be careful at the dance," Paul said, laughing, "or they could all be killed in the crush to take them out onto the floor."

"Be quiet, you," Rose hissed, "and go and give your hair a good brush."

Paul ran his hand over his thick curly hair. "Sure, it's fine. Didn't I brush it only this morning?"

"Well, you need to go and damp it down and brush it again," Rose told him.

Martha turned to her granddaughter. "Be sure and put on one of your nice outfits now," she said in a low voice.

Rose looked surprised. "But I thought I'd be better to keep them for special occasions, like the dance tomorrow night . . ."

"There's no point in having nice things and not wearing them. And you could easily outgrow them by next summer and you'll hardly have worn them." She raised her greyish-white eyebrows. "You can be sure that Hannah will be dressed to the nines when she arrives. She doesn't spare any effort with her appearance."

"She always has everything perfect," Rose said ruefully. "Matching bags and shoes and hats, the whole lot."

"Well, you have plenty of nice things now," Martha said, giving her granddaughter an encouraging smile.

"It's a pity about the shoes. I really need something new for the dance but I won't be able to afford anything for the next few weeks." She gave a little sigh. "Cathy offered to go halves with me on them, the way we did with the black and white handbags at Christmas."

"That was a good idea and it let you swap around without having to buy two."

"It was a good idea," Rose agreed, "and we are the same shoe size but I just didn't fancy sharing shoes. It's not the same as sharing a handbag or bit of jewellery. Ah, well, I'll make do with the black sandals – if I give them a good polish they'll do grand. And I can dance in them, which is the main thing."

Martha's face tightened. "I wish I had the money to buy you a new pair of shoes . . ."

"I'll be grand," Rose reassured her. "And don't go saying anything to Mammy because I know she felt bad she didn't have the money to spare either. I felt terrible that I'd even asked her." She raised her eyebrows. "I felt real selfish – especially when I think of all the lovely things the Bentley woman gave me."

"Ah, Rose!" her grandmother said, reaching out to touch her arm. "You're anything but selfish and any girl would want to look her best when they're measured up against that Hannah."

Rose looked at the door to check there was no sign of her father or brother, and then she whispered, "I'm not really looking forward to her coming again . . ."

"You'll be grand." Martha touched the young girl's hand with her own damp one. "Although she has notions about herself, she's not as confident as she appears."

Rose wrinkled her brow. "Do you not think so? I always think that she's far more confident than me."

"Not at all." The old woman shook her head vigorously. "She's all wind and water, *and* – not that I'm encouraging you to be swell-headed or anything – you're a far better-looking girleen than she is. It's just that she makes the best of herself, stuck for hours in front of the mirror dolling herself up and doing that fluffy hair of hers."

Rose blushed at the compliment while inside she felt an unaccustomed surge of delight. "Actually, that Mrs Bentley told me I was good-looking as well, so you're the second person to tell me that recently."

Martha put her finger to her lips and motioned out to the hall. "I don't want your father to think I'm giving you notions or anything like that," she said quietly, "but I've noticed that the last few times after Hannah has been here you've been down in yourself. You shouldn't let her get to you – you're every bit as good as her if not better."

"Well, I won't let her bother me," Rose decided, smiling broadly. She looked at the clock now and pulled a face. "I'll go and put on a nice blouse and go on down to meet her."

* * *

The coach was almost empty now as people had disembarked every few miles all the way out from Galway.

When she guessed she was only a few minutes from her stopping-off point, Hannah pulled her navy duster coat on and then stood up to lift her case down from the luggage rack. Then – just as she had anticipated – the smartly dressed man sitting across the aisle from her got up quickly to his feet.

"I'll give you a hand with that," he said, his gaze moving from her pretty face to the three undone buttons on her blouse.

"Oh, that's very good of you." Hannah lowered her blonde head slightly and looked up through her eyelashes at him. It was a pose she'd seen actresses adopt in magazines or in films and she had practised it to good effect.

He stretched up to lift the heavy case from the rack and placed it in the aisle between them.

"By the size of that suitcase, you look as though you're planning on staying a while!" he said as he sat down again.

"I'm here for the week," said Hannah, then turned her gaze back to the window, checking how much further they still had to go.

"And I suppose you'll be at the dance tomorrow night?"

"I might be . . ." Hannah said vaguely.

Then the bus turned a corner and started to slow down.

Hannah quickly stood up, tucked her black clutch bag under one arm and reached for her case.

The man in the brown suit was up on his feet immediately. "I'll take the case off the bus for you."

They moved to the front of the coach.

"Is there somebody meeting you?" the driver asked as Hannah made her way past a seat that had wired boxes filled with half-grown chickens. On the other side were boxes filled with spring cabbages and tomatoes that were obviously being delivered to a local shop.

"My cousin should be here," she told him.

"Have you far to go?"

"About a ten-minute walk," she replied as she followed the man in the brown suit down the steps.

"Well, sure, we can wait until they come!" the driver called. "I wouldn't like to see you stranded out here all on your own and we're not in any great hurry this evening. We're that little bit early since we were dead on time setting off."

"That's grand," Hannah said. She thanked the man for carrying her case and then turned away from him to do up the top of her blouse and button her coat against the spring chill.

Dismissed, he went back to stand by the bus and chat to the driver.

A slight tinge of anxiety ran through Hannah now. Where on earth was Rose? Surely they weren't going to leave her to carry the case up the hill on her own!

"Hannah!" a male voice suddenly called.

She swung around. It was Paul, a big grin across his face.

"Howya, Hannah!" he said, coming towards her with outstretched arms.

Hannah's blue eyes lit up. She rushed forward into his embrace and gave him a big kiss on the cheek. "I can't believe how much you've grown since I last saw you!" she exclaimed. "You've got so much older looking – quite the man now!"

Paul's cheeks immediately flamed up, embarrassed at the unaccustomed physical closeness. "And you've got even better looking – if that's possible," he stuttered, his dark eyes shining. "Is that your case over there?"

"It is. You don't mind carrying it for me?"

"Hannah!"

It was Rose, slightly breathless and pink-cheeked.

"Rose – how are you!" cried Hannah, moving quickly to hug her as well.

But as she hugged Rose, she was suddenly conscious that there was something very different about her. She pulled back to have a quick look at her and could see that it was the way she was dressed. Rose was wearing a beautiful black and white floral dress with a fashionable wide black belt just like her own and a neat little black cardigan with diamante buttons. But there was something else very different. Then it dawned on her that Rose was wearing perfume – and not just any old cheap perfume – it was a good one.

"I hope you haven't been here long," said Rose. "I can't believe the coach got in before us. It's never on time."

"No, no – we're only here a few minutes. I've just got off it." Hannah suddenly felt flustered. This wasn't the old, plain Rose she was used to.

To save having to react to the situation before she had time to think about it, Hannah turned back to the driver and the other man.

"Thanks, lads!" she called to them. "I'm all sorted now!"

"Ah, you're off to leave us now you have a younger man!" the bus driver called.

"Sure, *he*'s not a young man," Hannah laughed, putting her arm through Paul's. "He's only my cousin! Isn't that right, Paul?"

"So there's still a chance for the rest of us?" the man in the brown suit called, raising his eyebrows.

Rose's felt her throat tighten. Her cousin wasn't five minutes in Kilnagree and already she had any men in the vicinity dancing around her.

"Go on with you!" Hannah called back, tossing her blonde head. "Sure, I'm thinking of joining the nuns up in Dublin when I go back home!"

Rose wondered now at how easily Hannah joked and flirted with males of all ages and yet had very little to say when it came to girls of her own age.

"They'd have to build some height of a wall around the convent to keep all the fellas away from you!" the man called back.

They all laughed now including Rose who felt she had to play along with the banter and then the three of them set off to walk back up the hill, Paul in the middle carrying Hannah's case high up on his shoulder to give the impression that it wasn't any weight at all.

Hannah told them about her journey down and about all the men who had helped her, including the man in the brown suit who she said had offered to walk her all the way up to Barry's cottage if necessary rather than have a delicate young thing like herself carrying the case. The man hadn't actually said it in so many words but she knew of course that he would have jumped at the chance if Rose and Paul hadn't arrived just when they had.

Then Hannah came around Paul to go between the brother and sister and linked her arm into Rose's. "You're looking very well in yourself, Rose," she said. "That's a lovely new outfit you're wearing. Did you buy it for the dance?"

Rose shook her head. "No, I'm wearing a different outfit tomorrow night."

Hannah's blue eyes widened in surprise. "Good Lord – have you come into money or something?"

"No," Rose said lightly. "The outfit was a present from a lady I helped. In fact, she gave me several outfits and two lovely presents."

They walked on and then Hannah asked, "Is that perfume you're wearing, Rose?"

Rose nodded. "Yes, that was one of the presents she gave me."

Hannah's brow wrinkled. "And who exactly is this lady." She was full of curiosity now.

Rose suddenly got the distinct feeling that Hannah would love to know someone like Leonora Bentley. She had a funny feeling that she would be all over her the way she was with the lads. "Oh, it's nobody you know . . . It's just a woman that lives up in Dublin and only comes down to Kilnagree every so often."

"Oh," Hannah said, looking a bit nonplussed. "It's just that I've never heard you mention her before."

"Would you look?" Paul suddenly said. "It's oul' Behan out at the door having a good gawk to see who's coming off the bus. He's like a rat peeping out of a hole."

"Is that the old fella that your father's always giving out about?" Hannah said, her eyes lighting up. "The lecherous oul' devil?"

"The very same lad," Paul confirmed. "He's always at that lark, watching everything that's going on, especially if it's women. He's well known for being nothing but an oul' leer."

"We should give him something to look at, Rose," Hannah laughed. Then, before either of them could stop her, she called out, "Yoo-hoo, Mr *Bee* – han!" Then she whirled around and lifted her dress up to show the tops of her stockings and even a flash of her knickers, just like a can-can girl.

"Hannah!" Rose was totally aghast at her cousin's behaviour. She moved quickly to haul at the hem of Hannah's coat to cover her legs. "What the hell do you think you're doing?" she said furiously. She took a deep breath to steady herself. "That was the stupidest, stupidest thing I've ever seen! If Larry Behan tells my father what you've done we'll all be in very serious trouble, and you're likely to be sent straight back home!"

Hannah looked stunned now, all the laughter and hilarity suddenly drained out of her. She had never seen her cousin in such a temper before. "I'm sorry, Rose," she said, a tremor now evident in her voice. "It was only for a bit of a laugh . . . I really never meant anything by it."

"But how could you think that something like that was funny?" Rose hissed. "That's no way for any decent girl to carry on."

Paul put the case down on the ground now and put

his hand on his sister's shoulder. "Calm down, Rose! Hannah was only codding and it was only oul' Behan that saw her. Sure, he's not going to say anything to my father. He's as odd as two left shoes and who's going to listen to anything he says?"

But Rose couldn't calm down. It was as if Hannah had turned on a switch in her head that she couldn't turn off. "That's not the point!" she snapped at her brother, her eyes flaming with rage. "It doesn't matter who it was that saw us – it's the fact that Hannah would do such a thing in front of any man – and especially in front of a lad who's her cousin!"

"Aw, Rose, there's no need for that!" Paul shook his head and then ran both his hands through his thick dark hair.

Hannah had tears in her eyes. "I'm sorry for being so stupid. I just got carried away with the excitement of being down here. I really didn't mean any harm . . ." She delved into her coat pocket now in search of a hanky. "I promise I'll never do anything like it again!" She dabbed her eyes with the hanky.

"Let it drop now, Rose," said Paul. "She's said she's sorry. We can't keep this carry-on up when we go back to the house."

Rose looked at the teary-eyed Hannah and wished that by some stroke of magic the girl would turn around and catch the bus back into Galway and go back home. But she knew that wasn't going to happen.

She took a deep breath to steady herself.

"Okay," she said in a stiff tone. "We'll forget about it so."

* * *

By the time they reached Barry's cottage, some kind of harmony had been restored and, in a strange way, Rose felt that the incident had cleared the air and set the tone for her cousin's visit. There had been many occasions when she wanted to tell Hannah off but the reasons had been so petty and small that she had let them pass. This particular occasion had let her vent her feelings very strongly and Hannah could not be in any doubt as to Rose's opinion of silly, cheap behaviour.

"We're here!" Rose called, as all three walked into the steamy kitchen which was filled with the welcoming smells of the evening meal.

Veronica and Eileen came flying out of the sitting room to excitedly greet their glamorous cousin from Offaly and then their father joined them and the whole crowd sat in the kitchen while Martha Barry poured from the big brown china teapot.

"Your Auntie Kathleen will be home in half an hour," the old woman told Hannah, "and then we'll all sit down to the dinner."

After a while, Paul lifted Hannah's case into his small bedroom where she would sleep with Rose in the double bed which almost filled the entire room. Paul was swapping over to sleep in Rose's single bed in the room she shared with Martha and the two younger girls.

Hannah spent a few minutes unpacking her case and then she came back into the kitchen carrying the various presents. She made a big palaver of giving the children the sweets and hair-ribbons she had bought for them and then she presented Martha with her box of fancy chocolates and a small bottle of sherry. Then she gave a bottle of Tullamore Dew to Stephen, saying, "My father sent that down especially for you."

"And you can tell him that I'm more than grateful for it," Stephen said, a delighted gleam in his eye. It was rare that a bottle of spirits came into the Barry household as there were too many other basic necessities to be met first. The whiskey would be tucked away at the back of a cupboard to be brought out on special occasions – like when the Parish Priest came for his six-monthly visit – and sampled in the smallest quantities.

Paul's face reddened with embarrassment when Hannah gave him a lovely Cross pen, saying, "You'll need a good pen when you start work soon."

"Oh, thanks, Hannah," he said, obviously delighted with the expensive, grown-up gift. "That's something I'll keep."

And then Hannah turned to hand the carefully wrapped bottle of perfume to Rose. She gave a tight little smile and watched in silence as her cousin opened the package.

"Oh, Hannah!" Rose said, smiling warmly. "That's really lovely. I've always liked *Soir de Paris*." She couldn't believe that in the space of a week or so she had become the owner of two bottles of perfume and a whole new wardrobe of clothes.

"Good," Hannah said. "And I've bought earrings and a nice *Coty L' Aimant* set with perfume and talc for Auntie Kathleen. It's one my mother wears, so I thought she would like it."

"Oh, she'll be delighted," Rose said, knowing that her mother had no perfume of her own at the moment.

Everyone chatted in the kitchen for a while and then Eileen and Veronica went off to meet their mother coming from work and Paul and his father went outside to look at a fence that needed mending.

Martha Barry moved around the kitchen checking the steaming pots and pans, and keeping an eye on the oven while the two girls set the table. There was a special dinner tonight as Stephen Barry had been given a parcel of pork steaks by a neighbour the previous day – one of their pigs had been killed and when it had been divided into the various cuts by the butcher in Gort, the family had given small meat parcels to several close neighbours. Kathleen had been both delighted and relieved as she had wanted to do a decent meal for Hannah arriving but was pushed midweek to find the extra money for something other than the basics. From the various comments she'd heard Hannah make, she knew her niece quickly got fed up of the bacon and cabbage and potatoes that was their staple diet.

She had planned to ask another neighbour to swap a big chicken for some of the home-grown potatoes and vegetables that they carefully hoarded in the barn and couldn't believe their luck and good timing when Stephen came back with the pork.

They were usually lucky to get a few slices of fish to eat on a Friday from an old man who knew Martha Barry's husband from years back. His sons owned a boat and they usually dropped a pile of fish out to him every Thursday evening. Then he would walk down to the Guards' Barracks and leave a nice package of fish for the Barry family. Stephen repaid him for it during the summer, when it came time to cut the turf and he and Paul would give him a few days' work.

The cycle of neighbours helping neighbours was one that had gone on in Kilnagree for generations, and those – like the Barry family – that had little extra to give in the way of meat or foodstuffs always managed to return the favours with their labour on the farms or out on the bog.

"Thanks again for the lovely perfume," Rose said, reaching across the table to put a large serving spoon in the centre for the vegetables.

Hannah made a little snorting noise and rolled her eyes to the ceiling. "I'm sure it's not as nice as the one you were wearing earlier," she said, her voice slightly wounded. She halted, then a little glint came into her eye. "I noticed you didn't have any perfume of your own the last time I was here and I saved up to buy it for you, thinking that it would be something special for you. But it seems I got that a bit wrong."

Rose stopped what she was doing. "But I told you I loved the perfume, Hannah!"

Hannah looked at her, then turned to stare out of the window "But it's not as special as it would have been before that strange woman gave you all those expensive things," she said in a low voice.

Rose's face darkened. "Where did you get the idea that she's a *strange* woman? I never said that."

Hannah gave a little shrug, then she glanced over at Rose's grandmother to check that she wasn't listening to their conversation. "Well, it seems a bit odd for somebody you hardly know to give you clothes and presents for no particular reason. In fact, it's a bit of a cheek in a way, as if she's suggesting that you haven't got decent clothes of your own."

"But it wasn't like that!" Rose stated, feeling a real surge of anger. How *dare* Hannah say such an insulting thing? "It was because I helped her and she said she wanted to show that she was grateful!"

Hannah suddenly felt Martha Barry's eyes piercing into her and she coloured up. She was very wary of the old lady, who she had discovered on one of her visits wasn't quite as deaf or as short-sighted as people thought. As she proved now.

"Rose always looks decent," Martha stated in a low, serious voice, "and Mrs Bentley told her that she was one of the finest-looking girls she'd seen in a long time, and that she gave her the good clothes because she knew they would look well on her."

"Oh, she looks well in anything," Hannah hastily agreed. She turned to Rose, her face beaming now. "You'll have to show me the other things she gave you," she said ingratiatingly. "The outfit you're wearing now looks lovely on you. . . . I said that the minute I clapped eyes on you."

Rose inclined her head slightly, neither agreeing nor disagreeing, then turned away from the table. She wasn't fooled for a minute. She knew Hannah had meant every word she had said earlier and now, feeling awkward, was trying to wriggle out of it.

Then the outer door to the kitchen opened and Kathleen Barry came in followed by her two young daughters. "Look what the wind blew in!" she said, coming over to give Hannah a slightly self-conscious hug. "Did you have a good journey down?"

For Rose, the rest of the evening dragged and she found herself constantly checking her wrist-watch, wishing it was bed-time. It was drizzly and damp which put paid to any plans for a walk down to the harbour and Rose was grateful when Paul suggested they have a game of cards around the kitchen table. The whole family joined in, apart from Stephen who was still out at the farm and Martha who sat in her high wooden chair at the edge of the table, encouraging and helping Eileen and Veronica on their choice of cards and enjoying the general banter.

Just after nine o'clock Stephen Barry came back, his outer coat and cap drenched from the rain which had now got heavier. They took a break from cards while Kathleen made everyone tea and Hannah's favourite supper of bread dipped in whipped-up egg and fried in the pan.

When the plates were being gathered up, Stephen looked at the kitchen clock and then at the two youngest. "It's time the pair of ye were in bed," he told them, "so go and get your Rosary beads now and we'll say our few prayers."

As she stood up to get her own beads, Rose noticed Paul's eyes darting across to Hannah. Then he rolled his eyes to the ceiling. Rose glanced at Hannah in time to see her wink at Paul and then, as she was standing up on her tip-toes to reach her Rosary box on the top shelf of the white-painted dresser, she heard her cousin say in a soft but enthusiastic voice, "I'll call the prayers tonight, Uncle Stephen – if it's okay? I often call them out at home."

"Good girl!" Stephen said. "It's nice to hear a young one showing a bit of interest in their prayers. You'd be waiting a long time before that Paul fella would think to offer."

"Ah sure, that's not fair!" Paul protested, a lop-sided grin on his handsome face

"Fair or not," his father said, raising his eyebrows, "it's the truth."

"I'll go and get my beads from my case," Hannah said, pushing her chair back. "I made sure to pack them when I was coming away. I never go anywhere without my Rosary beads."

"And that's the right way," Stephen said.

Hannah went out into the hallway towards the bedroom with Paul hot on her heels and Rose could hear them laughing and giggling, knowing perfectly well that they were mocking her father because he had believed her little charade over the Rosary. She had seen that side of Hannah before and, while she was capable herself of complaining about her father, she felt annoyed that Hannah should rope the impressionable Paul into her subterfuge.

A few minutes later Hannah and Paul came back to join the others and the family knelt down.

Blessing himself with the cross on his Rosary beads, Stephen led off with the Apostles' Creed and the other preliminary prayers, then he gave Hannah a nod to begin the first decade.

"Are the Joyful Mysteries okay?" she asked in a low voice.

"Whichever you like," said Stephen.

Rose watched as Hannah closed her eyes and started: "The first Joyful Mystery – The Annunciation. *Hail Mary, full of grace, the Lord is with Thee . . .*" And off she went in a calm, clear voice, the others chorusing the responses. She said the whole five decades of the Rosary with a serious, determined face and her eyes shut tightly against any distractions as her fingers slid from bead to bead.

Rose found herself confused as she had expected Hannah to give a giggle or at least a smirk. She wasn't sure whether she had totally misjudged her cousin or whether she was a very clever actress whenever the occasion called for it.

After the Rosary, the night finished with all the adults playing a game of cards for pennies. As though sensing that Rose was annoyed with her, Hannah sat close beside her and was more serious and sensible.

"I forgot to tell you that I brought a knitting pattern for a nice cardigan down for your friend, Cathy," she suddenly said. "I was telling her all about it the last time I was here and she said she'd love to borrow it."

"Oh, that was good of you," Rose said, slightly taken aback by the fact that her cousin had even remembered the conversation, because there were times when she only seemed to be half-listening to anything other girls had to say. "She'll be delighted about that – Cathy is always knitting."

"It's that white, lace-patterned cardigan you might have seen me wearing before," Hannah went on. "I have it in the case to wear while I'm here. The pattern looks complicated but it's easy enough once you get the hang of it."

Rose suddenly brightened up – the knitting pattern would give them an excuse to walk over to Cathy's tomorrow afternoon. She had been feeling awkward about turning up at any of her friends' houses with Hannah in tow.

"If it's fine tomorrow afternoon we might take a walk down and drop the pattern off," she said, her relief evident in her voice.

Chapter 10

The following afternoon the girls left the house to walk the half-mile down to the post office to post a letter for Martha and then to walk the two further miles out to Cathy Brennan's house.

At first the conversation was slightly stilted but as they strolled along the path the atmosphere between the two cousins became more companionable and easy, Hannah stopping every now and again to shield her eyes against the weak sun and admire the lovely view.

She was wearing a blue and white blouse with a dark blue skirt, with the white lacy cardigan slung casually over her shoulders, while Rose was wearing another of Leonora Bentley's outfits – a nice black blouse with pink flowers on it with a plain black skirt. She wore the outfit with her sturdy black sandals which were the best for walking and she carried an umbrella with a long cane handle.

Hannah had appeared for breakfast that morning in her flower-printed winceyette pyjamas with half a dozen pink rollers dotted over her hair.

"Oh, I didn't wash it," she explained to Rose and

Martha when she saw them eyeing the rollers. "I only dampened it to give it a bit of a lift." She looked at Rose. "You're so lucky having straight hair that always hangs the same way whether it's newly washed or a week old." She rolled her eyes. "My hair can be a complete nightmare. If it gets wet it just goes completely limp and, when I've slept on it, it sticks out in all the wrong places."

"Well, it always looks grand to me," Rose told her.

Hannah's eyes lit up with the compliment. "Ah, you're very good saying that . . ." She smiled and touched the back of her hair. "Funnily enough, I never think my own hair is nice but a few people have told me that, when I curl it, it makes me look a bit like Marilyn Monroe."

There was a silence which was suddenly broken when Martha Barry went into an unexplained fit of coughing.

Rose smiled to herself now, turning her head away from Hannah as they walked, remembering the expression on her grandmother's face.

When they came up to Diana Tracey's imposing white house which towered over the smaller houses and cottages, Rose was about to say, "This house belongs to the daughter of the lady who gave me the presents," but she caught herself just in time. She and Hannah were getting on so much better today and she didn't want to give her an opening to say something that just might annoy her. The way that Hannah had reacted to the clothes had made her feel self-conscious and touchy. Even though she had gushed about how gorgeous and beautiful they were and how well they suited her, Rose got the feeling that Hannah looked down on her for having someone else's clothes. Her grandmother had said that Hannah was only jealous as the clothes were more expensive and flattering than anything she had herself, but Rose wasn't so sure. She just knew that she would feel more relaxed and happier wearing them when her cousin had gone back to Offaly and she no longer had to feel that she was scrutinising every item that she wore.

Rose then thought back to the day that Leonora Bentley had given her the lovely things and remembered how the older woman had told her that she had worn second-hand clothes herself. She had said it without the slightest embarrassment. Rose wished she had that confidence. She suddenly had the feeling that if she spent a lot of time in the company of people like Mrs Bentley and her daughter she would probably end up not caring what Hannah, or anyone else, thought of her.

Rose knew she was unlikely to see much more of the Dublin woman but she decided that she would try to adopt her attitude and in future would do her best to shrug off Hannah's remarks.

Two seagulls fighting over a dead crab suddenly caught Hannah's attention and then they were past Traceys' house, saving Rose the need to comment or give Hannah any information about it.

They left the path and went the short distance down to the shore to walk barefoot on the rocks and pebbles. Rose warmed more towards her cousin as Hannah exclaimed with delight at the rock pools, the shells and lacy scraps of pink and purple seaweed.

"You are so lucky living in such a beautiful place," Hannah said, as the two girls sat down on a large rock to put their sandals back onto their damp feet. They sat for a few moments, their legs dangling over the rock, staring out over the wavy water.

Rose lifted her gaze to check the sky. "On a fine day I love walking down here more than anything else in the world."

Hannah suddenly became serious and gave a dramatic sigh. "Oh, I'd love to live here! Walking along the strand, watching the waves and the seagulls, somehow seems to make all your problems seem a long way off."

Rose turned towards her and was surprised to see a bleak, despairing look on Hannah's face. She paused for a moment, wondering what on earth could be wrong. She felt she should say *something* but she wasn't quite sure what it should be.

"I wouldn't have thought you have too many problems, Hannah," she said lightly.

"Nobody ever does," the blonde-haired girl said, her voice tight and croaky. "And according to my mother, me being *me* is the biggest problem of all."

Rose's brow furrowed. She'd never heard her cousin talking like this before. Hannah was usually bright and bubbly and brimming with confidence.

"Your mother always seems very nice to me," she said quietly. It wasn't quite true because there had been occasions when she had noticed that Sheila Martin could be a bit snappy and intense, but on the whole her aunt seemed no more unreasonable than the next person.

Hannah pursed her pink lips together. "If you were a fly on the wall in our house at times you would have a very different opinion."

"Ah, sure all families have their ups and downs!" Rose said, trying to err on the side of caution.

There was another pause this time – a longer one – then Hannah suddenly shook her head and laughed. "Ah, sure, you're right! I must sound like a real old moan."

"I think we'd better make a move anyway," Rose said, looking up at the greying sky. "If we don't head off we might end up soaked through because there's little or no shelter on the way out to Brennans'."

Hannah made a praying gesture with her hands and looked up at the sky. "Please God don't make it rain! I don't want my hair looking a mess for the dance tonight!"

* * *

God must have heard Hannah's prayer as the rain held off and it was still dry and bright two hours later as they started their return journey, Hannah carrying a bag with eight scones in it that Cathy had given them and Rose swinging her long-handled umbrella. In fact, the weather forecast looked to be spot-on as the sky had cleared and the sun was starting to come through.

The visit had been a great success and Cathy had been delighted with the cardigan pattern, though Rose noticed that she still behaved in a slightly reserved manner towards Hannah.

"Cathy's a very nice girl when you get to know her, isn't she?" said Hannah suddenly.

"Yes, she is. She's been my best friend since we were at school."

"You're lucky. I've quite a few friends at home in

Tullamore but I wouldn't say I was closer to one than another. And they're not reliable at letting you know when there's a dance on or anything like that. They've often let me down when we'd planned to go to the pictures."

"That's not very good, is it?" Rose mused, not quite sure what to say.

"That's why I like coming down here. The girls are a lot friendlier and – don't get me wrong – they might be a bit plainer than the girls I went to school with but they're more decent and dependable. I felt really relaxed with Cathy, as if I'd known her for years."

Rose took a deep breath, amazed that Hannah hadn't caught onto her friend's coolness with her. She obviously thought that they liked her and considered her a real friend. Was it possible that she didn't know the difference between a good friend and somebody she barely knew?

"I've brought a couple of magazines in my case," Hannah suddenly remembered, "and I'm sure there are patterns in them as well – I must cut them out for her."

"Oh, she'd be delighted," said Rose, trying to conceal her surprise.

They were just rounding the bend again that would take them back to Tracey's house and then on to Slattery's pub when Hannah announced that she'd love to have another barefoot walk on the seashore. Rose checked her small Timex wristwatch, wondering if they should hurry home for the dinner, but it was only half past four and the dinner wouldn't be ready until her father came in at six.

It was a Friday so it would be fish tonight. Occasionally, if Martha's old friend had no fish to spare – and Stephen hadn't had a decent week's work to allow them to buy any – they made do with fried eggs, potatoes and onions for the day of abstinence.

Although their meals were very basic and repetitive and they had very few luxuries, Stephen and Kathleen Barry's family never went hungry. One way or another they had always got by.

"Give me the scones and your sandals," said Rose. "I'll carry them for you so you can have a walk down at the shore. I'll keep up with you on the path."

"Oh, thanks, Rose!" Hannah said, handing the bag to her and slipping off her shoes.

In a few moments Hannah was far enough away for them to have to call to each other over the noise of the sea. Rose slowly ambled along, occasionally waving to Hannah but most of the time enjoying the peace and quiet.

Her thoughts wandered to the dance tonight and she felt a little ripple of anticipation as she thought of how she would look in the blue and red dress she planned on wearing. Instinctively, she lifted her gaze further down the coastline to the big white house ahead where Leonora Bentley's daughter lived.

Her mind turned to the Dublin woman again, wondering what sort of house she lived in and whether she had people working for her. She smiled to herself, thinking that she could still hardly believe the luck that had befallen her, and the fact that it had all come about because she had given the woman a drink and a chance to lie down and let her head clear. Sure, any decent person would have done the very same thing, wouldn't they? She shrugged to herself, suddenly feeling all light and happy again, just as she had the day that Mrs Bentley had brought the bags of clothes and the presents. It was something she would never forget because no one had ever treated her so generously before. And the clothes had already made such a difference to her. She had never felt so confident in Hannah's company as she had these last two days. Whilst she had always admired her cousin's nice clothes she hadn't realised just how much she had felt in her shadow until her own clothes matched up.

Suddenly she heard a voice crying out and she turned quickly to see Hannah's blonde head bobbing between two large rocks.

"Rose! Rose!" she called, waving her hand. "You'll have to help me!" Her voice was high and almost hysterical. "I've done something serious to my ankle!"

Chapter 11

Rose dropped her umbrella, the bag of scones and Hannah's sandals at the side of the road. Then, as quickly as she could, she picked her way over the rocks and pebbles until she reached her cousin.

"Are you okay?" she asked, scrambling down beside her.

Hannah had got herself into a sitting position on the rock now, her good navy skirt all wet from the damp sand and seaweed. "I slipped on a bit of seaweed and tumbled off the fecking rock!" she said to Rose, struggling to hold back tears. "God almighty!"

Rose knew it must be bad because she had rarely heard Hannah swear.

"Is it very painful?"

Hannah nodded. "I can't put my weight on it at all. I think I'll have to wait a few minutes to see if it eases."

Rose perched carefully on the rock beside her cousin and bent to inspect the damage. Already, she could see the skin around Hannah's ankle was pink and painful-looking, and it was starting to swell.

Hannah looked up at Rose with a stricken face.

"Imagine if I've come all the way down from Tullamore and I'm not able to dance!"

"Never mind worrying about dancing. You're going to find it hard enough to walk back up home."

Hannah bent down to rub her swollen foot now. "Maybe if I start to walk on it, it might ease a bit?"

Rose looked doubtful. "You can try, but you'll have to be careful with the rocks and pebbles until we get back onto the path."

"I don't believe this has happened," Hannah moaned, shaking her head sorrowfully. "I've never twisted my ankle before in my life!"

"Do you want me to help you up to your feet? You could take my arm and lean on me."

Hannah rolled her eyes and sighed. "I'm going to have to move somehow. I can't stay here all flamin' night." She touched her swollen foot to the ground and then let out a yelp. She closed her eyes for a few moments, then steeled herself and did the same again. This time she didn't complain so loudly although the pain was evident on her face. She leaned over and slid her arm through Rose's, keeping her other hand on the rock to steady herself.

"We'll take it slow and easy," Rose told her.

Then, very carefully, they got Hannah into a position where she could limp along, leaning on Rose, back onto the path.

Then, just as Hannah was struggling to get her sandals on with Rose's help, large, heavy raindrops started to fall unannounced from a suddenly grey sky.

"Jesus!" Hannah groaned, throwing her hands skywards. "How much worse can things flaming well get?

My hair's going to get ruined now and I won't have time to do it again before we go out."

"We've got the umbrella," Rose reminded her. "I can hold it up over us with my free arm."

Rose was about to put the umbrella up when she suddenly noticed two Golden Retrievers coming bounding towards them. There was a figure some distance behind them, presumably their owner. Rose couldn't tell if it was a man or a woman. "Don't move!" she told her cousin, suddenly remembering Hannah's fear of dogs.

Hannah turned to look as the dogs came tearing in their direction and her face paled. "Oh Rose," she said in a quivery voice, "they look real vicious . . . I think I'm going to be sick . . ." She closed her eyes and put her arms up in front of her face.

"Don't worry! I'll wallop them with the umbrella if they come anywhere near us."

"Toby! Dizzy!" a stern female voice called now.

Both dogs stopped in their tracks as a woman in a rain-jacket with the hood up appeared.

"Get back here!" she yelled, waving the dog leads about. The dogs quickly turned and went to heel and the owner attached their leads to their collars.

"It's okay, Hannah," Rose said. She dropped the umbrella to the ground and put her arm around her cousin. "The woman has them. They won't be able to come near us. You'll be grand."

Rose stared now with narrowed eyes, trying to make out who the person was. Then, the woman pushed her hood back as she came closer and Rose suddenly realised that it was Diana Tracey.

"I'm so sorry," she said, stopping a few feet away with them. "I hope the dogs didn't frighten you?"

Rose felt her face flushing up. "No, no," she lied.

The vet's wife put her hand on one dog's head and made it sit and then did the same with the other. She pushed a strand of hair back from her face, then frowned. "Is anything wrong?" she asked, looking at Hannah.

"I twisted my ankle," Hannah said in a faint voice, "and I can hardly walk . . . I was down at the rocks and I slipped on some seaweed."

"Her ankle is very swollen," Rose volunteered.

Diana Tracey's face suddenly lightened. "You're Rose, aren't you? The girl from Slattery's shop who helped my mother."

"That's right," Rose confirmed, finding herself tongue-tied with embarrassment. There was a silence, then she forced herself to say. "How is she? Mrs Bentley . . ."

"Oh, right as rain," Diana Tracey said, in a brisk manner reminiscent of her mother's. "She's usually as fit as a fiddle but there are occasions when those migraines really hit her hard." She turned back to Hannah. "Can you walk at all?"

Hannah rubbed the back of her hand over her forehead. "Not very well," she said, her voice breathless and quivery.

Diana Tracey pointed back to the big white house. "Do you think you could make it up to the house? I could bandage up that ankle for you and run you both home in the Land Rover." She smiled at Rose. "It will give me the chance to repay your Good Samaritan act for my mother."

Rose was *really* embarrassed now. "Oh, no . . . we couldn't ask you to do that –"

Hannah suddenly cut in. "That's really good of you," she said, delighted with the offer of a lift and the chance to visit such a fancy big house. She attempted to straighten up but as soon as her sore foot touched the ground she let out a gasp of pain. Rose immediately went to her aid, one hand holding her elbow and the other around her shoulders to take as much weight off her foot as she could.

Diana Tracey pursed her lips. "Actually, you might be better off waiting here and I'll bring the Land Rover down to you. I think trying to walk on that ankle just might cause you more trouble in the long run. I'll bring a long bandage with me as well to give you a bit of support."

Hannah gave a sigh of disappointment that had a little sob at the back of it, as her chance of seeing inside Diana Tracey's house evaporated.

"That's very, very good of you," said Rose.

"It's nothing. It will only take me five minutes." One of the dogs started to strain on the lead a bit now and she pulled it back sharply. "I'll put the two boys back in the house first so I'll be a few minutes. I hope the rain doesn't get any heavier. You have an umbrella there anyway, haven't you?"

"Oh, we'll be grand," Rose said.

As Diana Tracey strode off with the dogs, Rose guided Hannah over to lean against a tree-stump, then she went to pick the umbrella up and bring it back to cover them both.

"Isn't she a nice woman?" Hannah said. "And wasn't she real kind to me?"

"She was, and it's very good of her to give us a lift home."

"I'd love to have seen inside her house, though. Wouldn't you? Or have you already been inside it?"

"Only in the hallway but it looked lovely."

"Does she have a piano?" Hannah asked. "She looks the type that would."

Rose shrugged. "I really don't know."

"Didn't she ask you in?"

"Yes, she did," Rose said, beginning to feel as if she were being interrogated, "but I was only dropping something off and there was no need for me to go inside the house."

There was a little pause, then Hannah said, "So her mother is the woman who gave you all the clothes and the fancy perfume?" She winced in pain even as she asked the question but seemed intent on getting as much information about the Bentleys as she could.

Rose nodded, deliberately keeping her gaze in the far-off distance. There was something about Hannah's curiosity about Diana Tracey that made her uncomfortable.

Then, before Hannah could ask any more questions, there came the sound of voices behind them and when the girls turned around they saw two bicycles heading towards them. Rose's heart sank when she saw that it was Liam O'Connor and Jack Kelly, a fellow from Kilnagree who always had an eye for the opposite sex.

"Well, isn't this our lucky night!" Liam exclaimed, as his bike came to a halt beside the girls. "The best-looking girl in County Clare along with her lovely cousin from Offaly! How are ye, ladies – and what has you down here?"

"We're waiting to get a lift home," Rose told him without smiling.

"Well, there's no need to be waiting in the rain for any lift," Jack Kelly told them. He slapped the bar on his bicycle. "Can't you hop up on a bike each and we'll bring you off home?"

Hannah gave a simpering little smile. "You're very kind, boys, but there's no need. We're getting a lift in a big car."

"And who has the car?" Liam asked.

"The vet's wife," Rose said. "She's just gone up to the house to get it."

"Diana Tracey?" Liam said, his brows raised.

"Yes," Rose nodded. She pointed towards her cousin's foot. "Hannah's hurt her ankle and she's not able to walk too far."

The two lads' attention immediately focussed on Hannah's leg and Rose noticed the little sly smile on Jack's face when he glanced at Liam. But Liam didn't respond.

"As Jack says," he ventured, "we could take you both on the crossbars and have you home in a few minutes. It would be no trouble – we were only going out to Jack's house to do a bit of work."

"Another time we'd be more than delighted to take you up on a ride," Hannah said, flickering her eyelids, "but we've already made arrangements with that very kind woman, haven't we, Rose?"

"Oh, you can have a ride with us anytime!" Jack Kelly said, grinning over at Liam again, although his friend remained serious.

Rose felt her face burn, wondering if Hannah was aware that the word 'ride' was often used as a rude word by the rougher lads. Whether she did or not, she just smiled innocently at the two boys.

Liam looked at Hannah. "I'd say you'll need to rest that ankle or you won't be fit for the dance tonight."

Hannah rolled her eyes dramatically. "Ah, don't!" she said, her voice sounding all anguished. "I've come all the way down from Offaly especially for it! Wouldn't it be an awful waste of time if I can't go?"

"It might be fine after you've soaked it in a basin of hot water," Rose suggested.

"And you needn't worry about tonight," Jack Kelly told Hannah, "because you'll have no shortage of lads willing to sit it out with you if you're not fit to dance." He shook his head. "Oh, you won't be short of company to sit beside you – no fear of it!"

Rose stifled a sigh of irritation now, wishing the two lads would go because she didn't want Diana Tracey to see them all standing together. She felt it just might look as though she and Hannah were very flighty and that they had encouraged them. Then they all fell silent when they heard the sound of Diana Tracey's car engine coming towards them.

The rain had eased off now, so Rose put the umbrella down. Then she put her free arm out to Hannah. "Are you ready?" she said, linking her.

"Ooooooh!" Hannah groaned as her foot touched the ground again.

"Hold on," Liam said. "It might be best if we lift her into the car."

The two boys dropped their bikes and came over to help just as the Land Rover pulled up beside them.

Rose was conscious of holding her breath now as she waited for Diana Tracey's reaction to the two lads standing there. Diana came out of the car, leaving the driver door wide open, and then came around the back towards the group, the hood of her jacket up against the rain.

"I see you've found some knights in shining armour to help you out," she said to Hannah. She pushed her hood back off her damp hair and then turned her gaze on the two boys. "Hello, Liam," she said, smiling warmly at him. "How are you getting on? I haven't seen you this long while."

Rose was surprised at her knowing Liam.

"Grand, thanks," he said, smiling back at her. "Keeping busy as usual."

Then Rose noticed a faint blush coming to his face. It was the first time she had ever seen Liam O'Connor embarrassed. Her brow furrowed. How on earth did Liam O'Connor know Diana Tracey?

"James was going to call out to you at the weekend," Diana told him, "so it'll save him the trip. He bought an old desk at the auctions in Galway that needs a bit of work doing on it. You might call out to the house some evening and have a look at it?"

"No problem at all," Liam said, nodding his head.

Diana rolled her eyes and gave a light laugh. "I don't know if it's worth working on. It looks as if it's seen better days – it's been painted over and varnished and God knows what."

"Ah, he usually has a good eye for wood," Liam said. "He knows what's worth buying. He's got some lovely pieces back at the house."

Rose glanced over at Hannah now and saw the look of

amazement on her face and realised she wasn't the only one to be surprised by the easy way Liam O'Connor and Diana Tracey were chatting with each other.

"Right, young lady," Diana said, looking at the injured girl, "we'd better get you into the Land Rover. Is the ankle easing at all?"

"Not really," Hannah said, her voice all thin and wavery again. "I'm sorry to be such a nuisance."

Diana turned to Rose. "If you want to get in first and slide into the middle, then we can lift your friend in after you."

"It's Hannah," Hannah piped up in a stronger voice. "I'm Rose's cousin from Offaly."

Diana Tracey looked bemused for a moment, then it dawned on her that the blonde-haired girl was highlighting the fact that they hadn't been properly introduced. "Of course," she said, smiling apologetically at her, "and I'm Diana Tracey."

Liam and Jack went on either side of Hannah and helped her over to the waiting vehicle. As soon as she was settled in, the vet's wife came around to the passenger side. Taking a long white supportive bandage from her pocket, she quickly and expertly wrapped it around Hannah's swollen ankle.

"Do you think the ankle will be all right?" Liam asked.

"She'll have to rest it for a day or two," said Diana.

Liam looked over at Rose. "You'll still make the dance, won't you?"

Rose shot a quick glance at Diana Tracey and coloured up when the vet's wife smiled knowingly at her. Flustered, she turned to Liam and said in a terse voice, "We're more worried about Hannah's ankle at the minute . . . we'll have to wait and see what happens."

A short while later all three females were in the Land Rover and heading off to Rose's house.

As they drew near, Rose leaned forward to direct the Land Rover down the narrow path that led to their house.

"Oh, what a lovely spot you're in!" Diana commented as she pulled up in front of the cottage. "You have a clear view of the sea. I don't think I've ever seen it from this angle before."

Rose smiled. "It's nice enough, but it's not as good as the position you're in right beside the beach, where you can just walk out of the house and it's all in front of you."

"Oh, we know we're very lucky with the location," Diana agreed. "James and I enjoy walking out on the beach and of course the dogs love their daily scramble across the rocks and in and out of the water. And as she probably told you, my mother absolutely adores Kilnagree – when she's here she's up and about first thing in the morning doing her long daily walk along the coast."

"I've seen her several times," Rose said, "and she looks very fit."

Hannah suddenly gave a little groan and the other two immediately turned to check on her.

"Is it hurting very bad?" Rose asked, her face full of concern.

Hannah bit her lip and nodded, as though in too much pain to talk.

"Let's get you out and into the cottage," Diana said, hopping out.

The door of the cottage opened and Paul came out, followed by his father.

The vet's wife halted on seeing them as she came around the car to the passenger door. "There's been a little bit of an accident, I'm afraid," she said, "but not too bad, thank heavens – Hannah has hurt her ankle." She halted for a moment, then she put her hand out to Paul. "Diana Tracey – I live down at the shore."

Paul's brain worked quickly, thinking of the correct response that someone of her kind would expect. "Pleased to meet you," he said, his voice trailing off in embarrassment.

His father came forward now to shake her hand. "I'm Stephen Barry, Rose's father – I've often seen you at church."

Diana nodded and smiled at them both, and then she indicated the Land Rover. "I think we might need a bit of help with the young lady."

Paul moved quickly to the car and opened the door. Then, when he saw his cousin leaning back in the seat with the back of her hand over her eyes, he asked anxiously, "Are you all right, Hannah?"

Hannah gave a weak smile. "I'll be all right," she said, but there was a little catch in her voice which indicated that she had suffered.

Rose – still seated in the middle of the front seat – leaned forward. "She fell on the rocks on the beach," she volunteered.

Stephen came over to lean on the opened car door. "Can you walk or do you need us to lift you out?"

Hannah threw her eyes heavenwards. "It's very painful – but I hate being such a nuisance to everyone."

Stephen's face softened in a way it rarely did with his own daughters. "Now, Hannah," he said, "there's no way you would ever be a nuisance in this house." He moved in towards her. "Lean yourself down on my shoulder and between me and Paul we'll get you into the house and get that ankle sorted out for you."

Rose came out of the driver's side of the car and stood silently beside Diana Tracey, watching as the men manoeuvred Hannah out of the vehicle. When they had her standing on the ground and moving towards the house very gingerly, Stephen turned back to Diana Tracey.

"Can we offer you a cup of tea or anything? My mother always has the kettle on the boil."

"Not at all. I have to get back home for the dogs. But thanks for the kind offer." She looked at Hannah and smiled. "I think you'll be all right now. You'll be well looked after."

"Thank you," Hannah said, smiling weakly at her. "I really appreciate all you did for me."

"It was nothing," Diana said.

Within a short while Hannah was sitting at the kitchen table with her foot soaking in a bowl of hot water. Martha Barry went searching in her bedroom and came out with a small packet of white powder that would ease the pain in Hannah's ankle. After a lot of coughing and choking from Hannah as she tried to swallow the unpleasant-tasting medication, she gave up with self-pitying tears.

"I'll be all right," she said. "I can't stand the taste of that horrible stuff."

Martha Barry looked at her solemnly. "Ah, you poor

girleen . . . and you hoping to go to the dance tonight . . . If you don't get that ankle sorted out, I think you might have to take to the bed until it's all better. And if there's no change over the weekend, we might even have to get you into the doctor in Gort to get an injection, so that you're fit to travel back home."

Hannah's face paled and then her eyes narrowed in thought. "I think I'll try the powder again . . ."

"Get poor Hannah a drop of cold milk to drink it down," Martha said to Rose, giving her grand-daughter a conspiratorial wink as she went past.

Rose hid a smile but she was worried. She knew that if Hannah wasn't up to going to the dance that she couldn't go either. How could she? Hannah had travelled all the way down from Offaly especially for it and it would be the height of bad manners for her to go out and leave Hannah in the house on her own with the adults. It was strange, because up until today she had wished that Hannah hadn't come for the dance in the first place. But this afternoon she had felt much easier with her cousin than she had for a good while and Hannah had also made a big effort out at Cathy's house. Hannah had also surprised her by not being too forward with Liam O'Connor and his friend or taking up their offer of a lift home on the bikes in preference to Diana Tracey's car. For once she hadn't been all flirty and vying for attention from the lads.

Martha Barry opened the small greaseproof packet that held the painkiller again, and this time Hannah let her pour the powder on her tongue. She quickly took a drink of milk, closed her eyes and swallowed the whole thing down.

"Ooooooh!" she said, pulling an agonised face. "That's the worst thing I've ever tasted in my life!"

Kathleen Barry came in from work a short while later and she looked most alarmed when she heard about Hannah's ankle. She made a huge fuss of her niece but Hannah told her she was feeling much better.

"I think the powder did the trick," the blonde girl stated, "because my foot feels a hundred times better." She suddenly stood up and miraculously managed to walk slowly about the kitchen unaided. "It's more or less back to normal," she said smiling. "So I won't need to miss the dance after all."

Kathleen pursed her lips together. "I'm not too sure . . . I don't know what your mother would think."

"Oh, please, Auntie Kathleen," Hannah said, putting her hands together in a praying gesture, "I'll be grand, honestly! And Paul has offered to bring me down on the crossbar of his bike so I don't have to walk far."

Kathleen raised her eyebrows in resignation. Hannah was such a nice mannerly girl that she hated to upset her. "Well, make sure you don't put any kind of a strain on it. You'll have to be sensible – won't she, Rose?"

Rose smiled over at her cousin – half in relief that she would make it to the dance herself. "Oh, I'm sure she'll be grand."

Later, as the whole family sat around the table eating the locally caught fish, Stephen Barry pointed his fork at his niece. "D'you know, Miss Martin, when I saw you in the front of that fine lady's car this afternoon, I wouldn't have given tuppence for your chances of making this dance tonight, and here you are, all hale and hearty again. You're not as delicate as you look at all. You're a fine, hardy girl!"

"My ankle really is much better," Hannah replied, looking around the table with a beaming smile. "And I won't be silly. I'll be happy to sit it out for the night and just watch everyone else enjoying themselves." She gave a little laugh. "I'll just have to not mind looking like a wallflower for once."

"Oh, that's the last thing anybody could call you," Paul said, shaking his head. "There will be a stampede the minute the lads see you in the hall."

Stephen frowned. "Well, just see that you keep a close eye on Hannah," he told his son. "We don't want any of those corner boys making a nuisance of themselves."

Rose felt a stab of annoyance. Both her brother and father took it for granted that boys would flock around Hannah wherever she went and there wasn't a word said about her. It wasn't that she wanted her father to be uptight about unsuitable lads having their sights set on her, because he could end up getting so annoyed by the situation that he mightn't let her go to the dance at all. It was more a case of everyone assuming that Hannah would be the main centre of attention even though there could be fifty other girls in the place.

As soon as everyone had finished their meal, Hannah carefully stood up. "If nobody minds, I'm going to go off down to the room to put a few curlers in my hair and have it looking nice for tonight." Then she looked over at her uncle, smiled sweetly and said, "I'll be ready in plenty of time if we're saying a few decades of the Rosary before we go out."

Chapter 12

Leonora lifted her head from her newspaper when she heard the phone ring. She listened as Mrs O'Shea's footsteps tapped their way down the hallway to answer it, then she heard the housekeeper chatting in a relaxed manner and she immediately knew that it was one of her children. All three – Edward, Jonathan and Diana – were extraordinarily fond of Lizzie O'Shea and always made the time to have a few words with her when they phoned. Leonora waited to see which one it was.

A short while later the housekeeper came down to the sitting-room. Since she knew Leonora was on her own, she opened the door without any formality and said, "It's Diana! I had a great wee chat with her."

Leonora took off her reading glasses and went outside to the phone.

"Hello!" she said. "I wasn't expecting to hear from you until the beginning of the week."

"Oh, I had a little bit of news I thought you might like to hear. It's about your little friend – the Barry girl from the pub."

"Really? Go on . . ." Leonora sat down in the comfortable velvet-covered chair by the phone, surprised at how eager she felt to hear about Rose. There was something about the girl that had left an impression on her.

"Well, it's nothing that exciting," Diana said. She gave a short laugh. "But, as you know, in small villages small things make for big news. It's just that I ended up playing the Good Samaritan to Rose Barry and her cousin this afternoon down at the shore."

"What happened?" Leonora was intrigued.

"The girl's cousin, Hannah, had slipped on one of the big rocks and twisted her ankle. It was swollen and painful and the girls were walking, so I came to their rescue and drove them home."

Leonora smiled into the receiver. "That was very kind of you."

"It was interesting because the two girls are so very, very different. Both very striking and beautiful in their own ways. The cousin is smaller and blonde, and although she seems around a similar age to the Barry girl, she's more sophisticated and more sure of herself."

"Really?"

"Now, having said that, it would appear that Rose Barry has caught the eye of at least one of the local boys. One I know, as it happens. Liam O'Connor – a very nice young chap. He's been up at the house on a few occasions doing a bit of woodwork and furniture-restoring for James." She paused. "You know the black ebonised sideboard with the painted flowers on it that we have in the hallway?"

"Yes, of course."

"Well, that's one of the pieces he did. It was in pretty poor condition when James bought it and Liam O'Connor spent quite a few evenings on it."

Leonora's brow furrowed. "And did Rose seem to have any interest in him?"

"Hard to tell. She was awkward and embarrassed when he spoke to her, and I couldn't tell whether it was because I was there or because she didn't like him."

"Well, I suppose she's at that age when she's going to start looking for a husband." She gave a little sigh. "And I suppose she'll end up with a local chap like the one you've described." For some reason Leonora felt a little flat at the thought and she was surprised at herself for caring so much about a girl she hardly knew.

"Probably. That's usually the way down here. If they haven't taken the plunge and emigrated, they tend to stick fairly close to their own area. I suppose it can't be easy with only bicycles for transport or walking."

"True . . ." Leonora paused. "Kilnagree is such a beautiful place to live and I do love visiting there. You and James have careers and a busy social life – but it's a very limited place for girls like Rose."

"I suppose it is, because the people I know in the village say what an attractive, clever girl she is and how it's a shame there's no suitable work for her. She should really have gone to college or university but there's no way the family could afford to send her. I suppose Slattery's has been a saving grace – without it she would have nothing outside of the home."

Leonora sighed. "Even if she were in Dublin, she might see a different side of life and stretch herself a little further. If she had a job, she could perhaps save up for college."

"That's a hard thing to ask a young girl to do. If I hadn't had you and Daddy behind me, I doubt if I could have worked and saved for my own education." Her voice lightened. "It's much easier to marry the first half-decent fellow you meet and get on with starting a family of your own."

"Do you think she's the type who could cope with living in Dublin?" Leonora asked.

"I really don't know," said Diana. "Until you met her I hardly knew the girl by sight." She gave a small laugh. "You've really taken to her, haven't you?"

"She's such a striking girl and she was so kind to me. But really, what she does with her life is none of my business."

"She'll survive," said Diana. "If she doesn't find a decent fellow here, she'll probably cast her net further afield."

There was a small pause.

"And how are you, darling?" Leonora asked. "Anything at all since we spoke a few days ago?"

"No . . ." Diana paused. "I had my period yesterday, so that's it for this month again."

"Oh . . . it's still early days" There was a little pause. "What did James say?"

"He was disappointed," Diana said in a low voice.

"Oh, I am sorry for you both . . . but I'm sure that one of these days you'll be on the phone telling me wonderful news."

"Hopefully. It's just so disheartening, month after month. I suppose we'll just have to wait and see." Then, changing the subject, she asked, "Have you heard from Edward or Jonathan?"

"Not since I last spoke to you. But I usually ring them on a Sunday, so I'll catch up with them then."

"Edward is very quiet these days," Diana said. "I've tried to broach it with him but he's not the easiest to get information out of. Have you any notion what could be wrong with him?"

"I have no idea," Leonora said, a weary note evident in her voice, "but he's definitely not himself." She gave a little sigh. "All we can do is hope and pray that whatever is wrong with him passes soon."

Leonora felt unsettled for the rest of the afternoon. She went out into the garden and pottered about, tying things up here and snipping things back there. Edward, of course, was on her mind, and so was Rose Barry. Even after telling Diana she knew it was none of her business, she still had an overwhelming feeling that she should try to help the girl in some way. The clothes and gifts she had given her would have made some small difference but she felt there must be something more she could do to help.

Maybe she could give her a position in Glenmore House – even if it was only helping Mrs O'Shea for a few months? It might not be much better than what she was doing now but at least she would get the chance to experience life on the outskirts of Dublin for a while. And who knows what else might turn up? Leonora could imagine herself and Rose Barry scouring the newspapers for suitable positions. An office might be the very thing, or maybe something along the lines of a doctor's receptionist. Leonora knew a few people through Andrew's work who might be able to help out.

She wondered if thinking about Rose was her mind's way of diverting her worries away from her eldest son. She shrugged. Did it really matter why she cared about the young girl? It wasn't doing anyone any harm.

She would give it some more thought. Then she might write to Rose Barry or ring Diana and ask her to put the suggestion to the girl.

Chapter 13

As they came in sight of Slattery's pub, Rose looked up at Hannah who was perched on the saddle of Paul's bike. Paul had walked the bike all the way down the hill from Barry's cottage. All were dressed in their best with Paul in his Sunday suit, Hannah in a pink checked dress with a little matching jacket and her hair all set in perfect blonde curls, and Rose wearing the blue dress splashed with brilliant red poppies. She wore it with a tight-fitting blue cardigan over it that was in the exact same shade of blue – she was sure that Diana Tracey must have bought it to wear with the dress because it was a perfect match and it had the same label on it.

Earlier on in the evening, Hannah's jaw had dropped when Rose took the dress out of the old wardrobe in her grandmother's room and quietly slipped it on. It fitted her to perfection, and the low cross-over neckline showed up the full, firm bust that Rose had always kept well covered up.

"Is that another one of the outfits that Diana's mother gave you?" Hannah had said, as if she'd known the vet's wife all her life.

Rose nodded and smiled. "Does it look all right?"

Hannah raised her eyebrows. "Yes, and it's a lovely colour." She paused. "But if you don't mind me saying, it's a bit on the low side. It's an awful lot more daring than anything I've ever seen you in before." She bit her lip now. "I think Diana Tracey would carry it off better, being a different build from you . . .you might be best to stick a safety pin in the front to bring the neck up a bit higher."

Rose's hand immediately flew to her chest as a hot embarrassed flush worked its way over her neck and face. "I really didn't think it looked that bad . . . but I would hate to have everyone looking at me . . ." She turned to the mottled wardrobe mirror to check again.

Then a tap came on the bedroom door and her mother came in.

"Oh, that dress is gorgeous on you, Rose! And needless to say, Miss Martin, you're dressed up to the nines as always. Is that a new one since you were last here?"

"Yes," Hannah nodded. "But, Auntie Kathleen, we were just wondering if Rose's dress was a bit low for tonight?"

Kathleen's gaze shifted to her daughter. "I think it's grand," she said, wrinkling her brow in surprise

Rose fiddled with the neckline now, pulling the sides closer together to cover herself up. "I'm not too sure . . ."

"Leave it be!" Kathleen said, smiling incredulously at her daughter's embarrassment. "And stand up straight and let me see how it looks."

Rose squared her shoulders now and closed her eyes as her mother inspected her.

"There's not a thing wrong with the dress. It has a nice neckline without being too low." She turned to Hannah. "I think that Rose fills it well. If someone like

Diana Tracey could wear a dress like that, then I don't think Rose needs to worry what anybody is going to think."

"Oh, sure, that's fine then," Hannah said, smiling back at her aunt. "I suppose I was just thinking that my Uncle Stephen might not be too happy – you know the way he goes on about the lads around here . . ."

"I think it's absolutely grand," Kathleen said. She patted Rose's arm. "Wear your cardigan buttoned over it until you get to the dance hall." She looked towards the bedroom window. "It's brightened up now but it's bound to be a bit cool by the time the dance comes around this evening and you don't want to get a cold on your chest."

Martha had echoed that opinion. "She looks lovely in that dress, doesn't she, Hannah?" she said. "She looks like a grown woman in it. You'll both be the belles of the ball tonight! God willing that your ankle is well enough for you to have a dance."

* * *

As soon as they turned the corner towards the hall at the crossroads in Kilnagree and saw at a distance the rosy lamp lit outside the hall, Rose felt a little knot of excitement in her stomach. There was something about the welcoming light shining in the semi-darkness that gave her a great feeling of anticipation about the night ahead. Rose had never had a bad night out in the hall yet but she felt that tonight was going to be extra special, despite having Hannah along with her.

They were just wheeling the bike past Slattery's bar when Hannah gave a groan. "I'll have to get down – I've got a bit of a cramp in my leg!"

Paul and Rose carefully helped her down onto the ground.

"I think I could do with putting my foot up on a stool or something for a few minutes," she told them. "Why don't we go into the bar and have some lemonade? I'll pay – I have extra money on me."

Rose looked at her brother. "I'm not too sure about that – my father wouldn't like to hear of us going into the pub before the dance."

"Surely he wouldn't mind it for just a few minutes?" said Hannah. "If there's any problem I'll explain to him later that it was my fault because of my ankle." She gave a little smile. "Besides, Rose, he can hardly complain about you going into the place you work in. If it's good enough for you to work in it, surely there's no harm in having a lemonade with the same people you serve?"

Paul shrugged. "Sure, what harm can it do?" he said dismissively. "And anyway, who's going to say anything to my father? He and his oul' cronies are only down at Slattery's on a Saturday night."

Rose bit back a feeling of annoyance, knowing full well that Paul would never normally talk about his father like that. He was obviously trying to sound all independent and grown-up to impress Hannah. She turned to her cousin.

"Are you sure you can't make it straight to the hall? It's only another few minutes or so."

Hannah started limping towards the bar door. "We're in plenty of time," she said, determination clearly evident in her voice, "and I know I'll feel much better when I've rested my foot properly."

Paul strode ahead and led the way with his sister and cousin following behind. The bar was half-full and, as usual, the door opening attracted the attention of everyone in it. Rose raised her hand in a self-conscious salute to anyone who caught her eye and in particular to Joe Slattery who was serving behind the bar.

"Rose!" he said, greeting her with a cheery smile. "And what has brought you in here on a night off?"

Rose indicated her cousin. "Hannah has hurt her ankle and she needs to give it a rest for a few minutes so we thought we'd come in here and have some lemonade."

"Sit yourselves down," Joe said, giving a friendly wink, "and I'll be over to you."

The three of them went over to a table with an empty wooden bench behind it and Paul helped Hannah to lift her leg up onto the bench to rest it.

A few minutes later the landlord appeared at the table with the three glasses of lemonade.

"Herself was saying that she'd like a word with you, Rose," he said.

Rose's brow furrowed as she wondered if she was in trouble with the fussy landlady.

Joe saw her expression and gave a knowing grin. "Ah, it's only something about giving her a hand with getting the house ready for some visitors that are coming over from England next week."

"Is she through in the house now?"

"She is." He leaned in closer to her. "And the best place for her! She'll be in here later complainin' and givin' out to me as usual."

Rose laughed. "I'll go in to her in a few minutes." As

Joe went off, picking up glasses and full ashtrays from the tables, she looked over at her cousin. "How is the ankle now?"

"The rest is definitely helping it. Another ten minutes and I'll be ready to try the bike again." Her face suddenly looked glum. "I think I might have to sit it out for most of the dance . . ."

Rose nodded her head, trying not to show her irritation. Even though Hannah had insisted on going to the dance, it was as if she wanted to cast an air of doom and gloom even before the night began. She lifted her handbag. "You'll be okay if I just go to have a word with Mrs Slattery? I'll be back in a few minutes."

Paul gave a beaming smile and then made a big gesture of putting his arm around Hannah's shoulder. "Sure, won't she be well looked after? There's no harm going to come to her when she has me to mind her."

Rose rolled her eyes. "Listen to Sir Lancelot!"

As she went through the back of the bar to the living area, Rose caught a glimpse of a group of lads coming into the pub and spotted the tall figure of Liam O'Connor in the middle of them. She quickened her step to avoid notice. She didn't feel like any further chat with him. No doubt the minute he saw Hannah he would make a beeline for her anyway.

As she knocked on the door which led into Slattery's kitchen, Rose fleetingly wondered if Ruairí and Michael Murphy were amongst the group that had just come in.

About twenty minutes later Rose emerged, feeling flustered about not being able to get away from Mary Slattery and expecting Paul and Hannah to give out to her for taking so long. When she glanced across to the corner where they were sitting, she stopped, totally bemused, because there was such a crowd around them that she could hardly see them. Joe Slattery saw the look on her face and laughed.

"That cousin of yours has them all dancing around her like bees around a honey pot," he told her, "bad leg or no bad leg. There's one of them even bought her a brandy to help the pain." He shook his head. "A *brandy* no less!"

Rose's face turned pale. "But my father will go mad if he hears we were in the pub and being bought drink by lads!"

Joe gave her a sidelong look. "Well, he's not going to hear it from me, Rose," he said, putting his hand on her arm. "Jack Kelly, the lad that bought it, meant no harm."

Rose felt her hackles rise when she heard the name. She might have known that someone like Liam O'Connor's friend would be involved.

"He said his granny takes a drop of brandy at night to help her rheumatics and that it might help the girleen," the easy-going landlord went on. "Now whether it will or not I don't know, but I don't think a small drop would do her a bit of harm."

"Rose!" Hannah suddenly called, beckoning to her.

Rose went over to her, ignoring the group of lads. She was so annoyed she didn't even notice whether the Murphy brothers were in the group or not. She sat down on a chair, angled away from the others. "Did you drink a glass of brandy?" she demanded in a low voice. She leaned in close, checking if there was a smell of alcohol on her cousin's breath, but she couldn't detect anything.

Hannah moved back, offended by Rose's suggestion. "No," she said, shaking her blonde curls. "Indeed I did not. I couldn't touch stuff like that – even the smell of it would put me off."

Rose looked bewildered. "But Joe told me that he served one of the lads a brandy that was meant for you – supposedly to help your ankle."

"Oh, one of them brought a glass over to me all right," Hannah confirmed, her tone unusually snappy, "but I told him I didn't want it." She shrugged. "I don't know what he did with it then. All I know is that he wasted his money." She indicated her glass of lemonade. "I'm happy enough with a mineral – I wouldn't thank you for a drink."

Rose felt a heavy hand on her shoulder and turned around to see her brother beaming at her. "Are we off again?" he asked, looking from one to the other. "To the dance? If we don't get a move on we won't be in time to get a chair for Hannah and she won't be fit to stand on that ankle all night."

Rose reached for her own untouched glass of lemonade. "I know I might as well not be here as far as you're concerned," she told her brother, "but since ye both dragged me into this place, I'd be grateful if you'd just give me a couple of minutes to finish my drink and then we'll all be ready."

"Of course we'll wait," Hannah said, smiling ingratiatingly.

"Oh, oul' touchy-touchy!" Paul said, leaning over to flick Rose's hair in a teasing fashion. "Did ye think we were going to go off and leave you?"

"If you don't shut up with your nonsense," Rose snapped, "it's me that'll be going back home and leaving ye!" Paul was really getting on her goat now, acting the eejit more than normal. He had a confident swagger about him that she had never seen before and she reckoned that he was playing to the audience because he wanted to impress Hannah and the other lads in the pub. Rose swallowed her annoyance along with a gulp of her lemonade now, and had only drunk half of it when she noticed a tall, dark figure coming towards them.

"Well, isn't this my lucky day? Would you look who it is again!" Liam O'Connor said, his gaze taking in every inch of Rose from her dark hair to her well-polished sandals. "And looking the belle of the ball as usual. Rose Barry – the Darling Girl from Clare!"

Rose rolled her eyes to the ceiling and took another drink from her glass, ignoring him. Then she noticed Michael Murphy followed by his brother Ruairí heading out of the door without even glancing in her direction. Her heart sank. They had probably noticed Liam O'Connor chatting to her again – as he seemed to be doing every time they were around. Michael would probably think she had an eye for him now and was encouraging him. She remembered what Paul had said about Liam O'Connor frightening the other lads off and felt a sudden rush of frustration at the whole situation.

Liam turned to Hannah now. "Well, Rose's lovely cousin from Offaly – how is the poorly ankle?"

Hannah looked at him through lowered lashes. "Slowly getting better," she said, giving him a shy sort of smile. "Although I don't think I'll be fit to do much dancing."

A short time later Hannah decided that she could continue the journey to the dance hall and the three made their way outside. Hannah seemed to be walking much better and Paul stayed glued attentively to her side.

They looked back when Liam O'Connor called to see if Rose would like a lift on his crossbar to the dancehall, since Paul had already helped Hannah up onto his cycle again.

"No thanks!" she called back briskly. "I'm quite happy to have a bit of a walk." There would be no chance of the Murphy brothers coming near her if she showed up sharing a bike with Liam.

A few minutes later the group of lads passed them by on their bikes.

"I think that Liam fellow has an eye for you, Rose," Hannah said, looking back from the saddle of Paul's bike.

"He can have all the eyes he wants," Rose retorted. "I have no more interest in him than in flying in the air."

* * *

Ten minutes later they parked the bike around the side of the hall and then, as they stopped at the door to pay their entrance money, Hannah insisted that she paid for all three. "My father gave me extra money to pay us into the dance," she told them, "and I've money to buy us all a few minerals as well."

"No chance of another brandy?" Paul said, digging his cousin in the ribs and laughing.

"Don't be so stupid," Rose told him, wondering what on earth had got into him to make him so giddy.

As they walked inside the darkened hall, Hannah said, "My ankle feels tons better. I can put my weight on it without any great pain. I might even manage a slow waltz."

"Well, be careful anyway," Rose told her, relieved that her cousin wasn't going to need her attention for the whole night.

A little ripple of excitement ran through her when she saw the three band members up on the small stage conferring about the order of the tunes they would play. There was already a fair crowd gathered, the girls sitting on the chairs that lined the perimeter of the room and groups of lads just standing around chatting. Thankfully, there were still a good few chairs up near the stage that they could claim for the evening. Mostly the lads kept to one end of the hall and the girls at the other, but from the way he was starting out glued to their sides, Rose could tell that Paul was planning on being a fixture with her and Hannah for the night.

"You keep seats for us," Rose instructed him, "while we put our things in the cloakroom and sort ourselves out in the ladies' room." To the side of the cloakroom there was a trestle table being set up by a local middle-aged woman to sell tea and biscuits and bottles of minerals halfway through the night. Rose gave a quick glance around the room and her gaze fell upon Ruairí and Michael Murphy. She caught her breath when she saw they were standing chatting to two very pretty girls who she knew were from Gort and probably knew Michael from going in and out of the bank where he worked.

Flustered, she took Hannah's arm. "Come on, and we'll put our coats in and get back to get our seats." She stole another glance across the hall but both brothers were too engrossed in chatting to the girls to be aware of anyone else.

"Do you think anyone will notice my ankle and the way I'm limping?" Hannah said as they moved slowly across the dancehall. The polished floor had a light layer of sawdust on it, to prevent the dancers from slipping "And I don't think my hair is sitting as well as it usually does."

"I doubt if anyone will be even looking at you," Rose retorted and immediately felt aware of the sharpness of her tone.

Then, before she had time to wonder if she had offended Hannah, a group of four girls rounded the corner from the ladies' toilet and came towards them.

"Rose!" Cathy Brennan exclaimed. "Your dress is absolutely gorgeous! I hardly knew you." She turned to the other girls, who were all looking on with great interest. "Isn't it totally different from the things she usually wears? The bright colours really suit her."

Rose's cheeks coloured up and she suddenly felt very self-conscious wearing the vivid blue and red dress. With everything that had happened this evening she had half-forgotten about her new outfit and wasn't at all prepared for being the centre of attention. "Thanks," she said, giving an embarrassed shrug.

"Sure she has a whole new wardrobe of clothes back at the house," Hannah put in. "Don't you, Rose?" She looked at the group of girls with wide, excited eyes.

The other girls looked expectantly at Rose.

Rose felt her throat tighten and she felt like killing her

big-mouthed cousin. "I think that's a bit of an exaggeration, Hannah," she said in as cool a tone as she could muster. She turned and looked back down into the hall. "I was given a few nice bits and pieces by a friend, that's all." She looked directly at Cathy. "The next time you're up at the house I'll show them to you."

"Oh, but we'd all love to see them!" Mona Tierney said. Mona was a slim, pretty-looking redhead who was inclined to be nosy and was always looking for a bit of news or scandal which she wasn't slow to spread.

"Well, I'm sure there's nothing that special about a few new dresses!" Rose said, in a deliberately vague manner. There was no way she was having a crowd of them turning up at the house to gawk at her clothes and then have to explain all about Leonora Bentley. Not that she minded any of them knowing that she had been given the clothes. All the girls around wore clothes that had been handed down to them by older sisters or cousins, or had been sent from relatives abroad. It was the big sensation that Hannah had tried to make of it that annoyed her and she knew that if she gave her the chance now she would elaborate further about Diana Tracey bringing her home in the car.

She also knew that Mona Tierney would relate every bit of news about her clothes back to all her family at home and before she knew it the whole of Kilnagree would know where every stitch on her back came from.

Rose turned to her cousin, pinning a carefree smile on her face. "Will we put our coats in now?"

By the time they had finished at the cloakroom and squeezed into the small ladies' toilets to check their hair and lipstick in the mirror, Cathy and the other girls had found seats for themselves near Paul and the band had struck up their first tune.

Hannah was still whinging about her hair not sitting as well as it should have done. "It's never the same when it gets wet with the rain, especially down here," she moaned. "It must be something to do with the water in Clare."

Rose glanced over to where she had last seen the two Murphy brothers but there were so many people in the hall now she couldn't spot them.

"Now, don't you be worrying about me," Hannah said, as they made their way back across the floor which was now fairly crowded. "I'll be grand sitting with Paul if you're asked up to dance. I wouldn't like to chance this ankle at the start of the night." She leaned closer to Rose and whispered in an excited tone. "You'll be delighted to know that Liam O'Connor and his friend have just come in the door."

Rose bit back the retort that came to the tip of her tongue and tried to pin a relaxed, friendly smile on her face in case anyone was looking at her.

They had hardly sat down on the seats that Paul had saved for them when Jimmy Flynn, a tall, heavy-set lad who often worked with Rose's father, came striding across the floor to ask for the first dance.

"Begod, you're lookin' grand tonight, Rose," he told her. "That frock makes you look like a million dollars."

Rose felt a little rush of delight as she got to her feet. Jimmy Flynn wasn't exactly the best-looking lad in Kilnagree but he was a friendly, dependable sort that always had a bit of a joke and a laugh. The start of the dances was always the hardest. If you weren't asked up fairly quickly, it had you worrying that you might be left on the side of the floor for the whole night. Not that it had ever happened to Rose but she'd had her moments when she'd been left sitting and it was always a horrible feeling.

She had three dances in a row with Jimmy and came back to her place laughing and heated up from the exertion. She had hardly sat down again when another fellow she knew from her class at school was at her side and she was up on her feet again.

Halfway through the dance Rose felt a slight dig in the ribs from a passing couple and she looked up to see Liam O'Connor winking at her.

"I'll be over for you shortly," he told her.

Rose lifted her eyes to the ceiling in a couldn't-care-less manner and guided her partner off in a direction that would hopefully keep her away from her unwanted admirer.

The last in the set of three dances was one where everyone changed partners several times and Rose was delighted when it was announced as it meant that she could move around the hall and dance with lots of different lads in quick succession. It also added a more light-hearted tone to the night as people never knew who they were going to encounter next. The music struck up and Rose and her original partner bade each other a mock-tearful goodbye after a quick round of the floor and then they went off in different directions. Rose danced with short fellows, tall fellows, fat fellows and fellows that seemed much too old to be at the dance. And occasionally she found herself dancing with fellows that were rumoured to be married. They were never local men from Kilnagree who, even if they were inclined that way, wouldn't have the nerve to be out on their own dancing with young girls.

At one point in the dance Rose found herself being swung around by the grinning Jack Kelly, who kept leaning in close to shout in her ear over the noise.

"I was chattin' to yer cousin," he told her, breathing beery fumes all over her. "She's some character, isn't she? I'd say she's a lot more forward than yerself. Not backwards at comin' forwards, like!"

Rose shrugged and smiled and continued to dance, keeping her face as far away from his as possible. The smell of the beer was off-putting and she was sure she could detect whiskey on his breath as well. Working in the pub had given her enough experience to know she was probably right.

"Did you have a turn on the floor with Liam yet?" Jack asked. "He was lookin' out for you." He gave a little laugh. "He doesn't give up when he sets his mind to anything, you know. He has his eye firmly fixed on you."

Rose pretended not to hear him and, as the dance progressed, he was eventually passed along the line to some other unfortunate girl. Rose danced with various other fellows for a few minutes at a time and, while she was grateful to have escaped Liam O'Connor, she was disappointed not to have had a dance with Michael Murphy. Then, just as the set was coming to its final reel, Rose turned to take her new partner and came face to face with Ruairí Murphy.

"Rose," he said, taking her into his arms and swinging her around, "you're on top form tonight, if you don't mind me saying! Myself and Michael were saying that earlier."

"Thank you," she said, delighted. "And are ye both enjoying yourselves tonight?"

"Ah, sure everybody enjoys a bit of a dance," Ruairí

laughed, showing the same white even teeth that his older brother had. "And it's been a long old depressing winter, so it's good to get out now that the weather is getting finer. There's times when the damp and the rain in this country would get ye down, especially when you think of the lovely weather they have out in America and Australia. Wouldn't it nearly make you think of packing up and going off there?"

"I suppose so," Rose said, a little surprised to hear Ruairí moaning. He was usually a good-natured lad who saw the best side of everything.

The dance ended, Ruairí gave a theatrical bow and went off into the crowd of lads that was now enveloped in a hazy fug of cigarette smoke.

Rose went back to her chair, only to find Liam O'Connor sitting in Paul's place, head bent, listening intently to Hannah. She took a deep breath and sat down beside them. "Where's Paul?" she asked Hannah without even acknowledging Liam. She felt she had seen and spoken enough to him today without having to be all over him tonight.

Hannah shrugged and looked at Rose with wide, innocent eyes. "He went outside with some of the other lads for a bit of fresh air a while ago but he might have come back in without me seeing him."

Rose pursed her lips and then, before either of them could engage her in conversation, she said, "I'm just going to have a bit of a chat with Cathy and the others, I'll be back shortly." Then she got up from her chair and moved further down the hall to join her friends.

"I'd say Hannah's in her element with all the attention she's getting," Mona Tierney said. "She's been like the

Queen Bee sitting up there with your Paul and all the other lads swarming around her."

Cathy leaned forward and then clucked her tongue in annoyance. "That's Michael and Ruairí Murphy up chattin' to her now."

Rose suddenly felt as though she had a lump of lead in her chest. The boys had made no effort to come over when she was sitting there and now Hannah had them all to herself.

"Liam O'Connor doesn't look too pleased," Cathy went on, giving the others a running commentary. "He's sitting well back in the chair now with his arms folded."

"Oh, he's a fine-looking fella," Mona said, tossing her curly red hair back over one shoulder. She looked at Rose. "Can't you wave to him to come down and sit with us? Cathy was saying you know him well from working in the pub."

"I know plenty of them well," Rose said, "but that doesn't mean I want to be sitting with them in my own time."

Cathy dug Rose in the ribs. "You wouldn't be saying that if it was Michael Murphy, now would you?"

Mona's pencilled eyebrows shot up in surprise. "Oh, have you an eye for one of the Murphy lads?" she asked, all interested.

Rose folded her arms and shifted her gaze to the ceiling. "I have my eye on *nobody*," she said as innocently as she could. "Sure, I only came here tonight because I enjoy the dancing."

"It's just as well," Cathy told her, "because none of the rest of us are going to get a look in now that

Hannah's around. Your Paul and Jack Kelly are back now, so she has five of the best-looking lads in the place hovering around her."

"I wouldn't exactly count Paul in when it comes to being good-looking," Rose said in an off-hand manner.

"Your Paul?" Mona said, her voice high in amazement. "Sure, he's turned into a fine-looking lad in the last year or so – he's tall and well-built and he has a lovely face. A lot of the girls are mad about him."

"And he's a good dancer," Cathy put in.

"Go away with you!" Rose said. "When we were at school the teacher said he had two left feet."

Then they all jumped as they heard Michael Murphy's voice saying, "Rose, can I take you up for the next dance?"

Rose was so taken aback she suddenly felt her throat run dry.

"Grand," she muttered, smiling embarrassedly at him. And then, making sure she didn't catch Cathy's or Mona's eye, she stood up and followed him onto the dance floor.

"I was looking for you earlier," Michael said as the band struck up a slow waltz.

"Were you? When?" Rose said quickly, then instantly regretted sounding so eager.

"A few dances ago," he said. "I went over to ask your cousin where you were, but you were dancing with somebody else." He raised his eyebrows and laughed. "I forgot how popular you are."

Rose felt a warm glow run through her and she was delighted that Hannah had been there to hear Michael looking for her not once, but *twice*.

She moved into his outstretched arms now and was

instantly aware of the heat of his hands as one took hers to lead her and the other slid around her waist. Then she caught her breath when she felt his hand tighten as they moved off into the crowd.

They danced in silence for a while, with Rose thinking that it seemed as though they'd danced together every weekend of their life.

And then Michael suddenly bent his blond head and said something that she didn't quite catch. She pulled away a little and looked up at his face quizzically.

"I said," he repeated, moving his lips close to her ear, "that you smell lovely . . . really lovely."

Rose felt her face flush. She was wearing the *Chanel* perfume that Leonora Bentley had given her. "Thank you," she said, delighted with the compliment.

He kept his lips close to the side of her face. "And the dress you're wearing is one of the nicest I've ever seen . . . the colours really suit you."

Rose's heart soared. This was more than she had dreamed of.

This night was turning into the best night of her life.

* * *

Paul Barry walked carefully around the side of the dance-floor, making sure that he didn't get in the way of any of the dancers. His eyes darted around the couples until they came to settle on his sister and he smiled with relief when he saw that Rose was still fully occupied waltzing with Michael Murphy and looking up into his eyes. Paul reckoned he could be in and out of the hall in a short time without her noticing anything.

As he neared the place he had been sitting with his cousin, he paused to let a couple weave past him. He craned his neck as he stood and through the smoky haze he could see Hannah sitting, as pretty as a picture, with her curly blonde head bent close to Liam O'Connor's. The sight of them both looking so cosy together brought a stab of jealousy to his chest. He reasoned with himself that it was not the sort of jealousy that a boyfriend might feel, because of course he knew how very weird that would be.

He was Hannah's first cousin after all and she was a few years older than him. It was more a feeling of someone muscling in on a close friendship, because he had discovered during the last few holidays that he and Hannah were very similar in many ways. They had the same sense of humour and they viewed adults in the same way. Paul could see straight through Hannah's sucking up to his parents – especially his father – with things like reminding them it was time for the Rosary and all that old-fashioned kind of thing. He could see that her making big issues of the small things they thought were important made them trust her, which meant that they turned a blind eye to other things. He had first teased her about it last year, when they were walking down on their own to meet Rose from work one evening. Hannah had raised her eyebrows and then – just when he thought he had chanced his arm a bit too far – she had given him a broad grin.

"Ah, well," she had told him laughingly, "'Aithníonn ciaróg ciaróg eile' – it takes one beetle to know another!"

"Maybe I should take a leaf out of your book," Paul had replied. "If it keeps them happy to think we're toeing the line then maybe they won't be watching every move we make."

"It's not as if we're exactly getting up to anything worthwhile," Hannah had sighed. "I'm always very well behaved . . . when I'm down here."

Paul had looked at her for a few moments, wondering if that meant she wasn't well-behaved at home.

"And anyway, you should consider yourself very lucky," Hannah had continued. "Your mother and father are easy enough to get on with. Your father might be very strict and they're both old-fashioned about things, but they're kind and nice in their own way and they really care about all the family."

"I'm sure yours are the very same. I know we don't see much of your father with him being tied up with the farm and everything, but your mother seems very like our own. You can tell a mile off that they're sisters."

Hannah's blue eyes had narrowed. "Oh no," she said, shaking her head vehemently. "They're not at all alike. You've never seen my mother when she's riled."

Paul had stuck his bottom lip out, thinking. "But I couldn't imagine my Auntie Sheila in a very bad mood. She always seems very quiet when she's here."

"That's because she doesn't want to show her true colours in front of ye all," Hannah had said, raising her eyes to the ceiling.

Paul stood watching Hannah and Liam O'Connor now, feeling awkward about interrupting them. Then he glanced back at the dimly lit, packed dance floor and shrugged. If he didn't make a move now, Rose would be back and his chance would be gone. He let another couple pass and then he quickly moved up towards his cousin.

When Liam O'Connor saw Paul approaching, he touched Hannah's arm and nodded towards him.

Paul felt a heat coming to his face as he went down on his haunches beside Hannah's chair. "How's the ankle?" he asked her.

"I think I'll chance the next dance," Hannah told him. "I've asked Liam if he'll guide me around the floor. He's big and strong and would be well able to catch me if the ankle goes on me again."

Just then, a lad who was standing on the floor with a group beckoned to Liam who, with a gesture to Hannah signalling he would be back, went over to join them.

Paul took his chance. "Do you still have that thing in your bag?"

Hannah looked at him and smiled. "Of course I do. I thought you'd forgotten all about it. I thought I might have to throw it away in the bushes on the way home."

"Don't be coddin' me," Paul whispered. He looked anxiously at the dance floor as the waltz came to an end. "I'll take it now or Rose will be back and I won't have it for the break."

Hannah gestured to her handbag on the floor. "Give it here to me," she told him. Then, when he handed it to her, she leaned to the side of the chair where she couldn't be seen, opened the handbag, took out a small brown paper package and handed it to him.

"You're one in a million," he told her, affecting the manner of an older, confident man. He noticed Liam coming back towards them now and, opening his jacket, tried to slide the flat package into his inside pocket, but when he realised it was too big, he put it under his arm and closed his jacket over it.

"I'll be back shortly," he told Hannah with a wink and, giving Liam O'Connor a nod, disappeared off through the crowd.

"Rose's young brother seems to be acting very shifty," Liam commented. "And is that what I think it is in the bag?"

Hannah's eyes widened innocently. "I don't know what's in the bag. He just asked me to keep it for him . . . I never asked what was in it." She paused, biting her lower lip in thought. "I don't think it's Paul's anyway – I think somebody just asked him to carry it for them."

Liam shrugged and offered her his hand.

Hannah rose with some difficulty but, when they moved out onto the floor and Liam was supporting her around the waist, she managed well enough.

"So, you really like Rose?" she said after a while, looking up at Liam as they slowly moved around the floor.

Liam nodded, glad of the chance to talk about Rose to her cousin on her own. "The very first minute I clapped eyes on her behind Slattery's bar, I knew she was the girl for me. And I thought tonight I might ask you to put a good word in for me . . ."

Hannah felt a stab of annoyance, as she wasn't used to lads telling her they were interested in other girls when they were with her. And it was even more annoying that it was Rose. She stifled a little sigh. It was obviously the second-hand clothes that had made the difference.

Liam O'Connor went on, delighted to have Hannah's ear. "I'd be grateful if you could tell her you and me had a great chat and that you think I'm a decent kind of a fella and that she should at least give herself the chance to get to know me a bit better."

Hannah shook her curly blonde head and smiled. "You amaze me now," she told him, "I wouldn't have put you and Rose together in a million years . . ."

"And why not?" Liam asked, his brow knitted together.

"You're not a bit alike. Rose can be a very serious girl, you know –"

Another couple bumped into them now, sending them off-kilter for a few moments.

"Are you okay?" Liam checked. "Is your leg all right?"

Hannah screwed her face up for a moment and then she nodded. "It's grand," she said in a thin, pained voice, "and no matter how bad it gets, I'm not going to let it spoil my night." She moved back into his arms and was heartened when Liam's grip tightened on her. *This is more like it,* she thought, moving closer to him. This was the way that most lads reacted to her and it was the way she liked it. Especially tall, muscular lads like the county football player.

"I'll keep a firm grip on you and make sure nobody knocks us off our stride again," he told her, laughing now.

As they moved around the edge of the room Hannah thought how lovely it was being held by such a handsome, strong lad. A lad her own age, with all his future stretching out before him. Not like Simon Connolly who was years older than her – and married with a family. Not like Simon Connolly who was her uncle and at times could be cross and awkward. She suddenly wondered how she had ever got involved with him in the first place. Had she really been that desperate as to court his attentions? Had she been totally mad?

Then she remembered that Simon was the one person who understood how vicious her mother was and how awful and depressing it was living with her. Her Aunt Ursula wasn't quite so bad but Simon had told her that although they were only sister-in-laws they still had the same mean streak running through them. He had also told her that it was okay for her and him to comfort and console each other because they weren't blood relations either. He was only her aunt's husband which meant he and Hannah were only related by marriage.

But it wasn't right, she thought, and it couldn't go on.

Deep down Hannah had always known that.

Looking back, she could see how easy it had been for them to become involved with each other. It was because Hannah had needed someone to make her feel better about things at home and because Simon had been a good listener. Over the last few months she felt he had saved her from becoming totally depressed. He had lightened her life up and made her feel sexy and attractive. He had told her she was the double of Marilyn Monroe and she had loved it. It had given her the confidence to go into school each day and not care what the other girls thought of her. They might be all giggly and whispering about lads who were in the local boys' school but they were young and silly and didn't have a good-looking mature man who adored them.

But as she felt the strong arms around her now, Hannah knew that the time had come when she preferred to have someone livelier and nearer her own age. She smiled up into Liam O'Connor's face, wondering if he thought she looked like Marilyn Monroe.

Chapter 14

Rose was elated.

She and Michael Murphy had spent the last few dances together and it seemed as though he would have danced with her all night if the halfway interval hadn't come when it did. And, unbelievably, he had told her that he would be back for another dance in a short while. But – best of all – he hadn't mentioned Hannah at all. Even though he and Ruairí had been chatting to her, he hadn't found it worthwhile to bring her into the conversation.

As she walked back to her seat, she found herself almost surprised when the full lights were switched back on and she was back amongst all the other dancers. For the last fifteen minutes or so, it was as if she and Michael had been in a little world of their own, dancing round and round the floor, occasionally chatting and smiling at each other. She had to remind herself not to keep smiling as she knew it would look very odd to the others.

Hannah was still sitting in the same place, with Liam O'Connor on one side and the annoying Jack Kelly on the other, but Rose was so happy that she couldn't care less who was there.

"Would you like me to get you a bottle of lemonade or a cup of tea?" she offered when she reached Hannah. She didn't bother to acknowledge the two lads, thinking that it would only encourage them to hang about.

"Liam's already offered to buy us one," Hannah said. She tilted her head to the side, studying her cousin. "You're looking very delighted with yourself. You're like a dog with two tails. What's happened?"

Rose immediately started to blush. "Nothing has happened," she said, a touch defensively. "I only offered to get you a drink. Where's the harm in that?"

Hannah smiled ingratiatingly at her now. She had made her point and didn't want to get into any kind of an argument. "I just meant that you looked very happy." Her eyes lit up. "When Liam and me were dancing, we were trying to get your attention but we couldn't catch your eye."

"Well, the lighting isn't very bright and the floor was so packed you could hardly make out one couple from another." Rose glanced at Liam now. "I never noticed either of you."

Liam stood up and Rose was suddenly conscious of how much taller than her he was. How much taller he was than Michael Murphy, who she had decided was the perfect height for her as they danced together.

"What would you like to drink?" Liam asked in flat, quiet voice.

"I can get my own," Rose said, looking around her, "or Paul will get us drinks."

Liam shrugged. "I'm getting Hannah one so it's just as easy to bring you one as well."

"That's good of you. A lemonade will be grand, thanks."

He went off with Jack Kelly sloping behind him with a kind of wide-stepped gait that made him look almost drunk. And yet he couldn't be. He'd only had a couple of pints earlier. She'd seen him down four or five pints on other occasions without it having any great effect on him.

Rose gave a little sigh. Why should she care what he had to drink? Why should she care about any of them? Something special had happened tonight with her and Michael Murphy, and she was determined not to let anything spoil it. Not Hannah, not Liam O'Connor – not anyone. It was just a pity that there had to be a break in the evening at all or she could still be up on the floor in that lovely little world with Michael Murphy.

She turned to Hannah. "How is the ankle?" she asked in a chirpy voice. "I heard you saying you were up dancing, so it must have improved."

Hannah nodded. "Yes, thanks. It's a lot better." She leaned down now to give the tender part of her foot a little rub. "Liam was very good when we were up dancing – he made sure he took all my weight." She smiled. "He's a lovely fellow when you get to know him, isn't he?"

Rose shrugged. "He's not the worst, I suppose, and it was nice of him to go and get us a drink."

Hannah leaned towards Rose now, crossing one shapely leg over the other, and said in a low voice, "I saw you up on the floor with that Murphy fellow. You were dancing very cosy with him. All lovey-dovey looking."

Rose's face brightened instantly. "Get away!" she

said, laughing, making out she hadn't even noticed the attention Michael had given her. She would have loved to have quizzed Hannah more about how she and Michael looked together but something made her hold her tongue. She hadn't even told Cathy her true feelings about Michael because she knew in many ways that he was out of her league. But tonight Rose was sure – absolutely sure – that he liked her. The way he had held her, the way he had leaned his head against hers as they waltzed. The things he had said to her.

"I don't want to you take this the wrong way," Hannah said in a low, conspiratorial voice, "but if I was you I'd watch that Michael Murphy. I think he's a bit of a ladies' man. He was over chatting to me earlier, giving me the glad eye. I told him my ankle was too sore to dance to get rid of him." She shrugged, tossing her blonde curls over one shoulder. "But he's not really my type . . . I prefer them a bit taller and older-looking. And to be honest, I've had a few better-looking ones up chatting to me tonight to be bothered with the likes of him."

Rose felt as though she had suddenly been punched in the stomach. Surely Michael Murphy hadn't made a total fool of her on the dance floor? Surely he hadn't been so nice to her, complimenting her – telling her he'd be back for her later – when he hadn't meant a single word of it?

Rose stared at her cousin now and when Hannah's eyes met hers she instantly knew that Hannah was lying. Oh, she knew that Michael and Ruairí had been over chatting to Hannah, but hadn't Michael told her that himself? He didn't know that Rose and the other girls had seen him, so he had no reason to make excuses or tell lies.

Rose's upset now turned to anger. Anger that this cousin of hers should come all the way down for a dance she wasn't even invited to. That she should push her way in with all Rose's friends, and laugh and jeer at her father behind his back. That she would do anything to get her own way.

It would be easy now for Rose to lose her temper and make a holy show of them both but she knew that that would be stupid, because Hannah would only deny everything. She would say she hadn't a clue what Rose was going on about. She would have no compunction about bringing Michael and Ruairí Murphy into the argument and, if all else failed, she would resort to tears to gain everyone's sympathy.

The wise thing would be to say nothing. Not to rise to Hannah's bait. To act as though Hannah hadn't even told those spiteful lies.

Rose took a deep breath. "Have you seen Paul anywhere?" she asked, glancing around the hall.

Hannah's eyebrows rose in surprise. She had been expecting some reaction to what she'd said about Michael Murphy. "He's been around about all evening," she said, shrugging. "He must be up dancing or over chatting to someone."

"Is he enjoying himself? I haven't seen him up on the floor much at all."

"He sat it out with me for a while," Hannah said, indicating her ankle. "He's such a decent, thoughtful young lad. He said he didn't want to leave me on my own but I told him to go and have a few dances when Liam and Jack came over to sit with me."

"I don't know what's worse," Rose said, forcing herself to sound carefree and light, "being stuck with our Paul or being stuck with Liam O'Connor and that Jack Kelly."

There was a little pause, then Hannah leaned across to Rose in a casual, friendly way. "Oh, that Michael Murphy must have something very special about him," she said, tucking one side of her curly blonde hair behind her ear, "because I've not heard you say a good word about anybody else." She put her hand on Rose's arm now. "I don't mean to be critical – but you're very hard on poor Paul at times. He's turned out to be the loveliest of fellas." Then Hannah looked over to the corner where a crowd was gathered at the drinks table. "And even though you're not too keen on Liam and Jack, they've been decent enough to sit with me and then go and get us drinks. There are some fellas who wouldn't make the effort."

Rose bit her tongue as Hannah rattled on about Liam and Jack as if she'd known them all her life. That was another irritating habit of hers – she was hardly introduced to somebody when she was calling them by their first names and talking as if she knew every little detail about them. And, if she didn't know, she had no problem in making presumptions about them – many of which were often well off the mark. Rose wondered now how she was going to get through the rest of the week, until it was time for Hannah to go back home, without blowing up at her.

Then Rose caught sight of Michael Murphy coming towards them and Hannah's words were lost on her. She smiled warmly at him and barely had time to wonder why he looked so serious when he bent down and whispered in her ear.

"Can you come outside for a few minutes, Rose?" Then he dug his hands in his trousers pockets and started to move in the direction of the hall door.

Rose turned to a surprised Hannah and said, "I'm just going outside for a few minutes with Michael." She glanced around her and then she gave a little shrug. "I'm sorry to leave you sitting all on your own – but you'll be all right, won't you? I won't be long." The look on Hannah's face told her that she had paid her cousin back for her earlier lies and nastiness.

She got to her feet and followed Michael towards the door, picking her way through the small groups, baffled about the look on his face and his strange manner. He hadn't even looked at Hannah – in fact his whole demeanour had been quite brusque. She wasn't at all sure what was going on. Was Michael asking her to go for a walk with him or just outside for a breath of air? Some couples did that. It was well known that certain types of girls and fellows wandered down to the beach or even around the side of the hall for a bit of privacy to get up to whatever they liked. Her brain ticked over fast. Did Michael Murphy think she was that type of girl?

Rose wondered now if she had read him wrong? She had both him and Ruairí down as well-mannered, respectable young men, the type of lads who would never take advantage of a girl. And however much she liked him, she was going to have to leave him in no doubt that she certainly wasn't the type of girl who went off on her own with a fella at the drop of a hat.

Michael slowed up as they neared the door and turned back to wait as she weaved her way through the crowd towards him. "I'm sorry now . . ." his voice was so low she could hardly hear him, and his face was still serious, "but there's a bit of a problem and I didn't want to go talking about it in the hall." He glanced at the groups on either side of him. "It would be easier to explain outside . . ."

A cold chill ran down Rose's spine. "What kind of a problem? What do you mean?"

He moved closer and put his arm around her. "It's nothing too serious," he told her, "but I thought I should call you to be on the safe side."

Rose stood rooted to the spot, her feet refusing to go an inch further until she knew. "Tell me!" she hissed.

"It's Paul . . ." Then, seeing Larry Hennessey looking over at them, Michael suddenly stopped speaking and led Rose on.

Larry grinned when he saw the couple coming towards him. "Is it getting too hot in there for ye?"

"Yeah – we're just going out for a bit of fresh air," Michael said.

Larry winked knowingly at him. "Nothing like it. Nothing like a bit of fresh air when you're feeling hot."

When they got safely out of earshot, Rose turned to Michael, her brow furrowed in anxiety. "What about Paul?" she demanded. "What's wrong?"

Without another word Michael Murphy took her hand and firmly led her out the door. And, as Rose followed him around the side of the hall, it crossed her mind that although he was holding her hand she wasn't enjoying it. This wasn't a romantic encounter. Michael Murphy was holding her hand because there was something wrong.

When they rounded the end of the hall and she saw half a dozen or so lads all gathered there with the pale yellow lights of the hall shining on them, Rose's blood ran cold. Then, as she got closer she could see Paul propped up against the wall and her hand flew to her mouth. Oh, my God, she thought, what's happened to him?

Slowly, she stepped towards him.

"He's all right," Francie Kane, one of the lads, said. "He'll be grand in a while . . ." His voice tailed off in a slur.

"Paul!" Letting go of Michael's hand, Rose rushed to her brother's side.

Paul was as white as a sheet, his head lying on his chest and his eyes closed as if he was in a deep sleep.

"What's wrong?" cried Rose. "What's happened?"

"Ah, he's all right now – he's been sick," Francie said.

"Oh, my God!" Rose said, kneeling down beside Paul on the grass, heedless of her new dress and good stockings. "Paul . . . Paul . . ." she said, putting a finger to his eyelid to open it. Then, as she moved her face closer to him she caught the unmistakable smell from him. The smell of whiskey. Rose's head started to reel with the shock. "He's drunk!" she whispered, hardly able to form the words. "Paul is drunk!"

"He didn't have that much," Francie said. "It's just that he's not used to it. It was Jack Kelly that encouraged him, telling him to take gulps out of the bottle."

But Rose wasn't listening. Her mind was racing,

trying to make sense of the situation, trying to decide what she would – what she *could* do.

"Ah, sure he'll be grand when he's slept it off," one of the lads said, by way of offering comfort.

Sleep it off? Were they mad? Rose thought. He won't get a chance to sleep it off. My father will absolutely kill him! She turned to Francie and his friends, her face stiff and angry. "Just go away," she told them in a shaky voice. "I'll look after him."

Francie shrugged. "It wasn't us that gave him the drink, Rose," he told her lamely.

"Leave us!" she told him again.

Then, as the group all started to slink away, Paul gave a moan and opened his eyes. "Rose . . ." he muttered. "I'm sorry . . . I kept seeing double of everything . . . I still do . . . and I've been really sick."

"You mean you've been really bloody *stupid*!" Rose snapped, her eyes blazing with anger.

Paul sat up straighter now and then lowered his spinning head into his hands. "I'm sorry . . ."

Rose felt a hand on her shoulder and she looked up. It was Michael Murphy. With all the drama she'd nearly forgotten about him.

"I'll go and get Paul a cup of strong black tea," he said, squeezing her shoulder in a comforting manner. "We have a while yet before the dance finishes to try to sober him up."

"Thanks, Michael, you're very good. Will you ask Hannah to come out? But please don't mention it to anyone else. The more people that know the more chance there is my father will get to hear about it."

Michael nodded. "You're going to have to get a bit of help with getting him home tonight."

Rose shook her head, tears coming into her eyes. "I can't believe he's done this – my father will kill him."

"It's out of character for him. He's always come across as a nice, sensible lad. I suppose anybody can make a mistake – I've done it myself."

"Not a mistake like this," Rose said, looking at her brother. "He doesn't know what he's done."

Michael went down on his haunches beside her now and put his arm around her properly. "He's coming round. It's not as bad as you think." Then, he suddenly leaned in closer to her and kissed her very gently on the cheek. "It'll be all right, don't worry."

Chapter 15

Hannah smiled to herself when she saw Michael Murphy coming striding across the hall towards her but she just kept sipping her lemonade through the straw in the bottle as if she hadn't noticed him. She was delighted to have had Liam and Jack hovering around her all night, bringing her lemonade and biscuits, and now she was beginning to wonder about the blond fellow that Rose obviously fancied. And even though he had looked very keen on Rose while they danced, he had come over to where Hannah was sitting many times when Rose wasn't even there. She wondered if he was just using Rose as an excuse to talk to her.

To her surprise, he bent and whispered in her ear. Within seconds her carefully made-up face had blanched of all colour. She felt a sense of impending doom and disaster when he described the scenario with Paul outside and when he told her how upset Rose was.

"I'm going to get him a cup of strong tea," Michael muttered, "and I think Rose might feel better if you went out to help her with him."

As soon as he went off, Hannah turned to Liam. "Will you come outside with me for a few minutes?"

Liam O'Connor looked back at her in a very confused manner. "Why?"

"Because Paul Barry has got himself into a bit of a state with drink, and Rose and me are going to have to try to get him home."

"Jesus!" Liam said, running his fingers through his hair. "Stephen Barry will go mad – totally mad. He doesn't hold with drink at all and he's fierce strict with the family – he's well known for it."

Hannah felt her chest tighten. This was all beginning to sound much too serious for her. It sounded as though it could even spoil the rest of the night. She put her lemonade bottle down at the side of her chair and lifted her handbag. "It's only halfway though the night," she said, sighing. "I only hope this isn't going to finish the dance off for us."

"We'd better go and see how the land lies," Liam said.

They moved slowly through the hall towards the door, as they were going against the tide of the crowd, who were all heading back in, eager for the second part of the night to get underway. Hannah was walking much better than she had been since the afternoon. They picked their way across the wild grass at the side of the building and around the back. Paul was now up on his feet – albeit very unsteadily – and leaning against the wall.

Rose saw Hannah coming and was about to say something to her when she caught sight of Liam O'Connor coming behind her. She stood bolt upright with her hands on her hips. "I hope that Jack Kelly's not with you!" she told him in a clipped, angry tone. "Because if he is, he better be prepared for what I have to say to him."

"Why?" Liam said, his brow wrinkled in confusion. "What's Jack done?"

"What's he done?" Rose's voice was high and indignant. She pointed at Paul. "Would you look at the state of him! And while I know it's his own stupid fault – the other lads told me that Jack Kelly had a hand in giving him the drink!"

Paul slid down the wall a bit and then staggered to the side to stop himself from falling back on the ground. Hannah went rushing to his side to help him back upright again.

Liam looked at him in amazement. "Sure, a few pints wouldn't do that to him – and he seemed grand enough back in the pub."

"But it wasn't only a *few pints*," Rose told him, on the verge of tears now. "It was *whiskey*!"

Liam slowly shook his head in bewilderment. "And you say Jack gave it to him?"

"That's what I was told," Rose stated, hating having to explain herself to the likes of Liam O'Connor, and hating having him see her so upset and her brother in such a state. "And he knows well that Paul is only a young lad just out of school and not fit for that kind of stuff. He never even tasted whiskey before in his life!"

"Look, I know Jack can be a bit of a chancer at times but I wouldn't have thought he would get up to something like that," said Liam. "But I'll certainly be having a word about it with him."

"Well, who's been a silly boy?" Hannah said to Paul in a high-pitched, school-teacherish kind of voice.

Rose's hackles flared up. "I think the situation is a lot more serious than to be calling him *a silly boy!*" she snapped. "He won't be so feckin' silly when my father gets a hold of him!"

There was a stunned silence now at Rose's outburst. Never had Paul, Hannah or Liam O'Connor heard Rose Barry swear. The fact that she did indicated more clearly than anything else just how distraught she was.

Michael Murphy suddenly appeared out of the shadows. He had obviously been standing there and heard every word that Rose had said, and she was glad to be in semi-darkness as her face was so flushed with embarrassment at him hearing her swearing. What on earth would he think of her now?

"I've brought the tea," he said, in a low, hesitant voice. "Is he fit to drink it now, do you think?"

"He better be," Rose said, taking the cup from him.

Hannah reached to take it from Rose. "I'll give it to him," she said quietly. "Just in case he drinks it down too quickly."

Just like the way he drank the whiskey, Rose thought ruefully, but she surrendered the cup and managed to bite her tongue.

"He looks a bit better," Michael said now. "At least he's up on his feet."

"He won't manage the bike home," Rose said, "so he may walk as soon as he's fit to."

There was a silence now as they all watched Hannah trying to encourage Paul to drink the tea, then Liam said,

"I'm going to go inside and have a word with Jack and see what the story is."

Hannah lifted her head. "Sure, there's no need to go making more out of the situation than needs be, is there?" she said. Her eyes darted from Rose to Liam, then she looked across to Michael for support. "There's little point in involving other people. It's best if we just concentrate on getting Paul fit enough to get home and forget about any arguments."

"I'll have a word with him all the same," Liam stated, almost as if Hannah's opinion was of no interest to him. "If he's involved in giving young fellas strong drink he needs to explain himself. I wouldn't have been in his company tonight if I'd thought for a minute he had a hand in causing all this trouble."

Rose said nothing. She could still hardly take in what had happened. One minute she was dancing around the floor in Michael Murphy's arms, almost making plans for their future together, and the next minute she was so ashamed she couldn't look him straight in the face.

She felt his hand on her shoulder. "If there's nothing more I can do here," he said, "then I'll get back inside myself. Ruairí and the other lads will be wondering where I've got to. We said we might give them a few tunes at the end of the night."

Rose nodded regretfully. She would have loved to have watched him and Ruairí up on the stage. "Go on in and enjoy the rest of the dance," she said, without looking directly at him. "And thanks for your help."

"Ah, sure it was nothing!" And then he went off around the side of the building into the darkness.

Without anything being said, Rose knew that that was the last she would see of Michael Murphy tonight. It would be the last she would see of the dance tonight.

The night she had looked forward to for weeks. All the dreaming and all the planning had come to nothing. All the effort she had put into making sure she looked her very best. The dress, her hair, her lovely perfume – all had come to nothing.

The night was ruined. And deep down in her heart, Rose knew that she might never get a chance like that with Michael Murphy ever again.

A short while later Liam O'Connor appeared again. He motioned to Rose to come to the side of the hall where they could talk without Paul hearing them. Rose just followed him, still numb from all that had gone on in the last half an hour.

"I've had words with Jack Kelly," he told her in low, very serious voice, "and you only need to look at him to tell he's had a bit too much to drink himself. I got this great rambling story out of him about a few of the lads bringing small bottles of whiskey in their pockets to the dance and they were drinking it around the back of the hall. And he also told me that Paul downed a large brandy earlier in the night."

"When?" Rose asked incredulously. The nightmare was becoming more and more complicated.

"In Slattery's before the dance." His brow furrowed. "Not that I would count Jack Kelly as one of my best friends or anything, but I feel bad because I was with him. In all honesty I never noticed what he bought at the bar or what he drank, although I did hear him telling all the lads about the medicinal brandy he had bought for your cousin. You weren't in the bar at the time."

And then Rose's brain clicked. Of course! The brandy that he had bought for Hannah. So Hannah had been telling the truth when she said *she* hadn't drunk it, but she had omitted to say that Paul had. That was obviously why Paul had been so silly and giddy on the way to the dance. She looked back at her cousin now who was still ministering to him, an arm around his shoulder, and coaxing him to drink the tea.

What else was there to find out? Was there anything else she didn't know now?

She thanked Liam and then hurried back into the hall to retrieve the coats and her handbag and Hannah's.

She felt mortified at having to tell lies. She had to tell Cathy Brennan and the girls a white lie and say that Paul wasn't well with a bad headache and Hannah's ankle was bothering her, so they were all going home.

Cathy walked her to the door. "What a pity you've got to go home!" she said. "And you were having such a great time! I saw you up on the floor with Michael Murphy and it looked as though the pair of ye were getting on great."

Rose raised her eyebrows and sighed. She had a pain in her heart now at the thought of what she had lost. "We were," she said heavily, "but I've got to head home. I've no choice." Then she felt guilty at not being honest with her friend. "Listen, I'll call up to you some evening when Hannah's gone and tell you the whole story."

Cathy put her hand on Rose's arm. "I don't mean to make you feel bad but I've already heard about Paul . . . some of the lads were talking about it."

Rose closed her eyes to stop the tears that had suddenly welled up. Her friend already knew she had lied. "I'm sick to my heart about it, Cathy. And if my father finds out . . ." Her voice was wavery and sad. She halted to look at her watch. "I'm hoping he'll be gone to bed by the time we get home."

"He won't find out. Who's going to tell him? Don't be worrying – I'm sure it'll all be fine." Then she smiled and winked at Rose. "I'm sorry you're going but on the other hand maybe the rest of us might get a few dances now we've got rid of the two best-looking, best-dressed girls in the hall!"

In the midst of her misery, Rose gave a watery smile. "I wouldn't go that far!" She blinked hard against the tears. "Who would believe it? I've been looking forward to this dance for weeks."

"There will be more dances," Cathy told her in a low, kind voice, "and more chances with Michael Murphy. You made a grand-looking couple on the floor."

Chapter 16

Rose didn't know whether to be angry or grateful to Liam O'Connor for accompanying them home. Although he was the last person she would have wanted, she knew that if she had to walk home on her own with Hannah and Paul she would end up completely losing her temper with them both. Dealing with her drunken *amadán* of a brother was bad enough, but having to watch Hannah fussing about him like a ministering angel was more than she could bear.

And there was always the danger that Paul might collapse or be too sick to continue. Or that Hannah's ankle might get worse – though, in fact, Hannah was so concerned about Paul that she seemed to have forgotten all about the problem with her ankle.

The black tea had sobered Paul up to some extent and the cold sea breeze helped to continue the process. Rose could hardly look at him and she was glad that Hannah was willing to coax and cajole him along on the long, dark walk home. Paul was leaning on the handlebars of his bike for support and Hannah had positioned herself at the other side of the handlebars in case he staggered and he and the cycle went flying into the ditch. That wouldn't do Hannah's ankle much good, thought Rose, but she said nothing.

Rose and Liam walked a couple of yards behind the other two, Liam pushing his bike. Rose held her breath as they passed Slattery's pub, terrified that she might run into her uncles or Mary Slattery. Apart from the state of Paul, she wondered how she would have explained the fact she was walking alongside Liam O'Connor who lived a good mile out from Slattery's in the opposite direction. Thankfully, they met nobody.

It crossed Rose's mind now whether Liam had actually come to help tonight so that he could spend more time with Hannah. Since she herself had made it perfectly clear that she didn't have any interest in him, had he transferred his affections to her cousin?

Liam said very little which Rose was very grateful for as she didn't feel at all like talking. Occasionally he asked Paul how he felt and at one point, when they reached a bit of an incline, he asked Hannah if she wanted to get up on his bike and he would push her up the hill to save her ankle. Hannah had declined, saying her ankle wasn't too bad and she preferred to walk along with Paul.

Rose walked every step as though she had a thorn in her shoe. Wanting to get home and at the same time dreading it. Tonight had changed everything. It had taught her not to take things for granted, and that one mistake – Paul's mistake in this case – could affect a lot of people.

Eventually they hit upon the last quarter mile of their journey and Rose went to check on Paul.

"Are you fit to walk in the house sensibly and quietly?" she asked him in a tone which was devoid of any sympathy.

Pal nodded. "Yes. I'll go straight to bed and –"

"Make sure you go to the lavatory first," Hannah cut in. "You don't want to have to get up in the middle of the night to find your way outside in the dark."

"I'll go as soon as we get to the house," Paul promised, "and I'll make sure I don't make any noise."

Hannah patted his shoulder. "You'll be grand," she told him in a comforting voice.

Rose listened to the exchange between them, thinking how quickly Hannah had rushed to Paul's side when she realised what had happened. And how practical and sensible she'd been helping him to drink the tea and walking the bike home with him. She supposed it was easier to be helpful when it wasn't your own brother. At the end of the day – apart from having to leave the dance early – it wouldn't really have had much effect on Hannah, whereas Rose would never see her younger brother in the same light again.

When they came within sight of the house, Rose turned to Liam who seemed to have grown quieter the further along they travelled. "I think you should head back to the dance now. You'll catch the last half an hour if you cycle back down to the hall."

Liam shrugged. "I doubt if I'll bother now . . ." He paused, looking at Paul who had just staggered again. "Do you want me to check he's okay going to the lavatory?"

Rose coloured up at the mention of such a personal thing. "No – no, he'll be grand. It's just at the back door, so he doesn't have far to go."

"Will he be able to see all right in the dark?"

"My father has an oil lamp rigged up inside the lavatory for Granny which will be lit. The door is left open so you can see the light when you go out into the yard." She looked up at the sky. "There's a good moon out tonight and plenty of stars so he'll be able to see grand."

He looked awkward for a few moments. "If you're sure, now, I'll head on . . ."

"We'll be grand, thanks. It was good of you seeing us back to the house."

Liam looked her. "Rose . . ." he said, in a low voice, "I want you to know I'd do anything to help you." His eyes narrowed a little. "And I know well you would have preferred it if Michael Murphy had been the one to walk you back home but since he didn't seem to be in the position, I thought I was better than nobody."

Rose looked back at him, completely taken aback by his forthrightness, and slightly ashamed of her distant manner towards him. "Thanks, Liam," she said in a sincere tone. "I'm actually very grateful to you." There was a little pause, then she said, "Goodnight, and I hope you get back for a bit of the dance." Then she turned and hurried after her brother and cousin.

The two girls waited outside the lavatory for Paul, in silence.

Then Rose's hands suddenly flew to her mouth. "Oh, God!" she whispered. "I forgot he was sleeping in my bed tonight . . . I was thinking we only had to get him into his own room and he'd be grand. How are we going to get him into the room without him waking Granny and the girls up?" Tears pricked at her eyes again and she felt tired and weary. "I could kill him! I could absolutely kill him. He's ruined this night for us all and made a terrible fool of himself and me. And you coming all the way down from Offaly especially for the dance and then having to leave it halfway through!" She bit her lip. "And Liam O'Connor is going to have strong words with that Jack Kelly tomorrow about buying strong drink for Paul. Imagine giving whiskey to a schoolboy!"

"In the morning it will all be different," Hannah murmured. "Maybe there's no point in making too much of it. He's not the first to have more than he should to drink."

Rose looked at her. "Are you mad? My father will murder him if he finds out. He doesn't even know Paul has the odd glass of beer!"

The latch creaked on the lavatory door now, making both girls jump.

Paul slowly emerged holding a hand up to his head. "I've just been sick again . . ." he moaned.

Rose closed her eyes for a moment, trying to fight back the urge to go over and give him the biggest slap across the face. "C'mon you," she said, taking hold of him by the arm. "You'll have to walk as straight as you can, and when you get into the room take off your jacket and your trousers and put them on the chair. Don't bother trying to take the shirt and shoes and socks off until you're lying safe on the bed" She then looked him straight in the eye. "And don't you *dare* make a sound!"

"I'll be behind to keep a grip on him," Hannah whispered.

Rose went in first, quietly opening the door which led

into the kitchen. The sweet spicy smell of her grand-mother's baking hit them as soon as they entered. And in the light of the dim lamp that had been left on, she could see the outline of several loaves of soda bread covered over with damp teacloths to keep them fresh and a large covered tray of scones. Often when they came in late, they would rake the range up to boil the kettle for tea and help themselves to a bit of whatever had been left out.

But tonight wasn't the night for normal things like that

They went across the kitchen floor, then Rose stopped and turned back to the other pair, her fingers pressed warningly to her lips. She slowly turned the handle to open the door into the hallway. Then just as the door swung open a figure loomed towards her from the darkness of the hall and her heart almost stopped.

She stepped backwards, sharply colliding into Hannah who then went backwards into Paul, sending him flying back against the kitchen table. Then he went sprawling over the kitchen floor.

Chapter 17

"What in the name of God has happened?" Martha Barry asked in a low, shocked voice as she gazed down at her grandson, who was gripping onto the leg of the kitchen table in an attempt to pull himself up on his feet again. "What's wrong with you, Paul? Stop that trick-acting and get up from the cold floor!" She leaned heavily on her walking stick, an indication that her arthritic hip was troubling her again.

Hannah moved to stand with her back against the cooker, her eyes darting from one to the other, wondering what was going to happen next. She was used to this unpredictable type of situation at home with her mother but she had never encountered it before in the Barrys' quiet, calm household.

Rose went over and closed the kitchen door quietly. "I'm sorry but I got a fright when I saw you, Granny," she explained in an urgent whisper, "and I stepped backwards into the other two and Paul got knocked down." She went over to her brother now, praying that he would appear normal, and said, "Up you get, Paul!"

"What time is it?" Martha Barry asked, turning to look up at the clock. "Sure, it's only half past eleven." Her gaze shifted back to Paul and she watched for a few moments as Rose tried to drag him up onto his feet. Then she glanced over at Hannah. "Did the dance finish early?"

Hannah's blue eyes darted across to Rose now, trying to gauge what she should say. When she saw that Rose was too involved in trying to sort her brother out, she decided to improvise. "It was my fault we came home early," she told the old woman in a high, breathless voice. "My ankle started to get very painful again."

There was a silence and Martha suddenly said. "Am I imagining it or has Paul been drinking, Rose?"

Rose pushed Paul into one of the kitchen chairs and then she turned to look at her grandmother. She had never told her a lie in her life – and as their eyes met she knew she couldn't do it now. Besides, there was no point. The evidence was there, slumped in the chair. "Yes," she said, tears now starting to brim up in her eyes.

"Oh, dear God!" Martha limped across the floor and sat in one of the chairs around the table.

"He's been a stupid *amadán*. Somebody gave him whiskey tonight and he drank it. He was in such a state we've had to bring him home."

"My ankle was hurting too," Hannah put in, "so we would have had to come home anyway. I didn't mind coming home early."

Martha gave Hannah a withering look. Then, turning to her grandson, she pursed her lips together and shook her head. "You're an awful eejit of a boy," she said in a low voice, a voice full of the experience of all her years. "An awful eejit to go doing something like this."

Paul looked up at her with glassy eyes. "I'm sorry, Granny!"

"Oh, I don't doubt you are sorry," Martha said resignedly.

Rose's eyes flitted towards the hall door, terrified that the noise would waken her parents up. "What are we going to do, Granny? If Daddy finds out he'll kill us."

Martha thought for a few moments. "Get your jacket and shirt and your shoes and socks off in here," she told Paul. "Then we'll get you down to the bedroom and into bed as quick as we can." She narrowed her dim eyes to look closer at him. "You don't feel sick or anything, do you?"

He swallowed hard. "I've been sick several times . . ."

"Good," Martha said, "and please God there's nothing more to come up." She turned to Rose now. "Go into the top press there beside the range, while he's getting stripped, and get the tin of Andrews Liver Salts out. Put a good big spoonful in a cup and then fill it halfway with cold water and stir it up until it's all dissolved."

In a few minutes Rose was leading Paul in his bare feet – and wearing only his trousers – on his unsteady way down towards the bedroom.

Then Martha turned to Hannah and said in a voice that brooked no argument, "You had better take yourself off to bed now. And you might as well stick to your lies about the ankle. Because it's the only thing that will save that fellow's neck if his father gets to hear about his nonsense."

Hannah looked at Martha Barry from under lowered eyelids, annoyed that she was being openly accused of lying. But she knew that there was no point in even trying to argue with the old woman. Besides, because of her age and circumstances in the Barry house, Hannah reckoned she was the least important person and not worth the effort of arguing with. Who cared what an old lady thought? She was in her eighties now and would be dead in a few years, so her opinion hardly mattered. Hannah lifted her handbag from the back of one of the chairs and, without bidding a word of goodnight, took herself off to bed.

Then Rose arrived back in the kitchen to report that Paul was safely in bed.

"Thank God," Martha sighed. She pulled a chair out "I'll make sure he sleeps on his back in case he's sick during the night and bring him down a cup of milk to settle his stomach in the morning." She nodded her head thoughtfully. "And I'll make sure to leave the window open all night because otherwise the bedroom will stink like a brewery."

Rose wondered where her grandmother had learned all the right things to do with a drunk man. Her father hardly drank and as far as she could remember her grandfather – who had died when she was twelve – had been a Pioneer of Total Abstinence. She knew her two uncles – regulars in Slattery's pub – liked a bit of a drink, but they didn't go mad. Martha also had a son in London who came home for a fortnight with his family every summer but Rose had never seen him drink – and two daughters in America who Rose had only met twice. They had gone off as ladies' maids as young girls but had married well and sent their mother home money every few months.

"Do you want a cup of tea or some hot milk?" Martha asked her granddaughter. "It won't take me long to get the range going."

Rose shook her head. "No thanks, I think I'll just head off to bed myself."

"Your night didn't turn out the way you expected?" Martha said quietly.

Rose shrugged. "It was going grand until Paul ruined it. Only halfway through the night and I had to come out of the hall to see to him."

There was a small pause, then Martha said, "Did Hannah have any hand in what happened?"

Rose shook her head. "No – in fact she was very good with Paul considering her night was ruined as well."

"Ah well, when his head has cleared make sure and let him know what he's done. He won't learn otherwise."

Rose picked up her bag and her coat and then she suddenly halted. She needed to talk to someone she could trust.

"I had been dancing half the night with a lovely, decent lad, Granny, when I had to leave." Her voice faltered now. "Paul made a right show of me in front of him. I don't think he'll bother with me now."

Martha's eyebrows rose. It wasn't often Rose opened up like this and it was the first time she had mentioned anything of a romantic nature. "Who is he? Is he a local lad?"

Rose felt her cheeks colour up. "It's Michael Murphy – one of the Murphy boys that live out on the Gort Road."

"They're a very nice family." Martha gave a little smile. "One your father would have no complaints about." She pulled the chair out beside her now and said, "Sit down for a few minutes."

Rose sank down on the chair, suddenly feeling exhausted. "It makes no odds now whether my father likes him or not, because I think I've missed my chance tonight."

"Do you like him a lot, girleen?"

Rose nodded. "I always liked him when we were at school together and he's even nicer now since he's got older. A real gentleman." She sighed. "He has a good job in the bank in Gort and he's a great musician." She pictured the two of them up on the dance floor now and suddenly her eyes filled up with tears. "He's everything a girl would want in a boyfriend and there are plenty of others who have their eye on him. He's probably up on the floor dancing with one of them now and leading her home."

"He didn't walk back with you?" Martha asked.

Rose shook her head, feeling utterly miserable now at the thought of him dancing with somebody like Mona Tierney. "He was to play a few sets with his brother in the second half, so he couldn't leave."

"So you ended up minding both of them? Hannah and her ankle and that drunken young eejit?" Martha clucked her tongue.

"Well, actually . . . there was another lad," Rose admitted. "Liam O'Connor. He walked back with us. He said he felt guilty that one of the lads he was with bought the drink for Paul."

"He was surely very *flaithiúil* with his money," Martha said. "Whiskey doesn't come cheap. He must have been a good friend of Paul's to be buying him expensive drink."

Rose stopped for a moment. That was a very good

point. Jack Kelly certainly wasn't a good friend of Paul's – he hardly knew him. Why on earth would he be buying him whiskey? It didn't make a bit of sense. Then, she suddenly gave a big yawn. Her head was too tired to do all this thinking. She'd tackle Paul in the morning.

"C'mon now, girleen," her grandmother said in an affectionate tone. "Get yourself off to bed now. It won't seem so bad in the morning."

"What if Daddy finds out?"

"Then Paul will just have to face the music."

Chapter 18

Rose woke up on Saturday morning to the sound of her younger sisters joking and laughing and the familiar, comforting smell of bacon frying. She turned in the bed and realised she was in her brother's room and there was no sign of Hannah. Then, like a tidal wave washing over her, all the memories of the previous night came flooding back. She sat bolt upright in bed, her heart thumping, wondering what had happened this morning so far and what reception would await her when she arrived in the kitchen.

She looked at her wristwatch and realised it was nearly ten o'clock. Her mother would be gone to work by now and her father would be up and about. She wondered whether anything had been found out about Paul. Then, when she could stand wondering no more, she threw the blankets back and got out of bed to face the day.

Amazingly, all seemed normal.

Her grandmother was by the range as usual and she told Rose that Paul was first up in the house after herself. He'd had two cups of tea and a piece of bread along with two aspirins that Martha made him take. And then, when

Hannah got up, they had both gone down for a walk to the shop, to get a newspaper for Stephen and a fresh sliced pan loaf for the fried breakfast that Martha had started to cook.

"All the soda bread I baked last night," Martha said, sighing, "and the pair of them have to walk a mile to buy a sliced loaf!"

"But what about Hannah's ankle?"

Martha raised her eyebrows. "As good as new it seems. It makes me wonder how bad it was in the first place. A bad sprain like that should affect her for days."

Rose felt really annoyed. Was her grandmother right? Had Hannah just been looking for notice?

Martha glanced around as if to check that there was nobody listening. "I think Paul needed the walk to clear his head and to give your father the impression he was as fresh as a daisy," she said in a low voice.

"So Daddy doesn't know anything about it?"

"No, thanks be to God and his Blessed Mother!"

Rose closed her eyes. She felt as though a great weight had been lifted off her. Suddenly, the day seemed sunnier and brighter than any she could remember this spring.

* * *

"So what's the chances of us going to Kinvara this evening?" Hannah asked Paul as they walked down the hill towards Slattery's.

Paul came to a halt, then looked at Hannah and started to laugh. "You're some character! I'm feckin' half-dead on my feet here this morning and you want us to cycle out to Kinvara tonight! My head is still reeling from the drink last night."

"Oh, come on," she said in a wheedling voice. "You'll be grand. Some of the lads said there's a pub out there with a piano and I'd love to play a few tunes on it – join in with the bit of *craic*."

"Ah, Hannah," he said, moving his bike forward again, "I wouldn't be up to it. My head and my stomach are in an awful state. I only came out this morning so Daddy wouldn't think there was anything amiss."

"You'll feel better after the walk. When we get back to the house and you've got a good breakfast inside you, you'll feel like a different lad. And if you get a couple of hours sleep later on, you'll feel better for tonight."

"But even if I do feel better, I've no money," he argued. "And anyway, Rose is working this afternoon and then again tonight. She won't be able to come out with us."

"Well, that's one of the reasons I'm asking you. Otherwise I'll be stuck in the house all evening looking at the four walls. Sure, I could have done that back in Tullamore!" She reached a hand out now to ruffle his hair, then touched her fingers lightly to his cheek. "Ah, come on, Paul! Let's go out and enjoy ourselves. I've plenty of money for the two of us. Surely you'd rather have a night out with a bit of *craic* than sitting in the house playing with your Rosary beads?"

Hannah touching his cheek brought a bright red flush to Paul's face, and when he looked at her he was unusually stuck for words. They walked on, then he eventually said, "Ah sure, I'll see how things go . . . see how I feel as the day goes on."

* * *

Rose was setting the table when the two of them

returned. Hannah took her coat off, hung it behind the kitchen door and then went outside to the lavatory.

Rose seized the opportunity to catch Paul on his own.

"Well, how are you this morning after all your carry-on last night?" she asked him in a low, angry voice.

"I'm sorry, Rose," he told her, glancing over to the cooker where his grandmother was busy with a full frying pan. "I'm really, really sorry. I was stupid touching that whiskey . . . I'm not able for it and I didn't know what I was getting myself into."

He sat down in one of the kitchen chairs now, his throbbing head in his hands.

"What on earth did you think you were doing getting involved with that Jack Kelly and his cronies?" Rose's voice went into a higher note. "Sure, they're well out of your league. Jack Kelly's been drinking for the last few years and you've never had more than a couple of bottles of beer." She tapped the side of his head. "You need you're flaming head examined – and so do those that encouraged you."

"I've learned my lesson. I won't be touching drink again."

"I'll make damned sure you don't," Rose told him. "I'll be watching you like a hawk from now on down in the bar and I'll be telling Joe Slattery to do the same."

Paul shook his head. "Aw, don't say anything to Joe, Rose! You'll really show me up in front of all the lads."

Rose bent her head down now, her mouth close to his ear. "And what do you think you did to me last night? How do you think I felt in front of Michael Murphy and Liam O'Connor? You didn't stop then to think of the show you made of me and yourself."

"I've learned my lesson," Paul repeated. "I'm really, really sorry."

"Just be grateful that God was on your side last night," Rose told him. "Because you wouldn't be sitting here this morning if my father had been about when you came in."

Chapter 19

On the same Saturday morning, the shrill sound of the phone made Leonora Bentley wake with a start out of a deep sleep. Heart pounding, she reached over to the bedside table on Andrew's side of the bed where the heavy black telephone had always been.

"Hello," a clipped female Scottish voice said, then went on to deliver a torrent of words at breakneck speed.

Leonora pushed herself into a sitting position with her free arm, then switched on the bedside lamp.

"Hold on a moment, please," she said. "I didn't catch one single word of that. You'll have to slow down and start all over again." As the caller caught her breath, Leonora glanced at the bedside clock and saw it was only quarter to eight.

"Can – you – understand – me – now?" the woman enunciated in a painfully slow but loud voice.

"Yes. That's much better."

"Thank Christ," the voice said. "Can – I – speak – to – a – Mrs – Eliza – beth – O'Shea?"

"Who is calling?"

"It's a neighbour," the voice was speeding up again, "of her brother Willie."

Leonora was wide awake now and realised there must be something dreadfully wrong for Lizzie to receive a call about her brother at this hour of the morning.

"And is there some kind of a problem with Willie?" she asked.

There was a silence on the other end of the line, and then the voice said in a suspicious tone, "And who would you be?"

"I'm Mrs O'Shea's employer," Leonora told her.

There was a muffled noise at the other end, as though the caller might be discussing the situation with a third party. "Well, I'm – not – too – sure – if – I – should – be – telling – Willie's – business – to – total – strangers," the voice said.

Leonora's eyes opened wide in indignation. Then she realised that that's exactly the kind of thing that Lizzie herself would say to people. It must be a peculiar manner that people from that area of Scotland had. She knew from long practice with Lizzie that there was no point in arguing as it would only prolong the conversation, and at the end of it all she would be none the wiser.

"If you would hold the line for a few minutes, please," she said, throwing the bedclothes back, "I'll go and get Mrs O'Shea for you."

She put the receiver down on the bedside table and then, in her white-and-blue-checked cotton pyjamas, hurried barefoot out of the bedroom and onto the landing.

At the end of the corridor she rapped loudly on Mrs O'Shea's door. "Lizzie!" she called, not sure whether her housekeeper was up and about yet. She rapped and called a second time and then she went to the top of the stairs. "Liz-zie!" she called again.

"Hold your horses, I'm coming as fast as my legs will carry me," the elderly housekeeper called from downstairs. Then her heels could be heard clattering along the Victorian tiled floor.

"Pick the phone up in the hall," Leonora instructed her. "There's somebody on the line for you from Glasgow – it's about your brother Willie."

"Our Willie? Oh, Jesus, Mary and Joseph, I hope it's not bad news!" Mrs O'Shea muttered, blessing herself as she went along.

Leonora rushed back to her own bedroom and picked the phone up again to hear Lizzie say in the same abrupt tones as the woman on the line, "Hello – who's calling?"

Leonora put the phone back down in its cradle and sat on the edge of the bed for a few minutes, debating whether she should get back into bed or not. She decided she had better not get comfortable again because there was obviously a problem with Mrs O'Shea's family in Scotland and it might be something serious. From the mysterious way the caller had acted, it might even be a death. Leonora stood up and went to find her slippers and her dressing gown.

She was in the kitchen pouring milk into a cup of tea when the housekeeper came in.

"What are you doing making your own tea at this hour of the morning?" Mrs O'Shea challenged. "You know fine well I always bring you a tray up on a Saturday with the newspaper." She looked up at the clock and clucked her tongue in disapproval. "I'm very sorry now that the phone wakened you up so early."

"Was there anything wrong? It sounded very serious."

"Och, it was about my brother," Mrs O'Shea muttered, a deep red flush moving from her chest to her neck. "It was something and nothing. He's not on his death bed or anything like that." She went over fussing around the teapot that Leonora had just filled from the boiled kettle on the range.

Leonora took her tea over to the window and stared out over the garden. She knew the way the Scotswoman's mind worked. It was just a case of being patient until she was ready to tell the whole story. Sometimes it was quickly and all in one piece and sometimes the story came out bit by bit. She took a sip from her cup and looked up at the cloudy sky, wondering whether the weather would hold to allow her out into the garden for a few hours.

"Are you going back to bed?" the housekeeper asked. "I'll cook you a bit of bacon and eggs and bring it up to you with some nice hot buttered toast."

Leonora thought for a moment. If she went now, Lizzie would definitely put off telling her any information until later in the day.

"No," she said, "I'm awake now. I might as well stay up. I can have my breakfast in here if the fire in the dining-room isn't lit."

"Oh, the fire's lit this half hour," the housekeeper reassured her. "But you haven't had enough sleep. And you were up late last night – I heard you coming up the stairs and it was well after one."

Leonora took a sip of her tea. "You were obviously awake yourself and you're up and about for a while," she said, her gaze still fixed on the garden.

"Aye, well," Mrs O'Shea said, "there's a difference between you and me as I've often told you before. I'm hardened to getting up early – it was bred into me when I was working in Glasgow when I was a young girl. But you're a different kettle of fish. You need to look after yourself. You should be taking it easier – you're not getting any younger, you know."

She went over to the fridge and took out the container with the bacon and sausages and a dish of dripping. Then she came back to the range and lifted the frying pan down from the rack above.

Leonora almost smiled, as her housekeeper usually took the opposite tack, telling her how young and fit she was. But that was Lizzie. Everything depended on the mood she was in and at the moment she could say absolutely anything. When she was worried about something big, her words poured out unchecked.

"If you don't mind me asking, Lizzie, is your brother ill?"

Mrs O'Shea cut a large piece of dripping and put it in the frying pan, then she pricked four sausages with a fork and put them in as well. "Oh, kind of . . ." she hedged. Then, she lifted out a roll of black pudding, cut four slices from it and put them in the pan. She stood back and surveyed her handiwork. "It's all his own fault!" she suddenly blurted out. "He disnae look after himself." When the housekeeper was flustered or upset, unconsciously her dialect returned to her Glasgow roots.

Leonora waited. Meanwhile she gave her attention to two blue-tits hanging upside down on a bag of nuts on the bird-table closest to the window. It was quite an elaborate, hand-carved one that Andrew had bought her one birthday. She could remember the day quite clearly and she now ran a sequence of pictures of them as they debated where to put it in. He outside walking around with the heavy bird-table resting on his shoulder like a crucifix, while she was inside motioning from the window to him, until they found the exact spot. It must have taken them a good half an hour to decide but they had laughed about it as Andrew fooled around, pretending to collapse under the weight of it. And, like most things they did together, the spot they had finally chosen was perfect.

Mrs O'Shea peeled four slices of bacon from the large packet and then carefully added them to the pan. She put one between each sausage, making a kind of pattern. When the fry started to sizzle, she stood back with a small sigh of satisfaction. "You see," she started off again, "our Willie is his own worst enemy. There was a lovely girl he could have married years ago but he dillied and dallied around for too long and she went off and married his best friend. So he has nobody to blame but himself for being left on his own in his old age."

"How old is he?" Leonora queried, her gaze still directed on the blue-tits. She took another sip from her tea.

The housekeeper narrowed her eyes as she calculated. "Ah, he's a few years younger than me – around sixty-three or four." She paused. "Och, there's no real point in me telling you all the details, for you widnae understand. It's a different world from all of this, the old Glasgow tenements and the way people live."

Leonora turned away from the window now and came to sit at the table with her half-drunk cup of tea. "We don't have to live the same lives to understand and sympathise with other people's situations," she said quietly.

The housekeeper nodded and muttered something to herself that her employer didn't catch. She rolled the sausages over with a well-worn wooden spatula and turned the bacon over. Then she whirled around to Leonora. "It's the drink," she announced. "When he's down in himself he turns to the bottle and then all hell is let loose. He's a different man with drink – he turns kind of belligerent like and annoys other folk." She gave a frustrated sigh. "And that was never our Willie. He was the most placid one of the whole family. And ye see, he can go six months without touching a drink, but when he gets into that kind of mood, he never knows when he has enough until he lands himself in trouble." She paused. "And that's exactly what he's done now."

"What's happened?"

"Well, for a start he's behind with his rent again. He's been spending every penny he gets on the drink." She looked directly at Leonora now. "And he's been served with an eviction notice."

"Oh, dear! Remind me now – does he still work?"

"Work?" Mrs O'Shea shook her head vigorously. "No, indeed he does not. He worked in the shipyards but he has a problem with his chest and the doctor signed him off about five years ago. That's when all this caper started. I think he has too much time on his hands and that's when he starts thinking too much. Dwelling on things and nursing grievances against the whole world."

"So what was the particular problem this morning?"

"Oh, seemingly he got rushed into hospital with his

chest again. Couldn't catch his breath. That was the next-door neighbour that phoned. She cleans one of the big offices in the town on a Saturday morning and she's able to use the phones when the bosses aren't in."

Leonora made no comment on this casual fact and the way Mrs O'Shea stated it, as though it was common practice. She briefly wondered if her housekeeper had taken such liberties herself but she dismissed the idea as soon as it came into her mind. Lizzie O'Shea was as honest as the day was long and she had always been told to use the phone if she ever needed it.

"Willie's neighbour is quite a hard ticket," the housekeeper went on, "but when you get to know her she's a decent enough woman and she's been very decent with our Willie." She rolled her eyes to the ceiling. "She'd have to be some kind of a saint to put up with him."

Leonora hoped the neighbour's bark was worse than her bite. "And how is he, did she say?"

"Not great. That's the trouble – they've had to transfer him to another hospital."

Leonora bit her lip and shook her head. "I'm so sorry, Lizzie . . . it sounds very serious."

"All self-inflicted," Mrs O'Shea stated, turning the items in the pan over again with a few vicious pushes this time. "They've had to transfer him to the psychiatric hospital because of his stupid carry-on." She went to a cupboard and rattled plates and utensils around, which was always a sign of her agitation.

There was a small silence now and Leonora was grateful that it was masked by the housekeeper's industrious rattles as she was lost for what to say next.

Mrs O'Shea went to the pottery dish where she kept the eggs, lifted two and then went back to crack them into the pan. Leonora knew that she would now have to face a much bigger breakfast than she had intended because she couldn't offend her housekeeper by not eating it.

"Do you think you might have to go over to Scotland?" she ventured.

The housekeeper's eyebrows shot up. "I certainly hope not! It doesn't suit me one bit to have to go over the water at this time of the year, and God knows what I would have to face in that pig-sty of a place that our Willie lives in."

Leonora knew that it would all pour out now, because Lizzie was on her high horse about her brother. By nature she was a private woman and most of the time kept her business to herself, but there had been occasions when she had let her guard down and spoken about her family back in Scotland and about her late husband. And on those occasions she had gone into details that had made her and Andrew feel concerned. They felt she'd had a raw deal in life and both made sure that they always treated her with respect and kindness, and in some ways she was regarded almost as part of the family. But very, very occasionally, their lassitude with the housekeeper had backfired when Lizzie was a little bit too familiar or critical when she had no business to be. Offering her opinions on guests or passing remarks on the amount they drank or about the state they kept the bedrooms in if they stayed overnight. And even passing comment on outfits Leonora chose, saying that she couldn't understand why she often chose to wear grey, as it didn't do a thing for her. And on those occasions, Leonora gently – but firmly – put her back in her place.

"Are you ready to go into the dining-room for your breakfast?" Mrs O'Shea asked now.

"It will be perfectly fine in here, Lizzie." Leonora's voice was softer than usual. "We can finish our chat off while we're eating."

"Well, if you say so," the housekeeper said but there was no disagreement in her tone. She would feel more at ease chatting about her problems in her own familiar surroundings.

When they sat down opposite each other at the old pine table, with their piled-up breakfast plates, Mrs O'Shea continued her story where she'd left off. "The last time I went over to Glasgow I spent the whole fortnight cleaning and tidying the place up. I even had to go out and buy a tin of paint to do up the kitchen. He'd let a pan of chips go on fire, and it scorched the whole wall and he'd just left it like that." She tutted viciously.

Leonora felt a pang of sadness to hear the truth about her housekeeper's holiday. When she'd been asked how she had enjoyed her holiday, Lizzie had put a brave face on and said she'd had a lovely time. Hearing the reality now made Leonora's heart go out to the poor hard-working woman.

"Och, it was an absolute disgrace! For a start, the day I arrived he had no electricity on, can you believe it?" Mrs O'Shea rattled on. "He hadnae paid the last two bills so they quite rightly cut him off." Her voice rose an octave higher. "You can't have people not paying their bills. I mean we've all had to go without, but if Willie didn't waste his money on drink he'd manage perfectly well the same as everybody else. So, Muggins here had to go to the Electricity

Board and pay the bloody bill or else I'd have spent the whole fortnight in the dark. The tenement flat that he lives in has very little light at the best of times, so you can just imagine what it would be like with no electricity."

Leonora couldn't imagine it at all. In fact, she was appalled at the very thought. Although she hadn't grown up in the wealth that Andrew had, she had never wanted for the very basics in life. There had been times when she hadn't been able to afford the clothes she would have liked, and she hadn't always been able afford to go out every time she wanted, but she knew nothing of the real poverty that her housekeeper was describing.

"Don't you think you should go and visit him if he's in hospital?" she suggested. "I could manage here perfectly well for a week or so on my own. I'm quite capable and you know I enjoy cooking."

"No, no, not at all." She cut into a sausage. "I don't want to go. And anyway, the money I would spend on my fare over would be put to better use paying his rent. The neighbour told me how much it is, so I'll send that over to him with a wee bit extra and that'll help him more than me turning up on the doorstep giving him hell." Then, her face suddenly brightened. "I'll knit him a nice warm jumper as well. Aye, that would be the very dab. I'll walk down to the shops over the next few days and pick the wool. I haven't knitted anything for a while. I'll get a good thick Aran style and it will keep my hands and my mind too busy to be worrying about him."

Leonora nodded. "That's a good idea, Lizzie." Privately, she wasn't too sure about the housekeeper's knitting talents. But it would help her relax. Leonora had always noticed that the Scotswoman seemed to go into a little world of her own when she had knitting needles in her hand and a knitting pattern in her lap.

"Aye," Mrs O'Shea said, delighted with herself now, "that's exactly what I'll do. I'll go upstairs this afternoon and have a root through the patterns and I'll pick one out that will suit him." She paused. "For all he's in a loony ward, there's not a tap wrong with him mentally, you know. He's as cute as a bag of monkeys is our Willie. He knows that the council can't evict him if he's in the psychiatric hospital – that they'll give him a bit of time to sort himself out."

"Is there no one else in the family who could help him out?"

"Ah, sure they're all too busy looking after themselves and their own families. I'm really the only one in a position to help him out." She gave a small, pained smile. "And for all I go on about him – and could kill him at times – I'm actually very fond of our Willie. Before he hit the drink he was a decent, hard-working fella who wouldn't do anyone a bad turn. And he's always had a good sense of humour – you can always get a bit of a laugh with him."

Leonora nodded and ate her breakfast as her housekeeper went on but she was saddened by the whole situation. Poor Lizzie had very little in her life – and looked for very little – and now she would have to give her hard-earned money up to help her ne'er-do-well brother.

Chapter 20

By the time it came around for Rose's lunchtime shift down at the bar, she was more than ready to get out of the house and away from both Hannah and Paul. She was disgusted with the great pretence they put on for her father when he came in for the breakfast, laughing and joking like two of the finest actors in the films. No one looking at them could have guessed the state that Paul was in the night before and all the trouble it had caused.

Later in the morning, when his father went off to help one of the farmers out with a troublesome tractor, Paul took the chance to sneak back to bed and have a few hours' sleep. Martha left the two girls with the washing up and went into the small sitting room to rest her legs while she listened to the radio and helped Eileen with a scarf she was knitting for school.

"I wish you weren't working," Hannah told Rose as they put the washed breakfast dishes away. "We could have gone out for a bit of a walk to Cathy's to hear how the rest of the dance went."

Rose had whirled around at her cousin. "Hannah, you never cease to amaze me. How you have the nerve to think of going down to Brennans' after what happened last night, I do not know!" Her eyes were blazing as she recalled the little digs Hannah had made about Michael Murphy, insinuating that he'd taken Rose as second choice. "Cathy's my best friend and I'm mortified at the thought of meeting her and have her asking how Paul is and how we got him back home with the state he was in." She raised her eyebrows. "Don't you feel any way awkward about that?"

Hannah shrugged. "He did no harm to anyone but himself. Anyway, I'm sure Cathy won't be that bothered. She's not that kind and didn't she say she had older brothers of her own? She'll know what it's like. I have brothers and I know lads do stupid things like that now and again. It's not the end of the world."

Rose looked at her and shook her head. There was no point in wasting any more time discussing it.

After she had finished all her chores, Rose changed into one of her nice skirts and blouses to brighten herself up. Then, just as she was putting her coat on to walk down to the pub, Hannah appeared at her side, smartly but casually dressed in navy slacks with a pale blue twin-set and the matching pearls and earrings that she had got for her sixteenth birthday.

"I might as well walk down with you," she said, "because I've nothing else to do."

"What about your ankle?"

"Oh, it's grand now."

Rose looked at Hannah – at her perfectly curled hair and her newly varnished nails – then she looked at her perfectly matched outfit with the expensive pearls and the little navy clutch bag and she suddenly a stab of real animosity towards her. Apart from still being annoyed at her about last night, it galled her that Hannah was all dressed up in her fashionable slacks. Even though she had persisted until Rose showed her every item in her wardrobe, she hadn't shown Rose any of the clothes in her suitcase. And she hadn't mentioned that she had new slacks.

Rose hated herself for being envious of Hannah but the slacks had made her feel that her cousin would always have one up on her when it came to clothes, because despite all the lovely things that Leonora Bentley had given her – the dresses and blouses, skirts and bags – there had been no slacks in the bag.

"No, thanks, I'd rather walk on my own," Rose told her abruptly.

"Oh, don't be like that!" Hannah said, sounding all hurt. "There's no point in us falling out over what Paul did and it's going to look bad if your mother and father find out that you're not talking to me." She gave a little shrug. "They're going to wonder what it's all about."

Rose went over to the table and lifted her handbag. She couldn't leave the house on her own now. As usual, Hannah had won. She had got her own way.

They walked down towards the pub, Rose silent while Hannah constantly tried to make conversation. When they reached the pub Rose walked on ahead, calling "See you later!" without a backward glance at her cousin.

* * *

Hannah went into the shop and emerged a short time

later with a box of Milk Tray in a brown paper bag under her arm. As she passed by the adjoining door to the pub, she glanced through the glass door to check whether Rose could see her or not. Then, when she caught sight of the back of Rose's dark head, she smiled to herself and went outside. Without breaking her step, she headed off to the right, towards the lane that led down to the beach.

She walked steadily along the lane, then onto the narrow coastal path until she came in view of Traceys' house.

She stopped for a few moments at a low wall, to put the chocolates down and take her compact out of her clutch bag. She reapplied her light pink lipstick and checked her hair. She had sprayed it well with lacquer before coming out and she was relieved that it had stayed in place. Then she put her make-up things back in her bag and set off on the last lap of her journey.

As she walked up the path to Traceys' house, Hannah steeled herself in case the dogs came rushing out at her again. She had reminded herself, as she lay in bed last night, that Diana had said that the dogs might make a lot of noise but they were as soft as putty. And in any case, it didn't make sense for a vet to have vicious dogs.

She rang the bell and stood for a few seconds – and then she heard the dogs break into loud, ferocious barking. But thankfully the sound was coming from the back of the house, where they were obviously penned in.

Hannah waited for a short while before ringing the bell again, and then she stood back and looked up at the top windows.

Then the big red door suddenly opened and Diana Tracey was standing there looking at her.

"Oh!" Diana looked taken aback. "You're the young girl with the ankle – the one from Barry's cottage."

"I hope you don't mind me calling," Hannah said, smiling confidently. She deliberately spoke clearly and in more leisurely way than usual – like an older, more assured person. In a similar way, she hoped, to the lady she was visiting. "But I just wanted to thank you for rescuing me yesterday." She held the brown paper package out. "It's just a small gift to show my appreciation."

"But there was no need – it was nothing!" Diana smiled now and took the present. "That's very kind and thoughtful of you."

"I'm sorry it's only boring old chocolates," Hannah said, pulling a little face. "I'm sure you might have preferred flowers or a nice plant, but I'm afraid there's not much choice locally."

Diana raised her eyebrows and grinned. "No, you bought the perfect gift – I absolutely adore chocolates!"

"Good," Hannah said, her hand fluttering to her throat. "That makes me feel much better."

Diana's gaze moved to Hannah's neatly clad feet. "How is it – the ankle?"

"Oh, *much* better. I decided to have a bit of a walk out to test it."

Diana's brow creased. "It's a long walk down from Barrys'. Are you sure that was wise?"

"Oh, I was with my cousin and I stopped in at the shop and rested it for a few minutes." Hannah gave a little shrug. "Rose is working this afternoon so I was at a bit of a loose end. The walk out here has given me something to do."

"Well," Diana said, opening the door wide, "if you're

not in a hurry, you must come in and have a cup of tea and give that ankle a rest right now."

"Oh, I couldn't!" Hannah said, making a little waving protest with her hand. "I'm sure you're far too busy."

"Not at all. I'm still on school holidays, and I was only catching up on some mail. I was planning to stop for a cup of tea soon in any case."

"Well," Hannah said. "If you're really sure . . ."

* * *

An hour later, Hannah came out of the big house with the red door, smiling and chatting away to Diana Tracey as if she had known her for years.

"Thank you so much for the tea and the lovely homemade shortbread," she said, then she patted her little blue clutch bag. "And I have the recipe safe in here. My mother will be delighted with it – shortbread is one of the things she never seems to get right."

"Well, you can bake a batch for her and show her how to do it."

"As long as I don't burn it!" Hannah laughed.

Diana laughed, then said more seriously, "Now, make sure you keep up your piano practice, Hannah. I think you're very talented and you mustn't give up."

Hannah put her head to the side, smiling shyly. "Thank you. I've had a lovely, lovely afternoon."

"And you're sure you'll manage the walk back to the cottage?"

"I'm positive. Besides, if I take a lift back there from you again, I'll only have to come with more chocolates tomorrow!"

Diana shook her head, her eyes twinkling with laughter. "You must really liven things up in the Barrys' house! I'll bet they really look forward to your visits."

Hannah went off down the path, stopping at the gate to wave back. Her visit had gone much better than she could ever have imagined. Everything had gone to plan and then it had just got better and better. She had found out everything that she needed to know about Diana Tracey and her wealthy mother. From the minute she had stepped inside the rambling country house she knew it was the sort of place that she could easily fit into. And it also confirmed her suspicions – that it was certainly not the sort of place for Rose.

When Diana Tracey mentioned that her mother was thinking of offering Rose a few months' work up in Glenmore House, Hannah had quickly squashed the idea.

"Rose told me just last night that she'd hate to live anywhere else but Kilnagree," she had said. "Between you and me, she won't even visit our family up in Offaly." She shrugged her shoulders. "Rose is lovely . . . but she can be a funny girl. She's not comfortable with people she doesn't know well. If you remember, when I had my accident yesterday, she hardly spoke, did she?"

Diana paused for a few moments. "I hadn't really noticed but now that you mention it she was rather quiet."

"She's more comfortable with her granny than anyone else. I don't suppose your mother would be similar to her granny? She's not old or housebound or anything?"

Diana's eyebrows shot up. "Indeed she's not!" There was indignation in her voice. "My mother is a fit, youthful woman. There's no comparison." She halted. "I think it's best if I don't mention my mother's idea to Rose at all. I'll tell her I had a word with you and we decided that it wouldn't work out."

Hannah had nodded and taken a dainty sip from her china teacup. "I won't say a word to Rose either. She doesn't need to know."

For all that Diana's mother had taken pity on Rose by giving her all those nice clothes and buying her the present, Hannah could see quite plainly that it had been nothing more than a charity mission. And the thought pleased her no end. Both Diana Tracey and her mother obviously saw Rose as no better than a cleaner or a servant. The job offer showed that.

But there was no way that Diana's attitude towards herself could have been described as patronising or in any way looking down on her. She had been treated and talked to in the way that someone like Diana Tracey would behave with a younger sister or friend.

She had been treated as an equal – and that's exactly what Hannah felt she was.

An equal to the top kind of people – and better than Rose in every way.

Chapter 21

In the late afternoon, Leonora had the urge to take a walk out. The dull morning had turned into a fairly fine day and her mind kept flitting back to the circular route she always took down at the shore in Kilnagree. She loved the feel of the sea air in her face and the strong breeze in her hair but here she had to make do with a walk down into the village to collect the gardening and fashion magazines she had on a regular order.

A short while later Leonora was striding down the driveway, shopping basket in hand, and grateful to be out in the fresh air and away from all the mundane household things that Mrs O'Shea loved talking about. The day was pleasant with a hint of warmth and the sunshine was strong enough for her to dispense with a coat and hat – instead she had opted for a Fair Isle sweater in creams and browns and lilac slung over her shoulders. And, for the first time this spring apart from when she was driving, she wore her sunglasses.

In Lucan she collected her magazines and bought some lovely fresh vanilla slices and chocolate éclairs at the baker's. When she came out of the shop she glanced up at the blue sky and wished she had somewhere exciting to go to fill a few hours. She thought of dropping in to see Terry Cassidy but quickly dismissed the idea. She was sure Terry wouldn't have minded but her routine way of doing things was too ingrained in her to call in on someone she didn't know that well without prior arrangement. She picked up her step, telling herself that she would be perfectly content to go home and sit out in the conservatory with her magazines, her cream cake treat and a glass of wine.

Halfway back home an idea suddenly popped into her head for her art commission. She could use the same battered tin jug – empty this time – to keep the continuity with the other painting and maybe have something that toned in with it. Her mind turned over as she headed for home and within minutes she thought of a tarnished silver vase she had in her gardening room. Perhaps if she filled it with bluebells – in her imagination of course, because they wouldn't be out again until next spring. She suddenly felt quite sure that the bluish-purple flowers would work well with the grey tones on the creamy background.

A little ripple of delight ran through her now. As soon as she got home she must give Terry Cassidy a ring and tell her what she had come up with. It struck her that there was something about the artist that she had really taken to. It was similar to the way she had instantly taken to Rose Barry. She had done nothing as yet about inviting the girl up to Dublin but she had the feeling she should trust her instincts and go ahead.

She wondered how Rose's family would react to a total stranger suddenly offering to help the girl out of the blue? She would have to pick her time and her words very carefully. She wouldn't want the family to feel that she was criticising them for not being able to give Rose the chance of a college education. From what Diana had told her, they were a proud, hard-working, decent family who did the best they could.

If she decided to help the girl out, she would have to speak to her first and then speak to the parents, explaining why she felt that a clever girl like Rose needed to spread her wings further than Kilnagree.

Leonora wasn't at all sure how they would react, but there was no rush. If and when the time came for her to make the offer, she would work out a way to handle it.

She asked herself why she should even care about the girl? But she had no answer. Had shedding some of the old friends left a space in her life for such new, different people?

She was just turning in the gates of the house when a noise made her stop and turn around. It was a car engine. A black Rover car she didn't recognise was coming towards her and obviously heading for Glenmore House. As she stepped back on to the grass verge to let the vehicle pass, her brain worked quickly, trying to remember which of her friends had bought a new car she might not have seen recently. But no one came to mind.

And then the car came closer and her heart quickened. Now she was in no doubt who the driver of the shiny black Rover saloon car was.

It was Daniel Levy. It would be very hard to mistake him for anyone else. He was a tall, well-built man with solid grey hair. Unlike Andrew's sandy hair, which had greyed at the temples and had a silver streak running from the front to the back, the psychiatrist's hair had faded from black to a dramatic silvery grey. Leonora supposed it was like his personality – all or nothing. He was one of the most forthright people she had ever met – similar to Andrew in that way – and at one time she had thought of him as an interesting and very entertaining man.

He had been widowed for a number of years and, although Andrew had met his wife on a few occasions before she succumbed to her serious illness, Leonora never had.

When they first met, he had brought a very attractive lady friend as his partner for dinner at Glenmore House a couple of times, but the romance had fizzled out, and she'd only ever known him to come to Glenmore House on his own since then.

Unconsciously, Leonora squared her shoulders and straightened her back until she was at her full height. Why is he here again? she asked herself. What has brought him back?

As the car drew to a halt beside her, she turned towards him, her face stiff and unwelcoming.

He rolled the window down. "I've caught you at home at last," he said, smiling warmly at her.

There was an awkward silence.

"What do you want, Daniel?" she asked, with a strained note in her voice. "I can't think of any reason that you have for calling on me."

He grinned. "Oh, come on, Leonora! You can't keep up this formal façade forever. I'm not going to give up, you know." He leaned over and opened the passenger door. "Hop in and I'll give you a lift up to the house."

"I've been out walking for the last hour or more," she

informed him, "and I'm perfectly capable of walking the last few yards home."

"Please," he said, raising his finely arched eyebrows which were still a shade or two darker than his hair. "I want to talk to you and it will be much more comfortable up at the house than standing here in the drive."

Leonora stood rigid, holding her shopping basket close to her. She was determined not to be talked into anything she didn't want to do.

His face softened. "Surely you're not going to refuse to speak to me? Or turn me away from Glenmore House?"

"You've no reason to be here. I haven't invited you and I've never given you the impression that you can just drop in any time you like." Her jaw was set now.

"Well, I can't see any reason for your hostility towards me," he said, his tone more serious, but not in any way harsh or over-defensive.

"I don't have to give you any explanations. And I'm entitled to say who I wish to have visit me or not."

He stared at her for a few seconds. "Fair enough. But I think you're wrong. You're very wrong. Whatever has changed since I last saw you, I just can't imagine. You were perfectly fine. You were relaxed and happy. We were both fine."

Leonora's face flushed a deep red at the memory and her throat suddenly felt like sandpaper. "Now that I've had time to think about it, I realise that what happened was all wrong." Her voice was almost hoarse now. "I've nothing more to say to you, Daniel, apart from the fact that I am entitled to my own feelings."

"But we did nothing wrong, Leonora."

She started to walk away. Daniel Levy moved quickly to open the car door and in a few strides he was behind her.

"Leonora," he said, gently taking her arm, "this is ludicrous. We had some lovely times together. We have so many things in common. Surely you're not going to throw all that away?"

Leonora looked up at him. "It was wrong."

"No, no!" His voice was rising now. "How can you say that? We were wonderful together. Last Christmas with you was the best I've had in years. And that night we spent together was magical for me."

Tears suddenly came into Leonora's eyes. "Stop! I can't bear to think about it."

"It wasn't wrong," he repeated. "Two grown adults making love is a beautiful thing. The sex we had together was a beautiful thing."

The tears were streaming down her face now. "Goodbye, Daniel," she whispered. Then she pulled her arm away from him and walked through the gates of Glenmore House without looking back.

Chapter 22

Slattery's pub had one of the quietest Saturday afternoons in ages and Rose was more than a little grateful for it. There had been a match out in Clarenbridge and from the chat she heard amongst the few customers, the team and the supporters had set off early to cycle over there and have a few drinks in the pub beside the playing field. So there were only the usual older men and the odd sightseers who stopped on their way through to Doolin or the Cliffs of Moher.

Mary Slattery had gone off to visit her sister for the afternoon and Joe took the chance to sit and enjoy a few drinks and a game of cards while Rose kept busy washing down shelves and cleaning the ladies' and gents' lavatories with hot water and plenty of disinfectant. She soaked all the bar towels in washing powder and generally used her time to give the place a good clean.

When the place was tidy she went to make a cup of tea. She dipped into the biscuit jar that Mary Slattery kept well stocked and took a Kit-Kat out to have with her drink. Then she sat herself down in Joe's armchair by the range and sat sipping her tea, enjoying the peace and quiet. So far the afternoon had gone well. Thankfully, the landlord had never referred to Paul or anything about the brandy that was bought the previous evening. Rose couldn't believe how lucky they had been to get away without anybody carrying stories about it.

A knock came on the door now and Rose looked up. There, coming through the doorway, with his head bent to avoid hitting it off the low wooden frame, was Liam O'Connor.

"I've only called in for a few minutes," he told her in a low voice. "Just to check how ye all were last night . . . how your brother was."

Rose felt her face suddenly hot and shifted her gaze over to the window. Was he really that desperate to keep close contact with her that he would use any excuse to come into the pub to chat to her? And then she silently chided herself. He had been a great help getting Paul home last night and he'd done it quietly and without any great fuss. And now he'd come to talk to her discreetly on her own rather than ask her at the bar in front of other customers.

She managed a faint smile. "We eventually got him to bed, thank God," she said quietly. "And he was up and about this morning, although I think he was putting a brave face on. I think his head and stomach were a lot worse than he was letting on." She rolled her eyes to the ceiling. "I hope they were a lot worse because it might make him learn a lesson."

Liam pursed his lips together and a little nerve started working just above his left cheekbone. "Listen, Rose, I'm not quite sure if you'll thank me for saying this, but there's something you should know about last night."

Rose looked directly at him now, her brow furrowed. "What?" she asked, her voice suddenly strained and weary.

"It was your cousin – it was Hannah – who bought Paul the drink last night. She gave Jack Kelly the money to buy the whiskey and she gave him the glass of brandy in the pub earlier too. All that mixed with the few glasses of beer he had earlier would be enough to put him in the state he was in."

Rose stared back at him, her eyes narrowed now. "Are you sure?"

Liam nodded his head. "Sure, Jack would have no reason to lie about it. He's a bit of a fool and worse when he's had a drink, but he's not the kind to go feeding drink to young lads." He paused for a moment and looked back towards the door to make sure there was no one around to hear. "I've checked it out. When you came through here last night and left them sitting on their own, Hannah asked Jack to buy the naggin of whiskey for her. She said she couldn't buy it herself because Joe wouldn't serve her and you would find out. She said she just wanted Paul to enjoy himself the same as all the other lads. And of course Jack was a bigger eejit to go and do it, but he has an eye for her and that's why it didn't take much to persuade him."

The colour drained from Rose's face. It suddenly made perfect sense. That was why Hannah had been more or less standing guard over Paul and why she had been so defensive of him later. It had all been her fault. And once again, she had lied her way out of it.

"I hope you're not vexed at me for telling you," Liam said, "but I felt you had to know. After seeing the state of Paul last night, and the way you were so worried, I just felt you were entitled to know the truth. And bad and all as he is, I don't think Jack Kelly deserves to take all the blame and let that cute lady off the hook." He made a little hissing sound between his teeth. "He was so stupid he was nearly going to let me give him a good beatin' rather than tell on her. But after a bit of persuasion, he came out with the whole story."

Rose nodded her head. "Thanks, Liam. I appreciate you coming in and telling me that."

"Well, I know she's your cousin and it's not easy when it's your own family. But I think you need to know what you're dealing with, when it comes to people like that. They can cause mighty trouble for other folk and then just quietly slip away."

There was a small silence.

"You better head off," Rose told him, "or you're going to miss the match."

"No fear of that, I'm playing in it." He winked at her, trying to lighten things now. "The brother has the van outside, so we won't be long in catching up on the others and overtaking them on the oul' bikes."

Rose watched him as he went back out into the bar, thinking that there was something different about him. And she suddenly realised what the change was. He had accepted the fact that she wasn't interested in him since seeing her on the dance floor with Michael Murphy on Friday night. And he had obviously decided not to pester her any more.

But even though she had made it plain that she had no interest in him, Liam O'Connor was still being nice to her. He was acting as though they were friends. The fact that he had taken the trouble to come in and explain exactly what had happened about Paul and Hannah showed that there was a lot more to him than met the eye.

* * *

Rose walked back to the cottage, feeling flat and fed up, and almost oblivious to the sunny afternoon. She couldn't remember ever feeling this way before and she wasn't quite sure what to do about it. Since Hannah arrived, she'd had to deal with things she had never imagined before. She could cope with all the small things like Hannah irritating her friends and Hannah being all over the lads and her little remarks about her clothes and things. But this business with Paul and the strange incident when she first arrived when she lifted up her skirt – plus all the lies – had left Rose bewildered and worried.

She could go home now and have a blazing row with Hannah over what Liam had told her, but a niggling feeling told her that she just might come off worse if her parents heard about it. She would have to tell them about last night and she knew somehow that she would end up being blamed for going into Slattery's with them. And then there would be the big row with Paul and afterwards her father going about silent and like a black cloud. All the things Rose couldn't bear.

As the white-washed cottage came in view, Rose could see her grandmother sitting outside on one of the kitchen chairs enjoying the late spring sun.

Martha sat up straight when she saw her grand-daughter approaching and waved. "How's the working girl?" she asked, a warm smile on her face.

Rose attempted a smile back. "Oh, grand," she said.

"Why don't you bring a chair outside and join me? It's lovely and warm in this little sheltered spot."

Rose got a chair and they sat side by side in the sunshine, chatting generally for a while. Then Martha reached over and took Rose's hand.

"Don't be worrying your head about Paul," she told her. "He'll be grand. He got a fright with what happened last night and it'll last him a long time."

Rose looked at her grandmother and then, before she could stop herself, she suddenly poured the whole story out about Hannah and the brandy and the whiskey.

Martha listened without saying a word and then she said, "I'm not a bit surprised at anything you've said. There's something very strange about that girl." She took a deep breath. "I don't like to say anything because she's your mother's niece and I feel it's not my place. But all I'll say to you is watch her, Rose. Don't let your guard down when she's around. She'll use and abuse anyone to get her own way." She held up a warning finger. "And be very careful when you're out with her, because she could involve you in things you'd never know about until it was too late. Look what she's done with Paul. Look at the trouble she's caused there."

"Ah, he's a pure *amadán*!" Rose said unsympathetically.

"He's only young and he's bound to make mistakes," Martha said, "but underneath it all he's a lovely decent young lad."

Rose looked at her for a few moments and then she shook her head and smiled. "Oh, I suppose you're right. He's not the worst."

"Now, I have something more to tell you about Hannah," said Martha. "While you were down working, Miss Hannah took herself off to visit the lady who brought her home in the big car yesterday."

"What?" Rose said, her eyes wide with shock. "She went to Diana Tracey's house? How do you know?"

"I heard her telling Paul and the girls." Martha smiled and shook her head. "Oh, Hannah doesn't notice when I'm around – she thinks because I'm old that I'm deaf, dumb and blind and can't hear or understand anything she's talking about."

"Oh, Granny," Rose said, squeezing Martha's hand, "I'm sure she wouldn't mean to be dismissing you like that."

"Oh, indeed she would!" Martha laughed. "She wouldn't think it was worth explaining anything to me – there are people who are like that with older ones, Rose, and Hannah is one of them." She made a little waving gesture with her hand, signalling that it didn't bother her. "Anyway, she was busy bragging about the fine house she was in and having a cup of tea with the lady and how she played a few tunes on the big grand piano."

Rose's face paled. "I can't believe it," she whispered. "We walked down to the pub together and she never said a word about any plans to go and see Diana Tracey."

"Of course she didn't, because she was afraid you would talk her out of it. She was determined, come hell or high water, that she was going to the house. She took a box of chocolates and all, and went in and sat with the woman and had her cup of tea as if she was the lady of the manor herself."

Tears suddenly sprang up in Rose's eyes. She gave a shuddering great sigh. "Oh, Granny, I'm so fed up with her! What am I going to do? How am I going to put up with her until she goes home next Thursday?" For a moment Rose considered telling her about how she lifted her skirt to show her stockings and knickers to the man down the road. But she decided not to, feeling that it might be the one thing that would cause ructions in the family.

"Just keep your eyes open and your mouth closed," Martha advised. "She'll get caught out soon enough. Make no comment about her going to the big house, even when she tells you. Just nod and agree with her. Don't let her know that she's upset you."

"I'll do my best but I can't promise – she gets on my goat so much!"

"And remember," Martha said, wagging a warning finger, "say nothing to your mother and father until the time is right."

Chapter 23

"Your father was in a fierce good humour tonight," Hannah said as she and Paul started off on the bikes that evening. She wore a dark skirt and flat shoes for cycling but had her black patent stilettos in the little bag on the back of Rose's bike. She had her blonde curly hair tied high in a ponytail to keep it out of her face as she cycled along. "He didn't argue in the slightest when I asked him if we could go over to Kinvara to see a film."

"You caught him in a good mood," Paul told her. "He's got a few extra pounds for the work he did on a tractor for a local farmer. It wasn't just the money, it was the fact that nobody else could fix it – he was delighted with himself."

"Not half as delighted as I am," Hannah said, making big eyes. "Two nights out in a row!"

"It's a pity Rose couldn't come. She loves the oul' films and *South Pacific* was one of her favourites when it first came out. I'd say she'd have loved to see it again."

Hannah gave a tinkling sort of laugh. "You should be

relieved she couldn't come. By the sour look on her face this afternoon, you're still in the bad books."

Paul looked awkward and then he started to laugh too – but there was a hollow ring to it. He and Rose had always got on well and now he'd caused a rift between them. "Maybe you're right," he said, nodding.

"I'm sorry about what happened to you last night," Hannah said, resting her hand on his arm. "Buying you the whiskey was only meant for a bit of *craic* – I didn't think it would make you so sick."

"Ah, well," Paul said, feeling more than a bit foolish now as he remembered, "I've learned my lesson. I won't be touching the harder stuff again. I've discovered I don't have the stomach for it."

* * *

Stephen Barry was down in Slattery's pub that same Saturday night playing dominoes with his two brothers and he waited until Rose had finished to walk back home with her.

"It's a grand night," he said, as they stood outside the bar. "Would you look up at that big yellow full moon and all the millions of stars!"

"It's lovely," Rose agreed.

They stood in silence for a short while, then Rose fell into step with her father as they moved across the road and up the lane towards their cottage.

"And it's been a grand day. I was delighted I was able to fix that oul' tractor and get it going for them again." He went on to describe all the to-ing and fro-ing that had been involved in locating the parts that were necessary.

Rose walked silently alongside her father, thinking that today had been one of the worst days she'd ever had.

"You're awful quiet," Stephen said at one point. "Are you feeling a bit put out that you had to work while Hannah went off to the pictures with Paul?"

"Not a bit," Rose said, a tad quicker than she should have. "I've been with Hannah almost every minute since she arrived, so I didn't mind having a break from her for the night."

"Ah, she'll be gone before you know it and you'll miss her," her father said, smiling at her. "Sure, it's nice for you to have a girl the same age as yourself around the house. And it's nice for your mother as well, because Sheila hasn't been coming recently and I think it bothers her." He shook his head. "Sheila can be a bit of a queer fish at times and your mother's just relieved that Hannah is a nice, friendly girl who makes an effort with everybody. Weren't those lovely presents that she brought us all?"

Rose suddenly wondered if she should tell her father the truth. But what would be the point? It would cause all sorts of trouble for everyone – herself included. Her parents, especially her father, would take her to task for having kept quiet and not speaking up as soon as she got home on Friday night. It would cause more upset than it was worth. Besides, as her father had said, Hannah would be gone in a matter of days and things would return to normal.

* * *

"*Bali Ha'i!*" Hannah sang, as the walked down the street, one arm pushing the bike while the other was outstretched making dramatic gestures in time with her singing.

"You are totally mad!" Paul laughed, as he wheeled his own bike along. "You were lucky they didn't put us out of the cinema for your giggling."

"Sure, I was only enjoying myself! I love all the singing and the music and everything. What's the harm in enjoying yourself? There's enough misery in the world without us joining in with all the moaners and the begrudgers."

Paul stopped dead. "D'you know something, Hannah?"

"What, my darling?" she said in a theatrical voice.

He looked at her for a few moments without speaking. "You really liven up our house. It's like a different place when you're in it."

"Oh, Paul! That's a lovely thing to say."

They started walking along again. "It's the truth," he said. "I didn't realise how serious everything was until you started coming on your own."

"Well, it was a lot more serious when my mother was around," Hannah told him, with a toss of her blonde hair. "She is the most miserable, vicious woman at times."

"Auntie Sheila has never seemed that bad to me."

"You don't know her . . ."

He wrinkled his brow. "How do you stand it at home if she's so bad?"

Hannah shook her head. "Oh, forget about Mammy! C'mon, let's get up on the bikes and we'll sing the songs from *South Pacific* all the way home!"

"It's easier if we push the bikes up that bit of a hill just ahead at the pub and then we'll have a straight run home on the main road."

They'd just reached the pub and were ready to mount the bikes when the pub door opened and a man came out.

His eyes immediately fixed on Hannah. "Well, look who it is!" he said, grinning at her. "Marilyn Monroe herself!"

Hannah stared – and then she recognised him. It was the man in the brown suit who had travelled out with her on the coach from Galway the day she arrived. "Of all the people in all the places!" she said, in a giggly voice.

"If I'd known you were out and about I'd have brought you in and treated you to a drink," he said, thumbing in the direction of the pub.

"Oh, I wasn't free," said Hannah airily. "We've been to see a nice romantic film – *South Pacific.*"

The man glanced at Paul, then, obviously dismissing him as of no consequence, leaned forward towards Hannah and said in a low voice laden with the sweet, warm smell of brandy, "Wouldn't it be nice if you and I were to meet up for a nice cosy night on our own?"

Hannah pretended to look shocked. "You and me?" she gasped. "Oh, I don't think that would be a good idea."

"And why not?"

She put a hand on her hip. "Because, one – I'm sure you're way too old for me. And two – I'd lay a bet on it that you're a married man." She glanced over at Paul now and nodded her head in a knowing manner.

The man raised his eyebrows. "Ah, well," he said, shrugging, "you don't know what you're missing." He leaned towards her again, slightly swaying on his feet. "There's an oul' saying – there's many a good tune been played by an oul' fiddle." He thumbed towards Paul again. "And it plays sweeter tunes than anything a young scut of a lad could play."

Hannah steadied her bike with one arm and stretched

the other over to put it around Paul's neck and pull him close to her. "I wouldn't be too sure," she said, kissing Paul on the cheek, "and he's far better-looking than you!"

Paul's face turned crimson as Hannah held on to him while fluttering her eyelashes at the man.

"Ah, go on!" the man said. "You're codding me now. I would have thought a girl like you would have gone for the more mature man." He winked at Paul just to let him know he was only rising Hannah and that it was nothing personal. "I wouldn't have thought that a young buck would be able to keep up with your notions."

"D'you hear that, Paul?" Hannah said, in a high breathless voice. "Imagine him saying we don't make a lovely couple!" She cuddled in closer now, her soft hand caressing his neck.

Paul suddenly felt very strange and awkward. The fella obviously didn't know he and Hannah were cousins. And while they could get away with codding him on about things, everybody knew everybody else in these small towns and villages and you just never knew the minute when you'd be found out. He'd had a narrow escape the night before with the whiskey escapade and being on the receiving end of his sister's temper, and he just didn't feel too confident at chancing his arm over anything else.

"Ah, go on, Hannah!" Paul said, suddenly finding his voice. He pulled himself out of her embrace. "You shouldn't be trying to make an eejit of the poor fella!"

"Oh, Paul, don't be like that!" Hannah said, batting her eyelids and giggling.

The man in the brown suit shifted his gaze from Paul to Hannah, a bemused look on his face.

"If the truth be told," Paul said, "me and this lovely girl are actually cousins."

The man raised his eyebrows and laughed. "Ah, it's you that's coddin' me now! Youse don't look a bit alike." He waved his finger around. "Sure, you're dark and she's all blondey."

Hannah had her hand up to her mouth, giggling away.

"No – we definitely are cousins," Paul said, an insistent note in his voice. "Hannah was only messing around earlier."

"Well, it didn't look like that to me," the man said, winking at them. "If you pair are cousins then you're what would be called *kissing cousins*."

Chapter 24

On Sunday morning Rose woke to the sound of her mother tapping on the bedroom door.

"Up ye get, the pair of ye," Kathleen Barry called in a bright cheery voice, "or you'll be late for Mass!"

"Coming!" Rose called back. She turned in the bed now. "Hannah?" she said in a low voice. "Are you awake?"

Hannah gave a low moan. "It's too early . . . I'm still asleep."

"Come on, lazy-bones!" Rose said, trying to sound normal and friendly. She threw the covers back on her own side and got out of bed. "We need to move now to be in good time for Mass."

Hannah struggled to sit up. "I hate Sunday mornings! It's torture not being able to have any breakfast or even a cup of tea before going to Mass. It spoils the longer lie-on, knowing you can't have a thing until you've walked all the way to church, sat through Mass and then walked all the way back."

Rose shrugged. "You'll just have to become a Protestant then, won't you?"

"It doesn't sound like too bad an idea."

"I'd like to see your mother's face when you tell her that!" Rose laughed.

"You ought to see her face even when she's got nothing to moan about," Hannah said, giving a great big sigh. "She can be the most miserable, crossest woman that God ever put breath into. I'm grateful every morning that I wake up in this house – even this morning when I won't be getting any breakfast for hours."

Rose moved towards the door. She felt awkward when Hannah went on like this about her mother. "I know you think your mother is very difficult but don't forget she's Mammy's sister."

"I know, I know," Hannah said, brushing her blonde curls out of her bleary eyes. She suddenly threw the bedcovers back and started to bounce on the bed. *"I'm down in Kilnagree,"* she sang to the tune of *Bali Ha'i*, *"and I am going to be haa-ppy today!"*

Rose looked at her cousin in amazement and then she started to laugh. "I wouldn't get that carried away, Hannah. Kilnagree's not a bad little place – but it's not exactly the South Pacific or anywhere like that."

Rose went down to her own bedroom to get the large cream enamel jug and bowl for her and Hannah to wash in. The bed that Veronica and Eileen shared with their grandmother was empty since the younger girls had gone up to the kitchen to have their dark hair done up in neat plaits as they did every Sunday.

Hannah glanced over to the single bed where Paul was still fast asleep.

"Paul!" Rose said sharply. "Get a move on or you'll be late for Mass."

"I'm coming . . ." Paul mumbled from under the covers.

Rose took the bowl to the other room and then went to the kitchen to fill the jug with hot water from the kettle, mixed with a drop of the cold water they kept in another jug by the sink. Then she carried the heavy jug and two towels back to the bedroom for her and Hannah to get freshened up for Mass.

Hannah slipped her clean knickers on under her nightdress, then, standing with her back to Rose, she pulled her nightie off over her head and put her bra on. After washing her face and hands and under her arms, she dried herself and then went over to her case while Rose got washed in her petticoat.

In a few minutes Hannah was dressed in another outfit – a smart one she had bought especially for Mass – a plain black dress with a short black and white hound's-tooth jacket edged with black braid. A pair of shiny, black-patent court shoes and a matching quilted patent clutch bag finished the outfit off.

"That's a lovely rig-out," Rose said, drying under her arms. "It really suits you."

Hannah raised her eyebrows and gave a little smile. "Come on," she said, "I'm waiting to see what you're wearing, now you have all those lovely clothes from Diana Tracey."

Rose felt a jolt of annoyance at Hannah's remark but she bit her tongue. She opened the wardrobe, then stood with her hands on her hips looking in. "I was going to wear my black and white dress," she said, "but I don't want to copy you, now that you've the same colours on."

"Let me see it."

Rose lifted the hanger out from the wardrobe to reveal a black and white flowered dress in a boat-neck style with a big broad belt. Then she reached back in and lifted out a matching half-moon-style black hat.

Hannah shrugged. "It might be the same colours, but your outfit is completely different." She paused for a few moments, then gave a small laugh. "You might as well wear it because it'll make us stand out from the crowd and give them all something to talk about in the church."

Rose frowned at the thought. "I wouldn't like to draw attention to ourselves like that – especially in a church."

"Don't be silly," Hannah said. "I just meant that all the other girls will be jealous because we both look so well-dressed."

Rose hesitated, suddenly feeling very uncomfortable about the thought of people noticing her more than usual. "I'm not sure if I'll wear that outfit," she said quietly.

Hannah shrugged and gave a little sigh. "It's up to you – I was only giving my honest opinion."

Rose put the dress back in the wardrobe and lifted out her lilac blouse with the bow-tie neck and her plain black skirt. She would wear it with the hat and a black cardigan and there would be no similarity to Hannah's outfit.

* * *

Rose and Hannah followed Kathleen and Martha out of the church, with Paul, Eileen and Veronica coming behind. Martha was holding on to Kathleen's arm with one hand and leaning heavily on her walking-stick with the other. As usual after Sunday Mass, Stephen Barry was in the vestry sorting out the collection baskets with a few other men.

"Rose, if you don't mind," Kathleen said when they got outside the church, "would you and Hannah go on ahead and get the breakfast started?" She patted Martha's hand. "Your granny's leg is a bit sore this morning, so we'll be a little while behind you."

"We'll be as quick as we can, girls," Martha said, smiling apologetically.

Rose usually took the chance to have a chat with Cathy and her other friends, but in a way she was glad of an excuse not to have to wait around with her unpopular cousin.

She nodded to this one and had a few words with another as they made their way through the groups of people congregated in the churchyard. Then, just as they reached the gate, Rose caught sight of Michael and Ruairí Murphy and her heart started racing. She really wasn't ready to meet Michael again after what had happened on Friday night. She slowed up, moving to the right-hand side of the gate and then she suddenly realised that she was close to Diana Tracey and her tall, slightly balding husband. Local people still found it strange to see the formerly Protestant woman at Mass with her Catholic husband. Rose turned her head in the opposite direction, feeling self-conscious and embarrassed, but it was too late because they had already been seen.

"Hello again, girls!" Diana said, coming over to them. "And how's the ankle today?"

Hannah was all beaming smiles. "Grand, thanks. It's as good as new again." She looked at Diana's husband expectantly.

"I'm delighted to hear it," Diana said. She looked

back at her husband. "You know Rose Barry of course – the young lady who helped my mother out the day she took ill."

"Of course, of course," he said, smiling broadly at her.

Rose nodded and smiled back, feeling really awkward. She had no idea what to say to them and hoped they would just say a quick hello and move back into the crowds. Then Rose was suddenly aware of Diana looking at her hat and she wondered if the vet's wife recognised some of the clothes that her mother had given her. The thought brought a hot feeling to her face and chest.

If Diana noticed anything, she didn't show it. She turned now towards Hannah. "And this is Rose's cousin – the young lady I was telling you about."

James Tracey came forward now and shook Hannah's hand. "Delighted to meet you, Hannah. Diana was singing your praises yesterday after the little performance you gave on our piano. You're a very talented pianist by all accounts."

Rose stood smiling politely, wondering how Hannah felt with her sneaky little visit being exposed.

But Hannah was oblivious to Rose's presence. She put her hand up to her mouth and rolled her eyes. "I'm not so sure about that . . . I couldn't remember the end of one of the pieces."

Diana looked at her and then shook a teacher's warning finger. "Now don't be so modest – the fact you could play those pieces from memory is all the more impressive."

"Well, thank you," Hannah said, smiling gratefully at her then at her husband, "but I think the beautiful grand piano might have helped. It probably makes the most amateur pianist sound fantastic."

Rose stood quietly as James Tracey, Diana and Hannah chatted as though they were old friends but the more she thought about the pushy and deceitful thing Hannah had done the angrier she became.

Then, after a few more minutes the Traceys said their goodbyes and went off to where their Land Rover was parked.

"Aren't they a lovely, lovely couple?" Hannah said in a breathless voice as she and Rose crossed over to the coastal side of the road and started walking briskly in the direction of the cottage.

Rose swallowed hard now to keep calm. "I can't believe you went down to their house on your own, without saying a word," she said, her voice quivering with anger. "They are total strangers to you and it was a very forward thing of you to do."

"I don't think it was forward or wrong," Hannah said, sounding shocked that Rose should dare question her. "It was just being polite. I only called to give her a small box of chocolates for bringing me home the day I hurt my ankle. It's the kind of thing my mother would have expected me to do."

Rose felt her mouth all dry and cotton-woolly. Once again, Hannah had a clever answer to any criticism. "Well, I still think it was forward," she said, "and what makes the whole thing odder is the fact that you didn't even bother to tell me or anyone else about it."

Hannah came to a halt. "Oh, Rose," she said, biting her lip. "I thought I'd told you!"

"You thought you'd told me?" Rose repeated in a high incredulous voice.

Hannah touched the palm of her hand to her forehead. "It's just dawned on me that it was Paul I told – not you!"

Rose gave Hannah a long, disbelieving look. "There are times when you would say anything to get yourself out of trouble. I don't think you had any intention of telling me." She started walking again, really fast now so that Hannah had to almost run in her heeled shoes to keep up.

"I'm really sorry, Rose. I can see how it must look but, honestly, with you at work and me and Paul taking the girls out yesterday afternoon and everything, it just went out of my mind. And then when I told Paul, it must have made me think I'd told you."

Rose turned her head away from Hannah's lies and looked out over the shimmering blue sea, trying to calm herself down before going back to the cottage. Hannah walked on and a few moments later, Rose followed her.

As they walked along in an icy silence, Rose decided that she was going to get her mother on her own and tell her what Hannah had done. If her mother felt that Hannah had done no harm then she would let the subject drop. If her mother agreed with her that Hannah had indeed been forward and dishonest, then she would ask her to have a firm word with her.

When they arrived back at the cottage, Rose went into the bedroom and changed her blouse for a short-sleeved jumper. Then she put her apron on top and went to start on the breakfast.

Hannah waited until Rose had finished in the

bedroom, then she too went to get changed into more casual clothes. Paul arrived in with the two girls and Hannah called from the bedroom to ask if he could help her to find her earring which had rolled under the bed.

In the bedroom, he got down on his knees on the linoleum. "Whereabouts is it?" he asked.

Hannah went over and closed the door. "I only said that for an excuse," she told him in a whisper. "I need your help . . . I'm in trouble with Rose. I need you to say that I told you all about the visit to Traceys' yesterday."

Paul sat down on the bed, his brow furrowed in confusion. "I know you were all excited when you were talking about seeing inside the big house . . . but why didn't you tell Rose about it?"

Hannah put her hands on her hips. "Never mind all that. I don't need another Spanish Inquisition like the one your sister just gave me. I just need you to explain that I told *you* about it yesterday afternoon." She shrugged. "I just don't know why Rose is making such a big deal about it." She prodded Paul in the chest now. "I stood up for you yesterday and told Rose not to be so hard on you – so you owe me a favour."

Paul thought for a few moments, then he shrugged. He hated being in the line of fire between his sister and his cousin and if he could do anything to ease the situation between them, he would.

"Fair enough. You *did* tell me yesterday, so it's the truth."

Hannah gave him an appreciative little smile. She bent forward now, her lips touching his ear. "What would I do without you, Paul?" she said in a low whisper.

Paul started to make a joke – but the words had stuck in his throat as he found himself acutely aware of Hannah's closeness to him. The musky smell of her perfume and the touch of her lips had suddenly sent a strange, tingly feeling all down his spine.

*   *   *

They were all sitting eating when the sound of the latch going on the gate made Kathleen move out of her chair to look out of the window.

"Stephen's here at last, thank God," she said to Martha. "I'll just get his plate out of the oven." She went over to the cooker, took a teacloth to protect her hands and then proceeded to lift out the hot plate of fry she had put aside for Stephen. She was placing it on the table as he came through the door, unusually smart in his Sunday suit and shirt and tie.

"Sit yourself down," she told him. "We've managed to keep the bit of breakfast hot for you without it spoiling."

"Well, ye can just put it straight back into the oven," he told her, in a deep serious voice. "There'll be no breakfast for me until I've sorted a bit of business out with Rose and Paul."

Rose felt a cold hand clutch at her heart.

Her father pointed to the door leading out to the hallway. "The pair of ye can go down into our bedroom right now."

Rose and Paul immediately got to their feet, Rose's legs shaking as she did so.

They thought they had been clever enough to avoid this but they obviously hadn't.

They had been found out.

Hannah's face had drained to a porcelain white as she looked at her uncle. She was well used to this kind of scene at home and had found ways of coping with it. But this was different. She'd seen her Uncle Stephen in a bit of a mood before but this was the first time she'd witnessed him on the verge of really losing his temper.

"But they haven't finished their breakfast yet," Kathleen said in a lame voice, her eyes darting from her husband to her two eldest children.

"Pity about them!" he snapped. "I don't know how they could dare to sit there all innocent after what I've heard about the pair of them." He thumbed in the direction of the door. "Get moving now."

Rose thought her legs were going to buckle under her as she walked the short length of the hallway with her brother close behind her. When she reached her parents' bedroom she opened the door and went in and stood by the bed, Paul standing only inches away from her.

Stephen Barry came in behind them. He stopped to close the door, then he suddenly whirled around and his curled-up fist caught his son on the side of the head. Paul staggered backwards onto the bed, his hand covering his ear.

Rose looked at her brother but knew she daren't show any sign of concern for him just yet. In the midst of this nightmare confrontation, the one thing that did strike her was that Paul hadn't cried when he received the vicious blow. The last time anything like this had happened – over a much more minor incident to do with breaking his father's bicycle lamp – he had cried bitter tears. Paul was obviously growing up and learning to take the downs of life with the ups.

Stephen Barry then turned to Rose. "Now, milady," he said, moving his face close to hers, "while that young gobshite is nursing his ear, you can tell me exactly what your part in all this shameful business is. You can explain to me how ye all ended up drinking in Slattery's pub on Friday night and how your younger brother came to be mixing with the likes of Jack Kelly – and how he ended up in a drunken heap at the back of the hall!"

Rose dared to look him in the face and she saw that her father's eyes were brimming with suppressed anger and disappointment. "Whatever you've been told," she said in a nervous voice, "is not the way it happened."

Stephen Barry carried on as if she had never spoken. "And then," he said in a low, ominous voice, "you can explain to me how the girl I've always been proud of allowed a drunken lout like that Liam O'Connor fellow to walk her home."

"It wasn't like that!" Rose said, horrified that whoever had related the story had put such a twist on it. "He was only helping me because of the state Paul was in." Immediately the words left her mouth, Rose regretted them, because her father's left hand shot out and caught Paul on the opposite side of the face now.

"You little bastard!" he hissed. "You've ruined our family's good reputation. You've brought the Barry name low in the eyes of all the decent people in Kilnagree!"

"But hardly anybody saw him," Rose dared to cut in. "As soon as I knew what had happened, I brought him home. Nobody in the hall saw him . . . it was all outside."

"Outside, outside!" her father repeated. "Around the back of the hall like the skulking rat he is!" He looked at

Paul with disgust and shook his head. "According to Larry Hennessey, half of the place knew because that O'Connor fellow went back down after leaving ye and he and Jack Kelly got into a drunken row over the whole thing!"

Rose was suddenly reminded of what Liam had told her yesterday afternoon – about confronting Jack over who had bought the whiskey for Paul. He hadn't told her that half of Kilnagree had been listening.

"Well, nobody made any mention of it to me at Slattery's yesterday," Rose said in what she hoped was a quiet, respectful tone.

"And ye both thought that nobody would make any mention of it to me either – didn't ye? Ye thought I was some kind of an *amadán* that wouldn't get to hear about it. Well, ye were very sadly mistaken." He paused. "And let me tell ye both, this isn't finished yet. Not by a long chalk. I'm going to make it my business to have a word with both the O'Connor lad and the Kelly lad, and I can guarantee you that neither of them will set foot near you or this house again!" He paused for breath. "And there's no lad going to be allowed to buy and feed drink to any son of mine!"

Rose couldn't stop herself. "It was Hannah! It was Hannah who gave Jack Kelly the money for the whiskey!" She watched as her father stood still for a moment, his eyes narrowed in thought.

Then Paul gave a loud moan and buried his face in his hands.

"Don't go bringing your cousin into all this mess," Stephen said in a low voice full of scorn.

"But Liam O'Connor told me!" Rose protested. "I knew nothing about Hannah's part in it until yesterday. I never saw anybody buying whiskey and I knew nothing about Paul drinking it until Michael Murphy called me outside to see the state he was in."

Her father's eyebrows rose. "The Murphy lad? Another decent family that know all about our business now. Dear Jesus!" He shook his head. "And not content with canoodling with that waster O'Connor, you're now trying to put the blame on your cousin!" Stephen Barry's eyes suddenly filled with tears. "How can this have happened? I know Paul has it in him to be weak and easily led – but that will be knocked out of him one way or another. But how did the girl I would have trusted with my life suddenly turn into this liar and cheat? How did she turn into the kind of girl who would cheapen herself with the likes of Liam O'Connor?"

"It's not true!" Rose said defiantly. "None of it's true!"

Her father's face suddenly paled and then he slowly raised his arm above her head. "Get out!" he roared, a single tear sliding down his cheek. "Get out before I lay my hands on you. Before you make me strike a woman for the first time in my life!"

Chapter 25

Leonora pulled up outside Terry Cassidy's cottage. She switched the windscreen wipers off and then the engine. She sat in the car for a few moments, wondering if she should wait for the rain to ease or whether she should just get out of the car and take her chances. She glanced up at the sky and the grey clouds immediately above and the darker ones in the distance told her there was no point in waiting. The rain was on for the afternoon. She lifted her waxed Barbour hat from the car seat and pulled it on over her ash-blonde hair. She was wearing black slacks that had seen better days and a beloved soft green turtleneck sweater that had frayed slightly at the cuffs. Clothes that were a little too good for the garden but not decent enough for wearing outside.

"Welcome, welcome!" Terry said, holding the studio door open wide. She was dressed in a huge blue stripy shirt with a black, paint-splattered apron over it. She had her long hennaed hair tied up in a turquoise and purple scarf. "You actually came! How are you feeling?"

"Better," Leonora said, rushing through the door to escape the rain. She was carrying two canvases in one hand and a bag with all her painting accoutrements in the other. She put her things down in a corner and then she removed her hat. "And hopefully I'm in a better frame of mind for working than I have been recently."

Terry smiled sympathetically and shrugged. "It happens," she said, "but if you really want it to, it always comes back."

"It's *got* to come back," Leonora sighed, running her fingers through her hair to revive it after the flattening it had received from the pulled-down hat. "I had to phone that poor man and assure him that I would have the paintings ready by next weekend. Thankfully, he was very kind and said there was no rush. And when I explained that I needed the original one to copy from, the lady who bought it said she didn't mind waiting a few weeks for it either."

"Sometimes it's better to have a deadline. I always work better when I know I have an exhibition coming up."

Leonora bit her lip now, knowing she sounded weak and very amateurish in comparison to the professional artist. Knowing that a real, talented painter would have dashed her little paintings off in an hour or two instead of agonising over them.

"I should have about fifty pieces ready for August," Terry continued, waving her hand at all the newly framed pictures around the room, "but if I didn't have the exhibition to encourage me, I would take weeks over one."

"Well, I really admire you because I could never do it," Leonora said. "I find the whole thing a terrible pressure. I just want to get it all over and done with."

Terry held her hands up. "Stop – stop!" She looked at Leonora, as a teacher would look at an irksome child. "Put your hat back on and we'll go into the cottage and have a nice cup of coffee and some cake – and then we'll start all over again."

"That's not fair. I'm only holding you back. The idea was that I'd just come to the studio and tuck myself into a quiet corner while you got on with your own work."

"I didn't stop for lunch so I need a break in any case." Terry opened the studio door. "Prepare to run! It's absolutely bouncing down!"

As she sat in the cosy chintz armchair in the surprisingly large sitting room sipping a comforting mug of sweet, milky coffee, Leonora felt herself relaxing. Terry had explained that she'd had a wall taken down to knock two rooms together some years back, to allow more light to flood in. Leonora's eyes moved around the soft yellow walls, taking in the myriad paintings and collages, and the shelves and window-sills full of carvings and sculptures, thinking that it was almost as entertaining as sitting in a small art gallery.

"You'll have a piece of chocolate slab cake, won't you?" Terry said, holding out a strangely shaped pottery plate with several square slices on it. "I made it only yesterday and if I say so myself it's really lovely. It has biscuit and nuts and raisins through the chocolate." She patted her rounded stomach and sighed. "You'll be helping me if you have it, because I'll only end up eating it all by myself and adding to my already significant tummy."

Leonora laughed. "When you put it like that, how can I refuse? Besides, I have a very sweet tooth that I find hard to control at times." She took a piece of the cake and put it on the smaller plate the artist had given her along with an embroidered napkin. "It looks lovely and just the sort of thing to give a bit of comfort on a wet, miserable afternoon."

Terry took a slice of the cake and came to sit in the matching chintz chair opposite. "If you don't mind me saying, you seem in need of some comfort today. Is there anything wrong? Anything I could help you with?" She took a drink of her coffee.

Leonora looked over. "Thank you . . . but no. There's nothing wrong as such." She glanced out of one of the cottage windows. "It's probably just the weather. I begin to feel hemmed in when I can't get into the garden."

"You'll just have to pour all your creativity into your painting this afternoon, instead of the garden. It's the same sort of thing and you'll feel the same at the end of it as you do when you've done a good afternoon's gardening." Terry took a bite of the chocolate cake now.

Leonora gave a little shrug. "I didn't feel good the last time I came and I left feeling worse than ever. I must have painted over my attempts and come back to a blank canvas about ten times." She sucked her breath in. "I'm actually very nervous about doing these paintings . . . I feel as though I'll never be able to do it again."

"Nonsense," Terry told her. "It'll eventually come all right."

Coffee and cake consumed, they returned to the studio.

"We have a new addition here," Terry said. She pointed over to the furthest corner of the room where a small gramophone stood on the end of one of her long tables. "It keeps me company and inspires me." She went over now and lifted the lid. "I tend to play the same one over and over again, as the wrong sort of music can completely kill the muse. Hopefully, it will help you to get back on track." She switched the gramophone on, and then she lifted the arm across to the very edge of the record. A few seconds later the soft strains of Handel filled the room.

Leonora unpacked her paints, set out her canvas and pieces of old newspapers that Terry kept in a pile on the floor, and donned her painting apron. After that she filled an empty jam-jar with white spirits and sorted out her brushes.

"Your little masterpiece is on the second shelf," Terry informed her, "and the bits and pieces you used for the still life."

Leonora went over to the shelf and lifted down the small canvas with the painting of the jug and the snowdrops. She now had to re-create this, plus another one with the jug and bluebells. She studied it for a few moments, wondering how on earth she had managed to produce such a realistic effort, then she shrugged and lifted down her little tin jug and took that and the canvas back over to the table.

Both canvases she had brought already had the whitish-grey background painted over them since her previous attempts, so at least she had that to start on. She propped the original painting up on a small easel on the table, and started on the process of copying it. Within a short while there was a satisfactory replica of the jug on one of the canvases and Leonora felt herself beginning to relax. Then she moved onto the part she had enjoyed most – painting the individual snowdrops.

She and Terry worked away companionably, with only the music relieving the silence between them. She had painted half a dozen or so of the small winter flowers when the opening bars of Grieg's "Morning" filled the studio. Leonora's paintbrush froze mid-air. A picture of herself and Andrew at a classical music concert in Dublin – listening to this very piece – flooded into her mind. The music took her back to the happy times in her life, the happy times in her marriage. And there had been many. There had been high days and there had been ordinary days. Peaceful and contented days. Why, she wondered, after all those good years, was she left with only the bad memories?

And then her eyes suddenly filled with unwanted, unbidden tears.

She blinked them away, and moved the brush back towards the canvas – but her eyes were blurred and she could not properly see what she was doing. Then more tears welled up. She wiped the back of one hand to her eyes, but only succeeded in getting a small stray spot of the paint in one eye. She then resorted to using the sleeve of her green sweater which didn't help either. She took a deep breath to steady herself, but with the stinging and the tears still coming, it suddenly all became too much. She put the paintbrush on the table and then, searching in her trouser pocket for her hanky, she sat down on the bench behind her.

"Are you all right?" Terry asked, looking over the rim of her glasses.

Leonora swallowed hard on the lump which had formed in her throat and composed herself enough to reply. "A bit of paint in my eye – very stupid of me." She dabbed the hanky to her streaming eye.

Terry looked at her thoughtfully. "How is the painting coming along?"

The strains of "Morning" were building up now, reaching a crescendo.

"Okay, I think . . ." said Leonora.

There was a choked note in her voice that alerted

Terry who carefully wiped her brush on a rag and put it in her jar of white spirits. She took her glasses off, thrust them on the top of her head, deep into the wild red hair that wasn't covered by her brilliantly coloured scarf and came towards her student.

"Something is troubling you, Leonora – isn't it?" she asked in a gentle voice. "I can feel it . . ."

Leonora looked up at Terry with watery eyes and nodded. "I'm just being silly." She closed her eyes now and the tears just spilled down her cheeks. Quickly she moved her hanky from eye to eye, but had difficulty in stemming the avalanche that she had been holding back for so long. Terry's comforting hand came to rest on her shoulder. "I'm so sorry," Leonora said. "I don't know what's come over me." And although she normally would have been mortified at the situation, a weariness descended on her that made her barely care.

"Age, dear," Terry said. "It's probably just your hormones. We women are very prone to it at this time of life."

Leonora shook her head and managed the vestiges of a smile. "That's all gone," she said, her voice quivery, "some years ago. I'm well past the change of life. Too old for it." At this very moment, Leonora actually felt too old for everything.

"Nonsense," Terry told her, sitting down on the bench beside her. "It can go on for years – so I read in an article recently."

Leonora rubbed her eyes hard now; glad she hadn't been wearing mascara. "I'll be fine," she said, a determined note in her voice.

"It might help to talk," Terry ventured. "I'm a good listener and I can assure you that not a word of what you say will ever be repeated."

Leonora was suddenly assailed by an overwhelming urge to pour out everything that was worrying her – old and new. But the old ways had a firm grip on her. She had never truly opened up to another woman before. She had only ever discussed things that were close to her heart with Andrew. And then later – to her regret – she had talked in a much too intimate way with Daniel Levy. He had caught her at a low point and she had let her guard down with him in more ways than one.

Apart from the two men, there had been no one that Leonora had trusted with the darker worries that kept her awake at night. But there was something about this artist that she instinctively felt was different. There was something about the way that Terry Cassidy made human failings and frailties seem a part of everyday life that gave Leonora consolation and comfort. Terry made very serious mistakes sound like something that everyone made at some point in their life – and she gave the impression that there was nothing in the world that would shock her.

Leonora looked up for a few seconds and then she took a deep breath. There were several things she could have started with but she chose the one that was easiest to put words to. "It's my son – Edward. The one in America. I'm very worried about him."

Terry waited. She didn't assume or ask anything. She simply waited for Leonora to tell her in her own time and in her own way.

"There's something wrong," Leonora eventually went

on. "I know it. I spoke to him last night and he didn't sound himself at all." She wiped at the corner of one eye with the damp hanky again. "You see, he went out to America initially to work with a friend of his – they had studied architecture together at Trinity." She smiled now. "Christopher Hennessey, a lovely chap. He went out the year before Edward, and at first I was delighted that Edward had gone out to join him in New York, even though I knew he would be so very far away. Setting up in partnership with Christopher was a marvellous opportunity, and I couldn't expect him to miss it . . ." She paused. "And Christopher had obviously settled well in America, because after a whirlwind romance he got married to a girl from Galway, Theresa, and now they have a baby girl. That made me feel even happier with the situation, because I felt that Edward wouldn't be lonely if he had a family home to visit and stay weekends."

Terry smiled encouragingly but said nothing.

Leonora's brow darkened. "But something has happened. Something has changed. He hardly mentions Christopher and Theresa any more, he's very evasive about his work and –" She halted. "He's actually very evasive about everything." She looked at Terry. "And it's not just me – it's not just the worries of a besotted mother. Both Jonathan and Diana have said that they've noticed a definite change in him. Diana said only last weekend that she thought his voice sounded very flat and he seems to have lost his sense of humour. He's always been very sharp and witty, you see . . ." Her voice trailed off and her eyes suddenly filled up with tears. "I don't quite know what to do. He's a grown man – nearly thirty years of age . . ."

"Have you asked him directly how he is? Have you said that you're concerned?"

"Oh, yes," Leonora said, blinking the tears back again. "I have. But he just fobs me off and says he's very busy at work and too tired in the evenings to phone."

Terry squeezed her shoulder. "You mustn't worry – at least until you find something worth worrying about. Give him time and it will all sort itself out." She paused, thinking. "Is there a possibility that the business isn't going as well as he thought? Maybe he's got himself into some kind of debt and doesn't want to tell you? Money problems can bring the best of people to their knees."

Leonora raised her eyebrows. "I must confess I haven't thought of anything like that." She gave a little shrug. "He must know that I would help him out financially if he needed it. In fact, I gave him some money when he went out – to help with his share in the business."

"Maybe he feels he can't come back asking for more," Terry suggested.

Leonora thought for a few moments. "You may well have hit the nail on the head." Her face began to visibly brighten. "I'll give him a ring in the next few days and see if I can manoeuvre the conversation around in that direction. See if I can get to bottom of it. If it's simply money, then I'm sure we can do something about it."

"Is that it?" Terry asked. "Nothing else niggling away there?"

Leonora smiled properly now. "No. I feel a weight has been lifted off me now." She looked at Terry. "You're a very easy person to talk to – and a very good listener."

"When you've been in certain situations yourself,"

the artist said, "you find it easier to empathise with other people. Over the years I think I've made every mistake in the book, but I've only really hurt myself. And if I ever did inadvertently hurt anyone else – like the married man's wife – thankfully they never knew about it." She rolled her eyes dramatically. "*Men* – they're more trouble than they're worth!"

Leonora was suddenly curious. "You've given up on them?"

"I think we've given up on each other. It's been a few years now. I suppose I don't really go anywhere to meet single men these days."

"What if the perfect man came along? Would you be interested then?"

"Of course! Wouldn't I be mad not to? Especially if he was the *perfect* man. Having someone to bring the coal in and light the fire, empty the bin – someone to bring me breakfast in bed. There are lots of lovely things about being married to the right person." She looked at Leonora. "What about *you*?"

"*Me*?" Leonora's voice was high. "You're surely joking! I'm past all that."

"Nonsense," Terry said. "You must be only a few years older than me."

"Oh, I reckon I'm probably ten years older than you," Leonora calculated. "I reckon you've a few years before you reach fifty and I left it behind a good few years ago."

"Well, I'm forty-six and in all sincerity you don't look much older."

"Well, that's very flattering," Leonora laughed, "but I'm ten years older than you nonetheless."

"Amazing!" said Terry, shaking her head. "You really look years younger and I'm certainly not one of those people who give false flattery."

Leonora felt a little glow of pleasure. "Thank you. That's very kind of you."

The conversation wound down and the two women went back to concentrate on the work in hand. And as Leonora's paintbrush moved deftly to shape one snowdrop after another, she noticed that the music suddenly seemed more uplifting and she was inspired to move the brush more quickly and with more confidence than she had ever felt. And as she went along with the warm flood of creativity flowing from her, she knew that Terry Cassidy's easy skill with words and compassion had eased all the tension and turmoil within her

Within two hours the first half of her commission was on a stand drying out and she had started confidently into the second painting with the bluebells and the vase and the same small grey tin jug in the background.

It was late in the afternoon when the two women eventually came to a halt.

"Will you come again tomorrow?" Terry asked. "You could have that second piece more or less finished."

Leonora hesitated. "I really don't want to take advantage . . ."

"Please come. You and I have a kind of *simpatico* together – I feel we are on the same sort of wavelength."

Leonora smiled, suddenly feeling like a young girl who has been asked to be someone's best friend. "Thank you. I would be delighted to come tomorrow."

Chapter 26

Hannah Martin lay on her bed in Tullamore, staring at the white-washed ceiling. How was it, she thought, that other people had such ordinary, easy families? How was it that her own was so difficult?

She had hoped that her grandmother coming to stay with them for a while would make things better. But instead it had just made things far worse.

Before, she could have time to herself when her mother went out, but now she had none. If she came into her bedroom and shut the door, she would barely have time to lie down and think, or open a school book or a magazine when her Granny Martin would come to the foot of the stairs and shout up – asking if she was all right or whether she should start peeling the potatoes or some other stupid question.

And she was in the middle of her important exams at the moment – her grandmother might at least leave her in peace upstairs or in the parlour with the piano if she said she was studying or practising. It didn't seem to matter – every twenty minutes or half an hour she would appear at the door demanding to know what she was doing.

Hannah had imagined it being quite different. She had thought that her granny would just sit quietly in a corner knitting or listening to the radio, and would always be willing to make a cup of tea for everyone. The way Martha Barry was. Hannah had even thought that after a while she might be able to talk personally to her – confide in her. The way she felt that Rose could talk to her granny.

But Bridget Martin wasn't a bit like that. She was up on her feet all the time, fussing around, checking things, and then going in and out to the yard to talk to Hannah's father. Mainly to moan about his brother and new wife who she claimed were trying to force her out of her own home.

The only blessing about it, Hannah thought, was the fact that it wasn't permanent – well, not permanent *yet*. For the time being, Bridget was going to spend six weeks at their house and six weeks at Ursula and Simon's.

And it had severely curtailed Hannah's jaunts out with Simon, because her grandmother liked to know every little detail about where she was going, who she was going with, and exactly when she would be back. Hannah found it excruciating having to explain every single thing she did, because if by mistake she gave her grandmother a different version of events when she came back, Bridget Martin would say, "But that's not what you told me when you were going out."

And for someone who was getting forgetful about leaving taps running or irons plugged in, her granny seemed to have no trouble remembering things that were none of her business. All little fiddly, annoying things that didn't matter. And everything was reported back to her mother – all the things that Hannah had said or done, the tunes she had played on the piano and the length of time she had been in the bathroom doing her hair.

To make Hannah's situation worse, there was little escape from the house in the evenings now, as she was no longer needed to baby-sit her younger cousins. Bridget said she would do any baby-sitting for Ursula and Simon that was needed as it gave her a few hours out of the house.

In a way, Hannah was relieved that she and Simon could no longer find any opportunity for their passionate encounters. Since her last trip down to Clare she found that she had gone off her uncle in many ways. He suddenly seemed older and not as attractive to her – not when she compared him with lads like Liam O'Connor and the Murphy brothers, or even Paul.

Hannah hadn't been out much recently. She had been to the pictures on a couple of occasions with girls from school and she had been to one farmers' dance in Birr which she hadn't enjoyed one bit as she had been with Dymphna Naughton, the daughter of one of her mother's friends and the type who would report on Hannah's behaviour to her mother.

Hannah shifted onto her side on the bed now, wondering when she could escape back down to Kilnagree again. It had been a few months since her last visit and the incident over Paul getting drunk surely would be long forgotten. She smiled to herself now, thinking how lucky she had been that her aunt and uncle hadn't caught onto the fact that she'd bought the drink for him. She hadn't meant any harm by it – it was only meant as a bit of a laugh and to make Paul feel that bit more grown up.

But it had been a mistake. She knew that she had crossed a dangerous line with Rose over the incident. And she knew that she would have to work hard to gain back the ground she had lost. She would have to make sure that she didn't make a mistake like that again.

Hannah heard the kitchen door open below now and then she heard her grandmother's heavy footsteps coming along the hallway to the foot of the stairs.

"Hannah! Will you come down and help me to sort out the washing that I've brought in from the line?"

Hannah closed her eyes and gritted her teeth together – then she gave a loud, shuddering sigh.

There was a few seconds' silence.

"Han-*nah!*" Bridget called again, her voice an octave higher. "Your mother said we had to bring the washing in if it started to rain – and the best half of it is yours!"

Hannah uttered several oaths under her breath and then she got up from the bed.

"Look at this pile of washing," Bridget Martin said, as her granddaughter came into the kitchen. She put her hand into the pile of damp clothing on the big farmhouse table and held up a mass of shirts and stockings that were tangled with various undergarments. "I don't know where to start with it. I'm not used to this amount of washing any more. I had enough of it in me day, when I had a houseful of me own to be cooking and cleaning for." She shook her head. "I didn't come here to be skivvying in and out of the house when there's a young one around more able for it than me."

"It's all right, Granny," Hannah said in a deliberately calm voice. A voice that totally belied how she felt. She went over to the table and started to sort the items out into various piles. "I'll put them up on the pulley over the range and they'll be dry in a few hours."

"I'll give you a hand," Bridget said, suddenly much calmer herself. "I'm grand as long as there's somebody there to tell me what I'm doing."

They worked together companionably for a while until the old woman picked up a white, lace-covered bra.

"Would you look at this!" she said, twirling it around on her finger and laughing incredulously. "Who in the name of God would get into such a small little scrap of material? Sure that would hardly cover a pimple, never mind a woman's chest!" She looked at Hannah, her bushy white eyebrows raised. "I presume it belongs to yourself?"

Wordlessly Hannah reached out, took the brassiere from her grandmother and threw it up on top of the pulley.

Without waiting for a reply the old lady went on. "I wouldn't think for a minute that it's your mother's." Then, she started to laugh even louder. "God knows what would happen if your father was to see her all decked up in an item like that! I'd say it would send his blood pressure soaring sky high." Bridget was laughing so hard now she had to reach for a kitchen chair and sit down on it.

Hannah looked at her grandmother in amazement – not quite sure how to react. She'd never seen her so giddy before – nor had she ever heard her carry on like that, making crude suggestions about her own son.

"It's only an ordinary brassiere, Granny," she ventured. "It's what all the girls my age wear." If this was how her granny reacted to a plain white lace brassiere, what would she have had to say about the fancy red and black ones she had hidden under the mattress upstairs?

Her grandmother's face suddenly became serious again. "Ah," she said, nodding her head thoughtfully, "I suppose it's the modern way. Clothes and fashions have all changed. Everything has changed. It's hard to know what's what these days when you're getting old. You get left behind and nobody wants you." She pursed her lips together. "You're only a burden to everybody. You're like an oul' mare that's been put out to pasture in your own field."

Hannah stared at her for a few moments. "But that's not true, Granny – we all like having you here."

Bridget looked at her granddaughter now and her pale grey eyes suddenly flooded with tears. "It's Finbar's woman that's caused all this trouble. Everything was grand until she made her appearance. I had my own house and my own bed until she marched into the place and took it over. She's turned his head until he doesn't know whether he's coming or going – that's what she's done!"

"Maybe when they've had a bit of time on their own?" Hannah suggested.

"Oh, there's no fear of anything changing back to the way it was, for it'll be childer next," Bridget stated. "That'll be the next thing. She'll want to make sure she has a good grip on him. They'll be announcing it any time now. I've seen it happen time and time again."

Hannah lifted a large bath-towel now and proceeded to fold it. What was she supposed to say to her granny, she wondered. Wasn't it only normal and right that Finbar and his wife should have children fairly soon after they got married? But she knew her opinion wasn't going to be appreciated.

"Don't let it bother you, Granny," she said in the most placatory tones she could find. "It'll all work out."

"Well, it's to be hoped that it does, because I don't want to be roamin' around like an oul' itinerant to this house and that house for the rest of me days." She stabbed her finger down on the table to emphasise the point. "I want to be back home where I belong, in me own kitchen. It's good of your mother having me here in this house, but I know well she'd rather I was back in me own. There's times when she's very highly strung and having me under her feet won't be helping."

"But I don't think Mammy is any different whether you're here or not. In fact, she's a bit more even-tempered when you're around."

"Well, that's heartening to hear at least," the old lady said. She paused, thinking. "I don't think your mother always feels at her best – it's the time of her life, you see. *The change*, as they call it. It usually comes around the late forties and it can hit some women a lot worse than others. The way that having a child hits some harder." She shrugged. "I was lucky myself not to be hit too bad by anything. I've always been the one way – kind of easy-going. Neither up nor down. None of my family ever complained that I was hard to live with."

Hannah turned her attention back to the damp clothes, trying not to smile. She was sure that the last word that Finbar Martin and his wife would use to describe his mother would be 'easy-going'. But what her grandmother had said about her mother's moods had made her wonder. When she thought about it, her mother's temper had got much worse in the last few years. Maybe it was to do with 'the change' and, if so, hopefully it would pass soon and everyone might have a bit of peace.

Hannah and her grandmother worked companionably on the basket of wet laundry and a short while later the wooden pulley had been filled.

"I'll put the kettle on," Hannah said, going over to the sink. "I'll switch on the electric one, it'll be quicker." She knew her granny didn't always hold with modern items like electric kettles. In fact, she had a brand-new electric cooker at home that was bought for her last Christmas, still in all the cardboard and polythene wrapping from the shop.

Finbar had bought it for her but up until now she was still refusing to open it, saying it was far too good for everyday use, but everybody knew that it was because her daughter-in-law had made a big palaver of it. She had gone on and on saying how wonderful it was and how it would change her mother-in-law's life and make things far easier for her. Naturally, Bridget had then held out even stronger against using it.

"You know, underneath it all, you're a good enough girl," Bridget suddenly said.

Hannah's face went pink with delight. It wasn't often she got a compliment in her own home, and praise from her stern grandmother was praise indeed. "I try my best," she said, giving a little sigh. She plugged the filled kettle into the socket.

The old woman's brows came down. "Your mother can be hard on you at times, I've noticed. I don't like to interfere – I've never interfered with any of the family's business." She gave a little shrug. "That's never been my way."

Hannah caught her breath at such a blatant untruth. Was it possible that her granny was totally unaware that she criticised her Uncle Finbar and his wife morning, noon and night? But there was no point in saying anything – and Hannah wouldn't dare. "Will we have a slice of apple tart?" she asked instead.

She had brought a cup over to her granny at the armchair by the range and was just pouring her own out when a loud, firm knock came on the door.

"Now, who the damn could that be?" Bridget Martin said, rising from the chair to look towards the door. "Who could that be knocking on the door? If it was any of the family, sure they'd just walk in." She looked at Hannah with wide, accusing eyes. "Well? Are you going to see who it is or are you going to keep us in suspense?"

Hannah hurriedly put the teapot down on the worktop with a bang, which resulted in the hot liquid splashing out all over her arm. "Jesus Christ! Look what you've made me do!" she said, rubbing her hand and arm furiously.

"Never mind your arm! It's your mouth you need to wash out, using blasphemous language like that!" Bridget Martin shook her head and raised her eyebrows. "Ah, well, you won't be so smart when your mother gets to hear about it."

Hannah turned and walked towards the door, her face tight with rage. Then her expression suddenly changed to alarm as she saw the familiar black hat through the square pane of glass in the door. Tentatively, she opened the door.

"Father McGinn!" she said in a loud voice, so that her grandmother could hear. "Are you on your house calls?" She opened the door wider now. "Come in, come in!"

Somewhere in his early forties, stocky with dark hair greying at the temples, Father McGinn was an amiable easy-going man who rarely interfered in the parishioners' business.

When Hannah ushered the priest into the kitchen, she glanced over to the range to see her grandmother standing as straight as a soldier, her face blood red.

"Oh, Father McGinn!" she said in a high, breathless, almost girlish voice. She looked at Hannah with wide, anxious eyes. "Isn't this a nice surprise for us?" She turned back to the priest. "Sheila is down the town and Bill is out in the field somewhere."

"Will you have a cup of tea, Father?" Hannah asked. "I made a pot only a few minutes ago."

"Ah, sure I might as well make myself at home for a few minutes," the priest said, smiling at them, putting his hat on the table and then taking off his coat and putting it on the back of a kitchen chair.

"Now, Father," the old woman said, gesturing with her hands, "sit yourself down in this nice comfortable chair by the cooker."

"I'm grand here," the priest said, pulling out a chair from the table. "You sit where you were."

Hannah went back and forth to the table, bringing the tea and a plate with several slices of buttered brown bread and another one with pieces of the apple tart, while her grandmother availed of the opportunity of asking about all the sick people the priest had visited either at home or in hospital. Then Hannah sat down at the table opposite the priest, smiling and making the odd comment when it was appropriate.

Father McGinn was just starting on his second cup of tea when he suddenly said, "Well, Hannah, I suppose you're in the thick of it at the minute with the school exams?"

"I've only a few more to go and I'm finished," she said. And then she held her breath, waiting for the question that everybody asked her.

"And what are you hoping to do?"

Hannah's eyes flitted across the kitchen to her grandmother who was listening intently. She shrugged. "I'm not quite sure yet . . ."

"Your mother was saying you were hoping for enough points for teaching – or for music college. Have you applied for both?"

"I'll just have to wait and see," she said vaguely.

Hannah knew perfectly well that she wouldn't get the points necessary for either teacher training college or Music College. She knew that so far she'd done only marginally better than last year when she had got such poor results. Not enough to get the much better Leaving Certificate everyone had hoped for – and certainly not enough to get her onto either of the courses her mother dreamed of. And two of the exams that were still to come – Irish and Maths – were her worst subjects.

Most of the time Hannah just blocked out any thoughts or worries about the results, telling herself they were months away. They were a whole summer away. Anything could happen in between.

"Now, Father," Bridget Martin suddenly cut in, "another person I was meaning to ask you about – Frank Mooney. He hasn't been outside the house this long time. I believe he finds it very hard to walk now – I heard both legs have gone from below him. How is he, the poor cratur?"

Hannah was delighted to be let off the hook.

* * *

Sheila Martin came in through the kitchen door like a bat out of hell. "What in the name of God," she demanded, "is the smell in this kitchen?"

Hannah looked up, completely startled. She had been sitting at the kitchen table for the last half-hour trying to decipher a poem written in the Irish language. "I didn't notice anything . . ."

"Didn't notice anything? Are you a complete *amadán*? The smell would knock you out the minute you come in the door." She looked suspiciously at her daughter. "Have you been burning oul' plastic or polythene or something that you shouldn't?"

"No, I haven't, Mammy," Hannah said in a wounded tone. "I only put turf and a few bits of wood on." Hannah was very careful about keeping the fire going, as it was one of the first things that her mother checked when she came in.

Sheila's eyes darted around the kitchen. "Where's your granny?" she asked in a low voice.

"I think she said she was going outside to have a word with Daddy."

"Maybe she put something into the range before she went out – she's forever putting stuff in it that she shouldn't. She's the same when we have the fire on in the parlour"

Hannah shrugged. "I didn't see her putting anything in it."

"Huh! That's nothing new. When you have your nose stuck in a book the house could collapse in on top of you and you wouldn't notice!"

Hannah felt her shoulders and back stiffen, as they often did when her mother was working herself into a rage.

Sheila Martin went over to the range, sniffing audibly as she did so. "Well, there's definitely something burning that shouldn't be. God knows what the pair of ye have thrown in. One's as bad as the other. At least she has old age on her side for her stupidity – you have no damned excuse."

"But I didn't put anything in it," Hannah protested.

Her mother's eyes narrowed. "Don't dare take that tone of voice with me, or I'll give you something to complain about."

Hannah was silenced. She turned back to the table and sat hunched over her Irish poem.

Sheila lifted the thin hooked poker and opened the top of the range to look in at the glowing red turf. To her bemusement and annoyance, there was nothing untoward – nothing burning that shouldn't be burning. She prodded the fire about for a bit, double-checking, then she slid the cover back on again with a disgruntled sigh.

The back door opened and Bridget Martin came in. "Oh, you're back," she said to her daughter-in-law. "You were gone so long I thought you'd got lost. I was just saying to Bill that you must have bought up half the shops in Tullamore."

"I was only gone a couple of hours," Sheila said in a curt tone, "and I told you I was calling in to the Parochial House."

The old woman's brows came down. "Did you? I don't remember you mentioning it." Her slow walk came to a sudden halt. "Is there something burning in here?" she said, looking around the kitchen.

"Thank God that it's not just me," Sheila said. "I smelled it the minute I opened the door." She threw her hands up. "I've checked the fire and everything, but I can't seem to find anything. But there's definitely a weird smell coming from the range. She paused for a moment, thinking. "Did either of you put anything in the oven?"

"No," Hannah said, "I haven't been near it." She looked over at her granny, and saw the shock suddenly registering on the old woman's face.

"Oh, Holy God!" Bridget Martin said, her hand coming up to cover her mouth. "I forgot all about it! It was when Father McGinn was in . . ."

Sheila's hands moved to her hips and there was a resigned look on her face. "What? What have you done?"

Bridget gestured towards the range. "I didn't want him to see it . . . I thought the poor man would be mortified so I put it in the oven and I must have forgot all about it."

"What did you put in the oven?" Sheila's voice was slow and deliberate. She moved towards the range again. "By the smell of it you could have set the whole kitchen on fire!"

"It was Hannah's . . ." Bridget said weakly. "I was only trying to . . ."

Hannah was out of her chair and up on her feet now. "What was mine, Granny? You never said anything to me."

"Sure the priest was in and I couldn't tell you, and by the time he left –"

There was silence now as Sheila Martin opened the oven door in a fearful fashion. Small clouds of thick black smoke billowed out into the room. Sheila immediately started to cough – and to Hannah's ears it sounded more dramatic than was necessary. "Open the window, quick!" Sheila commanded. "Before we're choked by the fumes!"

Hannah rushed over to open the nearest window.

Sheila shoved the hooked poker into the oven and a few seconds later it came back out bearing the charred remainders of a once-white brassiere and a pair of knickers.

"They're my things – they were on the end of the pulley," Hannah exclaimed. "The rain had come on and we had to bring in the damp washing and hang it up."

"Would you listen to her – all this 'we' business," her granny suddenly asserted. "You brought in no washing. You were upstairs hiding in the bedroom as usual, and you left me to bring the washing in on my own. Your mother knows only too well what you're like."

Sheila held the blackened underwear out to her daughter. "Look at that!" she said in a strangled voice. "That could have burnt this whole house down. What kind of an eejit am I rearing?" Then, as if her mother-in-law wasn't even present, she said, "What on earth did you let her anywhere near the oven for? Haven't I told you to keep an eye on anything dangerous when I'm out?"

"But I knew nothing about it," Hannah protested,

trying carefully to tread the fine line of telling the truth and not getting herself into trouble for cheek. "Granny must have put them in the oven when I was at the door with the priest." She turned towards her grandmother now. "Isn't that right, Granny?"

Bridget shrugged. "All I know is that I didn't want the priest to be looking at young girls' underwear – or any kind of underwear – and I pulled them down from the pulley and shoved them into the oven. It was only lukewarm at the time."

Sheila was still holding out the poker with the charred evidence of Bridget's neglect.

"Well, it was obviously an accident, Mammy," Hannah said, "and I don't think the things could have gone up in flames in the oven or anything – the nylon in them has just kind of melted." She gave what she hoped was a placatory smile.

"The nylon in them has caused poisonous fumes that could have choked us all!" her mother hissed. "If it had been left long enough God knows what would have happened – and all you can do is grin like an eejit!" Sheila's voice had a recognisable crack in it and there was a slight but definite tremble in her body. "Nobody would believe the things I have to contend with. One of these days I'm going to walk out of this house – and if I ever get the guts up I'm going to just keep on walking."

"Now, now," Bridget Martin said to her daughter-in-law, "sure there's no need for talk like that. It was only a bit of an accident. There's no harm done and I'll give Hannah the money to buy new underwear." She looked at her granddaughter. "We'll all be that bit more careful from now on, won't we, Hannah?"

Hannah stole a glance at her mother, wishing with all her heart that she would carry out her oft-repeated threat to walk out on them. She wished that she would either change into a more kind and understanding mother or just go. But Hannah knew that there was little chance of that happening. She ground her teeth together in silence as her mother passed her by on the way to the bin with the blackened, offending articles.

Then she closed her eyes tightly and tried to block out the pain when her mother hit her on the back of the head with her knuckles as she came back in again.

Soon, Hannah thought, I'll be old enough to leave here. And when that time comes, I'm never, ever coming back.

Chapter 27

It was June before Rose began to see a thawing out in her father.

The subject of the dance had never been referred to again and neither Rose nor Paul had dared to mention any subsequent dances locally or in the surrounding area. They had kept to a strict routine of work and home and church.

"He'll get over it eventually," Martha Barry had told her granddaughter several weeks after the event. "I let him know about Hannah's little underhand tricks – although I had to be careful with her being a close family connection of your mother's. But your father – like a lot of people – can see no wrong in the girl. And he's very stubborn, you know. Even if he thinks there might be a grain of truth in it, he would find it hard to admit that he had the wool pulled over his eyes."

Rose had nodded. "I've tried to talk to him about it several times and so has Mammy, but he won't listen. He still says that Paul was entirely to blame and that even if I'm telling the truth I was a bigger fool to have it happen under my nose and not notice." Her voice was strained now. "Mammy was willing to believe what I told her even though Hannah is her sister's daughter. Why couldn't he? And apart from all of that, he still believes that me and Liam O'Connor were up to no good." She lifted her eyes to the ceiling. "When I think of that night that he caught hold of Liam down in Slattery's – I was mortified. He didn't let him say a word of explanation – he just threatened him and told him to stay away from me and Paul."

"Don't take it so bad," Martha said, patting her grand-daughter's shoulder. "All fathers can be like that at times. He was only protecting his own."

"I know that but I'm nearly nineteen years old and if I'm not allowed out to dances or anything like that I'm going to end up an old maid." Her mind flitted straight to Michael Murphy now and she felt her cheeks start to burn up. He had been very careful since the night of the dance. Word had obviously got out about her father reading the riot act about Paul and everything that had gone on with Liam O'Connor. Michael had still been polite and friendly enough when he and Ruairí came into the bar but it was almost as if the night he had danced with her and kissed her had never happened.

Martha moved closer now and gently put her arms around her granddaughter. "You might not think it now, but things often have a way of working themselves out for the best."

* * *

When Rose arrived in Slattery's for her evening shift the following Friday afternoon, both the landlord and his wife were in a strangely light – almost euphoric – mood. In fact, when Rose thought about it, they hadn't been their usual selves for the last couple of weeks. There had been an air of heightened tension around the shop, the pub and the house. It had been hard to pin down. It wasn't that there had been a bad atmosphere in the place, more of an unpredictable feel about things. Both of the Slatterys had seemed kind of distracted, as if their thoughts were a million miles away from the small pub on the shore of Galway Bay.

On a number of occasions, when she had gone into the kitchen, Joe had been talking on the phone in a hushed voice with Mary, brow furrowed, standing close by his side trying to listen in on the conversation. On each occasion the landlady had motioned Rose to go back into the bar.

But all now seemed brightness and light.

Rose went into the kitchen to get a basin of water to wash down the bar and the tables. The landlord and landlady were sitting in armchairs by the fire drinking tea and eating slices of a chocolate cake that had been bought from the travelling van that morning.

Joe got to his feet the minute Rose came in, as though he had been waiting for her. He put his mug of tea up on the mantelpiece. "Now, Miss Barry, sit you down here for a few minutes," he said, taking her by the shoulders and guiding her into the warm armchair he had just vacated.

Mary turned to her husband. "Pour Rose a cup of tea now and make sure you give her a saucer," she ordered, then she waved towards the table, "and she'll have a bit of that nice chocolate cake." No matter how often Mary told him to use the fine bone china cups, Joe always ended up offering people the same big mugs he drank from himself.

Rose immediately sensed that there was something

serious in the air. Mary Slattery always had chores waiting to be done in either the pub, the shop or the kitchen. And while she didn't mind Rose having a cup of tea, there was always an unspoken agreement that it was only deserved after a few hours of work had been put in.

Joe came over with the cup and saucer and handed it to Rose. She felt her hands shaking a little as she took them and sat them in her lap. And then she felt slightly flustered when her boss came towards her with a small plate with a thick slice of cake on it.

"Here," Joe said, sitting the side plate down on the wide arm of the chair. "You haven't hands enough to hold it – you'll manage it easier on there." Then he went over to get his mug from the mantelpiece and, pulling one of the wooden chairs over beside Rose, he at last sat down.

Rose was feeling really nervous by this time.

"We've a bit of news we wanted you to hear," Mary Slattery suddenly said. "Now, it's nothing for you to worry about." Her eyes flickered warningly in her husband's direction, lest he should jump in with his two big feet and say the wrong thing. "Nothing for you to worry about at all –"

Joe couldn't help himself. "We'll make sure you're all right –"

Mary held her hand up to silence him. "The fact of the matter is – we've sold the pub."

Rose's mouth opened in an 'O' of surprise. There was a small silence. "You've sold the pub?" she repeated, her voice cracked and high.

Joe nodded, then his hand came up to cup his chin – a sure sign he was uncomfortable with the conversation.

"We only got official word this morning that the sale had actually gone through."

"But it's not straight away," Mary butted in again. "We won't be going for a while. It could be weeks or months."

Rose slowly nodded her head, trying to digest this wholly unexpected news. Trying to work out what it would mean for her. Would it be no job? Would it be new bosses? Whatever it was it didn't bode well. "What will you do?" she asked, looking from one to the other. "Will you still be living in this house?" Then she had a sudden thought. "Will you keep the shop going?"

Joe made a little hissing sound between his teeth. "Ah, no, the whole thing is going in the one deal."

Rose nodded her head, suddenly feeling her lack of years and inexperience of life.

"Now, don't be worrying, Rose, there's a lot more to all this," Mary said. "There's good news as well." Her face broke into a beaming smile. "Joe and I have bought a nice hotel in the middle of Galway, with sixteen guest rooms and a reception area, a nice bar and dining-room, and we have four live-in staff bedrooms at the back for anybody that's living out of Galway. It needs a bit of work on it but when we do it up it'll be a little palace."

Joe sat back in the wooden chair now and folded his arms high across his chest. "And you were the first person we thought of for the staff quarters. We want you to move with us to Galway, Rose."

Rose caught her breath. It was all too much to take in. "*Me*? Me move to Galway?" Away from her mother and father? Away from her grandmother and Paul and

Veronica and Eileen? Away from Michael Murphy? Rose felt her throat suddenly dry and she gave a little cough to clear it. Then, for want of something to do, she lifted her forgotten cup of tea and took a sip from it.

Joe raised his eyebrows and nodded. "Sure, wouldn't it be a great chance for you? A clever girl like you! We could give you a try in the reception if you like." He winked over at Mary to signal that all would eventually work out. "Well, what do you think?"

Rose felt her cheeks flush. She was totally over-whelmed with the bombshell about the pub being sold and now she found herself having to make a life-changing decision about moving away from Kilnagree.

"I don't know," she told her boss. "To be honest, it's all a bit of a shock . . ."

"Well, take a bit of time to think about it," Mary said. "There's no immediate rush. We don't have to make any decisions for a week or two."

"Will you have to let the new owners know what I'm doing? If I was to go Galway, I suppose they'd have to look for somebody new." She forced a little smile. "They might be glad of somebody here who knows all the customers."

Joe shot an anxious glance across the room to his wife and his hand tightened on his jaw. "Well, it's not as straightforward as that," he said. "They have two lads of their own – a year or two older than yourself."

"They said they don't need any outside staff," said Mary. "They have enough between their own family to run the pub and shop." She gave a little sniff. "You can never depend on small places for a long-term job. So, as

306

you can see, it's just as well that you have the offer of the hotel job with us in Galway."

Rose looked down into her teacup and nodded her head slowly. Suddenly she could see it all quite clearly. The future that she thought was all mapped out in Kilnagree was now all falling away from her. The bit of independence she had from her small wages would now go. There was no other work in the village or in the surrounding villages that she knew of. Work was scarce and particularly so for young women.

Rose suddenly felt very stupid. Why had she not realised that this might one day happen? What had made her think that she was so special that she would hang on to one of the few paid jobs in the area? It had only been a part-time job and there had never been any likelihood of it being anything else.

"Can I think about it?" she said in a voice which was barely louder than a whisper.

"Of course you can," Mary Slattery told her. "We won't be looking for staff for the hotel for a week or two yet."

"And you'll have to talk it all over with your mother and father," Joe said. "It's a big step moving from a little village to the big city. And it's a bigger change leaving those that are close to you behind."

Mary suddenly made a move from the chair, signalling that the unscheduled conversation was now over. She went over to put her cup and saucer in the sink. "Take a few minutes to finish your tea and chocolate cake," she told Rose. "I'll see to the bar until you're finished."

Rose looked at the slice of cake and she knew that if she started to eat it, it would choke her.

Mary stopped as she reached the door. "Rose, we'd ask you to keep the news to yourself except for your family. We don't want them all chatting about it in the bar just yet until we've finalised things. We'll gradually tell them all in our own time."

"Oh, I won't say anything," Rose reassured her. Soon there would be no need. News travelled quickly in Kilnagree.

News like this would travel even more quickly.

Chapter 28

Rose put on her good lilac blouse, her black straight skirt and a brave face for her last Saturday night in Slattery's bar. She made a particular effort with her appearance to bolster her spirits because Mary Slattery had warned her that the new owners were coming out for the evening to be introduced to the locals.

"Just keep your head high and a smile on your face as usual," her grandmother told her, as she was preparing to leave the house.

"It's not easy to do that," Rose said, with wide, anxious eyes, "when Mrs Slattery is still being very cool with me. Joe's been okay but she's hardly broken breath to me since I told her I couldn't take the job."

Old Martha Barry's face darkened. "I suppose it's awkward for her – they would have liked to have somebody familiar in the new place who they knew was a hard worker and who they knew they could trust . . ." Her words hung in the air as she stood lost in thought, dusting white flour off her hands.

"Even if I *had* wanted to take the job," Rose said,

"my father wouldn't hear of it. He said the only way I would leave this house is when I have a husband to support me." She went over to the small glass bowl on the dresser and lifted out a black velvet ribbon. Then she gathered her thick dark hair back, low on her neck, and deftly tied the ribbon in a neat bow.

"I suppose your father is only looking out for you . . . wanting to keep you close to home," Martha said in a low voice. "Maybe when he sees how it is when you have no work . . ." Then, afraid she would say the wrong thing, she turned back to the two large lumps of dough she was kneading. Whilst for her own selfish reasons she was glad that her granddaughter wasn't leaving home to go to the big city in Galway, there was a little voice at the back of her head that told her that Rose was too clever to be stuck at home every single day in a small place like Kilnagree. But she knew that she would miss Rose desperately if she decided to go.

There was a noise at the back door and they both glanced up to see Kathleen coming in carrying a basket of fresh laundry that she had just taken from the line. "You're off down below?" she said, smiling at her daughter.

Rose lifted her coat from the back of the door. "I was just saying to Granny that I'm a small bit anxious about it – Mrs Slattery is still very cool with me."

"Well, don't be anxious," Kathleen told her firmly. She brushed a strand of hair that the breeze had caught back into place. "They had no right to put you in such a position." Her eyes flickered towards the hall door. "She knows well what your father is like and she should have known he wouldn't fall in with any plans like that."

Rose shrugged. "It's not just my father – I don't want

to leave Kilnagree." Her eyes filled up with tears. "But I don't want to be out of work either . . ."

Her mother came towards her, touched the top of her long dark hair and then affectionately ran her hand down the ponytail. "Leave it be for just now," she advised. "We might hear something back about the cleaning job in the doctor's house in Gort."

Rose felt her heart sink. Cycling over to Gort every day to do cooking and cleaning was the last thing she wanted. And it wasn't just that it would take her an hour to cycle over there, it was more to do with the fact that Michael Murphy worked in the bank in Gort, while she would be working in a lowly menial job in the same town.

While it wasn't exactly a professional occupation, working in the pub and the shop had a bit more substance to it than being a housemaid.

But she couldn't really say to her mother that she didn't want a cleaning job in Gort in case Michael Murphy suddenly suggested that they start courting. And she knew it was stupid of her to even think it, because he had really shown no interest in her since Easter. Since the night of the dance. She had even begun to wonder if it had all been in her imagination – if, in fact, Michael had really been interested in Hannah. If perhaps he had only latched onto her at the dance because her cousin had shown more interest in Liam O'Connor. But she knew there was no point in going over it all again. What was done was done. The way things were with her father and lads since the night of the dance had ensured that Michael Murphy wasn't going to approach her.

* * *

Rose was brushing around the tables in the empty bar when Joe Slattery came through from the store-cupboard carrying a crate of beer.

"I think we could be busy enough tonight," he panted, lifting the crate up onto the bar counter. "I let it be known that there would be a few free drinks for any musicians that turn up this evening and I've heard there's fellas travelling out from Kinvara and Ballyvaughan." He put his hands on his hips now. "And no doubt we'll have the usual crowd from around Kilnagree as well. It should be a good night – we want it to look good for the new people."

Rose leaned her brush against a table and then lifted her hands behind her head to tighten the black velvet ribbon. Michael and Ruairí Murphy would be there of course, as they were most Saturdays. It had been that way every Saturday for the last year or so. But things were going to change in a big way now. She would have little or no opportunity to see the brothers from now on. It would only be from across the churchyard at Mass on Sundays or at the occasional dance if she was ever allowed back to one. She lifted her brush again to continue with her work and it was only then that she realised the landlord was staring at her.

Joe Slattery rubbed his chin with one hand. "To be honest now, I'm vexed about you, Rose," he suddenly said, "and so is Mary. We were tryin' to give you a bit of a chance offering you the job in Galway."

Rose lifted her head sharply and he held his hands up.

"What I mean is – we thought it would have suited you as well as it would have suited us. You're a fine, intelligent girl who knows the right thing to do and say – you'd have been a great addition to us in the hotel. And we thought it would it would be a great opportunity for you – more money, for the job would be full-time, a nice uniform for working on reception, and your own little room. And you could easily catch the bus home on your weekends off back to Kilnagree." He shrugged and raised his eyebrows. "Sure, it could have been the making of you."

Rose's grip tightened on the brush. "It's very good of you both to have thought of me," she said, "but I couldn't move away to Galway just now . . ."

"I know, I know," he said, nodding his head. "I spoke to your father and he told me that you were needed up at the house and about your granny not being well and everything." He paused. "But you have a life to live as well and they'll have to let go of the reins at some point. And it wasn't as if you were leavin' the country or anything – sure it's only a hop, skip and a jump into Galway on the coach. And while we would give you a job next year or the year after, there's no saying that we'll be needing staff when it would suit you to come." He waved his hand towards the window. "Sure, there's nothing around here for young ones – it's a dead-end alley. Anybody that has anything about them – any kind of ambition - is heading off to England or America."

Rose started moving the brush in a circle around the table. "I suppose they are," she said in a vague manner. What else could she say? It was obvious that Joe and Mary Slattery saw her as immature and lacking in ambition – and maybe she was. But she wasn't ready or prepared for a move to Galway or anywhere else at this particular minute in time. In fact, Rose doubted if she ever would be ready to leave Kilnagree – and why should she? It had to be one of the most beautiful places in Ireland and it held all the people she knew and loved.

Rose was grateful when the sounds of half a dozen bicycles skidding to a halt at the front of the pub brought the conversation with the landlord to a close. And as a group of lads came through the door, Rose's heavy heart lifted when she saw the two fair-headed brothers at the back – Michael carrying the fiddle and Ruairí with his squeezebox. They both had tin whistles in their top pockets as well.

The music started off a bit earlier than usual which immediately set the tone for a lively night in the bar. Rose's uncles came in and, after ordering their pints of beer, went to their usual table. A short while later her father appeared and Rose was relieved that he seemed relaxed and easy enough in himself. And she was even more relieved when Liam O'Connor arrived with a group and her father didn't seem perturbed by it. Liam was quiet and polite when he ordered the drinks but all the usual familiarity was suppressed in Stephen Barry's presence. The night he had been wrongly accused of leading Paul astray was still very raw. Rose felt guilty that he had been dragged into the family dispute and she felt almost grateful when Liam gave her a discreet but friendly wink as she handed him his change.

The new owners of Slattery's turned out to be very nice people – which in a strange way was the opposite of how Rose had hoped they would be. She would have found it much easier to walk away from her job if the Purcells had been aloof and distant towards her. She would have been able to tell herself and her family and friends that she was better off having left when the Slatterys left – that the new owners weren't the kind of people she would have liked to work for. But instead they were friendly and nice and she couldn't say a bad word about them. The prospective landlord – Dermot – had asked her to come through the back and he and his wife Agnes had explained all about how sorry they were that they had to let her go.

"We just wouldn't have enough work to keep you on a regular basis," Dermot had explained, "but if we're busy over the summer or at Christmas or, God forbid, if anybody's sick, then you'll be the first we'll call."

Rose had blushed and been all embarrassed and said she understood, and that really she was busy at home. She had been even more embarrassed when she was introduced to their two short, stocky sons – Gerald and Tom – who weren't much older than her. They had been equally nice and said there probably wouldn't even be enough work for both of them and that they were intending to buy a small boat to have a sideline in fishing.

In spite of all the awkwardness Rose was pleased in a way that the pub was full and busy and that there was a great atmosphere. There were at least a dozen musicians and they had kept the music going all night. Joe Slattery had generously bought them several pints of beer each and the regular customers were delighted to be given a farewell drink on the house by the Slatterys and then another round as a welcome from the new landlord.

"This night will be well remembered for years to come," Stephen Barry said to his two brothers, when Rose brought the second free round of drinks to their table. "I can't ever recall a bar being so generous before."

Rose was kept busy rushing back and forth behind the bar and every so often she had to go out on the floor to collect glasses from the tables. She noticed that her father seemed more relaxed than normal and had turned his chair around to face the musicians. Whether it was due to the extra free drinks, Rose didn't know, but she was just grateful that he wasn't serious and cross-looking as he had been for weeks after the dance at Easter.

Mary Slattery's mood towards Rose had also thawed out and she had been as nice as pie to her for most of the evening. At first Rose had thought the landlady was only putting on a front for the Purcells, but when Mary – flushed from the brandies she had downed – put her arm around Rose and said she would miss her, Rose was delighted.

"And we'll do our best to find you a job in the hotel if you change your mind," she said. "It might only be cleaning the rooms or working in the kitchen to start off, but we would give you one of the more professional jobs as soon as we had a vacancy." She had also told Rose to make sure she waited behind at the end of the night as she had her severance pay to give her and a small present.

When the Murphy boys finished one particularly difficult round of music, her father actually got up out of his seat and went over and shook their hands, and then he stood chatting to both the boys for a while. Later, when Ruairí went to join in with the musicians again, Rose noticed that her father and Michael continued chatting. She mused to herself that it was strange that today of all days she should feel easier about things than she had for weeks.

It was towards the end of the night – when the musicians were starting to pack away their instruments – that Michael Murphy came to the end of the bar where

Rose was mopping up a spilled glass of beer. When she looked up at him, she noticed that he looked slightly hesitant and not quite so sure of himself.

"I'm glad I've caught you on your own, Rose," he told her, "because I wanted to ask you something . . ."

Rose put her cloth down and waited nervously.

"Well, it's just that I received an invitation," he started off. "One of the girls in the bank . . ."

Rose felt her face stiffen. Why on earth should he be telling her about another girl inviting him out?

"It's a wedding," he went on, his face starting to redden. "I've got an invitation to a wedding in Gort – and I've been told I can bring a partner . . ."

Rose looked at him, wondering if she was hearing him correctly.

"It's in three weeks' time and I wondered if you'd like to come with me?"

It was Michael Murphy's turn to wait now as Rose stared at him in surprise.

"You want me to go to a wedding with you?" she said in a high, incredulous voice.

Michael nodded. "I'd be delighted if you could come . . ."

Rose felt her throat tighten and she glanced across the room to where her father was sitting chatting to his two brothers. Was there any point in asking him, she wondered. And how could she explain to Michael that her father had banned her from leaving the house apart from church and family visits?

Then, as if he had read her thoughts, he suddenly said, "I hope you don't mind but I had a word with your father about it. I thought I'd take the chance when we were standing talking earlier."

Rose caught her breath. She couldn't believe that he'd had the nerve to approach her father.

"He said it would be no problem," Michael continued. "He said if you wanted to go, then he had no objections, just as long as I saw you home and made sure that you weren't drinking or anything." He paused. "What do you say?"

Rose couldn't stop a beaming smile from spreading on her face. "I'd love to come!" she said, then immediately knew she had sounded too enthusiastic. But it didn't matter, because he was smiling back just as warmly.

"Grand," he said. "I'll bring the invitation with me to Mass on Sunday and we can make plans for travelling over to Gort on the day."

"We can cycle over," Rose suggested.

He shook his head and smiled. "No need. One of the lads in the bank will be coming out this way in his car and he said he'd be happy to give us a lift. It's more or less organised."

"That all sounds lovely," she told him.

They had a few more words together and then Michael went off to join the others, leaving Rose with a warm glow inside her. Then, as she glanced over in her father's direction again, their eyes locked and he winked over at her.

Rose's heart soared. He had – after the long, cold weeks – forgiven her. He had also given his blessing about her going to the wedding with Michael Murphy. At long last he was seeing her as a grown woman.

The day she had dreaded – her last day in Slattery's pub – had suddenly turned into one of the best days she'd ever had. The new owners of the bar had said she would be the first one they would call if there was any extra work. And Joe and Mary Slattery had both intimated that they would find her some kind of work if she changed her mind. They had also given her a present of a beautiful silver brooch in the shape of two leaves with a row of tiny pearls in the middle.

And her father had decided it was time to forget about the mistakes that had been made back in the spring.

But the best thing of all was that Michael Murphy had now openly declared an interest in her by asking her officially to accompany him to a wedding. This was more than Rose had ever hoped for.

Something deep down told her that it was the start of something new in her life.

Chapter 29

Leonora padded barefoot across her bedroom floor. She slid her feet into her slippers and then lifted her dressing-gown from the hook on the back of the door and put it on. Then she went downstairs as quietly as possible so as not to disturb her housekeeper.

It was three o'clock in the morning and Leonora had lain awake for the last half an hour staring into the darkness. Her mind had started to wander and worry. She knew the signs and she knew that there was only one thing that would help.

She went into the kitchen and switched on the kettle. Then she went into the sitting room to the cupboard where the drinks were kept. She lifted a bottle of Bushmill's Whiskey and held it up to see how much was in it, then she put it on top of the cupboard while she retrieved a bottle of brandy from further back on the shelf. She then measured both bottles up, deciding which one Mrs O'Shea was likely to notice least.

She decided on the brandy and put the whiskey bottle back in its place.

As she carried the bottle through into the kitchen, she wondered why she cared about Lizzie's opinion on her having a drink whenever she felt like it. It was her own house after all – it was her own business. And it certainly wasn't her housekeeper's business to comment on or to keep tabs on her drinking habits. And she knew perfectly well that Lizzie wasn't the type of person to be critical about anyone having a drink – she enjoyed the odd one herself. And she had never given Lizzie's opinion a thought when she and Andrew sat up many a night having several drinks.

As she poured a good measure of the brandy into a large mug, it suddenly dawned on Leonora that it wasn't really Lizzie who was disapproving about the drink – it was *herself*.

She had already drunk two large whiskeys before going to bed – and several glasses of wine earlier in the evening.

Leonora knew that she was drinking too much and she was doing it too often.

But as she poured the boiling water from the kettle into the mug, she knew that it had helped her to get through the last few years. It had been her comfort and her sedative.

It had helped her to get through the long and lonely nights.

She carried the mug very carefully up the stairs and tip-toed back into her bedroom. She put the mug down on the bedside table at her side, plumped her pillows up straight to support her back and then climbed into bed. She sat for a while sipping the hot brandy, then she put the mug back down on the table and got back out of bed. She went over to a mahogany tallboy in a corner of the room and opened the bottom drawer. Then she took out two photograph albums.

Back in bed again, she took a good mouthful of her

hot drink, put her glasses on and opened the albums. Leonora did this so often she could visualise every photograph before she turned the pages. The photographs that marked every stage of her life.

The photographs that marked all the precious things she had lost.

Leonora sipped her brandy as she turned the pages and by the end of the second album, her tears had obscured her vision. She let the album slip out of her hand to join the other one down on the floor, then she lay back amongst her pillows with her eyes closed.

She lay for a while, and then she suddenly sat bolt upright. She turned to check the time on her alarm clock. It was just after half past three. That meant that it was just after half past ten in New York.

She reached across to the black phone that Lizzie had carefully polished that afternoon, lifted it onto her lap and dialled the operator. A minute or two later, she hear Edward's number ringing.

It barely rang twice when it was answered. Then, as she went to speak her son's voice quickly rushed over hers.

"Christopher . . . thank God you rang back . . . I was really worried that you were angry with me for phoning the house but I honestly would have hung up if Theresa had answered. I couldn't wait any longer to speak to you. I feel I'm going mad . . . it's ages since we've had a whole night together." There was a pause. "My life is so fucking pointless when I'm not with you . . ."

Leonora felt a cold, heavy weight descend upon her chest, and her free hand came up to cover her mouth. *No, no!* she thought. *Please don't let it be that . . . not that . . .*

Edward went on in a hushed, desperate voice, "It's weeks since I've seen you and I just can't bear it . . . Since we finished working together, my life is falling apart I'm going into this new office every day and I find myself just staring at the walls thinking of you. I can't concentrate at work and I can't sleep at night."

He paused again for a few terrible moments, allowing Leonora's brain to reach the only possible conclusion. And then his next words underlined it, so that she was left without the smallest, kindest, sliver of doubt.

"I know you're worried about Theresa finding out about us."

Unaware that she had been holding her breath, Leonora suddenly took a loud, deep gulp of air.

"Christopher?" Edward whispered into the phone. "Speak to me . . . *please* speak to me . . ."

Silently, Leonora hung up the phone.

Due to the cruellest coincidence in timing, she was now left with no doubt as to what had caused the change in Edward. Quite clearly, he and his old school friend, Christopher Hennessey, were having some kind of clandestine affair. She had to face it now – they were obviously having a *homosexual* affair. And however awful and difficult it was for her to face the fact that her eldest son was not living a normal life, it was made far, far worse by the fact that Christopher Hennessey had a wife and a child. Leonora buried her head in her hands.

The thing she had dreaded most had come true.

* * *

Leonora heard her housekeeper go downstairs just after

seven o'clock. She gave her a short while to get the fires going and then she followed her down into the kitchen.

"You're up very early," Mrs O'Shea said with some surprise.

"I couldn't sleep . . . I've been awake for hours." Leonora tightened the belt of her dressing-gown.

"It's a bit cold for you to be up at this time," the Scotswoman said. "The fire is barely lit in the sitting-room."

"I'll be fine. We hardly need fires at this time of the year. Yesterday was fairly warm." She went over to the window to look out over the garden. "It looks as though it's going to be a reasonable day again."

There was a little silence, then Mrs O'Shea said, "Are you all right? If you don't mind me passing a remark, I'd say you're looking a wee bit peaky this morning."

A wee bit peaky? Leonora thought wryly to herself. I suppose anyone would look at least a wee bit peaky when they've just had a bombshell drop into their lives. "I'm just a bit tired with not having slept too well."

"I could tell by the kettle," Lizzie said.

Leonora turned back from the window to look at her with some bemusement.

The housekeeper tapped the side of the kettle. "It was still lukewarm when I went to put it on this morning."

"Oh . . ." Leonora said in a flat voice, "I got up around three o'clock to make myself a hot drink." She pulled a chair out from under the kitchen table.

Mrs O'Shea looked at her with narrowed eyes. "You need to look after yourself a bit more. I'm forever telling you that. You've been doing too much out in that garden. You should leave all that heavy digging to Tommy. It's no work for a woman of your standing."

Leonora looked at her and managed the vestige of a small smile. "I enjoy it. It's a hobby and it gives me great pleasure to watch all the things I've planted growing. The garden is a great source of peacefulness and delight to me – I don't know what I'd have done without it these last few years."

"Well, I have to admit that it does look lovely," Mrs O'Shea said grudgingly, "although if I'm honest, the bit of the garden that I'm most interested in is the drying green." Her eyes lit up. "As long as the grass is kept neat and tidy and Tommy keeps the weeds out of the paths so that I can get in and out with the lovely fresh laundry, then I'm happy." She glanced out of the window now. "I'll get the washing out early this morning and then I'm going to tackle the inside and outside of the kitchen windows. I wasn't too sure about doing them yesterday with it being the first fine day we've had in a while, but I'm going to get stuck into them today."

She rattled on about laundry and cleaning windows as she made tea and boiled two eggs each for them, while Leonora sat at the table nodding and smiling – her mind far away from Glenmore House.

Far away in New York.

At one point as they sat at the table over breakfast, she fleetingly considered confiding in her housekeeper about Edward but dismissed it quickly. She knew that the Scotswoman adored all her children but had a particular soft spot for Edward, being the eldest. Mrs O'Shea had looked after all three children as if they were her own, and would undoubtedly judge Edward's situation with the same love and understanding that a mother would. But something held Leonora back from telling her.

However hard it was for her to find understanding of her

own son's sexual leanings, it was going to be much harder for Lizzie. She was an older woman with no children of her own – and a Catholic to boot. Not that the Church of Ireland would be any more tolerant of the situation. In any case, Lizzie had enough on her plate at the moment with her brother back in Glasgow. And although she didn't say too much about it, Leonora knew that it was always there at the back of her mind. It was worrying her enough to visit the local church on a daily basis. If she didn't make morning Mass, then she went for a walk down to the church in the afternoon or evenings to light a few candles for Willie.

It wouldn't be fair to add to Lizzie's heavy burden and she knew the housekeeper would feel that Edward's serious situation would warrant a mountain of candles.

Whilst the housekeeper wasn't the right confidante, Leonora knew she would have to discuss the situation with someone. But *who*? Who could she discuss such a shocking subject with?

If only Andrew was still alive. He would have known *exactly* the right thing to say and do. He always did. Even when things had gone cold between them, she found she had still been able to discuss their children openly and honestly. But Andrew wasn't there any more, and there was no point in going down that regretful road.

The other person who would have been a wise and caring confidante about any subject was Daniel Levy – but their once friendly, trusting relationship was no longer available to her. That was the price she now had to pay for allowing him to come too close.

She supposed she would have to tell Diana at some stage – and Jonathan. And then she halted to wonder if she actually had the right to tell them. She could almost hear

Andrew's voice telling her that Edward was a grown man and his sexual persuasion was his own private business.

The fact that fate and coincidence had stepped in to alert his mother about the situation was one thing – the decision to tell his family and friends was another.

By the time she had forced half of the breakfast she didn't want down and had gone back upstairs and got washed and dressed, Leonora knew that she had to take some kind of action to get Edward away from the horrendous situation in America. She had to get him back home, where she could help and advise him, and try to get him to change the destructive course he was plunging headlong into.

She was going to seek advice from the one person who she knew would not be shocked by her news. She would go and see Terry Cassidy.

* * *

As soon as she saw Leonora's stricken face, the colourfully dressed artist ushered her into the cottage and poured them both a large port – the only alcoholic drink she had available in the house.

"Start from the beginning," she said, straightening the bow on a floral scarf she had tied her hair up with, "and take as long as you need."

When Leonora had finished telling her story, Terry stared at her for a few moments.

"I know you might find this a bit strange and personal – but do you have any kind of an illness at all?" she asked. "I know you mentioned some time ago that you had an appointment with your doctor."

"Illness?" A flush came over Leonora's face and neck.

"No – thankfully I'm in reasonably good fettle," she said, her brow furrowed in confusion and her tone a little prickly. "I've never had anything serious." Anything to do with her health made her feel slightly vulnerable and conscious of her age.

"It's just that if you did have some kind of an illness, it would be useful to play it up now and use it as an excuse to bring Edward home."

The penny dropped. "Ah . . . I see what you're getting at . . ." Leonora raised her eyebrows. "Well, actually, I haven't told anyone this – but the last time I went to the doctor he said that the symptoms could indicate a mild heart condition – angina. He wasn't too worried but said if it reoccurred he would send me to the hospital for tests."

"Perfect!" Terry said, clasping her hands together. "It means you don't have to feel guilty about lying – you're merely exaggerating. All you have to do is phone Edward and tell him that the doctor says that you shouldn't be left alone as it's possible you may need surgery – or something along those lines. Tell him you're so worried that you can't sleep at night and would be grateful if he could take some time off work to be with you."

"What about Mrs O'Shea? He knows I have her for company."

"Tell him that she's too old to be responsible for you," Terry replied.

"Doesn't it sound a bit weak?" Leonora asked. "He may think *I'm* beginning to get old and frail."

"It doesn't matter what he thinks," Terry told her. "As long as you get him away from the destructive situation he's in back in America."

Chapter 30

On the morning of the wedding in Gort, Rose's thoughts moved to Leonora Bentley as she checked her appearance in the wardrobe mirror. She was wearing one of the outfits the Dublin woman had given her – the black and white flowered dress with the fashionably broad belt. She had a small black hat pinned on her newly washed, gleaming, dark hair, and she carried the small beaded black evening bag for the first time. As a finishing touch, she had lavishly dabbed on her *Chanel No. 5.*

Rose was so, so grateful for the outfits Leonora had given her, because she could never have afforded to buy a new rig-out for the wedding, especially now that she didn't have regular work. But she had been able to afford to buy a beautiful pair of black patent leather shoes from a good shoe shop in Galway. Her mother had insisted that she buy them from her last pay-packet.

Rose was over the moon to get the shoes and luckily, as things had turned out, she had recently got quite a bit of work down in Purcell's Bar – as it was now called. Mrs Purcell's mother had taken ill and she had gone over to

Ennis to look after her for a couple of weeks. Dermot Purcell had said that he would be glad of Rose showing his two lads the ropes in both the bar and the shop, as they hadn't a clue when it came to operating the tills and dealing with the delivery vans.

Rose had been particularly glad that she'd agreed to help the Purcells out because the doctor's wife in Gort had phoned Kathleen Barry at the Guards' Barracks, to ask if Rose could come out to work at the house on a month's trial. Rose had been eternally grateful that her mother had explained that she wasn't free to take up the position at the moment due to a prior commitment. Seemingly, the doctor's wife had gone off in a huff, saying that she had any number of girls who would be glad of the position. Rose reckoned that if the woman was so awkward on the phone she would have been even worse to deal with as a boss. And she was secretly relieved that she wouldn't have to work as a menial cleaner and cook in the town where Michael Murphy worked in the bank.

Rose sat at the kitchen table with her mother and granny waiting for Michael Murphy and the other lads to appear. Every so often she glanced down at her feet and felt a surge of pride as she looked at the patent stiletto-heeled shoes. They were the highest heels she'd ever worn and she couldn't believe the difference they made to the length of her slim legs. She felt all elegant wearing them with the hat and the fancy little bag. She had borrowed her mother's pearls and matching earrings and she also wore the Slatterys' silver and pearl brooch pinned on her dress. She had put the lightest touch of powder on, along with a new pink lipstick and black mascara she'd bought the day she went into Galway for the shoes. As she checked her make-up in her small compact mirror, she was glad her father was off working a few miles away with Paul, because she knew he wouldn't approve of her being all made up. He would probably have said nothing because it was for a wedding, but Rose would have known what he thought.

When Veronica and Eileen came running in to say the car was on its way up the hill, Rose had looked from her mother to her granny. "Oh, I suddenly feel really anxious," she told them, her stomach all tight and fluttery. "I won't know anybody there apart from Michael . . ."

"You'll be grand," her mother told her, going over to open the door. "Once you get into the car and get chatting to the other lads, you'll be the finest."

"You'll be the belle of the ball!" her granny told her and as Rose passed by her, she grasped her hand and whispered, "Hannah couldn't hold a candle to you, the way you look today!" Then the old lady had winked.

* * *

By local standards, it was a big wedding. The church was packed and it was obvious to Rose that Michael was well known in the town as she noticed numerous people glancing over to see who the dark-haired girl with him was. When the crowds all poured out after the wedding ceremony into the churchyard to watch the photographs being taken, Rose felt slightly nervous at not really knowing anyone but then Michael introduced her to some of the girls he worked with and their boyfriends and they were so nice and friendly she immediately felt much better.

When the photographs were finished, everyone walked

around to the local hall where the reception was being held, and Rose felt a little thrill when Michael held his arm out for her to link as they strolled along.

"I'm sorry I can't walk too fast in these shoes," Rose said, as they encountered the stony path that led into the hall.

"Ah, sure there's no big rush," he told her, smiling. Then he leaned in towards her and said in a low voice, "Rose, you look lovely today. You always look lovely – you're one of the best dressed girls in Kilnagree – but the dress and shoes, *everything* you're wearing today looks very elegant." He squeezed her arm. "You look a million dollars and I'm proud to have you as my partner for the wedding . . ." He broke off then, slightly embarrassed, as though conscious that he had got a bit carried away.

But Rose didn't think he'd got carried away – in fact her heart had soared at the compliment. "Thank you, Michael," she said, and then offered up a silent prayer of thanks to Leonora Bentley.

* * *

After the meal and the speeches, Michael and Rose joined his friends in the bar.

The two girls decided they would have a sherry each, then the lads looked at Rose.

"A lemonade would be lovely," she told them.

Pauric put his hands on his hips. "Sure, you're at a wedding, Rose," he told her. "You're supposed to be celebrating – you're allowed to have an oul' drink today! Why don't you have a sherry or a glass of wine or something a bit more adventurous?"

Rose glanced over at Michael and when their eyes locked she knew he was remembering back to the night of the dance when Paul got drunk.

He smiled and then winked at her. "Trust me, one drink will do you no great harm."

Rose thought for a moment. "Okay. I'll go mad so and have a sherry." Her father hadn't actually said anything about her drinking at the wedding but she reckoned that no one would tackle her over one little drink. There was no fear of her going any further.

The boys came back from the bar a short while later and Rose noticed that the girls' glasses had a more generous measure than would have been served in the bar, but she said nothing.

She sipped on the drink very slowly and carefully, having only ever had the odd mouthful of alcohol to see if she actually liked the taste. This wasn't too bad at all. The sherry was sweet and warming and by the time she was halfway down the glass Rose could see exactly why people could be easily tempted. She discovered that it gave her a lovely warm glow inside and made her feel more relaxed and carefree. But that, she knew only too well, was the danger and it made her even more resolute that she would definitely stick to just the one drink.

As the band were setting up to start playing, Rose decided to go to the ladies' and was delighted that she didn't feel too self-conscious – she even stopped to chat to one or two people on the way over. She checked her appearance in the mirror and then went into one of the cubicles. Just as she was closing the door, she heard two women come in all laughing and chatting as they checked their hair and make-up in the large mirror over the sinks.

Rose paid no heed to them as they talked about this one and that one at the wedding. Then, just as she was about to come back out of the cubicle, she heard one of them say something that made her hand freeze on the door handle.

"Did you see the young, good-looking fella that works in the bank?"

"The Murphy fella from Kilnagree? I surely did!"

"And did you see the fine-looking girl he has with him? He's fairly landed on his feet with her. They make a lovely couple. I think half of the girls in Gort will have their eyes put out when they get to hear that he's courting somebody like that."

"Did you see the lovely rig-out she's wearing?" The woman had lowered her voice now but Rose could still hear.

"Oh, I'd say her family must be well-to-do. You wouldn't buy that outfit for small money."

A big, beaming smile spread over Rose's face. It was one thing hearing a compliment from people who might just be trying to be nice to you but it had to be genuine when they didn't even know you were listening. She stood very still now, waiting for them to leave.

"I can tell you now that that young one is from a very ordinary family. One of the women I was talking to earlier said her husband has seen the girl working in the pub in Kilnagree. Wouldn't that surprise you?"

Rose's smile faded at the turn in the conversation and a tight little knot started to form in her chest.

"You're codding me! She looks like a real lady!"

"Well, she's not. But she might well have some rich relations somewhere, because how else could she afford those clothes?"

"Your guess is as good as mine. Apparently her mother is the housekeeper in Kilnagree Guards' Barracks and by all accounts she's still a fine-looking woman, too."

Rose felt the slightest tinge of relief at the compliment to her mother and hoped they would leave their discussion at that point.

There was a small pause, then the woman went on. "According to that lady at the table who knows them, there was some talk about her mother recently . . ."

"Indeed . . . what kind of talk?"

Just then, the outer door of the ladies' room swung open and two young girls ran in giggling and laughing, bringing the gossiping ladies' conversation to an abrupt halt.

Rose waited a full five minutes until she was sure there was no one around, and then she slowly came out of the cubicle and went to stand in front of the mirror. Her face was pale and solemn. She was so self-conscious now she felt like sneaking out of the side door of the hall and walking all the way back home.

But she couldn't, of course.

She couldn't do that to Michael Murphy. It wasn't his fault that people were talking about her. She stared at herself in the mirror and had to blink back hot tears. What on earth had that woman been insinuating about her mother? What could people possibly have to say about her? Only that she was a hard worker who looked after her husband and family well.

Then a burning feeling of indignation began to grow

inside her. Those two women were obviously a pair of old gossips who looked for the worst in people. Rose knew one or two like that in Kilnagree. She supposed there were people like that everywhere. Why should she care what they thought about her clothes or about the fact that she worked in a bar? Wouldn't it have been far worse if they had been saying that her clothes looked terrible and that they didn't know what Michael saw in her? If it were Hannah, she wouldn't give a damn what other women said about her – in fact she would have laughed and said they were only jealous.

Rose decided that on this occasion she would have to adopt her cousin's attitude or ruin the whole wedding for herself – and for Michael. She looked in the mirror now and made herself smile. Then she took out her powder puff, dabbed her face again and reapplied her pink lipstick. She took a deep breath to relax, squared her shoulders and stood tall with her head held high.

She was going to go back into the hall now – every bit as confident as when she had walked out of it. She would sit down at the table and finish off the rest of the sherry and get that nice confident glow again, and she would enjoy the remainder of the wedding. She would remind herself that Michael Murphy could have had the pick of any girl in Kilnagree or in Gort – but he had chosen her. And he had told her that she looked lovely earlier on and given her lots of compliments.

When she strode back into the hall – back straight and head held high – Rose could see Michael watching her anxiously and when he caught her eye he waved.

When she reached the table he looked up at her. "I

was getting worried in case you'd got lost," he smiled, "or in case some other fellow had lured you away."

Rose forced herself to laugh. "Not at all," she said. "I'm not that kind of girl! I got chatting to two women in the ladies' and I couldn't get away." Then the band struck up an old-time waltz and, as the groom led the bride onto the floor to much applause, Michael leaned forward and took her hand. "Miss Barry," he said, squeezing her hand gently, "shall we take to the floor?"

As Rose looked back at him their eyes met and all her worries about what people thought simply melted away. She stood up and followed him onto the dance floor. The rest of the afternoon and evening passed in a lovely sociable haze of chatting to the other girls beside her and dancing with Michael and his very pleasant workmates. When the end of the night came, Michael took her up onto the floor for the last waltz and he held her so close she was sure she could feel his heart beating.

"I've enjoyed every minute of today," he whispered into her ear. "You're great company. Will you come out with me again, Rose? There's a film-show of all the outings in the parish for the last ten years in the hall next Friday evening. I think it would be a great oul' *craic*. Do you think you'd be allowed to go? "

Rose looked up at him and nodded. This was what she had been hoping for – what she had been dreaming about. She would now be officially courting Michael Murphy and as long as she did everything correctly, she was sure her father would have no objections.

If things went the way she hoped with Michael, then she could just tick along in Kilnagree, seeing him regularly until things became more serious. She would be content with doing the odd shift down at Purcell's bar, knowing that better things lay ahead for her. Knowing the way that romances went in the small villages, there was every chance that their relationship would eventually turn into marriage. And if that was the case, there would be no need for her to think of going to Galway or anywhere else for work.

It was all a matter of time and patience. As her granny was fond of saying – *All good things come to those who wait.*

* * *

The following Friday night Rose was all dressed and waiting for Michael at half past seven as he had said he would cycle up to collect her at the house and then they would walk down to the hall together. As Rose had anticipated, her father was quiet when she'd asked if it was all right for Michael to call at the house for her but he had not voiced any objections. He had just warned her not to be out too late and to behave herself according to the way she had been brought up. Her mother and her granny had been delighted and when Stephen wasn't around had quizzed her endlessly about the wedding and about how she and Michael had got on. She got the same reception from her friend, Cathy.

"If you play your cards right," Cathy told her, "you'll be set up with Michael Murphy from now on. He's had an eye for you for years and you suit each other down to the ground!"

Rose had just smiled and shook her head but said nothing either way. She didn't want to jeopardise her big chance by being too confident.

Half past seven came and there was no sign of Michael and then the hands on the old kitchen clock turned to quarter to eight. They were supposed to be down at the hall for eight o'clock. Rose tried not to look too anxious – in any case things never ever started on time in the village.

But when eight o'clock came she started to get worried.

Then, around quarter past eight she heard the bicycle wheels crunching on the gravel outside and she flew to the door.

"I'm sorry I'm late," Michael told her, all out of breath and red in the face, "but I had my uncles and everybody calling out to the house this evening to talk to me and Ruairí and I couldn't get away." He paused for a moment to catch his breath. "The letter we were waiting for came through this morning – we had applied for it last year but we thought it had all fallen through." He raised his eyebrows now and shrugged. "It seems that a friend of my uncle in Boston managed to pull a few strings and everything is organised for the pair of us now to head over in September."

Rose looked at him in bemusement. "What are you talking about?" she asked.

"About Ruairí and me going to Boston. I'm sure I mentioned it to you a few months ago." He paused, his forehead wrinkling in thought. "On the other hand . . . maybe I didn't mention it because I thought it was all off."

Rose's face paled and her throat started to close. "You're going to America?" she repeated, her voice suddenly croaky. "Do you mean for a holiday?"

Michael shook his head "No, not just for a holiday," he said, an awkward sort of smile coming to his lips. "We're emigrating."

Chapter 31

It was several weeks before Leonora found the right time – and the courage – to make the phone call to bring Edward back to Ireland.

She had planned to do it earlier but the last time she spoke to him he had a heavy cold and sounded so flat and ill that she knew she couldn't broach the subject then. She had cut the call short, telling him to go straight to bed with a hot drink and some aspirins.

Then she had lain awake all night worrying about him being sick and depressed on his own and she had to have a couple of strong drinks to help her sleep.

She dialled his number this time, determined to see things through.

"Edward, how are you?" she started off. "I do hope you're feeling better."

"The worst of it has gone and I'm fine now," he told her. "Actually, I was just thinking about you."

"Were you?" Leonora was relieved that he sounded brighter.

"I was at an art exhibition last night – a client I did

some work for. It wasn't particularly good I have to say – ludicrously abstract things. And I was just thinking about the paintings you had sold."

"Oh, I'm sure you wouldn't think mine are very good either," she said. "They're just amateur little pieces."

"I think it's great that you've taken art up at this time of your life. Dad would have been very proud of you."

Leonora suddenly caught her breath. Oh, how she wished she had Andrew here to make this phone call instead of herself! "Did you go to the exhibition with anyone?"

"I met up with some people I know," he said vaguely.

"Were Christopher and Theresa there?"

There was a pause. "No," he said.

She closed her eyes and thought of the words she had rehearsed. "Edward," she said, "I've called you tonight because . . . well, actually, because I'm afraid I need your help."

"How?"

"I've not been terribly well recently," she said, a tightness in her chest now. "I've had some tests done and it seems there's a problem with my heart . . . it's leaving me very tired and washed out. I don't feel I'm coping the same with the house. If things don't improve with medication, the doctor thinks I may have to have a fairly serious operation."

"Mother," he said, totally shocked, "why haven't you told me before?"

"Because I didn't want to worry you. You're so far away and you have your own life and your work, and everything. I wouldn't have said anything but, well, I'm suffering from a great deal of anxiety and finding it impossible to sleep. I feel sure if you were here I'd be able to relax."

"Have you told Jonathan and Diana?"

"Not really," she hedged. "And I know if I do, they'll only insist that I move to live with them. They've both asked me but, in all honesty, I'm not ready to do that yet."

She paused. "I just wondered if you might be able to take some time off work to have a spell back in Ireland." She took a deep breath. "I thought since Christopher knows the family, he would be more understanding about it. Now, obviously if you're in the middle of a big contract or anything I wouldn't expect you to drop everything."

There was a silence for a few moments while Leonora wondered if he would tell her that he and Christopher were no longer business partners.

"Edward?" she eventually said.

"Leave it with me, Mother," he said in a low voice. "I'll get back to you as soon as I can."

When she put the phone down, her chest felt tighter than it had felt in months and she felt breathless. She would have to take her angina medication.

Divine retribution, Leonora she told herself. *Divine retribution indeed.*

Two days later Edward rang back.

"I'm coming," he told her in an unemotional, business-like manner. "I've booked my ticket for next week."

"Are you sure? Was Christopher okay about it?"

"We've been working independently for the last few months," he said, "and I've just come to the end of a contract. Things are a bit slack here at the moment, so what I do won't affect him." He paused. "He's under some pressure at the moment in a number of areas – if I'm gone, it might be one less."

"Really?" she said, trying to sound surprised. "Oh, dear . . . I'm sorry to hear that." She swallowed hard. "Maybe if you stayed for a while you could get some work in Dublin . . . just until things improve."

"We'll see," Edward said. "We won't make any plans until we see how things work out with your health."

Chapter 32

Hannah was kneeling up on a stool cleaning the kitchen window when Kevin O'Reilly, the local postman, wheeled his bike into the yard. The sight of the friendly man made her blood run cold. It was the one day she had been dreading.

The day that would bring the results of her Leaving Cert exams.

Slowly, her heart thudding, she moved off the stool to stand by the side of the window.

Then, when she heard her mother call out to the postman from the clothesline where she was hanging out washing, Hannah's hands flew to cover her mouth. She stood rooted to the spot, watching as her mother dropped the item she was hanging up back into the basket, then walk across the yard to meet the postman.

Sheila Martin took two brown envelopes from him and put them into her deep apron pocket, then stood chatting to him for a minute. On occasions, the postman would be invited in for a cup of tea but Hannah knew that this was not one of those days. Her mother would not be in the mood for idle chat with the brown envelopes burning a hole in her apron pocket.

Hannah had beads of sweat on her forehead and cramps in her stomach by the time her mother came into the house and was still standing by the half-cleaned window. If only her granny were here! But Bridget Martin had gone to stay for a while with Ursula and Simon.

Sheila Martin came across the floor to her daughter, her arm outstretched. "Since it has your name on it," she said in an even tone, "you can have the privilege of opening it."

Silently, Hannah took it from her. Then, with a thudding heart and fumbling hands, she tore the top part of the envelope off to reveal a white flimsy sheet of paper. Her eyes were narrow as she started at the top of the page and then widened as her gaze moved downwards.

"Well?" her mother's eyebrows were raised. "Have you passed?"

Hannah took a deep breath. "I don't think it's too bad," she said, her voice high and trembling. "I think I've passed most of them."

Sheila Martin's brows came down. "You only *think* you've passed? You've either passed or you haven't. Give me the thing!" She moved forward and whipped the sheet of paper out of her daughter's hands. She quickly scanned the page. Then a steely look came into her eyes as her gaze flickered over in her blonde-haired daughter's direction. "You're either completely stupid or a very good actress, because all I see on this page amongst the bare passes is one big failure . . . and not one of them at Honours level."

Hannah's throat tightened and she began to feel dizzy. "But I've only failed the Irish. You know I've never been good at that. Mrs Conroy told you that there was still a chance I'd get into one of the colleges without it . . ."

Her mother's eyebrows rose higher. "But not the teaching college," she said, in a strange faraway voice. "You won't get into college to teach music with those results."

"But I never really thought I would –"

"*You never really thought you would*?" her mother repeated incredulously, as though hearing this announcement for the first time.

Hannah looked back at her mother with wide, terrified eyes. Every chance she'd got she had tried to warn her mother that she wasn't expecting anything great, that if she got a pass in most of the subjects she would be only too delighted.

"Mammy – when Mrs Conroy came out to the house she told you that I mightn't get the Irish – but that in her opinion I was doing the best I could. And she told us there was a good chance she could get me into the secretarial course in Galway . . ."

Sheila Martin stared at her daughter, her eyes hard and glinting. Then she slowly moved her gaze back to the sheet of paper. Her hand jerked upwards, crushing the disappointing results into a ball. Her gaze moved back to Hannah and there was a brief but deadly silence. Then her fists shot out to rain blows over her daughter's head and shoulders, as she cried out, "Well, *feck* Mrs Conroy into hell and back! Feck her and all her own family that have gone to university and college! Because it's not her that has to contend with a stupid ignoramus of a daughter like you!"

"Mammy – don't!" Hannah screamed, holding her

arms up over her head and face to ward off the blows. "I'm sorry! I'm really sorry – but I did my best!"

"Did your best? Did your best?"

Hannah moved backwards to try to escape the onslaught but, before she had even registered the obstacle behind her, she was tumbling backwards over the stool she had been standing on to clean the window.

As soon as her head hit the floor, Hannah blacked out instantly. She lay in a state of unconsciousness, oblivious to the sound of her mother's wailing and screeching.

Chapter 33

Leonora put her book down on the empty, unslept-in side of the bed and then she took her reading glasses off and laid them beside the book. She stretched across to switch her bedside lamp off, then lay back on her feather pillows and closed her eyes.

Twenty minutes later she was still awake, staring up at the ceiling, which she had decided would have to be added to the list of painting jobs when she could muster up the interest to contact the local painter she used.

When she checked the clock an hour later and discovered that it was still only two o'clock, she decided that she would go downstairs and make herself a cup of hot milk or Horlicks or whatever Mrs O'Shea currently had in stock.

When she opened the kitchen door she was greeted with the comforting warmth from the range and the sweet smell of cinnamon and vanilla from the house-keeper's late evening baking. Leonora glanced over to the table where circular soda loaves lay on a rack, each covered with a clean tea-towel. On a well-used but scrupulously clean tin tray beside them Mrs O'Shea had placed a coconut cake and an apple tart. Standing close beside the cakes was a Pyrex dish filled to the brim with a vanilla-flavoured rice pudding.

Leonora turned on the kettle and then padded across the stone flags and came to stand in front of the freshly baked fare. She tightened the belt on her dressing gown and then folded her arms across her chest and shook her head. How would three of them get through all that amount of bread and cake before it went stale? Edward had very little appetite at the moment and Lizzie and she couldn't eat it all. Poor Lizzie, she thought sadly as she switched on the kettle. Keeping busy was her way of coping with the difficulties in her life. As if she didn't do enough during the day with all her polishing and cleaning and cooking, she had to fill the rest of her waking hours with knitting, crocheting or baking.

The kettle boiled and Leonora found herself automatically heading out towards the drinks cabinet in the sitting-room and was down on her knees rummaging around for the half-filled bottle of whiskey she knew was there when she suddenly remembered that she had planned to have a milky drink. She stopped for a moment, staring at the bottle, and then she shrugged to herself. What harm could a hot toddy do? It was practically another day after all and, really, she hadn't been too bad for the last week or so – just a couple of drinks at the end of the night. In fact, she had drunk much less since Edward came back home because she felt slightly awkward pouring herself a drink in the evenings when he was around. Especially since the evening he had first asked her if she drank wine with her meal *every* night.

"Usually," Leonora had told him. Then, trying not to

sound defensive, she had added, "Your father and I often had wine with our meals . . ."

"And you've continued to drink it *on your own?*" He ran a hand through his dark hair in a slightly agitated manner.

"Yes. I actually find it helps my digestion and also helps me to relax and sleep better at night –"

"It doesn't seem to have helped much," he said quite sharply. "You told me you couldn't sleep at all before I came home! And surely drinking that much can't be good for your heart? Have you checked with your doctor or heart specialist?"

Leonora had flushed a deep red. Not only was she mortified at being questioned about her social drinking habits by her son but he had unwittingly reminded her of the fact that she was still living a lie. That Edward was still under the illusion that she had a serious heart complaint.

She touched the back of her hand to her forehead, trying to think of an answer that would halt the uncomfortable conversation. "I really hadn't thought about it," she said quietly, "but I will certainly check it out on my next visit. Under no circumstances would I do anything that would aggravate the situation." Then, mercifully, the phone had rung and she was able to escape from the dining room and her son's concern.

Since that evening Leonora had limited herself to just a glass when she and Edward were eating together. If he was out, she relaxed and drank several glasses. Thankfully he hadn't mentioned the subject since.

Leonora walked back along the dimly lit hallway to the kitchen as quietly as she could and then closed the door behind her. Her shoulders relaxed as she put the bottle down on the worktop and went to get her favourite large mug from one of the cupboards. She had a particular glass she used but she knew that it would immediately give away the contents whereas the mug looked more innocent if anyone walked in on her.

Fifteen minutes later she was sitting in the armchair in the sitting room, warmed through and feeling much more relaxed. She had a busy but pleasant day ahead starting with her art class at ten o'clock, and then she and the other members of the group were invited to one of the ladies' houses for a lunch to celebrate her fiftieth birthday.

She was looking forward to getting out of Glenmore House for a decent length of time. If she was honest, she was finding the situation with Edward a little wearing. She couldn't help worrying about him. She was concerned about the weight he'd lost. He was a naturally slim young man but his medium-height frame was looking almost gaunt these days. She found herself watching him and trying to anticipate his moods and at times wondering who he was writing to or speaking to on the phone. When the post arrived she caught herself scrutinising the envelopes, first to see if one had an American stamp and then to check if it was Christopher Hennessey's handwriting. She knew for definite that Edward had received two letters from him to date – and on both occasions he had seemed much brighter after reading them. She didn't know whether that was a good sign – that they had patched up their differences and were now back to being just ordinary – normal – friends. Or whether it was a bad sign and that Christopher was missing him and his letters were full of all the things that Leonora felt one man should never think about another, far less say or write it.

In the first week or two she had made a few gentle remarks about him looking for work but he had been so touchy about it that she had decided to leave him until he was ready. So the question of whether Edward intended to stay long-term or not remained quite murky and this kept her on edge.

Yes, she thought, a day away from Glenmore House and Edward will do me no harm at all.

Feeling quite mellow now, she was suddenly tempted to have a bath. That would surely relax her completely and besides, if she had a bath now, it would save time in the morning. She decided she would. And she would use the downstairs bathroom for fear of wakening Edward or Mrs O'Shea.

She went back along the corridor to the kitchen to wash her mug first, then paused for a moment and decided that she might just make another hot toddy – a very weak one – to sip as she lay soaking in the bath. She put the switch down on the kettle to re-boil it and then went down to the bathroom and started running the bath. As she poured some pink-flecked salts into the water, a picture flew into her mind of an evening in winter when she had put five-year-old Diana into this particular bath. Later – dressed in her warm fleecy pyjamas – the little girl had sat toasting bread in front of the sitting-room fire while Leonora had brushed out her long brown hair. She smiled to herself at the lovely memory. Then she thought for a moment. She was sure she had photographs of Diana and the two boys in their pyjamas in one of the albums. Could it be in the sideboard in the sitting room, she wondered?

She went back into the kitchen to finish making her

drink and then, with the whiskey bottle tucked under one arm and the mug held safely in her free hand, Leonora went off into the sitting room in search of the photograph.

* * *

It was daylight when Leonora was jolted into wakefulness by Mrs O'Shea's voice out in the hallway. She sat bolt upright in the armchair, completely bewildered and not at all sure where she was or what time of the day or night it could possibly be. She looked down at herself – still in her pyjamas and dressing-gown. Her heart started to race as she realised that something was wrong. She ran her hand through her hair as her brain tried to work through the foggy memories of the night before.

Before she had a chance to gather her thoughts together the sitting-room door was suddenly thrown open.

"We've a flood!" Mrs O'Shea shrieked, her voice raised a full octave. "There's water everywhere and I don't know where it's coming from!"

Leonora stumbled to her feet, the empty mug that had been in her lap now falling onto the floor. Oh God, she thought, I must have slept here all night. Did I not go to bed or did I go and get up again?

The housekeeper was staring at her.

"What's happened?" Leonora asked, kicking the mug to the side of the chair, hoping that the housekeeper wouldn't see it.

"It's a flood!" Mrs O'Shea repeated. Then she suddenly halted, a look of extreme alarm on her face. Her gaze moved downwards to her feet. "Jesus, Mary and Joseph! The carpet is soaked through in here as well. It'll be ruined! And all the good furniture!" Her hands came up to cover her mouth, as though she was afraid to voice her thoughts. She started back out into the hall. "It must be coming from the kitchen . . . we must have a burst pipe or something."

Leonora followed the Scotswoman. She looked up and down the wooden floor which was submerged in several inches of water. "But this is dreadful . . ."

They made their way to the kitchen, almost up to their ankles in water.

Leonora stood at the threshold looking in at the swimming floor while Mrs O'Shea checked under the sink.

"No, no," said the housekeeper, shaking her head vehemently. "There's no water coming from here."

Leonora tightened her dressing-gown belt. Then, it suddenly hit her. "Oh, my God!" Her face looked stricken. "It's coming from the bathroom along the corridor . . . oh, how stupid of me . . ." Her whole body started to tremble at the realisation of what had happened. "I couldn't sleep and I thought I would have a bath . . ." She gestured towards the sitting-room. "I sat down for a few minutes while it was running . . ." She had to stop to catch her breath. "I hadn't slept since I went to bed . . ."

Mrs O'Shea's eyes widened. "Surely you're not telling me that you fell asleep and left the taps running?" She didn't wait for an answer. Leonora's stricken face told her all she needed to know. She started moving down the hallway as fast as her spindly legs could take her.

*   *   *

What Mrs O'Shea had left unsaid, Edward had no

trouble in voicing as they sat at the kitchen table together having their first cup of tea of the day. All three members of the household had pitched in and helped clear up the worst of the mess. When the end was in sight, the Scotswoman had insisted that Leonora and Edward leave her to finish off and go and have their breakfast.

"You're telling me that you fell asleep downstairs and left the bath running for hours?" he asked incredulously.

The tone of his voice made Leonora shrink inside her dressing-gown. "Unfortunately . . . yes," she said in a low, strained voice. How could she defend herself? There was no denying what had happened.

He shook his head. "The damage . . . the furniture and the carpets and floors!"

"I know, I know," she said, her hands coming up almost to cover her ears. "I don't need to be told – I'm aware it's entirely my fault." She took a deep breath. "But in my defence, I've never had anything like that happen in my life before."

"That information doesn't exactly help us deal with the mess we have here," Edward said, shrugging his shoulders. "But maybe we need to look at *why* it happened."

Leonora looked back at him. "I simply fell asleep waiting for the bath to fill. It was a stupid accident – but an accident nonetheless."

He paused, looking straight into his mother's eyes. "Had you been drinking again?"

Leonora felt a cold hand clutch at her heart. "What do you mean?" she asked indignantly.

Edward was unflinching. "I'm asking you straight out: were you drinking when this happened?"

"I can't believe you've asked that," Leonora said in a low, shocked tone. She stood up out of her chair. "I refuse to be interrogated like this in my own home and I damn well resent my own son accusing me of being a drunk!"

"It's not just me who has concerns over your drinking. Mrs O'Shea told me that she found a bottle of whiskey beside the armchair where you were sleeping. When I went in later, there was a mug lying on the floor which you had obviously dropped."

Leonora felt something snap inside her. "I've given you the respect of listening to you, Edward, but I'm certainly not listening to criticism from my housekeeper. I'm going to have a word with Mrs O'Shea right now." She pushed her hardly-touched plate of toast disdainfully towards the middle of the table and tightened her dressing-town around her. If she couldn't relax and have a drink in her own home at the end of the day, then her life had indeed sunk to a new low. In fact, it suddenly sounded almost unbearable to her.

"We're only concerned about you," Edward called as his mother swept out of the kitchen and headed down the hallway to the bathroom where the housekeeper was still mopping up the excess water.

"Mrs O'Shea!" Leonora called in a high, authoritative voice she rarely used.

"I'm coming, I'm coming!" the housekeeper called back.

Leonora reached the bathroom door to see Mrs O'Shea holding her mop aloft, her face and neck red with all the exertion. She kicked a damp, rolled-up bathmat out of the way. "We're nearly there now . . . I think I've managed to soak the worst of it up." She looked at Leonora's stony face. "Was there something you wanted?"

"Actually, Mrs O'Shea, I want a word with you."

"Yes?" Mrs O'Shea was looking alarmed.

"Edward tells me that you have some concerns about my –"

"Oh, hold on a wee minute!" Mrs O'Shea said, flustered and flapping a hand in the air. "I just want to open the window to help to dry the floor while we're standing chatting."

"I haven't actually come to see you for a cosy chat," Leonora said sharply, then halted as the elderly house-keeper turned towards the window.

Then Leonora watched in frozen horror as, catching her foot under the rolled-up bath mat, Mrs O'Shea went face down onto the wet floor.

"Edward!" Leonora shouted along the corridor. "Edward, come quickly!"

By the time they had helped the housekeeper up into the kitchen and cleaned the worst of the blood up, it was quite apparent that she had broken her arm and possibly her nose. Leonora had worked very hard to keep her outward calm but inside she felt panic-stricken and laden with guilt. She knew perfectly well that if she hadn't gone down to the bathroom in such a manner poor Lizzie would not be in the state she was in now. And however strongly she denied it to anyone else, she could not deny to herself that her drinking had caused the whole dreadful situation.

"I think we need to get you straight to hospital, Lizzie," Leonora said in a firm but gentle tone.

"I'll be fine," the Scottish woman protested.

"We have to get that arm seen to. Don't you agree, Edward?"

"Most definitely. I'll drive and you two can sit in the back."

"Oh, I don't want to cause any fuss," Mrs O'Shea said, her voice muffled due to the fact she was speaking through the handkerchief that Leonora was still holding to her bleeding nose. "And I hate hospitals . . ."

"You'll be a bloody sight safer there than you are at home," Edward muttered to himself.

Leonora half-caught his words and stifled the indignation that shot up inside her. He really was pushing the point too far.

"You've nothing to fear from the hospital," she told the housekeeper. "I'll be with you, and I'll make sure you're well taken care of."

Mrs O'Shea looked up at her employer with anxious eyes. "You won't leave me?"

Leonora bent down and put her arms around the older woman. "No, Lizzie, I promise I won't leave you. I'll be there as long as you need me." And she meant it sincerely. It was the least she could do when she was to blame for the whole sorry situation.

* * *

Leonora was true to her word. She and Edward stayed with the housekeeper while she had several sets of X-rays done on her arm and her nose, and then while she went to theatre to have her badly broken arm reset and put into a plaster cast.

It was late evening by the time Mrs O'Shea came round from the anaesthetic and then she insisted that both of them go home.

"I'll be fine," she told Leonora, "and I'll sleep easier in here if I know you're in your own beds in Glenmore House."

"But I know you don't like being on your own in hospital," Leonora protested.

"Well, now I'm here, I don't mind it so much," said Mrs O'Shea. "The wee nurses are in and out to me every few minutes, and they're so nice and friendly. It's not at all like I imagined – I'll be fine."

Leonora looked back at her housekeeper and her thin frame shrouded in the white hospital bedclothes reminded her of a young, vulnerable child. She was suddenly reminded that Lizzie O'Shea didn't have a blood relation anywhere near her to visit or one they could even contact about her accident. Willie was the only one she talked about regularly and he was hardly in a fit state to visit anyone.

"You'll be fine," Leonora said emphatically. "The doctor said that your arm will be as good as new when the cast comes off." Then, before she had time to think better of it, she leaned forward and – for the first time in all the years that they'd known each other – she kissed Lizzie gently on the cheek and was pleased to see her flush with pleasure.

When she and Edward arrived back at Glenmore House Leonora was prepared for almost anything.

"We need to have a serious talk, Mother," Edward said as they walked into the house.

"Yes," was all she said but she gave an involuntary shudder which he noticed.

"If you put the kettle on," he suggested, "I'll round up an electric fire for the sitting room. Then we can have our supper in there."

"There's all that baking that Mrs O'Shea did last

night," Leonora said, half to herself. "It hasn't been touched yet . . ."

A short while later Leonora came into the sitting room with a tray with sandwiches, cake and mugs of tea. She put them down on the coffee table which stood in front of the empty fire grate. To the side of it stood the electric fire that Edward had plugged in.

"Mrs O'Shea should be a lot better by tomorrow," Edward said, a hopeful note in his voice.

Leonora gave a small sigh as she handed him a mug of tea, saying, "I really hope and pray that she is."

"She's a strong, hardy type of woman. She won't give in too easily – it's only a broken arm when all's said and done. There's a good few years left in her yet."

A sudden picture of the stricken, pale-faced Lizzie lying in the hospital bed flew into Leonora's mind and made her chest tighten. There was a small silence during which she tried to think of something to say that might make things better, but nothing fitting came. Instead she lifted her mug to her lips with a shaky hand and took a small sip of tea.

"Are we going to have to get you some kind of help?" Edward suddenly said.

Leonora's eyebrows shot up. Surely he wasn't suggesting that she needed to speak to someone about her drinking? A doctor or someone in the same line of work as Andrew. Her heartbeat quickened – and then she was flooded with an overwhelming sense of guilt. He was within his rights, of course, to suggest it after what had happened last night – all the damage that had been done to carpets and furniture, not to mention poor Lizzie.

"What do you mean?" she asked in a low voice.

Edward waved his hands around the room. "You're not going to be able to manage all this on your own. Now that Mrs O'Shea's out of action, you're going to have to get someone to help you sort things out properly."

Leonora swallowed a sigh of relief.

"There are carpets that are going to need cleaning or replacing and the linoleum in that bathroom and the laundry room will have to be lifted to allow the floorboards to dry out." He shrugged. "Of course I'll get Tommy Murray to help me to shift furniture and lift carpets and that kind of thing, but there are certain things that you need a cleaning-woman for. Mrs O'Shea isn't going to be able to do much for months."

Leonora nodded her head, wondering how long they could evade the inevitable discussion. "I will sort something out in the morning. I can ring the women who help at the church – they might know someone down in the village who would be glad of a few hours' work." She pursed her lips together. "Lizzie might even be able to recommend somebody from her own church."

Leonora felt a sense of frustration about the fact that she was going to have to get a total stranger in to help in the house, when she could have had Rose Barry actually living in the house with them and she knew instinctively the girl would fit in beautifully. But Diana had told her that it wasn't worth asking Rose because she was too tied to her family in County Clare – so that was that.

There was another silence, during which Leonora handed the plate of sandwiches to her son. Their eyes met for a second and then Leonora suddenly felt a sense of shame wash over her. Had it really come to this? Had she really sunk so low that she would put her son in the embarrassing position of having to preach to her about her drinking?

No, she decided. It was totally unfair of her to leave the problem with him. She had never behaved like that with Andrew. They had always faced issues fair and square. Even when the cold war came between them, Andrew had immediately owned up and taken full responsibility for the mistakes he had made.

It was unthinkable and cowardly that she should evade responsibility for all that had happened in the last twenty-four hours and Edward had more than enough weight on his shoulders as it was.

Leonora decided to take the bull by the horns. "Edward . . . I am so sorry about all this and I take full responsibility for the mess the house is in and for what has happened to poor Lizzie . . ."

Edward's eyes came to meet hers again and Leonora saw the young, confused boy in them who didn't want to criticise his mother. This served to intensify her guilt.

"You really don't need to say anything," she went on. "I hold my hand up to all your accusations about my drinking habits. You're perfectly correct, I have been leaning on it rather too heavily and this incident has really brought it home to me with a bang."

"What's brought it all on?" Edward asked quietly. "You never used to drink like that when my father was alive . . . is it because you miss him so much?"

Leonora swallowed hard. How could she explain that she drank to drown all the anger that had built up inside her *before* Andrew had died? How could she explain that she was angry with his father for dying before making things better again?

"I don't really know why," she said, evading the question. "The only reason I can pin-point is that I felt a drink helped me to sleep." She raised her eyebrows and shook her head. "And it wasn't really causing a problem until unfortunately I fell asleep in the wrong place at the wrong time."

"I think that it was a case of an accident waiting to happen . . ."

Leonora lowered her eyes to the floor.

"I noticed your voice slurring on a number of occasions when I spoke to you on the phone when I was in America," he said.

Leonora felt a small dagger pierce her chest as she remembered the phone call she had made to him late at night – the phone call with the crossed wires. The phone call that revealed all about Edward and Christopher Hennessey.

"In fact," he went on, "I mentioned it to both Diana and Jonathan but thankfully they said you had always been okay when you've been visiting."

"I'm glad to hear it," Leonora said, the strain of the recent long hours evident in her voice. "I was beginning to lose confidence in my judgement over the whole situation. I was beginning to think that *everyone* saw me as a complete drunk . . ."

"Now there's no need to talk in such an extreme way, Mother," Edward told her, leaning over to pat her hand. "No-one has said anything of the kind – although Mrs O'Shea did say that she was '*a wee bit concerned*' about you drinking on your own late at night."

Leonora closed her eyes. *Please, please . . . let it go.* "I really do understand . . ."

"Apart from everything else," Edward went on now, "we have to think of your health. Your heart condition . . ."

She caught her breath. Yet another horribly wrong thing she had done. Yet another hole she had dug for herself. She had hoped that at some point she would find the right time and the right situation to confess that she had exaggerated her heart problems in order to bring Edward home. But this was not the right time. She couldn't approach such a sensitive – such an explosive – situation now. It would simply look as though she were trying to divert the attention away from her own behaviour and focus on his.

"Yes, yes," she said. *How much more can I take of this? The point has been well and truly driven home. I have made mistake after mistake, and now I'm paying for it.*

Chapter 34

Hannah felt a huge surge of excitement as her uncle's car headed through the town towards the railway station at Tullamore. But for the moment she would show no sign of her feelings – she would keep them under control until it was safe to let go. In twenty minutes' time she would be on the train to Galway and gone from here forever. Her cousin Paul would be waiting for her at the end of her journey, to take her to Slattery's Hotel in the centre of the city where she would start off her new life working as a chambermaid for the summer.

She would have over three months working in the hotel alongside Paul and then she would pack her belongings and move across the city to college where she would start a secretarial course – a course which would qualify her for a worthwhile career and would give her the means to earn a decent, independent living. Hannah would be eternally grateful to her old schoolteacher, Miss Flynn, who had organised all this for her.

Only a short time ago things were so very different,

so bleak and dark that she could never have imagined a way out.

* * *

The morning that her mother had so viciously attacked her she had lain unconscious on the floor for nearly fifteen minutes. Her mother had panicked and phoned an ambulance and by the time that Hannah had started to come round she was on her way to the local hospital.

Her father, who had been in the town on farming business, had come rushing up to the hospital when he heard the news, to be told that his daughter had all the classic signs of concussion with double vision and vomiting and would have to remain there for observation.

Hannah's mother had been white-faced and tight-lipped about the whole situation and, when forced to recount the incident, had concocted a story about how Hannah had been cleaning windows and had clumsily fallen off the chair and banged her head.

It was a few days after she was released from hospital before Hannah got the chance to tell her father the truth.

"I didn't fall off the chair at all," she had said, blinking back the tears. "Mammy attacked me when she read my results – she hit me around the head and the face and then she knocked me backwards and I fell over the chair and banged my head."

Her father's hands came up to halt her. "Now, now, Hannah," he said, shaking his head. "This has all got out of hand – it was only a bit of an argument that got out of hand."

"No, Daddy!" Hannah said, the tears she had fought

springing into her eyes. "Why do you never believe me? You know it's not just a bit of an argument. You've seen what my mother can be like!" There was a choke in her voice now.

Every time she went to her father for support and a sympathetic ear he always tried to make out that she was exaggerating. He always evaded the main point Her two brothers weren't any better – they just told her that she should walk out when her mother started and come back when she'd cooled down. But while that tactic might work with the lads, Hannah knew that a show of defiance like that from her would never be tolerated – it would only make her mother worse. "You've heard the way she goes on to me," she said now. "She really *really* hates me."

"Ah, now, Hannah," he said again – at a loss for something else to say, "your mother was only disappointed for you. She was anxious that you'd get the chance to do better at school than she did herself." He rubbed the side of his nose now, an unconscious gesture he often made when he felt awkward. "She had great notions that you'd be a music teacher. I think she told a few people in town that you were definitely going to the music college, and now she feels she's lost face."

"Well, she had no business telling anyone that," Hannah said in a strained voice. "I tried to tell her often enough that I wouldn't get the marks to go to music college. The teachers at school told her that too. I asked them to explain because I knew she wouldn't believe me." She moved the back of her hand to her eyes now. "I did my best – I tried as hard as I could – but nothing I do is ever good enough."

"Ah, she'll get over it," he said, running a rough, farm-worked hand through his sparse grey hair. "Just give her a bit of time."

Hannah looked directly at her father through tear-filled eyes. "I'm leaving," she told him. "I can't stay here any longer. I'll go mad if I do. I'll end up doing something terrible . . . like killing myself."

Bill Martin looked more than a little alarmed. "Now, now, there's no need for talk like that! Things aren't that bad at all."

"They *are* that bad!" Hannah said, her voice almost screeching. "And you need to listen to me, Daddy! I'm a nervous wreck when I'm in the house on my own with her and since the night I had to go to hospital I can hardly sleep. And I'm still getting headaches after that bang on the head."

Hannah was exaggerating. She did have headaches after the incident but they had more or less gone. But she felt she had to remind her father exactly what had happened because if she said nothing he would take the easy way out as usual and forget all about it.

"I've got to get away from this house," she repeated. "I'll never feel safe here again after what happened."

Her father had moved towards her now and put his arms around her. "Now, don't be worrying. I'll have a few quiet words with your mother and, when she realises how you're feeling, I'm sure she'll be determined to make sure nothing like it ever happens again." He gently patted the back of her head. He wasn't a man given to displays of affection and the endearment indicated to Hannah that he was taking the situation more seriously than he was letting on. "It'll all work out if ye both give it time."

Whatever her father had said to her mother, it had made a bit of a difference. Her mother was now civil and seemed a lot quieter in herself. All the pent-up anger seemed to have died down but Hannah felt it was a bit like a volcano, which, having erupted had now settled down for a while. She only hoped that she was a long way from Tullamore before it all built up again, as it undoubtedly would.

Hannah's affair with Simon had continued, though sporadically. She had wanted to finish it, but in the end had taken the line of least resistance and given him just enough of her time to string him along and avoid confrontation. After all, she might need his help at some time in the future and she didn't have any other allies in Tullamore. Besides, the money he occasionally slipped her was useful. So she had sought Simon's sympathy and advice over the situation at home but quickly discovered that he was not inclined to get involved in family business.

"If I was to poke my nose in," he told her, "it would only make them wonder why you had come to me with your problems. It might just make your mother or Ursula suspicious, and they would be watching every move we made." He had rubbed his chin. "It's hard enough for us to get a few hours together to meet up as it is. We don't want to go rocking the boat with the women and end up not able to see each other at all. Sure, we have a nice little set-up between us here and we don't want to go spoiling things. It suits us grand the way things are. This business with your mother will sort itself out." To Hannah's dismay Simon then had had the nerve to smile and wink at her. "Ye women are all the same – at each other's throats one minute and the best of friends the next."

Whatever doubts Hannah had had about the illicit relationship she had with her aunt's husband were now confirmed. He had no understanding whatsoever of her situation and was only interested in her for one thing. His attitude clearly showed that he didn't want to know about any difficulties she had at home and she had the horrible feeling that he would not want to know about any difficulties she had in the future. He was only interested in her body, not in her troubled mind. She now knew that Simon was not a person to be depended upon. He was someone she wanted out of her life. His unsympathetic attitude had sealed the fate of their relationship.

Hannah now knew that she needed someone who was in the position to help her to make the move from home – and her tyrannical mother – to a totally independent life. After weighing up all her options she had gone down to her music teacher's house and poured her heart out about the situation back home.

"I'm used to it," Hannah had sobbed. "She's always lashed out at me when she's in a bad mood – since I was a little girl – but this was the worst. The doctor at the hospital said I was lucky, that the bang to my head could have easily left me with some kind of damage."

"You have to get out of that house," the spinster teacher said. "Have you an aunt or anybody you could go to in Dublin or somewhere like that?"

Hannah shook her head. "I have an aunt in County Clare but she lives in a small village and there's no work there or anything."

Miss Flynn thought for a few moments. "Have you any idea of what you would like to work at?"

Hannah had shrugged. "I don't know . . . maybe a nice shop or something like that."

"Oh, I'm sure you could do better than that," the teacher said. "How would you feel about working in an office?"

Hannah raised her eyebrows. "I've never really thought about it." She suddenly pictured herself sitting behind a desk, dressed in a nice smart skirt and blouse and high heels. "I suppose I could answer phones and things like that all right – but don't you have to know how to type and do shorthand? I can't."

"You could easily learn," Miss Flynn said, smiling broadly. "And I might just know someone who could help you out there. Give me a couple of days and I'll see what I can do."

For the first time in years – since she had left her innocent childhood behind – Hannah actually felt hopeful that something good might happen. She couldn't believe that things might be about to change in her life – and all because she had got up the courage to tell someone about her mother.

It happened that Miss Flynn had a brother who worked in a college in Galway that ran courses in secretarial studies. She had spoken to her brother and within forty-eight hours he had somehow secured a place starting in October for Hannah. Hannah's parents would have to come up with the money for the course and for her accommodation but, after the treatment the girl had suffered at her mother's hands, Miss Flynn reckoned that it was the least they could do. They would have had to pay for Hannah going to music college in any case, so it was simply a matter of sending the funds in a different direction.

"I don't know what my mother will say," Hannah told the teacher.

"I don't think we will have any problems with your mother," Miss Flynn assured her pupil.

Sheila Martin had been shocked when the teacher turned up at the farmhouse and even more shocked by the fact that she knew all about the incident which had ended up with Hannah being hospitalised.

"It was an accident," she stated. "Hannah fell over the chair . . ."

"Well, whatever happened," Miss Flynn said, raising her eyebrows, "she was a very lucky girl."

They had sat in a strained but polite atmosphere, sipping tea, and then the teacher had made her suggestion about Hannah and the secretarial college in Galway.

Sheila Martin's eyes had widened in surprise. "And would they take *her*?" she had asked. Her daughter's poor marks had convinced her that she was only fit for staying at home helping out on the farm or for minding her grandmother. And the idea filled her with dread, because she had no idea how she would cope with having the stupid girl around her feet all day.

"I've actually checked that there is a place available for her and I think that Hannah would be very suited to a secretarial course. It could open all sorts of doors to her for the future."

"Well, if it would mean that Hannah was qualified to do *something*," her mother said, although there was a doubtful note in her voice. Hannah had never lived up to any of her expectations in life and it was hard to imagine that she would stick a course out which might lead to a decent job. The only thing she had been any good at was music but she could only ever really play by ear and that was not what the examiners were looking for.

Bill Martin had arrived in from the farmyard at that point and, after several sleepless nights worrying about his pretty but undependable daughter, he grasped the opportunity that Miss Flynn was giving them with both hands. By the time the teacher left, everything was settled and it was agreed that Hannah would start college in Galway in the autumn.

She was elated. There was only one problem: this wonderful new life didn't start until October.

Then fate had lent a further helping hand. The following day a letter had arrived from her Auntie Kathleen with all the latest news from Kilnagree. Amazingly, her mother had handed the letter over for her to read herself.

"There's nothing much in it, as usual," she'd said, putting it down on the kitchen table in front of Hannah.

Hannah read down the first few pages of Auntie Kathleen's letter, full of boring things about Rose's granny's sore leg and her recent breathlessness.

The last page of the letter was the only one of interest to Hannah. Her eyes lit up when she read that Paul was living and working in Slattery's hotel in Galway. Apparently they had a couple of spare rooms for the staff and Paul had been lucky enough to get one. Hannah felt a great surge of excitement at the news. This meant that she would have someone that she knew really well when she moved down to Galway. And someone that she liked a lot and could have a bit of craic with. And a lad as well. Paul was only her cousin but he was someone who could introduce her to other lads, and he would be someone to go out with if she had nobody more exciting. Oh, my God, she thought. For once in her life things actually looked as though they were starting to go well.

Hannah wasted no time in contacting Paul. Her aunt had given the address of the hotel and that very day Hannah wrote him a letter telling him all her news about coming to college in Galway and saying that if he knew of any summer work that was going that she would be available to start straight away. She told him she wanted to be as far away from Tullamore as possible. She had to stop herself writing *'and as far away from my mother as possible'*, restraining herself just in case the letter ever fell into the wrong hands and was reported back home.

As she posted the letter in the main post office in Tullamore, Hannah could never have imagined that within a few days she would be leaving home forever. Paul had phoned her from the hotel the following afternoon, shortly after he received her letter, and amidst Hannah's uninhibited shrieks of delight – due to the fact that her mother was out – he went on to tell her in a breathless voice that one of the chambermaids in the hotel had been dramatically sacked two days ago and there was now a position that needed to be filled immediately.

"And did you mention me?"

"Yes, the minute I received your letter I had a word with Joe. I said you were my cousin and that you were looking for work and he said he remembered you well. Anyway, he spoke to Mrs Slattery and the next thing was she came through to see me, and asked if I could get in touch with you by phone as she needed somebody straight away."

He gave a little laugh. "I think she was impressed when she heard you had a phone at home. She said you'd be ideal working with the guests since you're used to high standards. But you'll have to help out a bit in the kitchen too."

"Oh, my God!" Hannah said again, thrilled with the excitement of it all. There was nothing better that she could think of than working in a fancy hotel where she would have a laugh with Paul and meet all the well-off guests. And since they were right in the middle of the city, she'd be able to walk to all the nice shops and on her nights off she would be able to go to the glamorous dances in the city. In fact she would be able to do anything she wanted now, without having to answer to anyone.

"You'll have to come straight away or they might give the job to somebody else," Paul warned her. "Mrs Slattery says she needs you for the weekend because that's the busiest time."

"Oh, I will, I will! My father's down the fields so I'll run down to him this minute and tell him all about it."

"Will I ring you back later? Joe said I can use the hotel phone since it's about work."

"Ring me back in a couple of hours. I should know then what's happening."

If Hannah had had her way she would have been gone that very night but her father was practical, telling her that she needed to wait until the following day to get everything sorted out.

"Are you sure about all this?" he had asked her as they walked back up to the farmhouse together. "It's all a bit sudden and quick. There's no need to be rushing away to the other end of the country because of a bit of a row with your mother."

"Daddy, I'm a hundred per cent sure," Hannah said in a firm and determined voice. Then, when her father gave a weary sigh, she turned to look at him and she noticed that his face suddenly looked very tired and very old. Something caught in her throat but she choked it back, knowing that she couldn't afford to be in any way sentimental at this point.

Fate had given her the chance to go – and go she would.

*   *   *

As the train station came into view now, Hannah felt her heart quicken. At last she could live the independent life she had imagined for the last few years, free from the feeling of being trapped in the small country life in Tullamore, free from all the girls at the local school who disliked her and who she knew were only jealous of her good looks, free from the constant feeling of failure that had been stamped into her since the day she started school.

And most of all – free at last from her domineering, unpredictable, vicious mother.

They pulled up right in front of the station building and Simon got out of the car and went to the boot to get Hannah's case. Hannah carefully climbed out of the passenger seat, taking care not to snag her stockings. While she waited for Simon, she looked at the back of her legs to check that her seams were straight, then she smoothed down her pink checked dress and tightened the white belt around her tiny waist. She glanced up at the cloudy sky, hoping that the weather report she had heard on the radio this morning was right and that she could look forward to sunshine when she arrived in Galway.

She was ready for anything, wearing a light pink cardigan and pearls, and carrying a cream raincoat and flowery umbrella. Then she smiled to herself, thinking that she really couldn't care less about the weather. A few drops of rain weren't going to dampen her spirits on such a wonderful day. In fact, she thought, it could thunder and lightning and pour with rain and she still wouldn't mind.

"I'll give it a few weeks," Simon said, slamming the boot back down, and walking towards her, "and then I'll take a run down to Galway to see you." He winked at her. "How would you fancy an overnight in a nice bed and breakfast? Wouldn't that be something for us to spend the whole night together and wake up in the same bed?"

Hannah felt her stomach tighten and the claustrophobic feeling she now had at the thought of any physical contact with her uncle almost overwhelmed her. "I'll let you know if I'm able to get a night off," she hedged. "Paul said that they're working flat-out in the hotel at the minute, and they're hardly getting any time off."

Simon looked at his watch now and then pursed his lips together. "It might be better if you give me a ring at the bank when you know what time off you have. It might look kind of suspicious if you phoned me at home."

"Grand," Hannah said, smiling warmly at him, knowing she hadn't the slightest intention of ringing him whether it was at home, the bank or Timbuktu.

* * *

As the train drew into Galway station, Hannah could see

Paul waiting by the wall, and she was impressed by how much taller and older he looked than the last time she had seen him.

When the train came to a halt and the doors started to open, he moved along the carriages, checking each one. His brow was in a deep, anxious furrow by the time he spotted the very glamorous-looking Hannah coming towards him,

"I thought you'd missed it!" he said, his face breaking into an embarrassed grin. He ran towards her and when he reached her stopped and suddenly looked awkward – not quite sure what to do. Then he suddenly moved to take the heavy case from her.

Hannah put her handbag over her wrist and then put both hands on her hips. "Don't I even get a 'hello' kiss from you?" she demanded.

Paul blushed. "Ah, don't!" he said, smiling and rolling his eyes. "You'll get me all embarrassed doing that in public."

"Come on," she said, pressing her index finger to her cheek. "You haven't seen your favourite cousin for months – surely I deserve a little kiss on the cheek?"

Paul shook his head. "Oh, you're some woman, Hannah!" he said. Then, when he realised that she wasn't going to move until he'd given her a kiss, he leaned forward and gave her the smallest peck on the cheek.

"I suppose that'll have do for now," she said, winking at him.

He blushed even more at that. "Was the train busy?" he asked to cover his embarrassment.

"Quiet enough," Hannah told him, "but I was quite happy reading my book and my magazines."

She smiled to herself, thinking how annoyed her

mother would have been had she seen her reading the
True Life magazines in public that she wouldn't let her
read in the house.

They walked out of the station into the sunshine and,
as they went along, Hannah hurtled one question after
another about where she would work and where she
would live.

"You'll see it all for yourself in a few minutes," Paul
teasingly told her.

"Is it very fancy?" Hannah persisted. "Tell me it is –
I'd love to work in a lovely hotel."

"Oh, it's nice enough, nicer than a lot of the other
hotels but it's not huge like The Great Southern or anything
like that. It has sixteen rooms and ten bathrooms and a nice
big dining-room and the bar is as good a size as any pub."

"And what are the guests like? Are they very posh?"

"Oh, they all have money, no doubt about it. You
couldn't stay for a week in a hotel if you didn't have big
money. And the price of the drinks and the lunches and
everything are more than you'd pay in an ordinary place."

"It's amazing to think that the Slatterys would buy a
hotel, isn't it?" Hannah mused. "The pub they had down
in Kilnagree was nothing special – it was just like a pub
you'd see anywhere."

A serious look crossed Paul's face a moment. "It
mightn't have been that fancy but it was a nice homely
place. It was the kind of pub that suited the area and
you'd be hard put to find a better view of the sea."

Something in his voice made Hannah look up at him.
"Do you miss Kilnagree?" she asked, a note of surprise
in her voice.

"No," he said, shaking his head vigorously. "What's there to miss? The sea is all around us here if we want it. Sure, I'm having the time of my life out here in Galway. I can do whatever I want, whenever I want." He grinned at Hannah. "And you'll be the very same."

Hannah gave a little squeal of excitement. "*I can't believe it!! I'm actually down in Galway!*" she sang in a high-pitched voice, whirling around in a circle like a little girl at a birthday party. Several people who were waiting on buses moved to avoid her bumping into them but most of them shook their head and laughed at the pretty, perfectly dressed little blonde. One or two even wondered if she might be an actress or somebody famous, the way she was carrying on, because you got all types of strangers in Galway.

After her few moments of madness, Hannah calmed down.

"So what else have you told the Slatterys and the other staff about me?" she asked, affecting a strict school-teacher manner. "I hope you've not told them anything terrible."

"Nope," Paul grinned. "I've left them all to find out what you're like for themselves."

* * *

After a quick tour of the hotel – which Hannah thought was a bit smaller than she had imagined but made up for its size with spanking new furniture, carpets and curtains – she was taken to meet the dozen or so staff who were working that day. They all seemed friendly enough, especially the lads, and Hannah immediately felt that she would fit in well in her new surroundings. Then she was taken to the basement through a series of low, dark corridors and shown to one of the four small, cell-like bedrooms by Joe and Mrs Slattery. A girl from Cork, who worked in the bar, had the room one side of Hannah, a lad from Kinvara had the one on the other, while Paul had the room down at the corner.

"They're not great," Mrs Slattery admitted, "but we spent so much on doing up the main hotel rooms for the guests that we couldn't put money out on the bits you don't see." Then she went on in a brisk manner. "It's only for the summer and you're getting free board, and you have the advantage of it being close for work for you since you have to be up early."

"It's grand," Hannah said, looking from the bare green-painted walls to the small wardrobe and chest of drawers and then to the single bed with the washed-out pink candlewick bedspread. Her new accommodation wasn't exactly glamorous but she felt better when she noticed that the white pillowslips and sheets were spotless and starched. "Is it okay if I put up a few little pictures and things like a nice mirror to brighten up the place?"

"You can do whatever you like with it, as long as you don't put any great holes in the wall or anything like that." She glanced around the sparsely furnished room and then she looked back at the perfectly dressed Hannah. It suddenly struck her that she was a lot more sophisticated in both her clothes and her manner than her cousin, Rose, and it mightn't look too well if anybody belonging to her dropped down to find her living in a cell. Hannah's parents and friends might well be the sort they wanted to attract as paying guests. Mrs Slattery had already learned that in the hotel business you never know where a good customer might come from. "We might have a spare little dressing-table and a chair that would fit in here." She looked at her husband and raised her eyebrows. "Maybe you'd organise that, Joe?"

"No problem," he said. "There's a few bits of furniture out in the sheds – me and one of the lads will see to it."

"That's very good of you," Hannah said, giving an ingratiating smile. She could tell already who the boss was and she knew that it would be in her best interests to keep on the right side of Mary Slattery.

"Oh," Joe remembered, feeling in his shirt pocket, "there's a key for the room as well." He raised his eyebrows and sucked his breath in through his teeth. "I hate to say it but you can't be too careful. You'd like to be able to trust the people you work with but it's not always the case."

"Well," Hannah said, taking the key from him, "it's better to be safe than sorry."

"Your main work will be up in the bedrooms," Mrs Slattery went on quickly, making the point that her husband was holding things up as usual, "but we need help in the kitchens in the evening with all the dinner dishes. It's all hands on deck there, so you'll just have to do whatever is needed."

"No problem," Hannah said, giving her new boss a beaming smile. "I'm well used to washing and cleaning at home." And not being in the slightest bit appreciated, she thought. And at least I'll get paid here.

"Well," Mrs Slattery said, "if you're half as good as your cousin Rose we'll have nothing to worry about." She looked at her husband. "We tried our best to get her to move here with us, but she was adamant that she didn't want to leave Kilnagree, isn't that right, Joe?"

"It is," he said, sucking his breath in through his teeth and shrugging.

Hannah kept her smile pinned on her face although she was irritated by the reference to Rose.

Joe told Paul to take Hannah over to the staff room to get something to eat and it was arranged that around half past two one of the chambermaids would take her around the rooms and explain what had to be done.

After picking at her lukewarm lunch in the empty staffroom, Hannah went back to her room and unpacked, then lay down on the bed with one of her magazines. After a while her thoughts drifted. She thought back to her last visit out to her Auntie Kathleen's, when Rose had suddenly produced all these fashionable, eye-catching outfits. It had really given Hannah a start, because although nobody could deny that Rose was a good-looking girl, she hadn't realised the difference that decent clothes would make to her. Strangely, Rose didn't seem to have any real awareness of how good-looking she actually was, and it was very strange that she hardly ever looked at herself in the mirror.

Hannah's thoughts then drifted towards her younger cousin, Paul. He was also very good-looking and had good thick, dark hair similar to Rose. And strangely enough – he didn't seem to know how good-looking he was either. It was a dreadful pity, Hannah thought, that they were actually related because she would have chosen him above any of the other lads she had met in the small fishing village. If he had been better dressed and had a decent haircut, she wouldn't even have minded the fact that he was a couple of years younger than her. But, she shrugged, he *was* her full first cousin, and that meant anything more than a friendship was out of bounds.

She thought of Simon for a brief moment, and it occurred to her that the fact she had been related to him – although only through marriage – had made it easier to see him regularly. It had also made it easier for her to pull away from him. If he ever confronted her and asked why she didn't want to keep in touch – she could always tell him quite truthfully that they should never have had a relationship in the first place.

But, Hannah decided, those sorts of thoughts wouldn't stop her and Paul being great friends and having a bit of a laugh together. They had always got on well. In fact she felt she got on better with him than she'd ever got on with Rose or any other girls. The only thing was that other people might find it odd that her best friend was a cousin – and a lad.

Hannah suddenly looked at her watch. She sat straight up on the bed, throwing her magazine to the side. She quickly changed out of her pink outfit into a plain black skirt, plain blue blouse and flat black shoes that she reckoned would do until she was sorted out with a uniform. Then she went back through the narrow, dark corridors towards the reception desk, where a small stout girl, dressed in a black dress with a frilly white apron and a cap, was waiting for her.

"I'm Sinéad," she said. "Mrs Slattery said to take you around the rooms and show you exactly how they've to be done for the morning." She rolled her eyes and sighed.

"We've got a big party arriving from Belfast tomorrow and she's very fussy."

Hannah smiled at her. "We'd better get started so."

A couple of hours later, Hannah knew exactly what way Mary Slattery liked the sheets on the bed folded, how the carpets were to be hoovered, how the curtains had to be tied back, and how the toilet bowls were to be cleaned. After she had finished, she was told she had a few hours off until seven o'clock when she was expected to help out in the kitchen. Hannah wondered what she would do with the time until she was back on. It was a wonderful feeling, knowing that she could choose exactly how to spend her own time. Never again would she have to dance to her mother's tune – in fact she might never lift a piano lid again unless it was to her own advantage.

Hannah thought that she might take a walk to the shops or at least have a look around and see where the dance halls and the picture house were. They were the things that interested her now, and there was no one around to stop her going.

"I'll have a nice chambermaid's uniform all pressed and ready for you this evening," Mrs Slattery said. She smiled now. "Lucky enough the girl that left had a nice neat little figure like yourself."

Hannah felt a surge of pleasure at the compliment. Surely if an older woman like the hotel-owner could see how attractive she was, the lads working in the place must have noticed too. "Paul has a few hours off too," the hotel-owner told her now, "so he might take you on a walk around the city and show you where everything is."

"That's great," Hannah said, feeling even happier now she knew she had company.

She went back through the low-ceilinged corridor back to her room. Then, just as she went to open her door, she changed her mind and walked further down the corridor towards Paul's room. She gave two little knocks on the door.

"Yep?" Paul called from inside.

"Can I come in?" Hannah asked.

"Hold on a minute!"

She could hear him moving around the room and then a minute or so later she heard the door unlocking. "Well?" she said, standing with her hand stretched up high on the doorframe like a model posing. "And what were you up to, that you couldn't answer the door straight away?"

"Nothing," Paul said, a redness rushing over his face. "It's just I didn't have a shirt on." He indicated the row of undone buttons halfway down his shirt.

Hannah looked him up and down, then she widened her eyes. "Are you sure? It's just that I'd hate to interrupt you if you were up to anything personal."

Paul looked back at her, then he shook his head and started to laugh. "I'm not going to ask you what you mean," he said, opening his bedroom door wide, "because if you're suggesting what I think you are, it's not something that a girl should know about."

Hannah started to laugh now too. "I don't know what you're talking about. I only meant if you were getting shaved or plucking your eyebrows or anything like that."

"*Plucking my eyebrows?*" he repeated incredulously. "Now you've got me thinking that you are really mad!"

They both stumbled into the room now, giggling and laughing.

Hannah eventually straightened up and had a look around the room, which was identical to her own. "Well," she said, patting the perfectly made single bed, "at least you're keeping it tidy. Most lads live in pigsties once they get away from home. We went up to Dublin once to where John and Kevin had digs and you wouldn't have believed the state of their rooms."

Paul shrugged. "Sure, it's easy enough to keep tidy, it's only a small room – and it's not as if I have that much."

"You're off for the next couple of hours, aren't you?" Hannah asked. "Do you fancy a walk into the shops?"

Paul raised his eyebrows in thought and then nodded. "Grand – it's not as if I'm doing anything any better."

"If you're nice to me, I might treat you. I had a few pounds put by and it's burning a hole in my pocket."

"You'll not buy me anything," Paul told her. "You need your own money. Girls have far more things to be spending their money on than lads do."

"I don't care what you say – I'm going to buy you a nice shirt," Hannah said in a childish voice. "Because we'll probably be going out on our nights off and if you're coming with me I want you to look decent."

Paul shook his head. "No way," he told her. "I'm not letting you pay for anything."

Hannah went over to the door and closed it. She leaned against it, one leg bent behind her and pressing on the door. Then, she suggestively half-closed her eyes and started licking her lips like a film star posing. "How about," she said, "if I agreed to let you kiss me? Would that make a difference?"

Paul stared at her for a moment and then he started to laugh. "You're an absolute devil, Hannah! Would you go off and don't be codding me like that!"

Hannah shook her head. "But I'm not," she told him. "I'm dead serious. If you agree to let me buy you a nice shirt then I promise that I'll give you a nice sexy kiss."

Paul looked around the small room now, as though he was checking it out for somebody listening to them. "But we're *cousins* . . ." he hissed.

Hannah shrugged. "So? It's only actually 'doing it' that counts – a kiss is neither here nor there!"

Paul shook his head. "We can't. It wouldn't be right."

But something in his voice told Hannah that he wasn't totally convinced of his principles.

"Oh, well, if that's how you feel, but you're the first lad that's ever turned down the chance of a kiss from me."

"Have you kissed many lads?" he asked, suddenly curious.

Hannah shrugged. "It depends by how much you mean by *many* . . ." She looked directly at him now and their eyes suddenly locked.

Then, as he moved from the bed towards her, Hannah knew she had won.

Without a word he came to stand directly in front of her and then he placed both his hands on her slim waist. "Are you sure it's okay?" he asked in a low, slightly croaky voice.

Hannah felt a hot ripple of excitement running through her that she hadn't felt since the start of her affair with Simon. "Who's going to know?" she whispered. She reached behind her to turn the key in the lock. "This is something that's completely private between you and me."

Paul bent forward and lowered his forehead so that it was touching hers, then he pressed it harder against her. They stood like that for a few moments and then his trembling hands tightened around her waist and he moved closer to her until their lips were only an inch apart.

Then Hannah moved her hands onto the small of his back and pulled him towards her. A small smile of satisfaction spread on her lips now as she felt his very obvious male hardness against her.

"Oh, God . . ." he moaned softly.

"Are you okay?" she asked, affecting innocence. She moved her stomach closer against him, knowing exactly the effect it would have on him.

Then, totally overwhelmed by her physical nearness, he took her by surprise when his hand came up to catch her curly blonde hair and his mouth crushed down on hers with a fierceness that took her breath away. He kissed her roughly, his lips almost bruising her.

Eventually he stopped to let them catch their breath.

"Have you any idea how long I've wanted to do that?" he said.

Hannah grinned and moved her head from side to side.

"*Years*," he said. "I've been dreaming about it since I was about fourteen."

"Never!" she said, her eyes dancing with delight.

He nodded. "And it was far better than I'd ever imagined."

"Well," she said, arching her eyebrows in question, "are you satisfied now?"

"You must be joking," he said, sounding full of confidence. "Sure, we're only starting . . ."

He took her hand now, leading her towards the bed.

"Paul," she said now, wagging a warning finger at him, "don't forget what I said about us being cousins. It's all right as long as it doesn't get too serious."

He sat on the bed now and pulled her down beside him. "And don't forget," he replied, his finger tracing her generous pink lips, "that you said it was all right as long as nobody else knew. That it was all right as long as we kept it completely private."

"Well, that wasn't exactly what I said," she giggled.

Then, before she could say another word, he shifted to lie straight out on the bed and then swung her around so that she was lying facing him.

"I think this is moving a little bit too quickly," she said now, attempting to sit back up.

His arms came around her again and his mouth sought hers again. They kissed for ages, Hannah enjoying it far more than she had ever imagined.

Over the years when she had teased him, Hannah had never really taken her young cousin seriously. Had never pictured them in any kind of romantic way. Her eyes had always been on the boys her own age or older. She had always thought they would be friends who had the same giddy sense of humour.

But she had never imagined them being like this.

A little voice at the back of her head was warning her now – telling her to tread very, very carefully. What she saw as an exciting little interlude over the summer could turn out to mean a whole different thing to her younger, less experienced cousin.

Chapter 35

Rose Barry's gaze was directed at the strip of blue sky peeping through the gap in the curtains in the bedroom but her thoughts were thousands of miles away in America. Away in a place she didn't even know the name of – as they had been every morning since Michael Murphy had left Kilnagree several weeks ago.

She had been awake even before her grandmother got up and dressed and went to start her daily routine in the kitchen. Twenty minutes later she had pretended to still be asleep when Martha stole back quietly into the room with a white, blue-rimmed enamel jug of steaming water which she left on the small table beside the matching basin.

Rose had continued to lie on for another while, even when she heard Veronica and Eileen moving around and chatting in Paul's old bedroom next door. The girls had moved in there when their brother moved to Galway, leaving Rose and her granny with a bit more space.

Then, with a sigh, she threw back the bedclothes. She washed and dressed in a short-sleeved red and white cardigan and a black skirt she had left out the previous night. She brushed her thick dark hair out and put a mother-of-pearl clasp in either side of her head.

A short while later she walked along to the kitchen to join the rest of the family.

Martha Barry gave her eldest granddaughter a beaming smile. "I was just going to send one of the girls down for you," she told her. "I have some lovely bacon and sausage warming in the oven."

Rose's nose wrinkled at the thought of the fried food. "I'm not very hungry, Granny, I'll just have a piece of bread."

Martha clucked her tongue in disapproval. "A piece of bread isn't enough to keep you going when you're on your feet all morning," she said quietly. "Try and force yourself to have a small slice of bacon – there's a good girleen." The old Irishwoman was concerned at her granddaughter's recent sombre mood and lack of appetite. She knew of course that it was all to do with the Murphy lad upping and going off to America. It wasn't a new story. Martha had seen it happen countless times to young girls in the area and, further back in time, to one of her own sisters.

After the lads had left for America or England, many of the girls would wait at home until they got word that all was going well abroad, and they could start to plan for a forthcoming wedding after which they would join their new husband in a new life. Other girls would patiently wait for their weekly letters which would gradually dwindle away as their intended was too busy to write, having got used to a more liberal way of life in their new surroundings. Eventually – as Martha's sister discovered – the letters stopped altogether and news would drift back usually via a third party that they had found romance closer to their work.

Rose picked at the plate of breakfast that her grandmother put in front of her but she only did it to please her granny as she had no appetite or any interest in food. In fact she had no interest in anything. From the minute she knew that Michael Murphy was leaving Kilnagree, all the light and colour in her life had disappeared.

And it wasn't just Martha Barry who had noticed the change in the dark-haired girl. Rose found she was constantly being asked if she was 'all right' and quite a few people had commented that she had lost a good bit of weight. Cathy Brennan had been very attentive, suggesting that they meet up for walks and that they could cycle over to Kinvara to see a film or Ballyvaughan to attend the weekly dances. But, much as Rose wanted to lift herself out of the flat mood she was in, she just couldn't summon up the energy.

"It'll pass," her granny told her. "These things are hard at the time but believe me, Rose – they pass. When you're older you'll understand all that." She had then gone on to tell her granddaughter all about her own jilted sister who had gone on to emigrate to London herself, where she had eight children and twenty-odd grandchildren. "One of the things you don't really realise," she had gone on, "is that, like Mary, you never really knew the lad." She had then waved her hand about. "In a way, it was only a bit of a dream."

Rose had looked up abruptly at her grandmother. "What do you mean? I went to school with Michael – I've known him for years."

"Ah, girleen," Martha had sighed, her face creased with

concern for her eldest, very naïve granddaughter, "sure, you only knew the young lad from a distance. When you're growing up at school you're only seeing them in the classroom or on the hurley field, or maybe dressed in their best at Mass on a Sunday. It's what they turn out to be when they're grown men that counts. In all honesty, you only met up with him on a few occasions before he went off to America. The wedding and the odd night out. It's not enough for you to have known what kind of a person he really was. You might have got fed up with him when you really got to know him. The fact he went off to America has made you think there was more to him than maybe there really was."

Rose had shrugged and shaken her head. "He was a decent lad with a decent job," she said a touch defensively, "and there's not too many of them around here." She gave a little sniff. "And whether anybody believes it or not, I liked him a lot."

What her grandmother had said had touched a little raw nerve of truth, because the evening that Michael Murphy had turned up at the house bursting with the news of his departure to America had actually made her feel she was looking at someone she didn't really know. And that night when he was going on about the great opportunities that he and Ruairí would have in this wonderful new place, she felt the quiet, solid banking-clerk had suddenly changed into an excitable, ambitious young man she hardly recognised.

"Rose," her grandmother said, putting an arm around her, "you have your whole life ahead of you. The right man will be waiting for you and he'll find you when the time is right."

"As long as I'm in Kilnagree, there's not much chance of

that happening," Rose said ruefully. "Sure, I hardly see anybody here, and when I go to Mass on a Sunday or work the odd day down in Purcell's it's the same old faces. If I want to meet any decent kind of a lad, I think I might have to look a bit further afield." She paused. "I'll have to start looking further afield for a job as well. I'm finding it awkward just going in to work for odd hours when Mrs Purcell is off at her mother's. Everybody must think I'm stupid that I couldn't get a job anywhere else and I feel it makes me look desperate for the few shillings they pay me."

"I'm sure nobody would think that, Rose. All the customers are used to you and they enjoy a chat with you, and they all know there's no work around here for anyone. Your mother's one of the few women to have a decent job and that's why she works so hard to keep it." Martha's eyes narrowed in thought. "Have you a mind to go into Galway? Joe Slattery said that he'll always have a job waiting for you."

Rose's dark, curly hair swung from side to side as she shook her head. "Not with Hannah and Paul both working in the hotel . . ."

"And if Hannah wasn't there?" Martha persisted. Now that she had Rose talking, she wanted to get to the bottom of all her unspoken thoughts. "Do you think you would feel better in yourself if you were in the city and earning more money and meeting more people?"

Rose turned her gaze towards the window. "I honestly don't know . . . At the minute, I'm just taking one day at a time." While she often talked about moving to a different place like most of the young people, the idea of actually leaving Kilnagree – leaving Clare – filled her with fear.

Fear of *what*, she wasn't quite sure, but it had something to do with going away and then coming back and finding that things had changed. She was afraid that her family and the beautiful sea village she loved would change irrevocably in her absence.

There was a few minutes' silence as Martha filled both their teacups again, and Rose continued to pick at the breakfast she didn't want.

Eventually Rose pushed her plate away. "I'm sorry, Granny, but that's all that I'm able for."

Martha nodded and smiled. "Well, at least you have something in your stomach. It's not a lot but it's better than nothing." There was another small silence while they both sipped their tea, then the old woman reached her hand across the table to catch Rose's. "You know you don't have to stay here because of minding me. I'm feeling grand at the minute, and Veronica and Eileen are well able to help me now. They're able to lift the potatoes into the kitchen for me and they're able to fill the range with turf." She looked Rose straight in the eye. "There's no need for you to be staying here if you've a mind to go to Galway. And while we would all miss you, you could easily catch the bus home at the weekends or on your days off. You're a good girl and you've always done the right thing but you can't always be putting others before yourself."

"But I'd miss everybody," Rose said, her voice suddenly softening, "and I'd really miss you, Granny . . ."

"But you have to think of yourself. And whether we like to think of it or not, I won't always be around you know . . . I've had a good innings."

Tears suddenly sprung into Rose's eyes. "Don't be

saying terrible things like that, Granny! How would I manage here without you? You're the only one that has time to listen to me –"

"Now you know that's not true, Rose," Martha cut in quietly.

"I know it's not Mammy's fault because she works hard but she's always busy when she comes home and I don't think she's even noticed how I'm feeling about Michael and everything."

"Ah, Rose," Martha said, "your mother might have a lot on her plate but she doesn't miss much. She doesn't like to be on at you but I can tell you that she asks me every day how you've been since the young lad went away."

Before Rose could respond the sound of a bicycle braking outside the house was heard and then the squeaky sound of the gate latch as it opened.

"It's Jimmy Quinn with the post," Rose said, rising quickly from the table.

"Tell him there's fresh tea in the pot if he has time to stop," Martha said.

Rose went out to meet the postman as he came towards the back door and a moment later returned followed by the small, stocky Jimmy.

"There's a letter for Daddy," she said, quickly putting it down on the table. "Granny, I'm just going back down to the bedroom to finish getting ready for work."

"And a letter for herself," Jimmy Quinn said, winking at Martha as Rose disappeared. "With an American postmark on it. A private letter, by the looks of it. Who could that be from now, I wonder?"

* * *

Rose couldn't believe that she'd finally received a letter from Michael – all the way from America! When she got down to the privacy of her bedroom, she turned the blue envelope over and over in her hands before eventually opening it with trembling hands. When she did, she found three fine sheets of paper filled with Michael Murphy's neat writing. And when she turned the sheets over, she was even more delighted to find that he had written on the back as well.

She made herself comfortable, propping a pillow behind her back on the bed as her gaze moved down through the pages. As she read, her mind became filled with the strange names of the people and places that were now part of his exciting new world.

By the time she got to the last page, she felt that she knew everything that Michael had done since he arrived in America.

Then, she read the last paragraph and her heart soared.

Myself and Ruairí are living in a fine big house in Boston and there's plenty of room for any visitors, so start saving now, and you could be out here for a holiday in the not too distant future.

Rose held the letter to her breast, feeling as though the dark world she had been living in had suddenly brightened up again. While her granny sat chatting to the postman, Rose spent the next ten minutes poring over Michael Murphy's letter again, taking in more and more details about his new life each time she read it.

* * *

Rose walked down to the bar with an unexpected spring in

her step and in her livelier, happier mood she found that the hours going between the shop and the pub flew in. As she finished drying off the last glass from the bar, Dermot Purcell came through from the kitchen.

"Could you help me out for a few hours tonight, Rose?" he asked. "There's a card game going on this evening and I'm expecting a bigger crowd than usual." He shrugged. "Agnes is staying at her mother's for a few days – some of her sisters are over from England and she wants to be there in the middle of them all – and it would happen to be the night that the two lads are in Galway for some match or other."

"Grand," Rose said, smiling at him.

Dermot Purcell was right: the bar was busier than their usual Friday night crowd. The regulars came in before their usual nine o'clock to make sure they got their usual seats and shortly after that a small coach pulled up outside with twenty-odd people from further out. The card games were underway when Rose caught sight of Liam O'Connor in the middle of a group of lads. She nodded over to him and he winked back. She felt the tinge of self-consciousness she felt every time she had seen him since the night of the dance at Easter, but the queues of customers at the bar thankfully gave her no time to dwell on it.

There was a big rush of orders during the break in the evening and Rose was glad when things settled down and she had time to catch her breath. She walked out into the warm night air and was just taking a sip from a glass of orange juice when Liam O'Connor came outside to stand beside to her.

"How are things, Rose?" he asked her in a quiet but cheery tone.

"Grand," Rose said, nodding her head a touch too quickly.

"Any news? How is Paul getting on out at the Slatterys' new place in Galway?"

"Grand," she said again. "He came out for the day last week and he said he's getting on fine in the hotel. It's busy at this time of the year with visitors coming back home and that kind of thing."

"Joe Slattery won't be complaining then," he laughed. "And your cousin? I hear she's in Galway now, too."

Rose raised her eyebrows. "She is – she has a summer job in the hotel and then she's starting college there in October."

"Doing music?" he asked.

Rose shook her head. "No. She's starting at a secretarial college."

"Sounds like she's fallen on her feet. Have you been there to see them yet?"

Rose shook her curly dark hair. "Not yet. Although I might take a trip some day soon." If the truth be told, the last thing she wanted was to spend a day with Hannah and she didn't relish the idea of being stuck between her and Paul who seemed to be more on the same wavelength as his cousin these days than he was with his own sister.

Liam looked at her for a moment, as though weighing the situation up. "I'm driving my brother's van now and again," he told her. "I'm actually hoping to get one of my own soon."

Rose looked at him in some surprise. "That would come in very handy for you, Liam," she said lightly. "There will be no holding you now."

He hesitated for a moment. "I could drive you over to Galway some Saturday or Sunday if you like?"

"Oh, no," Rose said, much too quickly. Then, feeling embarrassed at her rudeness, she added, "I wouldn't ask anyone to drive me that distance. And the coach is handy enough for me."

He straightened up to his six foot height. "It would be no trouble. I'd enjoy a day out in Galway myself." His eyes met hers now.

Rose felt herself blush. "I'm not sure . . . I'll have to see . . ."

He moved a few inches closer to her. "Is it your father?" he asked, his brow wrinkling in concern. "Are you worried what he'll say because it's me?"

Rose's eyes betrayed her now as they darted towards the pub window, checking whether her father might be watching her from inside.

"Because I don't mind speaking to him," said Liam. "I won't do it tonight when I've had a few drinks. And you needn't worry – I'll do it respectfully and decently – man to man. I'll come up to the house and speak to him."

Rose's heart lurched. This was not what she expected or what she wanted. She thought Liam had got the message that she wasn't interested in him long ago. "No," she said, "it's not just my father . . . I don't think it's a good idea. I'm not very interested in lads at the moment."

Liam eyes narrowed. "Surely you're not still holding a torch for that Murphy lad?" he said incredulously. "I thought you'd have seen sense about him, after he went off to America without as much as a backward glance for you. You deserve better than that, Rose."

His forthrightness made Rose catch her breath. "You know nothing about me and Michael Murphy," she said sharply. "Who told you that he went off without a backward glance?" She stood up to her full height now, which was still a good six inches shorter than him. "For your information, Michael has been writing to me every week and has asked me to go out to America to visit him as soon as I like."

"That's big of him," he said in a low voice.

"What do you mean?" Rose asked.

"Rose," he said shrugging, "if he had any real feelings for you, he wouldn't have gone off to America at all."

"Michael had planned to go to America with his brother before we started courting," Rose told him sharply, "and I wouldn't have wanted to hold him back." Her voice was confident and didn't betray the fact that he had struck a raw nerve.

"So you're going to wait for him?"

Rose turned her head away. "I don't think that's any of your business."

Liam closed his eyes now for a few seconds, then he shook his head. "Don't say you're going to close yourself off at home and wait for him? Surely you're not that stupid?"

Rose held her hand up, her face like thunder. "You've said enough," she said, her voice trembling with anger.

As she suddenly moved to pass him and go back into the pub, he caught her hand.

"Hold on, Rose . . . please," he said. "I apologise, I had no business saying such a thing."

She turned towards him now, snatching her hand away, then tilted her head and looked him straight in the eye. "You've no right saying such terrible things to me.

You were good with Paul when he was in trouble and that's the only reason I gave you a hearing, but you've overstepped the mark now –"

"Rose, please –" he cut in. "I'm sorry for saying all that, because I came out to talk to you about something else."

"I already told you that I don't want to go for a drive into Galway with you!"

He nodded. "Okay. But it wasn't just that . . . I wanted to tell you that I've been offered a job up in Dublin. My uncle has got me in with a big company that makes furniture and restores antiques."

Rose's face brightened up and she felt a sense of relief tinged with guilt. He had probably been asking her to go to Galway for a day out before he left. "That's great news for you," she said warmly. "You must be delighted. When are you going?"

"If I decide to go, it will be in the next week or so." He swallowed now and his gaze moved to somewhere behind her. "But I haven't made up my mind yet. I wanted to check a few things out . . ."

"I suppose you've got to sort out where you'll be living and all that. It's a big step moving up to the city."

"That's all been organised for me," he said quietly. "I'll be sharing a big house with a group of lads out in Ballsbridge."

"And is that in the centre of Dublin?"

"Fairly close . . ." He looked distracted now. He looked at her again now, an uncertain look in his eyes. "I need to check something with you before I make a final decision, Rose." He took a deep breath. "I need you to be completely honest with me and completely honest

403

with yourself . . ." He paused, checking his words carefully. "Is there the slightest chance that you might change your feelings towards me when you've got over this thing about Michael Murphy?"

Rose stared at him, lost for words at his suggestion.

"I've never made any bones about the fact that I have a notion for you and I wondered if you might come to consider me in the same way."

Rose couldn't listen to any more. "No, Liam," she said quietly. "I don't think that could happen."

"I'm prepared to wait for you," he told her, "to give you time. I can put the Dublin job off for a few months." He looked at her with narrowed eyes. "It's a good offer, Rose. I know you've never seen me in the same light as the Murphy fella and I'm not a bank-clerk or anything like that . . . but I'm a hard worker and I've got good prospects." He waved his hand around. "There's not much around here for any of us but I'm lucky to have work in Galway and now I've got the chance of a really decent job in Dublin. If you'd just give me a chance, I could give you the kind of life that a fine girl like you deserves."

Unexpected tears suddenly welled up in Rose's eyes and she felt the same confused way she had felt the night he had been kind to her and Paul. She felt terrible hurting him but there was nothing else she could do. For all he was a tall, good-looking lad that lots of the local girls were mad about – he wasn't for her. They weren't suited and they never would be. Besides, her father would never allow her to see him while she was living under his roof. Nothing could ever happen between them and it would be wrong to string him along.

"I'm sorry, Liam," she said, her voice almost a whisper, "but there's no point in you waiting for me. I think you would be wiser to take up the job in Dublin."

There was a small but painful silence.

"If that's your final word on it, then grand," he finally said, with an edge to his voice. "But I'll tell you this much and then I'll tell you no more. I've never understood what you ever saw in Michael Murphy and I think that you've had a lucky escape. Apart from being a decent musician, he was a very boring kind of a lad and, underneath it all, full of himself." Before Rose had time to catch her breath, he carried on. "I'm frightened you're going to end up being one of those old maids who waste their best years just waiting and hoping, while he's out in America enjoying himself. And then at the end of the day, you could end up married to a staid oul' farmer because there's nobody else left around." He moved closer towards her now. "And I'll tell you something else, Rose Barry, I could have the pick of the girls in County Clare but I know deep down that you and me are perfectly suited, but you're too blind and too cowardly to see it!"

Rose swung her arm to the side and threw the remaining orange juice from her glass onto the ground, then she looked up at him. "Are you quite finished, Liam?" she said, calmly and quietly.

"Well . . ." he said, sounding blustery and awkward, "I felt I had to say it plain and square."

"And you have," she told him. "You've certainly made your feelings plain and square on a number of things. And I'd like to make mine now." Her voice was steely and low. "Regardless of whatever happens between me and

Michael Murphy, I have absolutely no interest in *you* and I never will." She paused for a moment. "And even though you've said some very harsh things to me, I still wish you all the best for your future up in Dublin."

And without a backward glance at him, she turned on her heel and walked back into the bar.

Chapter 36

After Mass, Rose helped her mother and grandmother with the Sunday dinner and when the dishes were all cleared away and everything was washed and back where it should be, she decided to take a walk down to Cathy's house.

Her mother came out to the gate.

"D'you know, I think I'll walk you down a bit of the way," she said, glancing up at the clear blue sky. "It's a lovely afternoon and the exercise will do me good and make sure I keep that little belly of mine under control." She started to untie her apron. "Give me two minutes to get my cardigan and let them all know where I am. They could have the Guards out looking for me if they think I've just disappeared without saying anything!"

Rose laughed, delighted that her mother had offered to come along with her. It was rare that they got any time on their own.

A few minutes later Kathleen came back out and Rose noticed that she had her dark hair combed, a touch of powder on her cheeks and she was wearing her favourite pink lipstick. As she watched her mother coming towards her, looking younger and fresher than normal, she suddenly realised why people often said that she and Rose were more like sisters than mother and daughter.

"You look really lovely, Mammy," Rose said, smiling warmly at her.

Her mother smiled back and tossed her hair in a mock preening gesture. "Ah, I suppose I'll do."

"You smell nice, too. You're wearing perfume, aren't you?"

Kathleen Barry laughed now and lifted her eyes heavenwards. "I'm going mad in my old age, wearing perfume for a walk out." She gave a little shrug. "Other women wear it for special occasions but what special occasions do I ever have? It's ages since we were invited to a wedding and we're lucky if there's a dance on in Kilnagree once a year. And trying to get your father to go to a dance is like asking him to have his teeth pulled."

Rose looked at her mother now and felt a little pang of sadness. She'd never thought about how little her mother had in life before. She was either working at home or working down in the Guards' Barracks – and yet she rarely complained. And Rose knew that her father was not an easy man to live with. Lately he seemed to have become quieter and more withdrawn into himself. And although her mother never spoke a wrong word against him directly to her, Rose had come upon her granny and her mother quietly discussing him on several occasions. Each time, her granny said how like his own father he was and how she understood that it wasn't easy for Kathleen being married to him.

They walked down the path towards Purcell's bar, chatting as they went.

"Are you all right, Rose?" Kathleen Barry asked, linking her daughter's arm in an unusual gesture of affection. "There are times lately when you seem very quiet in yourself."

"Oh, I'm grand," Rose said automatically. It was rarely she complained about anything to her mother.

"You still don't seem like your old self. I thought the letter you got on Friday from America would have cheered you up a bit."

"It did," Rose said. "I was delighted to get it – I was delighted that he took the time to write to me when he's so busy. It can't be easy settling into a new job – in fact a new *life* – in such a different country."

"And it was a long enough letter," Kathleen said smiling. "He didn't write all that in a few minutes. He must have been thinking about you to take the time to produce that."

"Do you really think so? To be honest, there's times when I think I'm only codding myself." She paused. "There's times when I think I'll never see him again."

"Well, I can only say that the few times I saw you together, he seemed very keen on you. But there's no point in saying otherwise – America is a long way away." Then, seeing her daughter's face darkening, she said, "can't you just write to each other for a while and see how things go?"

"Well," Rose said, "I don't think we really have much choice – do we?"

As they strolled along in companionable silence for a bit, Rose wondered about her mother's own marriage. She had always thought they were very happy. Well, she thought, up until recently they seemed happy enough. But it was hard to tell whether her parents were really happy *now*.

When they reached the bottom of the road, Kathleen Barry looked at her watch. "I think I'll take a walk up to the barracks and set the breakfast table for the morning. It'll save me a few minutes."

Rose looked at her mother. "Surely you're not going to go into work on a Sunday?"

"Well, it's hardly work setting a table, is it?" her mother laughed. "And it means I won't be in such a rush in the morning."

"I'll walk you round that way. It's as easy to go on the main road as round by the shore."

"No, no, Rose," Kathleen argued. "I know you love the walk by the water."

"I can go that way when I'm coming home," Rose stated, continuing to walk alongside her mother.

The Guards' Barracks looked quiet and deserted as it often did on a Sunday. Then Rose noticed a bicycle leaning on a wall at the back of the building.

"I think one of the Guards must be in," she said in some surprise.

"I doubt it," her mother replied. "There's never anyone around on a Sunday."

Just then a figure appeared at the corner and disappeared just as quickly.

"I'm sure that was Guard McGuire," Rose said.

"Are you sure?"

Rose shrugged. "I'm sure it was him – but maybe it was one of the other Guards."

"I wouldn't want to go in if I thought it was Sergeant

Doherty," her mother said. "He'd end up giving me the Spanish Inquisition about what I was doing here."

"It definitely wasn't Sergeant Doherty," Rose stated. "I'm sure it was Guard McGuire – he's darker-haired than the others."

"Maybe I should go back home," Kathleen said now. "I feel a bit awkward going in there when I'm not supposed to be working." She sucked her breath in. "And I don't think your father would like it if he knew I was in there on my own with one of the Guards on a Sunday . . ."

"But why would he mind?"

"He can be a bit funny like that at times . . ." Kathleen turned back now towards the road she had just walked. "Oh, I think it would be best if I head home."

Just then, Guard McGuire came out to the side of the building and held his hand up in greeting. "You're surely feeling fit for walking on a Sunday," he laughed as he came towards them. "I'd say you're ready for a sup of tea? I have the kettle boiled."

Rose looked at her mother and noticed that her cheeks were pink and she was smiling.

"I said I'd walk Rose this far and I thought I'd come in and set the table for the morning."

"Well, you can come in and keep me company over a cup of tea," he said. "I've to write up an oul' report about a bit of a fight that I was called out to last night between two neighbours." He shook his head and laughed. "Two oul' fellas ready to kill each other after a few pints. Sure, neither of them would be fit to blow the skin off a rice pudding! And both of them so jarred that neither of them had a leg to put below them."

Rose and her mother started laughing now.

"I'll leave you to it," Rose said now, happy that her mother had the company of the nicest of the Guards.

* * *

That evening, when Rose was coming back home from Cathy's, her mother came to meet her at the gate.

"Don't say anything to your father or your granny about me having gone in to the barracks this afternoon, Rose," she said in a heated whisper. "Your father's in a bit of a funny mood and I don't want anything setting him off." Then she hesitated for a few moments, as if considering whether to continue. "Poor Guard McGuire is having a bit of a hard time of it himself. Seemingly, from what he tells me, that wife of his can be very awkward. She's gone a bit religious in the head and she takes notions about things. He says he often goes in to the barracks to get a few minutes' peace to himself." She raised her eyebrows and then smiled. "I felt a bit awkward going in when I saw him but I don't think he minded, and I'd say the cup of tea and the bit of oul' chat did the pair of us good."

"You needn't worry about me causing any problems between you and Daddy," said Rose. "I won't mention a word."

Chapter 37

A few days after Mrs O'Shea came out of hospital, Leonora decided that a trip away while the carpets and linoleum were being replaced and the damaged paintwork redone would solve a lot of problems. One, it would prevent Mrs O'Shea from attempting to do housework – nothing short of removing her from Glenmore House would ensure she rested and recuperated. Two – it would get Edward and herself away from the house and hopefully give them a break from their worries. And a third reason – which she could hardly admit to herself – it would help her to get out of her nightly routine of needing several stiff drinks to get to sleep. It would also save her the indignity of watching the men ripping up the water-damaged floor coverings and making the other necessary repairs.

She wondered whether a trip to Donegal might be a good idea or maybe Waterford. Somewhere that Mrs O'Shea might enjoy but which wasn't too far. Just as she was mulling over her plans, the phone rang and Diana came on the line.

After their initial light chat, Leonora took a deep breath and then launched into the deeply embarrassing story about her falling asleep and leaving the bath running. Then she went on to explain about the damage it had caused, playing the whole thing down as much as was possible without actually lying.

Diana expressed all the expected concerns and was genuinely upset to hear about the housekeeper's accident. Leonora reassured her that Mrs O'Shea was well on the way to recovery and that she would be allowed to do absolutely nothing until she was fully back to herself. She then mentioned her idea about the three of them going away for a week's break to have the house put back in order and to help speed things up.

"Donegal?" Diana said with some surprise when her mother suggested it. "Why don't you all come down here? It's every bit as nice here as Donegal and it would be lovely to see you and Edward – we haven't had a proper catch-up since he came home."

Leonora hesitated for a few moments. "Are you sure? I really hadn't thought of coming to Clare . . . even though it is my favourite place."

"Well, you should have. You know James and I love having you down and I would be absolutely delighted to look after Mrs O'Shea for a change. She's been so good to all of us down through the years, so it would be nice to return the compliment."

"I had thought of booking us all into a hotel for the weekend," Leonora explained, "but I must say I was slightly wary of approaching Lizzie with the suggestion. I'm not too sure whether she would feel comfortable in a hotel or a guest house – when she goes on holiday to Scotland it's always to stay with her family."

"She would be far more at ease here. And we'll make sure she relaxes and has everything she needs."

"That really is very kind of you, Diana," Leonora said, "And you're perfectly correct, she would be much happier coming to you than going anywhere else." She halted. "I'll tell you what – I'll ring you back as soon as I've had a chance to discuss it with Mrs O'Shea and Edward."

"Before you go, Mum, I was ringing you because I had a bit of news . . ." Diana's voice dropped. "Is there anyone close who can hear us?"

Leonora looked down the hallway, then stepped back to get a view into the front part of the kitchen. "No, there's no one around. Is there something the matter?"

"No, no," Diana reassured her, "it's just that . . . well, my period is late. *Really* late for me. It's over a week now and that's never happened before."

"Oh, Diana . . .' Leonora's hand came to her mouth. She wanted to choose her words very carefully because she knew that to be too encouraging might add to her daughter's disappointment. "It certainly sounds very hopeful. Have you spoken to the doctor? Have you told James?"

"No, I haven't seen the doctor yet, and yes – James knows."

"Oh, I really hope that it's a good sign . . . it would just be wonderful."

"I'm going to give it another few days and then I'm going to go to the doctor. But if anything happens in the meantime, I'll keep you up to date."

"Good girl – and I'll be keeping my fingers crossed for you."

* * *

As expected, Mrs O'Shea put up a good fight about going away.

"No, no, I've far too much to be getting on with around here," she said, gesturing around the kitchen with her good arm. "And what would Diana want with the likes of me as a visitor? If I can't be of any help to her then I wouldn't feel right about going."

Leonora sat opposite the small, frail-looking Scottish woman at the table and waited in silence until she had got all her objections into the open.

"Now, Lizzie," she began, in a gentle but firm tone, "are you quite finished?"

"I'm only saying," the housekeeper blustered. "We've got a few days' work here to get the place back to normal."

"It's all organised. I have Tommy Murray coming in to let the workmen in and keep an eye on things and his wife is going to clean up when everything is done." She gave a little shrug. "It's a local shop that's doing the carpets and flooring and the owner said he'll call up here to make sure it's all done properly. So there's really no need for us to be here. We'll come back next week and everything will be back to normal."

"And what does Edward think of all this?" Lizzie asked. "How does he feel about us abandoning ship?"

"He agrees with me, Lizzie."

"Oh, well," the housekeeper sniffed. "It looks like it's all done and dusted then, doesn't it?"

Leonora smiled and shook her head. There was no way that the housekeeper could give in and accept something nice graciously. "You'll enjoy it – and we'll all enjoy looking after you for a change."

On Friday Edward had a meeting with a group of architects in Dublin, so it was agreed that they would leave on the Saturday morning. He was unusually chirpy as he set off for the city which lifted Leonora's dampened spirits.

"Good luck," she told him, as he went out towards the car.

"Oh, it's nothing definite," he said, raising his eyebrows. "But they are useful contacts and it might just help set me off in the right direction work-wise if I decide to stay in Ireland for a while " He leaned forward and kissed his mother on the cheek. "Don't worry – everything will work out fine. The house will be sorted, Mrs O'Shea will be sorted and we'll all enjoy the trip down the country. I'm really looking forward to our walks along the shore with the dogs."

As she waved him off, Leonora offered up a little silent prayer of thanks that Edward had decided to let the issue of the flooding drop – and the issue of her drinking. She was also pleased that he was making enquiries about work, which indicated that he was getting over Christopher Hennessey.

While Lizzie O'Shea had a rest in the afternoon, Leonora decided to pay a quick visit down to see Terry Cassidy. She had completed all her commissions and was now experimenting with using different materials and finding it very discouraging. She knew a talk with Terry would boost her confidence. She decided to give her a ring to make sure she was at home.

Just then the phone rang. For a brief moment she

wondered whether it might be Edward ringing to say that he had been offered a partnership with one of the Dublin architects but as she hurried to answer it she chided herself for building her hopes too high.

A warm, friendly voice came on the line. "Mrs Bentley?"

Instantly Leonora's whole body stiffened. She took a deep breath to steady herself. "Yes . . ." she said, her voice sounding strange to her own ears.

"It's Christopher – Christopher Hennessey. Edward's friend."

Leonora's throat ran dry. She swallowed hard. She would have to be very, very careful here. "Hello, Christopher," she said, trying to sound the way she had always done with him. "And how are you?"

"I'm very well – couldn't be better!"

Leonora closed her eyes. "Good . . . good," she told him. Thankfully, things must be going well with work and with his wife for him to be so chirpy. She wondered if she dared ask him anything. And then she realised that in order to sound normal, she would of course have to. "And how is Theresa and the little one?" she ventured. "Both well?"

"Oh, they're both very well," he said. There was a pause. "I don't suppose Edward is around?"

"No, I'm afraid he's not. He's gone up to Dublin . . . some meeting or other to do with work."

"Have you any idea when he will be back?"

Leonora's mind worked quickly. She wanted to say that Edward had moved out of the house and that she didn't have a contact number for him as yet but something stopped her. "I'm not sure," she hedged. "Later this evening I should think."

"I wonder, while we're chatting, if I could ask you a favour?"

"Yes, of course . . ."

"I'm actually coming over to Ireland in a fortnight and I wondered if I could possibly impose on you to stay for a few nights when I'm up in Dublin?"

Leonora's head started to swim. Had she heard him correctly? "Did you say you're coming over to Ireland?"

"Yes," he confirmed. "I have a few things I need to sort out and I thought I could catch up with Eddie while I'm over. I'm actually going to book the flights tomorrow, so I thought I'd have a chat with him before I did to see what dates suited him best."

"And are the family coming with you?" Leonora asked quickly. "You're all very welcome . . ."

"No . . . no . . . I'll be on my own."

Leonora felt faint now. What on earth was he doing coming all the way over from America to Ireland on his own for? The distance, the expense. He had to be coming for a very good reason. Please, please God, she thought, don't let him be coming over for Edward.

"Theresa will be staying with one of her brothers who lives near us in New York." Then, a crackling noise came on the line. "Would you tell Edward that I'll ring back later? Actually, it could be quite late as I've got to go out. With the time difference and everything it could be ten or eleven tonight before I get the chance to ring. You will tell him, won't you?"

"Yes," she said. "Yes . . . I'll tell him."

"I'll look forward to seeing you in a fortnight or so," he said.

When she went to put the heavy black receiver back in its cradle, Leonora's hand shook so badly that she dropped it with a loud thump onto the wooden floor. She picked it up and, with two hands, put it back in place.

She walked along the hallway and into the kitchen where she went over to stand at the window by the sink. Her mind was numb – blanking out the dark thoughts that she couldn't bear to acknowledge – and so she just stared out over her colourful, well-tended garden trying desperately to glean some bit of comfort from it.

A while later she went back out into the hallway to the phone and dialled Terry Cassidy's number. She felt a great wave of relief when she heard the artist's voice. "Hello, Terry," she began in a falsely cheerful tone, "I was going to call down for few minutes and I wanted to make sure you were in."

"Oh, Leonora! It's lovely to hear from you but I'm afraid I'm tied up with visitors at the moment." She went on to explain. "My brother and his family are here as it's the anniversary of my mother passing away and we have the early Mass in the morning. We thought it would make sense for them to stay overnight. Was it anything important?"

"No," Leonora lied, "it was just to let you know that I'll be away for the next week or so."

"Somewhere nice?"

Leonora could hear children's voices in the background and then some loud laughter. She made a monumental effort to sound cheery. "County Clare – down to Diana's. Edward and Mrs O'Shea are coming as well."

"Oh, lovely," Terry said over the noise. "Some people have all the luck. So I'll see you when you get back?"

"Yes. I'll be in touch."

After hanging the phone up, she slowly walked back towards the sitting-room. She went in, sat on the corner of the sofa and lowered her head into her hands.

* * *

Mrs O'Shea had lain on the bed for the last hour or so, dozing on and off, but unable to drift off into anything more than a light sleep. She eventually decided that it was a wasted exercise and, being mindful of her strapped-up arm, she carefully manoeuvred herself into a sitting position. The hospital routine of the last few days had totally upset her usual time schedule, and she was afraid to keep sleeping now in case she ended up lying awake all night. It was preferable to struggle on now, rather than pay for it later on.

She decided to start sorting out her bits and pieces for going to County Clare.

After ten minutes – although she would never have admitted it to anyone else – it was obvious that even the effort of packing was too much for her. Going back and forth between the chest of drawers and the bed, where she had her small weekend case lying open, caused her to have to sit on the bed on several occasions. And it wasn't just the physical effort that made her feel dizzy and weak – it was the overwhelmingly dependent situation that she now found herself in.

Lizzie O'Shea had always been a very independent woman and from a young girl she had always worked, even when she was married. But this recent accident had made her look at everything in a different light. And it was a light she didn't like. For a start, the accident had made her realise that she wasn't invincible. For a woman who was proud of the fact she had never been in hospital in her life, it had sharply brought home to her the fact that good health could no longer be taken for granted.

And to complicate things further, she had suddenly realised that Glenmore House was now – and had been for a number of years – the place that she actually felt was her real home. In the hospital – in the dead of night – she had also faced the fact that it was her *only* home.

For years now, she realised she had comforted herself with the fact that if things went wrong at Glenmore House – if she felt that the people and the place no longer suited her – she could always go back to Glasgow. But where would she go? Back to live with one of her married sisters who had families of their own? Back to live with Willie? The thought had made her shudder.

And then, just as the dawn came up over the top of the faded green hospital curtains, the housekeeper had realised just how dependent she was on Leonora Bentley and her family. And that realisation had made her feel both vulnerable and very old.

Now she came down the stairs one at a time, stopping every now and again to catch her breath. She had already accepted that there was no point in rushing things because she couldn't afford a setback to her recovery. The doctor in the hospital had said to take things slowly and steadily until the arm was fully healed and she knew she had really no other option.

When she reached the bottom she turned towards the kitchen but she had only taken a few steps when an unfamiliar sound stopped her in her tracks. It was the sound of crying coming from the sitting-room. Leonora Bentley crying. The housekeeper stood silently, making sure. Then, when there was no doubt as to what the sound was, she pursed her lips together and shook her head. There was something going on. Something more than just the business with the flooding and her own resulting accident.

Leonora had seemed fine this morning when Edward was setting off and fine at lunchtime. Mrs O'Shea wondered what had brought this latest crisis on. She stood in the hallway for a few minutes listening to her employer's muffled sobs and trying to decide what to do. Most of the time their relationship worked on the basis that neither of them interfered with the other's business. And over the years it had worked very well. There were very few instances when they ventured into each other's territory, and yet they looked after each other well.

Mrs O'Shea had more or less decided that she should go quietly into the kitchen and mind her own business, when Leonora's crying suddenly turned into a fit of coughing. She stood for another few moments listening to the racking sound and then, unable to stop herself, she went towards the sitting room. Deciding there was no point in knocking or any such formality, she walked straight in.

Leonora was curled up like a child in the corner of the deep sofa, her face buried in two cushions. She either didn't hear the housekeeper coming in or she was too upset to care. Mrs O'Shea went straight over to sit beside her and place a comforting hand on her shoulder.

"You'll be all right," the Scotswoman said, patting her gently as though she were a child. "It'll work out . . . whatever it is. It'll all come right in the end."

"Not this time, Lizzie," Leonora sobbed. "I'm afraid this time it won't."

And since there was nothing more that Mrs O'Shea could say to make the situation any better, they just stayed there together in silence. Eventually, Leonora's crying ceased and she moved herself into a sitting position.

The housekeeper turned to look at her employer's red, swollen face. "I don't think a wee drop of brandy would do you any harm," she said.

Leonora shook her head vehemently. "No, no . . . not after all the trouble we had last week. I've not touched a drop since."

"Now, now, don't be so hard on yourself," the Scots-woman said in a low, soothing voice. "That was only because you'd got into the bad habit of drinking late at night and on your own. Nobody ever suggested that you had a problem with the drink or anything like that. Take it from me, I would know if you had. I've seen enough of it over my lifetime. And anyway, this is different, it's to help you. A small drop would do you good and help to steady your nerves a wee bit." Mrs O'Shea got up from the sofa now and went over to the drinks cabinet. With her good hand she carefully pulled open the door and lifted out the half-drunk bottle of brandy. She put it on the table and then went back to get a glass. "You can think of it more as a medicine than a pleasure."

"Get two glasses, Lizzie," Leonora said. She gave a half-hearted smile that didn't reach her eyes. "If you join me, at least I won't be accused of drinking on my own."

Mrs O'Shea got another glass and the bottle of dry ginger.

"It would do you no harm to talk – and you know you can trust me," she said as they lifted their glasses. "There's not a soul I would breathe a word to."

Leonora took a sip of her drink and then sat back in the sofa, trying to steady her breathing. She was going to have to talk to somebody or she would go mad.

She closed her eyes, wondering how the older woman would react to such a shocking revelation. "We have a serious problem about . . . about Edward," she began, her voice faltering.

The housekeeper's eyebrows shot up. "He's not sick or anything, is he?"

"No. It's more a situation he's got himself into."

Mrs O'Shea took a sip of the brandy and dry ginger and then put her glass down carefully on the coffee table. "And what sort of a situation would that be?"

Leonora felt her throat and chest tighten and she just caught herself before she started off into another fit of coughing.

"Take your time," Mrs O'Shea said gently, "and take another mouthful of your drink."

"While he was in America, he was . . . he was involved with another man," Leonora said. And then, lest she should drag the awful explanation out any longer than need be, she added for clarification, "*Romantically* involved."

"Oh, dear . . ." the housekeeper, nodded her head. "Oh, dear . . . dear."

"Well, Lizzie," Leonora said in a hoarse voice, "there you have it. I told you it was a dreadful situation – could it possibly be any worse?"

"Indeed it could," the housekeeper stated. "It could be an awful lot worse."

Leonora's eyebrows shot up. "How? How could this bloody awful situation be worse?"

Lizzie O'Shea looked back at her. "Is it that Hennessey lad?"

Leonora's breath was taken away. "How did you know?"

She shrugged. "They were always close. I saw it when they were teenagers."

"Are you saying that you *knew* there was something going on between them? Something *unnatural*?"

Lizzie nodded her head. "I had a good idea . . ."

"But did you ever see them –" Leonora halted, unwilling to put words to the horrendous thoughts. "Did you know for sure?"

"Well, as good as," Mrs O'Shea said, giving a little sigh. She leaned forward for her glass again.

Leonora was aghast. "But you should have said something!" she said accusingly. "You should have told me or Andrew. We might have been able to do something about it . . . to stop it long before it reached this stage. We're his parents – we should have known."

"I never saw anything *that* terrible. And I didn't think it was worth all the trouble that telling would have caused. The way I looked at it is that these things are part and parcel of life – whether we like it or not. I'm not denying that it's hard when it's on your own doorstep but these things aren't as unusual as we would all think – it's just that nobody talks about them." Her voice dropped. "Looking back, I probably thought it was something they would grow out of."

Leonora closed her eyes. "Oh, God . . ." she said, wishing with all her heart that Edward had grown out of it.

"And you and Andrew had no idea yourselves?" Mrs O'Shea ventured. "Did it never dawn on you that they were a bit too close – that they had a different way of going on from the other lads that they were friendly with?"

"Nothing like that ever crossed my mind – and Andrew and I certainly never discussed it." The words were hardly out of her mouth when several incidents flew into Leonora's mind and she now remembered Andrew commenting that he thought Edward and Christopher spent a bit too much time on their own. Then she remembered another occasion when he suggested that Christopher stay in one of the spare rooms instead of bunking down on the floor in a sleeping bag in Edward's room. Had he suspected? she wondered now. She bit her lip, her brow knitted into a deep 'V'. "But it's illegal . . . isn't it?" she said now, her voice dropping. Oh, dear God, she thought. What kind of trouble is descending upon the family? And no Andrew here to sort it all out.

The housekeeper shrugged and shook her head. "That's something I would know nothing about . . . but I've never heard of anybody being put in jail for it. Not anybody I know, that is."

"That Oscar Wilde fellow – all the furore about him when it was discovered – and, like Christopher Hennessey, he was a married man."

"But isn't Christopher back in America? So what's the problem about him now?"

Leonora distractedly ran a hand through her greyish-blonde hair. "The problem is he rang this afternoon and said he's coming over to Ireland in a few weeks – *on his own*. He asked if he could stay here."

"That must have been a bit of a shock for you all

right. Imagine, coming all the way over from America – and the cost of it. An aeroplane ticket over here will cost him a fortune. And does Edward know about it?"

"Not yet." She halted. "At least I don't think he knows. But for all I know they could have written to each other or phoned and planned it all."

"Tell me now," Mrs O'Shea said in her forthright Scottish way, "have you discussed all this business with Edward?"

"He doesn't know that I know," said Leonora and then realised what she had admitted to.

Mrs O'Shea frowned. "So how did you find out – if he didn't tell you?"

"Oh . . . I can't say . . ." She couldn't bear going into the whole story about the crossed phone lines and the intimate conversation that she'd overheard. She feared that recounting it would tip her over an edge she felt she was very close to. She took a big mouthful of her brandy.

Mrs O'Shea nodded, accepting that there was something Leonora didn't wish to disclose. "What are you going to do?"

"I really do not know," Leonora answered honestly. "I don't have the faintest idea what I'm going to do – but I think I'm going to have to say or do *something*. I can't have this awful situation going on in my house and turn a blind eye to it. Bad enough they're both men – but the fact that Christopher Hennessey is married just makes it a complete abomination." She took a deep shuddering breath. "The whole situation is just dreadful, dreadful . . . dreadful."

"It's not the end of the world, it's not the end of the world . . . It's just an awful pity that you don't have

428

Andrew here with you at a time like this. He would have known what to say and do." Mrs O'Shea made a little clucking noise with her tongue. "He was a rare man – he had an answer for everything."

"Not *everything*, Lizzie," Leonora said quietly. He hadn't been able to find the correct answer when their marriage ran aground.

"There aren't too many men like him around anyway." Lizzie O'Shea's eyes suddenly narrowed in thought. Then she clicked her fingers together as she thought of an answer. "Daniel Levy! Why didn't we think of it before? He's the very man who could advise you."

Leonora shook her head. "No . . . no, I couldn't."

"But he's in the same line of work as Andrew was – he's a psychiatrist – he'd understand all about those kinds of things. And he's bound to know about the legal situation and all that – he'd know that from dealing with clients with that kind of problem."

Leonora wished with all her heart that she did have someone she could turn to, but not Daniel Levy. That would only complicate things further. Her hand moved to soothe the throbbing in her temple.

"Well, if I were you, I would ring him and have a chat with him." Mrs O'Shea patted Leonora's arm again. "Maybe you could even go out for a nice meal together – the way you used to. He's a very nice man and would be good company for you . . ."

"Enough, Lizzie!" Leonora said, her tone suddenly authoritative. She knew perfectly well that Mrs O'Shea would love to see her and Andrew's old friend matching up together but that was never going to happen.

The housekeeper gave a resigned sigh. "I was only saying . . ."

"I appreciate your concern but this is a very delicate situation and I have to be extremely careful who knows." She rolled her eyes. "God knows what would happen if this got out, we could end up visiting Edward in Mountjoy Jail. Dear God, it doesn't bear thinking about!"

"There's more of it about than you think," Lizzie said now. "I can name a few men in Scotland who were like that – and even a *woman.*"

"No!" Leonora said, her face aghast.

Lizzie nodded her head gravely. "Oh, aye. There was a woman who lived near to us, and you wouldn't have known what she was." She lifted her shoulders up and then winced in pain as the action told on her sore arm. "Big bulky woman she was, with a deep voice and a tight haircut, but nice in her own way. And then there was a fella that worked in the local paper shop – well, his family actually owned it." Her face lit up at the memory. "A lovely fella – and very good looking and particular about his dress too. His name was Angus McNab – a Protestant of course. You could always tell by the names in Scotland." She shook her head. "Oh, it was terrible waste. Never married or anything, and the local girls were all dying about him between his good looks and him being a great dancer, and the family owning their own business. When I think of it . . . his father died and the poor soul ended up running the shop and pushing his mother about in a wheelchair. Oh, he was devoted to her!" She raised her eyebrows. "They often are – those kind are very good to their mothers. All the elderly people around us in Glasgow used to say that they'd give anything to have a son like Angus McNab."

Leonora cleared her throat. "Well, thank you, Mrs O'Shea, for that, but I'd much rather *not* picture Edward pushing me around in a wheelchair and stuck looking after me for the rest of his life." A feeling of dread suddenly washed over her as she remembered the shameful lie she'd told Edward about her heart condition. She wondered if it had crossed his mind that he might have to stay in Glenmore House looking after her for the rest of his days.

"Oh, for goodness sake!" The housekeeper's face was a picture. "You know I wasn't thinking of you and Edward. I could never imagine you needing looked after by anybody. You're one of the most independent women I know!"

A silence fell over the room as both women lifted their drinks and sipped on them, silently pondering their own situations.

After a while, Mrs O'Shea put her head to the side, a thoughtful look on her face. "Do you think it would be worth speaking to Edward about it?"

Leonora's brows came down. "About looking after me?"

"No, no . . . I mean about the phone-call business. Talk to him straight and say you're very worried about him." She looked at the marble clock on the mantelpiece. "When is he due in?"

"I don't actually know. And I'm not quite sure what to do." She leaned forward to the coffee table to put her drink down. Then she turned to face the elderly Scottish woman. "Lizzie, I want to tell you that I'm very grateful for your concern and for your kindness. I feel better having talked things over with you . . ."

Lizzie put her good hand up to halt her. "Now, now, there's no need to thank me for anything. What did I do?"

Leonora smiled fondly at her and then she took the house-keeper's hand. "I don't think I've ever said it before, Lizzie, but I feel you're as close to me as some of my sisters and aunts . . . and I know you always have my best interests at heart." She squeezed her hand now. "I know you have *all* the family's best interests at heart and that's why I was able to tell you something that I would find it hard to tell most other people. I thank you for that."

Mrs O'Shea's eyes suddenly filled up with tears, but she quickly blinked them back. "But there's no need for that," she said in her awkward, blustery way. "No need at all."

Later, when Mrs O'Shea went back upstairs to have another rest in her room Leonora went into the kitchen, mulling the situation over in her mind again and again as she washed the glasses they had used. Time was going on and she was no wiser as to how she could handle the situation. But handle it she had to do – and before Christopher Hennessey phoned back again. Before he made plans to come and visit Edward and stay in Glenmore House.

She felt almost paralysed by the indecision of it all. When she had finished tidying around, she wandered over to the window to look out over the garden. After a few minutes, she went out to the porch and changed into her gardening clothes and headed out to deadhead some rose bushes.

As she worked methodically picking the faded blooms and clipping some of the wayward branches, she felt herself relaxing and was grateful when she eventually lost herself in the tasks.

An hour or so later, she knew the answer to her problems lay in a phone call. Mrs O'Shea was right, of course. Edward's future and happiness was much more important than her own pride. There was no point in pretending that she was coping on her own – she clearly wasn't. Turning to drink had only made things worse. And the problems she was dealing with were bigger than anything she and Andrew had dealt with together – and certainly much bigger than she had dealt with on her own. She needed help and advice from the right sort of person. And she had no time to waste. Edward could walk through the door at any time, and Christopher Hennessey would be ringing Glenmore House looking for him.

Chapter 38

Leonora felt so anxious she couldn't sit down on the chair by the phone. Standing made her feel just that little bit more in control. So she stood as she dialled the familiar number.

Daniel Levy's voice was warm and welcoming, as though there had never been any awkwardness between them. "Leonora! I'm delighted to hear from you."

"I need your advice, Daniel," she started in a quick, low voice, "your *professional* advice."

A slight pause told her that he was well aware of the point she was making. That the call wasn't a cosy, friendly one.

"Fire away," he said.

She suddenly faltered, not knowing where to start. "It's difficult," she said, feeling an intense heat rise over her chest and neck. "It's actually about Edward."

"Okay . . ."

Leonora swallowed hard. "He's home from America – back living in Glenmore House. There was a situation in America . . . an . . . an unhealthy relationship, and I had to find a reason to get him away from it."

"Okay," he said, his voice now interested and encouraging. The way Andrew's voice had often sounded when he was working a situation out. "And what was that reason?"

She felt her shoulders slump now with the weight of the whole thing. "I had to tell him that I was ill – quite seriously ill."

"And are you?" His tone had suddenly changed. "Are you ill?"

"No . . . not really. I've just had a few small problems with my heart. An irregular heartbeat – perhaps a touch of angina – that sort of thing. I know it was wrong but I had to say something to get him back to Ireland . . ." Her voice cracked now. "To get him away from the horrendous situation."

"Please tell me about it, Leonora," he said, his voice gentle and concerned. "It might help."

Her hand came up to her throat. "It's very difficult. It's not something I ever imagined I would have to deal with."

"I promise you that I won't be shocked."

Leonora felt a wave of misery wash over her. She gripped the edge of the table to steady herself. "There's no way of dressing this up. No way of saying it that will make it sound even a modicum better." She took a deep breath. "The fact is, Edward is a homosexual."

There was no weighing up of the situation – his reaction was instinctive. "Whilst I'm not going to judge Edward's sexuality in any way – please let me say from the outset that I understand perfectly how you feel about it. It's a difficult situation for any parent to face but I have no doubts, Leonora, that you will face it – and face it bravely."

Tears sprang into her eyes again and she struggled to control them. "He doesn't realise I know, Daniel. I found out by accident."

There was a silence, and then – as if he knew how vulnerable she felt having divulged the information – he went on in a more matter-of-fact tone. "Edward is not by any means alone. There are plenty of professional young men who are of the same persuasion. And while the rest of the world feels that the male and female relationship is the normal and natural one, we have to understand that their feelings for their own sex are natural to them."

Leonora cleared her throat now. "I can't find anything in the slightest bit natural about it," she told him in a choked voice. "I just cannot understand a man wanting to sleep in the same bed as another man."

"You mentioned earlier about a relationship. Is Edward involved with someone at the moment?"

"Oh, yes," Leonora sighed, "that's the worst part of all. The man he is involved with is an old school friend – a man who happens to be married with a child."

"Ah . . . I suppose that does rather complicate things."

"He was desperately unhappy about it, really falling apart – perhaps on the verge of making some terrible mistake – and that's the reason why I had to get him back home to Ireland."

"And how have things been since he came home?"

"He was a bit strained at the beginning," she confessed, "but he has improved. He's actually in Dublin today meeting up with a group of architects, presumably to discuss work. He hasn't made any definite decisions about staying, but I had hopes of him settling back into a business here, starting all over again and putting the American situation behind him."

"Ah, Leonora . . ." he said, his voice trailing off. "I'm afraid it may not be solved as easily as that."

Leonora closed her eyes again. "So I've discovered. The man – Christopher Hennessey – rang this afternoon to say he's planning a trip over to Dublin in the next few weeks. He's asked if he can stay here!" She paused. "I have the most dreadful feeling that he's planning on leaving his wife and child." She heard a sharp intake of breath on the other end of the line. "That's why I rang you, Daniel . . . I couldn't think of another person who could advise me on this. Someone who would keep it totally confidential."

"Well, I'm pleased you thought of me – and flattered. The confidentiality goes without saying."

"Thank you, Daniel. The thing is, I don't want to lose Edward – I don't want to ostracise him in any way from me or the rest of the family."

"I'm delighted to hear you saying that. It's exactly the attitude I would expect from a woman such as yourself – and it's the right one." His voice dropped a little. "You have my sympathy, Leonora. I know this is not an easy route but I'm confident that you will survive and flourish again after all this."

Leonora gave a small, cynical laugh. "Oh, I think my time for flourishing is long gone. And if Edward insists on going on with this – this unnatural situation, then I suppose I will have to resign myself to living the rest of my life with shame and secrecy and lies."

"I promise you that it's not that bleak," he reassured her quietly. "Life has a way of working things out."

"But what if Christopher Hennessey decides to leave his wife and child and move back to Ireland? They can't possibly have a life here. No decent people would accept them. They would be breaking the law . . ." Her voice dropped to a whisper. "God forbid, Edward could end up in prison."

"No, Leonora," he told her firmly. "That's most unlikely to happen. I know for a fact that the law is rarely acted upon and only when minors are involved or if it is without consent – that kind of thing. There would be little or no legal involvement when it's between two consenting adults. You can rest assured on that one."

Leonora felt a huge wave of relief washing over her. "Well, thank God for that," she said, suddenly realising that the thought of Edward being prosecuted had been her greatest fear.

"Will you be at home with Edward this evening when the call comes?" Daniel asked now.

"Yes. We'll be having dinner together this evening." She hesitated, reluctant to involve Daniel any further in her domestic affairs. "Actually, we've had another piece of bad luck in Glenmore House. Mrs O'Shea has had an accident – she fell and she broke her arm quite badly."

"Oh, no! The poor woman! And is she recovering?"

"Slowly. We're going down to Diana's tomorrow to give her a short break. While we're at home, she's constantly trying to do things she's not able for."

"Ah yes, she's that kind of person. And a break might distract her from her worry about her brother – she confided in me about that recently."

Leonora raised her eyebrows in surprise. Mrs O'Shea obviously felt more comfortable with Daniel Levy that she had realised, because she wasn't the sort to go bandying her business about to just anyone.

"Actually, I must go now," he told her, as if suddenly realising the time. "I really hope the situation works out well for you."

She felt a little flustered at the abrupt change in his tone. "Thank you. I'm very grateful to you for both your advice and for your time."

"There's no need for any thanks. We're old friends, Leonora, and it's what Andrew would have expected of me."

* * *

That evening, after spending some time among the things that gave her solace – the trees, the shrubs and the flowers – Leonora felt more relaxed and in control than she had for days.

After waving away any offer of help in the kitchen from her housekeeper, she had come up with a very reasonable dish of macaroni cheese – an old favourite of her eldest son's. Then, remembering a plate of leftover boiled potatoes in the fridge from the previous day, she sautéed them in a pan with onions and some of the herbs that she had bought the day she and Edward went to the Italian stall in the city market.

She had just put both dishes in the oven on a low heat when she heard the car wheels crunching on the gravel at the front of the house.

The calm she had felt after the phone call evaporated

when she saw Edward's tired and weary face as he came down the hallway. She pinned a smile on her own.

"How did it go?" she asked.

"A total waste of time," he said, dropping his briefcase onto the floor. "I don't know why I even thought it worthwhile going."

Leonora's heart sank. She knew it was unlikely that he was going to walk straight into a position but she hoped that he might have made some contacts – got a foot in the door. "What was so bad?" she asked, moving towards the kitchen.

"It's a closed shop," he told her, loosening his tie and following her. "They're not open to any new ideas and they're about fifty years behind the Americans." He shrugged. "It was okay starting off in Dublin as a newly trained architect, when I didn't know any better, but I just can't imagine fitting in here ever again."

"Don't you think it's a bit early to say that?" she ventured. "Maybe in a few weeks' time you'll feel different."

He raised his eyebrows, but before he had a chance to reply, the phone rang. "I'll get it," he said, moving towards the hallway again.

Leonora's heart quickened. She hadn't even had time to tell him about Christopher Hennessey's earlier call. She held her breath for a few moments and then she heard Edward call, "Mother, it's for you!"

As she went out to the phone, she smiled at him and said, "You had a call from your old school friend in America."

Edward's whole face lit up. All the weariness and disappointment he had poured out a few minutes ago had instantly vanished. He put his hand over the mouthpiece on the phone receiver so that the caller couldn't hear them talking "*Christopher*?" he said.

The way he said his friend's name brought an ache to Leonora's heart. She nodded.

"Did he say if he'd call back later?" he asked eagerly.

"Yes," she said, reaching forward to take the phone from him. His obvious delight caused a wave of anger to wash over her. Why can't he just be a normal man, she thought.

Terry Cassidy spoke in a low voice. "I've been thinking about you and I just wanted to apologise again for not being available earlier on. I still have a very busy house, but I'm looking forward to catching up with you when everyone has gone."

Leonora quickly reassured her artist friend that there had been no problem and Terry's soothing tones helped her relax and feel more normal. They chatted for a few minutes and then the front doorbell sounded. "I'm sorry, Terry, but I hear someone at the door and I must go," she said, feeling slightly flustered again. She had no idea who could be calling at the house this evening and unexpected guests were the last things she felt she could cope with.

As she walked down the hallway towards the door, Leonora felt an ache across her shoulders and a tight feeling in her head and she knew that it was from all the tension. She suddenly wished she could detour into the sitting room and pour herself a very large whiskey.

When she opened the door and saw Daniel Levy standing there – dressed in casual trousers and a dark blue shirt and a tartan tie – she felt both surprised and hugely relieved at the same time.

"I hope you don't mind me turning up un-announced," he said, "but my meeting finished much earlier than expected and I felt you could do with a little support at this time."

Leonora looked back at him for a few moments in silence and then she said in a low voice. "I'm very grateful that you have turned up, Daniel. I think you're the only person who could possibly help me." She opened the heavy wooden door wide for him to come through.

As he passed he held out a bottle of very good white wine – one which Leonora had chosen in a restaurant when they were out together. "I thought a glass or two of this might help things to look a tad rosier," he said, giving a wry smile.

Leonora recognised the wine. She looked up at him and smiled, "that's very kind of you." She lowered her voice. "You bring it in, and *please* suggest to Edward that we have a glass straight away, because I'm feeling more than a little fraught at the moment."

He put his hand on her arm. "Things are never as bad as they seem."

"Edward!" Daniel said in a warm, friendly voice when he walked into the kitchen. "I heard you were back home and, since I was out this direction, I thought I'd look in on you all and see how things are going." He held the bottle of wine out. "It's already chilled, so I'll let you be the barman."

Leonora felt grateful to Daniel when Edward passed her a generous glass of wine and soon she felt reasonably relaxed as they sipped their wine in the sitting room. Edward had just started to explain how difficult he was finding the return to Ireland professionally when Leonora heard Mrs O'Shea moving around upstairs, so she excused herself and left the two men chatting together. As she went into the hallway, it dawned on her that she felt lighter than she had ever felt since Edward had come back home – as if a weight had been lifted from her shoulders. And in a way it had. Daniel Levy's presence in Glenmore House had made a big difference. To have another person there who she could trust with Edward's very fragile situation was a great comfort to her.

As Mrs O'Shea came carefully down the stairs, Leonora thought she looked a little brighter.

"How are you feeling?" Leonora asked.

"I had a wee sleep," Mrs O'Shea replied, "and I feel the better for it."

"That's great to hear!" Leonora looked towards the sitting-room and lowered her voice. "You'll be pleased to know that I took your advice."

The housekeeper looked at her sharply. "And what advice was that?"

Leonora leaned in closer. "Daniel Levy," she said, whispering now. "He's in there chatting to Edward."

Mrs O'Shea put her hands together in a praying gesture. "Thanks be to God! He's the very man that might just help to put things right." She paused, thinking. "Is he here for dinner?"

Leonora looked flustered for a moment. "I hadn't really thought . . ." She looked at her watch. "I suppose we should ask him."

"Right," said Lizzie. "What's that I can smell in the oven?"

"Macaroni cheese – with sautéed potatoes."

"Vegetables?"

"No – I didn't bother."

"We can do mushrooms and tomatoes in the pan," said Lizzie, all business now. "I take it you'll be eating in the kitchen?"

"Should we?"

"Well, I know for a fact that Daniel enjoys eating there – he's told me that on many an occasion." She raised her eyebrows in a meaningful manner. "It might feel more relaxed for everybody."

"Okay – but on one condition: that you join us."

"Not at all! I can eat later when you've all finished."

"No, Lizzie, I insist! Daniel has been asking about you – he'll be delighted to see you up and about on your feet."

"Well, it looks as though I don't have much choice," the housekeeper said, but there was a pleased tone in her voice.

* * *

They had just finished their main course and Leonora was in the middle of taking a warmed apple pie out of the oven when the phone rang.

"I'll get it," Edward immediately said, getting to his feet.

Leonora glanced over at Daniel and when she caught his eye he winked back at her.

"Well, Mrs O'Shea," he said, turning to the housekeeper now, "I'm delighted to see you're on the mend. You've made a good recovery already."

As Daniel and Mrs O'Shea chatted about her health and the upcoming visit to Clare, Leonora put the apple tart in the middle of the kitchen table and took the cream from the fridge. Then she laid out dessert plates and cutlery.

"It's a while since I've been to Clare," Mrs O'Shea was saying, "and Diana is always asking me to go. At my age, if I don't go now when I have the time on my hands, I might never get to see it again."

Daniel leaned over to pat the housekeeper's good arm. "You've more than a few years left in you yet, Mrs O'Shea. But you've made a good point there that applies to us all." He looked directly at Leonora now. "There's an old Latin saying, which I think is a very true one: *Carpe Diem*. 'Seize the day'."

Leonora could feel his gaze on her. "Would you like cream on your apple pie, Daniel?" she asked.

"Yes, please. As I just said, we must seize all the little pleasures that life offers us."

The others laughed and Leonora passed him the cream.

She was just pouring tea for the three of them when Edward came whistling into the kitchen and she immediately knew what he was going to say.

"Christopher is planning a trip over to Dublin in a couple of weeks," he said casually, "and I said he was welcome to stay here. He said he mentioned it to you when he rang earlier, so I presume it's okay?"

Leonora felt her throat tight and dry. She took a sip of her tea. "Of course," she said, feeling her reaction was being discreetly watched by both Daniel Levy and Mrs O'Shea. "Christopher has always been welcome here."

Edward leaned over and lifted the teapot to pour himself

a cup. "Actually, I'm delighted because I wouldn't mind catching up with him, and getting his opinion on the business situation over here." He poured milk into his cup and then sat back down at the table. "I was explaining the situation to Daniel earlier and he could see the difficulties of slotting back into the system here after being out in America."

"Definitely," Daniel agreed. "Being in such a huge, progressive country for a few years must make it hard to return in any business, especially something like architecture."

Edward nodded. "Can you imagine working in the country that produced someone with such advanced ideas as Frank Lloyd Wright?"

"That's the chap who designed Fallingwater, isn't it?"

"It is indeed." Edward sucked his breath in through his teeth. "Can you believe that he designed that building back in the 1930s?" He gave a little sigh. "Lloyd Wright is Christopher's biggest hero – there's nothing about his work that he doesn't know – and I have to admit I'm a great admirer of him myself. We had actually planned to travel to Pennsylvania to see Fallingwater together some time."

"Perhaps you'll get the opportunity to do that in the future," Daniel said.

"Who knows?" Edward shrugged. "I might mention it to Chris when he's here."

Leonora felt a little flutter in her chest now and she felt conscious of not being able to add a single thing to the conversation.

Mrs O'Shea put her teacup down now. "If you'll all excuse me," she said, standing up, "I'm just going to go back upstairs as I want to finish writing a letter."

Leonora knew that the housekeeper was just being

discreet. She had always had the knack of knowing when she should absent herself.

Leonora stood up now as well. "And I think I'll leave you two men chatting, as I must go out and give my poor rose beds a drink of water." She put her hand on her son's shoulder. "There's brandy and cigars in the cabinet in the sitting room if either of you feel so inclined."

A half an hour later, Daniel strolled across the lawn to where Leonora was checking out a row of lettuces in the vegetable patch. She lifted her head and, when she saw him coming towards her, she felt her pulse quicken.

"Thank you for such an unexpectedly lovely evening," he told her, smiling warmly. "Your meal was excellent as was all the company."

"It was very basic," she told him, "but thank you for being so polite about it."

"I wasn't just being polite. It was really delicious – another hidden talent you have that I didn't know about."

Leonora looked back with a quizzical look on her face.

"Your art – Edward told me all about it. I believe you've had a number of commissions."

Leonora's hand came up to cover her face. "You've embarrassed me now," she said, her face flushing. "I'm only dabbling at it and the people who bought the paintings probably don't know the first thing about art . . ."

Daniel shook his head. "You're an extraordinary woman, Leonora."

They started to walk back in the direction of the house. "It's me who should be thanking you," she told him. "Having you there when Edward was discussing his friend really made things seem more normal."

"But they are normal. Edward's relationship is very normal for him. It's just unfortunate that society in the main doesn't see it like that, but I'm quite sure that in the future it will all change and people will have a greater understanding about these things and accept same-sex relationships much more readily."

"I wish it was now," Leonora said. "And I wish it wasn't my son." She paused. "Did he say anything to you about Christopher Hennessey?"

"He talked about him all the time and he confided in me about his friend's marriage difficulties – and how his wife felt that America wasn't working out for them."

Her head jerked up. "Really? Did he say anything about their friendship?"

"No, and I wouldn't have expected him to. He doesn't have a deep enough relationship with me to divulge something so personal and know it won't go any further. Years of keeping that relationship secret will be deeply ingrained in both men. They have a lot to lose by telling it to the wrong person." Daniel ran a hand through his silvery hair. "I think he will have to admit it to someone closer to him – someone he loves and trusts. Do you think he might talk to Jonathan or Diana?"

Leonora thought for a moment. "Maybe he'll speak to Diana about it over the next few days when we're down in Clare."

"If they care about him, they'll accept it. It might come as a shock to them at first, but they'll gradually come around to it."

"I hope they do, because I'm afraid I don't feel that I will ever be able to cope with it."

"You will," he said, putting a comforting hand on her shoulder. "You're much stronger than you think."

"You have been so good – you've got me through a very difficult evening. You came out of a meeting and drove all the way out here just to help me out. " She looked up at him. "I honestly can't thank you enough."

"Well," he said, "I can think of a way you can repay me. I have two tickets for the Czech National Orchestra in the Concert Hall in Dublin the Sunday after next, and I could do with a partner to accompany me." He saw the hesitation in her face. "You'll be back from Diana's before then, so hopefully you'll be free. And before you say anything, I'm not presuming anything more from the occasion than your excellent company. I'm perfectly aware that you don't see us as anything more than friends and I hope you can put any awkwardness you feel about our previous relationship behind you and enjoy what we have now. And," he added, "I think a night listening to some inspiring music might just give you a break from worrying about Edward and Mrs O'Shea, and help you to relax."

Leonora felt herself tense up at his suggestion. "Thank you for asking me, Daniel but with everything that's happening," she said, affecting a certain vagueness, "I just don't know if I'm free. I'll have to give it a few days to see how Mrs O'Shea is and that kind of thing."

"Perhaps you could ring me from Clare when you know where you're up to?"

Leonora nodded. "That might be best." she said. She lowered her gaze. "But if you have someone else in mind who might be free, I perfectly understand."

Chapter 39

Hannah paused at the door of the bedroom and then, with a very critical eye, looked slowly from left to right – checking that every single thing was in exactly the right place. After several weeks of working in the hotel, she had adopted a standard that was even higher than Mrs Slattery's and prided herself on being the fussiest chambermaid in the group of four who worked on the rooms. A solicitor and his wife were staying in the room and every morning they had left it in a terrible mess which had really annoyed her.

Satisfied the job had been done well Hannah closed the bedroom door and went out into the hallway to pick up a tray full of used tea things and glasses that she had cleared before starting to clean the room. She was just bending over when she heard footsteps coming along the corridor behind her. She turned to see the good-looking, well-dressed man who was staying in the room she had just cleaned.

"I've forgotten my watch," he told her. "It's in my other jacket pocket." She let him into the room and when he came out he halted at the door. "Actually, I'm delighted I've caught you, Hannah," he said, smiling warmly at her. "Sarah and I are heading off tomorrow and we wanted to give you a small token to say thanks for all the hard work you've done cleaning the room after us." He gave a small laugh. "It's been a pleasure coming back to a tidy room every afternoon. As you can see by the disorganisation, we're too used to having other people helping us out."

Since he had mentioned the words 'small token', the annoyance she felt about the mess she had spent ages clearing up evaporated and Hannah gave him a sweet smile back. "Oh, you're very welcome," she gushed. "It's been a pleasure looking after you both." She found it quite easy to be nice to him because he was handsome and he had a lovely manner.

He dug into his pocket and took out a ten-shilling note. "Treat yourself to something nice – or have a night out on us."

Hannah felt a surge of delight at the tip. "Oh, it's too much!" she protested in a high, girlish voice.

"No, no – I insist. You deserve it."

"Well, that's very generous of you," she said, putting the note into her white frilly apron pocket "and I really appreciate it."

Hannah heard a noise further down the corridor and glanced around to see Sinéad, the small stout chambermaid, watching her. Damn, she thought, I'm going to have to put this tip into the communal dish now! The Slatterys had a rule that all the staff had to put their tips into a big jar that was kept in the staff room. Every Monday it was divided up into equal amounts for all the staff, since the owners thought it was only fair that the staff working hard behind the scenes in the kitchen and the laundry got a share in the tips as well. Mrs Slattery had also came up with the idea of dividing the money on a Monday, as a lot of the staff spent the bulk of their wages over the weekend and were glad of the bit extra at the start of the week.

When she had first started, Hannah had thought the idea was great, but the longer she worked in the hotel, the more she realised how unfair the system was. She worked her socks off cleaning baths and toilets until they shone, making and changing beds – and being very, very nice to the guests. Sinéad and the other chambermaids didn't work half as hard as she did and they were the type that got all embarrassed and kept their heads down when any of the guests spoke to them. Hannah reckoned that she deserved to keep all the tips she got and resented having to share them.

The guest checked his watch now. "Must run now, we're heading out to the races for the afternoon." He rolled his eyes. "I hope it keeps fine as Sarah is all dressed up in her fancy flowery hat and shoes and we wouldn't want her to come back like a drowned rose."

"Oh, I think it's to be fine all day," she said, giving him a final, beaming smile. Then, as she watched him rushing off down the corridor, Hannah felt a sharp stab of envy of Sarah, the pampered wife, who spent all her days riding horses or getting dressed up to go to the races.

By the time she had finished the other rooms, Hannah had accumulated over a pound in tips. As she went downstairs to the staff-room for her lunch-break, she decided that Sinéad had been too far down the corridor to have seen the amount the guest had tipped her. She would do what she'd done a few times before – she'd make a big issue of the tip she had got from the couple and say wasn't it amazing that they'd given her *five* shillings. That would still be regarded as a very generous tip. She stopped for a few moments at a vacant lavatory and went inside to put the ten-shilling note inside her brassiere, just in case she should inadvertently drop it or lift it out of her apron by mistake. She had around eleven shillings in silver that she'd got between the other guests that had checked out that morning, so she would just say that included the five shillings tip.

A picture of a nice handbag she'd seen in *Moons* shop window earlier in the week flashed into her mind. It was more expensive than any handbag she'd ever had. She decided that she would put the five shillings towards it, and over the next few weeks she'd do the same with any big tips that she could keep out of the staff pot.

The staff room was busy with nearly all of the seats taken at the long, narrow table. Paul waved from the bottom end of the table as soon as she walked into the room to signal that he had kept her a seat beside him. Hannah gestured back to him and went over to the hot cupboard to see what today's offerings were. Two dishes, bacon and cabbage – which didn't appeal to her as she had it too often at home – and chicken in some kind of a tomato sauce. She settled for a piece of chicken and a scoop of mashed potatoes.

She went back to the table to sit beside Paul and, after a few minutes of eating and chatting to him and one of the waiters, she noticed the three chambermaids opposite whispering amongst themselves and occasionally throwing glances in her direction. They were quite obviously talking about her and she got the feeling that whatever they were saying wasn't complimentary. Used to this sort of treatment from girls at school, Hannah ignored them and kept her attention on the two lads.

"Hannah," Sinéad suddenly called out, "I was just saying that you got a very generous tip from that guest upstairs. Have you put it in the pot yet?"

Hannah turned to look at her with a puzzled expression on her face. "Yes, it was generous," she said, "and no, I haven't had time to put it in yet."

"Well, just in case you forget," Sinéad said, looking back at the other girls for support. "Because there's been a few times when we calculated the amount we thought we should get and the money in the pot didn't tally."

Hannah's eyes narrowed. "Why are you telling me? I always put any tips I get into the pot." She stared at Sinéad for a moment then shifted her gaze onto the two other girls until they looked away. "I presume you've been reminding everybody here about the tips and not just me?" She turned to Paul and the waiter and they both shrugged.

"We have a little dish behind the bar that any cash we get goes straight into," Paul said, "and when it gets full Joe puts it straight into the pot."

Then Sinéad said, "I was only reminding you because we were all delighted to hear that you got a really big tip – a ten-shilling note – and it's not often we see one of them in the pot."

A feeling of rage ripped through Hannah. She was now going to have to hand up the five extra shillings that she'd planned to save towards her handbag. She felt like leaning across the table and giving Sinéad a good slap across her big fat face! But years of submerging her feelings from her mother ensured that no on else had the slightest idea of just how angry she was. "Well, as soon as I've finished my lunch," she said in a deliberately light voice to show she wasn't annoyed at the suggestion that she had been planning to keep the money, "then you can all go to the pot and admire it." She gave a little tinkling laugh. "In fact, I might even ask Mrs Slattery to put it in a frame and hang it on the wall."

Everyone at the table laughed and any previous tension evaporated.

Hannah sat chatting to the two boys again for a while as people started drifting out, either back to work or to have a few hours off before beginning the evening shift. Eventually there was only her, still sipping her cup of tea, and Sinéad, finishing off reading the newspaper, left in the staff room.

Hannah turned to the side and on the pretext of adjusting her brassiere strap, retrieved the folded-up ten-shilling note. A minute or two later she slid it down into the deep pocket in her apron. She finished off the remainder of her cup and then turned back towards her work-mate.

"I'm going to put that money in the staff pot now, Sinéad," she said, "if you want to come and witness it."

Sinéad lifted her eyes from her newspaper, "Not at all," she said, a pink tinge of embarrassment coming to her face. "I wasn't suggesting anything by what I said . . . and if you thought it, then I'm sorry."

"Oh, no need too apologise!" Hannah said. Then she started to laugh. "It's funny – you know that fella that gave me the big tip?"

Sinéad nodded. "The solicitor?"

"Well, he was really odd," Hannah said, wrinkling her nose. "D'you know what he said to me?"

Sinéad put her paper down, all eager to hear.

"He said he and his wife thought I was far too good-looking and intelligent to be stuck here working as a chambermaid full-time." Hannah paused for a few moments to let Sinéad take this in. "You see his wife was chatting to me when I was cleaning the room and I told her I was only working in the hotel until it was time for my college course to start."

Sinéad stared at her.

"Well, she just said she was glad to hear that I was going into a professional career because I stood out from all the other girls in the hotel, and that I would be wasted in a place like this." Hannah shook her head. "I couldn't believe it . . ."

Sinéad's eyes suddenly blazed. "She had a feckin' cheek!" she stated. "I wonder if Mrs Slattery knows that she has such a low opinion of the hotel and the staff?"

Hannah shrugged. "God knows. But then she said that I should think of being a model." She gave another big helpless shrug. "For some daft reason, she seems to think I look like Marilyn Monroe. She even said if I was interested in anything like that, she could introduce me to a friend who had a modelling agency up in Dublin."

The stocky-looking Sinéad started to fold her news-paper up now, her lips set in a tight line.

"But I told her I had no interest," Hannah said, getting to her feet. "I said I was quite happy in Galway, thanks very much." She went over to put her cup in the sink. "I couldn't believe it," she said, laughing again. "Can you imagine me being a model?"

She watched Sinéad from the side of her eye now as the chambermaid came over in a very subdued manner to put her cup in the sink. Hannah suddenly felt a sense of elation and realised that the money for the bag didn't matter to her any more. It was worth it for the feeling of superiority she now felt towards the plain girl standing beside her. The girl who had tried to put Hannah down in front of the whole staff group.

Hannah had suffered enough put-downs at the hands of her own mother and the day she had left the family home in Tullamore she had vowed that no one would ever treat her like that again. Whatever happened now, Hannah knew she would get even with anyone who ever put her down again.

The issue over the tips had been well worth the five shillings.

Chapter 40

Leonora felt it had been a long time since she had been able to relax in a car as a passenger. Since Andrew had died, she had more or less driven herself everywhere. When Edward offered to drive her car down to Diana's she found herself eagerly accepting his offer. He was a very competent, sensible driver and she found she could lose herself in the beautiful scenery during the quieter moments while he concentrated on the driving and Mrs O'Shea dozed in the back seat.

As they drove along the narrow country lanes towards Kinvara, Leonora thought how much brighter Edward was since the phone call from Christopher Hennessey. He seemed more positive and hopeful about life again and he had even arranged another meeting in Dublin when they returned later in the week. Exactly what he planned to do if someone offered him work or a partnership in a business Leonora neither knew nor was prepared to ask him.

She turned towards the side window now, unconsciously giving a small low sigh.

"Are you all right," Edward asked, a touch anxiously. "You sound a bit tired."

"Do I?" Leonora said, giving what she hoped was a bright smile. "I'm actually fine, thank you, and I'm really looking forward to seeing Diana and James."

"The sea air will do you good," Edward said comfortingly.

"Hopefully, it will do us all good . . ."

"Are you very worried?"

Leonora looked at him. Had he guessed that she knew? "In what way?" she said carefully.

"About the heart thing. You're due to have more tests done soon, aren't you?"

She felt suddenly flustered. "I must check on the dates," she hedged.

"Do you feel okay? Do you feel any different?"

"Just a little breathless at times and a strange kind of a feeling."

"Well, hopefully it will be all sorted out soon and we'll know what steps need to be taken for the future."

"It was very good of you coming back from America but I feel a bit concerned that it might not have done your career any good – especially the way things sound in Ireland."

"I hope you're not worrying about that? Because if you are, you can stop it now." He took one hand from the steering wheel, reached over and took his mother's hand and gave it a reassuring little squeeze. "I'm absolutely fine. In a funny way, the break away from America has done me good. It's given me a chance to look at things from a different perspective. I know I've ranted on a bit about things being so behind the times over here but, after talking to Chris last night, I can see that coming back to Ireland hasn't been a bad thing."

Leonora caught her breath. "And do you think Christopher might come back to Ireland?" she gently probed.

"Who knows?" he said, shrugging. "We'll have the opportunity to talk about it when he comes."

Leonora took a deep breath. "And what about Theresa? Do you think she wants to move back?" She noticed her son's jaw suddenly tighten at the mention of Christopher Hennessey's family and she wondered if she had delved too deep.

"I honestly don't know," he answered. "I haven't gone into anything too personal with him at this stage. I'll find all that out when he comes over."

* * *

"Lizzie?" Leonora said in a gentle voice when they were only a few miles from Kilnagree. When there was no response she turned around in her seat and stretched back to lightly touch the housekeeper on the knee. "Lizzie," she said again, and when the older woman's eyes fluttered open, she said, "We're nearly here."

Mrs O'Shea looked around her for a moment as though not quite sure where she was and then she smiled. "Would you believe, I had the loveliest of dreams. I dreamt I was back in Glasgow at a wedding, and me and our Willie were up waltzing around the floor." She gave a little laugh. "I was wearing the most beautiful outfit – a lovely pink dress with a matching little jacket. I must get myself one like it the next time I have an occasion to buy myself a new rig-out.

Knowing our family, I could have a niece or a nephew getting married or maybe even a christening in the next year." She paused. "Please God I'll be in the whole of my health again soon and I'll be well enough to travel over to Glasgow if there's any kind of an occasion." She tapped her plaster cast.

"Hopefully this oul' arm will be as good as new when they take the cast off."

A short while later they were entering the small fishing village and Edward slowed down so they could all get a good look at the shimmering sea as they drove the final stretch to Diana and James's house. As soon as they pulled in the driveway, Diana was out at the door, waving vigorously.

"No sign of the dogs," Mrs O'Shea said in some surprise. She looked this way and that to see if she could see them. "And I've brought them two big bones as well that the butcher dropped off for me along with the meat the other day. I kept them all wrapped up in the fridge."

"Oh, they're probably around at the stables – she often keeps them there," said Leonora. It had just dawned on her that Diana probably felt the dogs were too much for the frail housekeeper and had decided to keep them out of harm's way until they were safely settled in the house.

"Welcome, welcome!" Diana said, rushing down to give the two women and her brother a hug.

"Did you have a good journey?"

"A perfect journey," Mrs O'Shea told her, "although I was in Scotland for a good part of it!"

Then, as they all walked up the stairs and into the house, the housekeeper went on once again to laughingly relate all about her strange dream.

Chapter 41

On the Monday morning, Rose was just finishing off her breakfast when her mother came rushing into the kitchen.

"Rose, would you be able to give me a hand down at the barracks this morning? I could do with you coming down along with me in about twenty minutes – they're having some officials down at the barracks and I've got to do a full roast lunch for them, and I've just remembered that the good white tablecloths and the napkins are at the bottom of the ironing basket. I've got to get them all ironed and starched and on the tables before they arrive." She turned to Martha Barry. "You'll be grand here with the girls for a few hours, won't you?"

"Of course I will," Martha told her. "I've plenty to keep myself busy."

"Well, don't be overdoing it," Kathleen warned her. "You know the doctor said you had to take it easy."

It was a beautiful sunny morning, and when she and her mother started walking, Rose felt grateful to be out in the fresh sea air.

"I won't need you for too long," her mother said.

"I'm going to drop over to Cathy's when I'm out that way. I want to show her my latest letter from Michael."

Kathleen looked at her daughter now. "Are you really still holding on for him, Rose?" she asked, in a slightly surprised tone.

Rose nodded her head. "What else should I do? I told him in the letter that I posted on Friday that as soon as I've saved my fare I'll come out for a visit and see what I think of the country."

"But it's going to take you an awful long time to save the fare – it could take a few years."

"Well, when Granny gets over this bad spell with her legs and her chest, I was thinking that I might be able to take on a job a bit further afield," she said.

Kathleen looked at her daughter. "I wouldn't pin your hopes on America, Rose. You never know what might happen . . ."

Rose's shoulders stiffened and suddenly the warm, sunny morning didn't seem quite so bright. "I'm not stupid, Mammy," she said quietly, "but there's nobody any better around, so it's not as if I've loads of choice."

"I'm just worried that you don't know this Murphy lad very well at all. And I don't think you should be pinning your hopes on him and maybe miss somebody better."

"Who?" Rose demanded. It was rare that she showed any anger with her mother but she'd already had all this from her grandmother and she didn't need to be told the same thing twice.

"You never know who you could meet over the next couple of years," her mother said, in a gentle, understanding tone. "There's no rush, Rose. I'd far rather you were at home and on your own, than off in a foreign country with somebody you hardly know." She shrugged. "Once you sign your marriage papers, that's it for life. There's no turning back. You don't want to go making a big mistake and end up miserable and far away from your family and friends. It's a long, long life if you're stuck with the wrong man."

"I wasn't talking about getting married, Mammy," Rose said now. "I was only talking about saving up to go for a visit to America."

"Well, I suppose there's no harm in dreaming. I suppose we've all had our dreams at some stage." She gave a little sigh, and then said, almost to herself, "I suppose I had my own at your age . . ."

Rose looked up at her mother now, wondering what had got into her. She wasn't usually this talkative about personal things and she wasn't usually so negative either. It suddenly struck Rose that her mother was talking about her own experience and it sounded as though she wasn't happy with the way things had turned out for her.

The morning went by quickly down at the Guards' Barracks. Rose set to work immediately on the linen-wear for the tables, sprinkling the rolled-up white tablecloths with a solution of powdered starch and water and then ironing them with a firm hand to make sure there was not a single crease left in any of them.

"If we get the tables set first, then the place will at least look decent if anybody walks in," her mother explained.

While Rose worked away at the big square tablecloths, Kathleen kept busy going between the large joint of beef that was roasting in the oven and the pots and pans cooking on top of the big heavy range.

Rose had moved onto the napkins and was busily ironing them into small triangles when her mother said, "Keep an eye on the potatoes on the top of the cooker, Rose, as I just want to tidy myself up a bit before the men all arrive."

A short while later Kathleen Barry came back into the kitchen wearing the lovely pink jumper that had come from Leonora Bentley and a string of pearls around her neck. Rose looked up to speak to her and was surprised when she saw her mother all dressed up. When she looked closer, she was even more surprised when she realised her mother was wearing powder and lipstick.

"You look lovely, Mammy! You rarely wear make-up to work."

"Just on special occasions,"

"And did you bring the jumper down as well?"

"I leave a few bits and pieces here for occasions. I can wash and dry them here and it saves me carrying them backwards and forwards."

Rose finished up the rest of the napkins and was just ironing a few linen teacloths when Guard McGuire came in through the back door. "I wonder what I've done this mornin' to deserve *two lovely* ladies." The jovial guard smiled warmly at them both. "And two hard-working ladies by the looks and the smell of all the cooking!"

"Rose," Kathleen Barry said now, handing her daughter a deep wicker basket, "would you bring me in the other towels and cloths that are hanging on the washing line, please?"

Rose went out into the garden and picked her way through the long wild grass to get to the line of items that were blowing in the breeze. As she took the pegs off each piece of washing and then put it in the basket, she was surprised at the length of the grass and wondered if the Guards themselves were the ones responsible for keeping it tidy or whether some other man came in to do it.

She put the last teacloth in the basket and turned back towards the building. Then she suddenly froze in her tracks. Through the window she could see her mother and Guard McGuire standing talking together. There was nothing in itself unusual about that – it was more the way they were standing. And the way Guard McGuire was looking at her mother. Then she watched in morbid fascination as the tall, dark-haired man moved his hand upwards to lightly touch her mother's cheek.

As she watched her mother step backwards out of his reach, Rose suddenly realised she had been holding her breath.

* * *

As she walked up the narrow path to Brennans', Rose could see Cathy around the back of the cottage hanging washing on a line that was strung between two silver birches.

"Look what the wind blew in! What brings you down here at this time in the day?" Cathy was obviously delighted to see her friend.

"I was giving my mother a hand up at the Guards' Barracks and I thought I'd drop in and see how ye're all getting on." She pushed away the uncomfortable picture of her mother and Guard McGuire that immediately flew into her mind.

"Well," Cathy said, pinning one of her father's shirts on the line, "any news?"

Rose smiled and nodded. "I got another letter from America."

"Let me just finish hanging these things out and then we'll go inside and get a cup of tea and have a bit of a chat," her friend said.

"Here, let me give you a hand," Rose said, going over to the peg basket.

In a few minutes there was a whole line of shirts and blouses and skirts blowing in the light morning breeze.

"That's another job done," Cathy said with some satisfaction.

They went into the kitchen and sat chatting over cups of tea for a while with Cathy's mother, and then Mrs Brennan went off to the bedroom with a cup of tea and some soda bread for her bedridden husband.

"Did you bring the letter?" Cathy asked as soon as her mother left the kitchen.

"It's in my handbag," Rose said, reaching for it.

Cathy waited, a small frown on her face.

Rose opened the pale-blue airmail envelope and slid the well-read letter out. "I can't believe he's kept his promise. He said he would try to write every week and he's been like clockwork. He's only missed the odd one or two weeks." She raised her eyebrows and shrugged. "I thought he'd be so busy with his new life that he wouldn't get the time to write. Or I thought the girls out there would be so glamorous that he would forget all about me . . ." She held the letter out. "Do you want me to read it to you or will you read it yourself?"

"Go on, you read it. You were always a quicker reader than me at school."

"I was not," Rose said, shaking her head, but they both knew it was true.

She had got halfway down the letter when she glanced up to see Cathy's darkened, serious face. "What's wrong?" she asked. "Is there something in it you don't like?"

"No, no . . ." Cathy said, suddenly looking all hot and flustered.

"What is it?" she persisted.

"Oh, Rose," her friend said, "I hate to tell you this . . . but you're not the only one he's writing to."

"What do you mean?"

Cathy walked over to the mantelpiece and lifted an identical letter which was standing behind a small, china Pekinese dog. "He's been sending me letters too," she said, holding the envelope out so that Rose could see the familiar writing and the postmark.

Rose's face went visibly white. "Well, sure there's no harm in that," she blustered. "You've known him for years the same as me – he's always been friends with your family."

Cathy hated to dash her friend's hopes but she couldn't keep it in any longer. "Oh, Rose, he's written half a dozen letters like yours to people in Kilnagree. I've seen a few of them from the other girls and from what you've read so far they all sound identical."

Rose looked down at her letter and she suddenly became aware of how shocked she was when she noticed the large, thin, airmail paper shaking in her hands. "But you didn't hear the rest," she said in a wavering voice that was unfamiliar to her own ears.

"Is it all about how you need to start saving up for your fare over to America, and how he'll take you out and about to visit all the famous places?" Cathy said quietly. "And did he say about how if you liked it, he might be able to fix you up with work if you wanted to move over there?"

Rose didn't have to say a word – her face told it all. She looked from her friend back down to the blue airmail paper. One big tear dropped on the thin paper, then another.

"Oh, Cathy," she whispered in a broken voice, "I've been an awful fool . . . I thought it was all special to me. I thought he really liked me." She scrabbled on the floor for her handbag again to get her hanky.

Cathy rushed over and put her arms around her friend. "I'm sorry, Rose. I feel terrible telling you such bad news but I didn't want you to hear it from somebody else. I was going to tell you but when you were so delighted with the last letter I couldn't and kept my mouth shut. But on Sunday after Mass I heard some of the girls going on about him inviting them over for a holiday and I knew then that he was sending the same letters to everybody."

"Has he sent you one nearly every week?" Rose asked in a choked voice.

Cathy nodded. "From what I've heard, I think he posts a pile of them at the same time. To some of the local lads as well as the girls."

"But the way he worded it made me think . . ." Rose broke off. She closed her eyes now and pressed her hanky tight against them. "I feel such an awful fool," she said, remembering the words that she'd pored over week after week, searching for meaning in them. Searching for something that showed he cared.

"I never took anything that he wrote the way that you did," Cathy said, "because I knew he never fancied me or anything. He used to call down to the house because he was friends with our Jim and I knew he was only writing to me for news because he knew that Jim was useless at writing."

Rose shook her head. "I feel so stupid – I really thought he liked me. I thought there was something special between us."

Cathy rubbed Rose's arm. "But there *was* something between you. He liked you more than any other girl – everybody thought that."

"He took me to the wedding in Gort," Rose said in a croaky voice, "and he told me I looked lovely. And he was taking *me* out the night he got the news about America." She closed her eyes, trying to force back the tears. "If he hadn't got the papers through to go, we'd still be going out."

"Of course ye would," Cathy agreed. She halted and took a deep breath. "But you can't change things, Rose. He *did* go to America – he actually chose to go there."

Rose nodded her bent head. "Do you think . . . do you think if I was to save up and go out there that maybe there might be a chance for us?"

Cathy pursed her lips together. "I don't know, Rose. All I would say is that you don't know how the land would lie by the time you organised everything – it could take a few years. Who knows what could happen in that time?" She shrugged. "I wouldn't like to say. All I know is that it's an awful long way from Kilnagree to go to America if you don't know what you're going to. Don't forget that Michael Murphy has a brother out there with him and relatives and everything. If you were to go out there, you wouldn't know anybody but him. If it didn't work out, you'd be up the Swanee then . . ."

"I can't believe it. It's what I've been thinking about first thing when I wake every morning and last thing in bed, every night."

"You'll get over it. And don't forget the old saying – 'It's better to have loved and lost, than never to have loved at all.'"

Rose couldn't manage a smile. "I don't know about that . . ." she said in a shuddering whisper.

"I've never even had a proper boyfriend," Cathy told her now. "So you're luckier than me. You've loads of lads after you. You'll find somebody else easily."

"I've no interest. After this, I'll be steering clear of lads." Then, tears suddenly sprang to her eyes again. "You won't tell anybody about this, Cathy? Everybody will just think I'm a complete *amadán* to have taken it all so seriously."

"You know I won't," Cathy reassured her. She hesitated. "What are you going to do? Are you going to keep writing to him – just as friends?"

"I don't think so. I think I've a bit more pride than that. I'd be watching every word I wrote to make sure I didn't say anything stupid and I'd only be wondering what he was writing in his letters to other people." She shook her head. "I won't be writing to him any more."

"If you don't mind me suggesting, maybe you could just drop him a short line or even send him a card at

Christmas, just saying how busy you've been." She bit her lip and looked awkward again. "It's just that it might look funny if you never write again – after you were writing so regularly to him."

"I don't care," Rose said bitterly. "He's had the last letter from me. He can write to whoever the hell he likes for news from now on."

* * *

When she left Brennans', Rose decided to detour around by the sea path instead of taking the direct route home. She didn't feel like going home yet and she felt that walking by the calming seashore might just help her to feel more normal for facing her granny. She knew that the old woman would instantly sense that there was something wrong and would worry about it until she told her. And of course that wasn't going to make Rose feel any better because both her granny and her mother had warned her about taking things too seriously. Even someone like Liam O'Connor could see that she was reading far more into the romance than there had ever been. When she thought back to the last night Liam had approached her down at the pub, she remembered how incredulous he was that she was still carrying a candle for somebody who obviously had no feelings for her.

Every time she thought about it now, a burning feeling washed over her. How could I have been so stupid? she thought. Imagine thinking that Michael Murphy could have had any feelings for her when he left Kilnagree with hardly a backwards glance. And when she looked back on it, he hadn't given any direct promises.

Everything he had said, she now saw in a totally different light.

Rose walked along the stony path now, trying to blank out the events of the last hour or two, the salty sea breeze whipping her dark hair up and making strands of it stick to the occasional stray tear that she couldn't control. She tried to focus her mind on other things but after a few moments it would all come flooding back again. Then she got a sudden picture in her mind of the way her mother and Guard McGuire had looked at each other down at the barracks this morning and she felt almost as bad again.

She was just rounding the bend in the road when she saw two figures in the distance – a male and a female – coming towards her. Then she caught sight of the two black Labradors bounding around on the beach close by. The woman had to be Diana Tracey. But, as they got a little closer, she realised who the woman really was. There was no other woman in the area who would be dressed in blue wide-legged linen trousers with a navy sleeveless top and a comfortably large blue-checked shirt over it. She had a straw hat dangling by her side, which left Rose in no doubt.

The girl's immediate reaction was to turn around and quickly walk in the opposite direction but she knew that wasn't an option. Leonora Bentley would definitely have recognised her by now, and it would be the height of bad manners to ignore the woman who had been so kind to her. If it had been any other day, Rose would have been delighted – if still slightly intimidated – to meet up with her benefactor, but today she didn't even feel up to talking to her own family. Rose lifted her handbag up and searched for her hanky again, then quickly rubbed her eyes with it.

She hoped there was no obvious sign that she had been crying but if Mrs Bentley said anything she would have to pretend that the sea air had been stinging her eyes.

When she saw that the well-dressed young man walking beside the Dublin woman was a stranger, Rose felt even more self-conscious. Then, as they grew nearer to each other, it dawned on Rose that she was dressed from head to toe in Diana Tracey's cast-offs and she wondered if Mrs Bentley would comment on them.

"Hello, Rose!" Leonora called, with a cheery wave of her hand. "I was hoping I might bump into you."

Rose gave a little wave and smiled back. Then she noticed there was something familiar about the way the young man held himself and she realised he looked very like Diana Tracey. He was obviously Leonora's son.

"Well, how are you?" Leonora tucked a strand of her blonde bobbed hair behind her ear. "I must say you're looking very well – even better than the last time we met. This sea air must keep you all young down here."

Rose felt herself blush. She obviously meant that Rose looked better in decent clothes. "I'm grand, thanks," she said, not feeling in the slightest bit grand.

Leonora turned to the man. "This is Edward, my eldest son."

Edward stretched his hand out straight away. "Delighted to meet you," he said, showing a row of even white teeth. He indicated the dogs who were playing on a large white rock, tugging a large piece of seaweed between them. "We thought we'd give the two boys a run out."

There was a little silence and, feeling awkward, Rose rushed in to fill the gap. "Are you enjoying your holiday?"

she asked, looking from one to the other. "Are you here for long?"

"Until the end of the week," Leonora told her. "And yes, we're having a lovely time. What are you doing with yourself these days?"

Rose felt her throat tighten. This was exactly the sort of question she hated anyone asking her. "Oh, keeping busy," she said, looking over towards the dogs who were now galloping their way towards the water's edge. "My grandmother isn't too well and with my mother working long hours I have to help out at home a lot." To her own ears it sounded as though she were a shirker. It sounded like excuses just to stay hidden away here in Kilnagree.

Underneath it all, she knew that the real reason she had remained at home was because of Michael Murphy. Even with him all those thousands of miles away in America, being in his home village made her feel closer to him.

Leonora nodded her head slowly. "Diana tells me that the bar and shop have changed hands."

"I help out there too whenever I'm needed," Rose said quickly. "The new people are very nice . . ."

The dogs – now a distance away – suddenly started barking ferociously at something they had found on the stony beach.

"Oh, bugger!" Edward said. "I'd better go and check on those two. We don't want to get in trouble with Diana if they eat something they're not supposed to or get attacked by a giant squid or something!"

They all laughed and the two women watched as he went off after the dogs.

Leonora turned now, her hands holding the straw hat

behind her back. "I'll walk back along with you," she said. "I think the dogs have had a good run and it's time we got back for afternoon tea." She looked at Rose now and suddenly smiled. "My housekeeper – Mrs O'Shea – came with me this time. She had a bit of a fall recently and unfortunately broke her arm so I thought the sea air might help her recover."

"Has she been here before?" Rose enquired.

"Oh, yes," Leonora said, "but it's always difficult getting her away – she always feels she has a mountain of things to do back at Glenmore House."

Rose gave a little sigh. "That sounds a bit like Granny – she can always find things to do."

"Well," Leonora went on, "this time Mrs O'Shea has no excuse to stay at home, as she finds most things difficult to do with her arm in a plaster-cast."

Edward called to his mother now and gestured that he was taking the two dogs back to the house. Leonora nodded and indicated that she would follow behind.

She and Rose walked along chatting, then just as they reached the Traceys' white house Leonora came to a halt. She looked directly at her young companion, as though something had just struck her.

"What plans do you have for your future, Rose?" she suddenly asked.

Rose's brow creased. "My future? In what way?"

"You don't plan to stay here now you have no regular paid work, do you?" Leonora said, her question more of a statement. "There's nothing here for an intelligent young woman."

Rose was very taken aback. No one had ever said

such personal things to her before. Well, apart from a very
pass-remarkable teacher who had advised her to go and
train as a geriatric nurse in England, since she obviously
had great patience with elderly people.

"I've always been happy enough in Kilnagree," she said
now. "I don't think I would like to live anywhere else."

"And have you actually been anywhere else?" Leonora
said pointedly.

"I go into Galway regularly," Rose stated, feeling most
uncomfortable at having to explain herself to this woman
who was more or less a total stranger. She also felt guilty
that she was now exaggerating to make herself sound better
travelled than she actually was, because in truth she only
went into Galway twice a year – once at summer and once
at Christmas. "I've also been up to Tullamore in Offaly
several times, and we took the train up to Dublin . . ."

Leonora recognised the defensive note in the Rose's
voice and immediately backed off. "Well, you've certainly
seen two major cities which is very good," she said, smiling
encouragingly at the girl, "and you've seen more of the
Midlands than I have. I wouldn't want you to think that I'm
criticising Kilnagree, because I'm not. I love coming here –
it's a stunningly beautiful place but unfortunately it's very
hard to make a decent living somewhere like this."

Rose nodded dumbly, trying desperately to keep her
mind off Michael Murphy, who was an obvious example
of what the Dublin woman was trying to say.

"It's a different matter for someone like Diana whose
husband has a profession that brings him to farming areas,"
Leonora continued, "and of course her own teaching work
is needed in these small, remote places too. But there's very

little other work for an intelligent girl like you." Her finger came up to press on her chin in a thoughtful manner. "Have you ever considered moving to Dublin?"

Rose shook her head. "Not really . . ."

"What if I was to offer you work out at my house?" Leonora suggested. "In the short term I think Mrs O'Shea could do with some help at the house for a few months but after that perhaps we could look at you attending college. You could live at Glenmore House and generally help out – and, in return, I would pay the fees for whatever course you decided upon."

Rose stared at the older woman in shock. "But I couldn't . . ." she stuttered. Then fear – absolute fear – took a grip on her. "I don't think my family would want me to go." She was almost babbling now – the words pouring out of her. "My brother has just left home to go to work in Galway and it would be too much for both of us to go in the same summer."

"Think about it," Leonora told her briskly. She could see the girl was afraid and obviously was being encouraged to stay put at home. She needed someone to guide her with a firm hand in the right direction. "You're a clever girl, Rose, and you won't ever get a chance like this again. Work and an education – and somewhere very nice to live. Your only problem would be deciding what sort of a course you would like to do. I think you would make an excellent schoolteacher or maybe a doctor's receptionist – something along those lines."

Rose stared at her for a moment. "I don't –"

"Think about it," Leonora cut in. She didn't know if the girl was overwhelmed by the generous offer – because by anyone's reckoning it certainly was – or whether she was struck dumb with shock at the thought of moving from the small village. Either way, she knew that there were bound to be lots of things to consider before Rose could come to a decision. "I'll be here until the end of the week. After that, you can contact me through Diana."

Chapter 42

Mrs O'Shea and Diana were in the Victorian wrought-iron conservatory when Leonora and Edward came back into the house.

Edward went off to make a phone call, so Leonora followed the sound of the women's laughter and found them both sitting at a small table playing cards.

"Well," Leonora said, in a high, mock-surprised voice, "so is this what you get up to when I'm out? Gambling now, is it?" She lifted a chair from under the larger cane table that was used for dining in the conservatory and came over to sit beside them.

"Did you know your daughter's a cheat?" Mrs O'Shea stated. "You'd have to have eyes in the back of your head to watch her."

Diana rolled her eyes to the ceiling and laughed. "Well, you were the one who taught me everything I know. I remember playing this years ago with you and Jonathan and Edward, and you used to show me little tricks to use when the boys ganged up on me."

"Isn't that a lovely thing to say, after all the years

I bathed and washed you and changed your nappies!"

Leonora listened to the good-humoured banter with a smile on her face, pleased to see that Lizzie O'Shea was definitely getting back to her old self. Every day there was an improvement in the housekeeper and every day Leonora thanked God for it.

Leonora looked across the small table at Diana now, and saw the shining, hopeful look in her eyes. Tomorrow morning she would get the results of her pregnancy test and Leonora hoped with all her heart that it would be positive news. It was the thing that would make the single biggest change in Diana and James' life – and they were more than ready for it.

"How about tea or coffee now?" Diana asked. "I have a lovely date and walnut loaf and a gorgeous coffee and cream cake that I specially ordered from the baker's van."

"Oh, you're making me feel guilty now," Mrs O'Shea said, shaking her head. "This is the first time I've visited you and not brought some home baking. I feel terrible, having come here empty-handed. I usually do that lovely coconut cake that James loves.""

"Now, Lizzie," Leonora said, putting a comforting hand on the housekeeper's shoulder, "the next time you come you'll be more than able to bake all James and Diana's favourites."

"Well," Diana said, "if things go the way they should, I'd be very grateful if you came down here to help me next spring."

"Why?" said Mrs O'Shea. "What's happening then?"

Diana looked at her mother and immediately Leonora knew she had good news.

"Have you found out?"

Diana nodded. "I had a phone call when you were out – the lab results came back earlier than they expected." Tears of delight sprung into her eyes. "It's definite – I'm having a baby and so far everything looks fine."

"Oh, Diana!" Leonora cried, and rushing over to hug her. "A new baby! How wonderful."

"A baby!" Mrs O'Shea said, putting her hands together in a praying gesture. "Thanks be to God and His Holy Mother! I've been praying for it for this long time."

Mrs O'Shea hugged Diana too and then all three women sat back to discuss dates and hospitals, and generally digest the good news.

"James?" Leonora suddenly said. "Have you told him yet?"

"I phoned him the minute I heard," Diana said. "Luckily he was still in the surgery so I was able to catch him before he did his farm rounds."

"How did he take the news?" Leonora asked.

Diana rolled her eyes to the ceiling. "Thrilled – almost as bad as me!"

"What a change it's going to make," Mrs O'Shea mused. "A new addition to the family!"

"Have you told Edward?" asked Leonora.

"Not yet – I thought I'd wait until you got back."

* * *

James brought two bottles of champagne and a huge box of chocolates with him when he returned home and insisted on opening them straight away, and everyone toasted the couple's good news.

"I'm so delighted to be here with you on this special day," Leonora said to Diana as they sipped the bubbly drink. Diana only had half a glass but she was so elated with her wonderful news that no alcohol could have lifted her spirits higher.

"We must ring your mother and father to tell them, James," Diana suddenly remembered, "and Jonathan and Emily in London." The couple went off into the hallway to make the phone calls and then Mrs O'Shea decided she would go up to her bedroom to change into more comfortable shoes.

Leonora glanced over to see her elder son with a very thoughtful look on his face. "That was a lovely celebration, Edward, wasn't it?" She went over and stood with her arm resting on the back of his chair. "Are you all right?" She suddenly got the urge to reach towards him and ruffle his thick hair – as she had often done when he was a young boy – but something stopped her in her tracks. Then a feeling of self-consciousness washed over her as she realised it was because she was worried that Edward would think she was drunk from the champagne. She had, in fact, been very careful and made sure that she didn't drink it too quickly, so she knew it hadn't had any great effect on her. But, she supposed, that was the price she paid for having abused her little habit for too long and for causing a fairly serious accident.

"It was a lovely celebration," Edward said, smiling at her, "and I'm so very pleased for Diana and James."

There was something in his voice that touched her and Leonora felt her heart go out to her son for the very complicated situation he was in.

He reached forward to the table now and lifted a three-quarters-full bottle of champagne. "Will we have another glass?"

Leonora looked at her glass which was almost empty.

He held the bottle out to her. "Go on," he said, "it won't do you any harm!"

Leonora took a deep breath. "I'm just being careful . . . I don't want you to think –"

"Look, Mother," he said, putting his hand over hers, "I know I had some concerns a few weeks ago about you drinking on your own late at night but that's all stopped. I really don't think you have a serious drink problem or anything like that." He squeezed her hand. "You have things back under control now, so I don't think we need refer to it any more." He held the bottle out. "I think a new baby in the family is definitely worth another glass!"

* * *

Leonora helped Diana with dinner that evening while Mrs O'Shea clucked around muttering about her 'damned arm' and saying how useless she was.

"But I'll make up for it," she promised, "and Diana and I have it all arranged, don't we?" She looked at the mother-to-be for confirmation. "We've decided that I'll come down for a fortnight and help her to look after the new baby. New mothers need their sleep and I'll be only too delighted to get up and feed it during the night."

Diana looked at James and then they both burst out laughing.

"That's very kind of you, Mrs O'Shea," Diana said, "but I was just telling James earlier that I plan to breastfeed."

"Oooooh!" Mrs O'Shea said, a look of astonishment on her face. Then she saw the funny side of it. "I think the poor child would be waiting a long while for anything from me!" she laughed now. "But I'm a dab hand at washing and bleaching nappies!" She nodded over to Edward. "I got thrown in at the deep end with that one." She closed her eyes and shook her head. "Oh, he had the worst nappies you've ever seen!"

"Enough!" Edward said, holding his hand up. "We change the subject immediately or I'm off out with the dogs." He winked over at James. "And I might just drop into the bar for a pint of Guinness while I'm there."

"That could be arranged," James said, winking back. "And you might need a bit of company in case you can't find your way back."

"Later," Diana told them. "We have dinner first and then you can go wherever you want."

Over dinner the conversation turned to the work that was being done in Glenmore House while they were away.

"I don't mind renewing the carpets," Leonora said, "because they are going threadbare in parts. But unfortunately there's been a bit of damage to some of the paintwork and old wood panelling in the hall, and the lower parts of some of the furniture." She shook her head. "I think that's going to take specialist work, because they are antique pieces and they will all need stripping down and polishing."

"I know the very man for the job," James said.

Diana gave him a quizzical look, then the penny dropped. "Of course!" she exclaimed "Liam O'Connor! He's just recently moved up to Dublin."

"No better man," said James. "He's done brilliant work on my antique pieces, Leonora. He's only a young man, a local chap, but he's gifted where wood is concerned – and the more intricate the piece the more he loves it. He regards it as a challenge. He can literally restore anything."

"And you say he's up in Dublin?" Leonora asked.

"He's working for his uncle up there making furniture," James said, "but he told me that he had organised some sort of a place to do his own work on antiques in the evenings and at the weekends."

"And how would I get in touch with him?" Leonora asked.

"I can easily get his address from the family," James said. He looked over at Edward now and laughed. "Coincidentally, his father and his brothers are often down in Purcell's bar in the evening. If we take a walk down there we might just come across them."

* * *

"Now, Mother," said Diana as she sat with Leonora in the sitting room late that evening, "I need to ask you something."

"What is it?" Leonora waited expectantly.

"Have you been keeping something from me? Edward tells me that he is concerned about your heart problem. So concerned he thinks he will have to stay in Glenmore House indefinitely . . ." She halted, a deep frown on her forehead. "So it seems there is more to the angina problem than you've told me."

Leonora took a deep breath. She had asked Edward not to say anything as she didn't want to worry Diana and Jonathan but she hadn't considered the fact that his need to share his concerns with his brother and sister might override that.

"I think Edward is over-worrying," she hedged.

She now realised she was in a very tangled web of her own making. What was she to do now? She couldn't tell Diana the truth without revealing what she knew about Edward and Christopher Hennessey. What if he wanted to keep it a total secret – and she had blurted it out? What if Diana couldn't handle knowing about Edward's sexuality? So many dilemmas and so many lies.

Perhaps she would try the truth.

"Diana," she said in a slightly breathless voice, "I am not seriously ill but I had a very good reason for asking Edward to come back home for a while." She looked up at her daughter. "If you would please just trust me for a while longer I will explain it to you when the time is right."

Diana looked more puzzled than ever. "Okay," she eventually said. "As long as you're all right . . ."

Leonora felt her head starting to throb. The last thing she needed now was a migraine. "I don't mean to fob you off, Diana," she said, wincing at the pain which had just developed over her eyes, "but I think the boys could be home any minute now, and it might be best to talk about this another time." She looked up at Diana. "Please, darling?"

"Oh, Mummy I'm sorry," Diana said, calling her mother by her old childish title, "I didn't mean to go on. You've got a headache now, haven't you?"

"Just a touch," Leonora said, attempting a bright smile. She looked at the clock. "You know, I think I'll head off to bed now, too."

As she walked up the stairs Leonora thought what a strange day it had been. A mixture of great highs and lows. The wonderful baby news – Mrs O'Shea sounding back to her old self – Rose Barry turning up her nose at the offer of having a free education and living in Glenmore House – and now Edward's situation coming to the fore.

All these thoughts whirled around in her head as she undressed and washed in readiness for bed. And by the time her head hit the pillow her thoughts had turned to Daniel Levy and his invitation to the concert at the weekend. She had to make a final decision on this and then get in touch with him.

Her head began to feel really tight.

It was all too much to think about now, Leonora decided.

It could wait until tomorrow.

Chapter 43

Rose went out into the vegetable patch in the garden, carrying a small trowel and a cream enamel basin, to pick some carrots for the evening meal and some small beetroots for her granny to pickle in vinegar. As she set about her task, she wondered how she should broach the subject of Mrs Bentley's offer with her mother.

The thought of it filled Rose with a kind of dread that she couldn't really explain. It had something to do with leaving Kilnagree – leaving Clare – and leaving all the people she knew behind. It was a fear that things would change irrevocably after she left and it would never be the same again.

She filled the bottom half of the basin with the earth-encrusted carrots, and the top half with the round, firm little beetroots, and then she set it down by the side of the vegetable patch and walked down to the bottom of the garden, where she had a clear view of Galway Bay.

She stood leaning on the dry-stone wall, staring into the distance and trying to make sense of all that had happened in recent months. Waiting for Michael Murphy had taken over everything – it had taken over her *real* life. She had put everything else in Limbo, just going through the motions of doing everyday things, when her mind was far off in a strange place she knew nothing about.

From the descriptive passages in Michael's letters she had built this world up in her head. It had only been words that had conjured up pictures.

Rose had often found herself doing this when she was a little girl. If she was going somewhere she had never been before – like a school outing on the coach to Salthill – she always got a picture in her head of what it was going to be like. But very often the reality turned out to be totally different. Sometimes it was better and sometimes it was much worse.

She wondered now if she had grown up at all – because she had obviously done the very same thing when she'd built up the scenario with Michael Murphy. She reckoned she was going to have to wake up and realise that her life was here and now – and not in some far-off place in the future. Cathy Brennan's honest appraisal of the situation yesterday had confirmed that. In one fell swoop, it had removed all the vivid pictures she had created of a life she was never going to live. The only problem now was the great empty hole all those banished images had left behind.

Rose had no idea how long she'd been leaning on the wall when her granny's voice brought her back.

"Rose!" Martha Barry called in a high, thin voice from the doorstep. "Have you got the carrots and the beetroots for me yet?"

"I'm coming, Granny!" Rose called.

Her granny had only gone a few steps back inside the

house by the time Rose caught up with her. "I was just having a look out at the sea," she told her. "It's a funny greenish-blue colour today."

"Ah, it's like people – it changes all the time," Martha laughed.

Rose lifted the basin into the white stone sink for her grandmother to wash the vegetables. Then she turned around and saw the old lady sitting by the table with her head bent. "Are you all right, Granny?" she asked.

"I'm grand, Rose," she replied. "Just catching my breath . . ."

Rose went over to the recently boiled kettle. "I'll make us both a cup of tea," she said.

A little later, as they sat at the table preparing the vegetables, the story of Cathy and all the similar airmail letters that Michael Murphy had written gradually came out.

"So you were right all along, Granny," Rose said, raising her eyes to the ceiling and sighing. "I've made an absolute *amadán* of myself thinking it was only me."

"Ah, Rose," the old lady said, shaking her head, "I never knew any more about it than you. I was only warning you about not waiting for him for years and years. I never guessed for one minute that he would be writing to various ones around the place." She put her hand on Rose's. "It's far better you know *now* so you're not wasting any more time on him."

"True enough," Rose said, wondering if it was possible to explain that with Michael Murphy now firmly out of her life, she felt as though her future was like staring out over a frighteningly dark and unfamiliar ocean.

Chapter 44

Leonora was awake before dawn on the day that Christopher Hennessey was due to arrive in Dublin. Edward was driving up to collect him and they were going to have lunch in the city before driving down to Glenmore House. She had planned a special meal for that first evening with her son's friend, thinking that all the ceremony of the dishes and sauce jugs being brought back and forth would distract her from her own anxieties about the visit.

Mrs O'Shea had now had her plaster-cast removed and was able to do some of her lighter tasks, and as long as someone helped her with lifting the heavier pots and pans she was delighted to be back cooking. Terry Cassidy had been invited and Leonora knew the artist would keep everyone entertained with her travelling tales.

She had considered asking Daniel Levy to the meal as well but decided that it was a little too conniving to have two guests who knew about Edward and Christopher's relationship without her son being aware of it.

Leonora had lain awake for hours, going over and over the situation in her mind, and she had decided that she could no longer put off the conversation she needed to have with Edward. She was going to speak to him that very morning.

When she had met up with Daniel Levy the previous week to go to the concert, she had used the occasion to spill out all her concerns about the two men meeting up again. They went into the bar in the Concert Hall for a drink before the evening's programme was due to start. Leonora had deliberately picked a corner to sit, where they could talk without being overheard.

Daniel had gone to the bar and brought back two glasses of gin and tonic and then he had sat back and just listened.

"I feel I can't have Christopher in my house and pretend that he is a normal married man who is having just a normal male friendship with my son – when I know the reality is so very different," she stated. "I feel it would be completely hypocritical of me to allow Christopher to come and go and say nothing. I'm not going to ban Edward from bringing his friend to Glenmore House but I feel he should know that I'm fully aware of their relationship."

Daniel had listened carefully and then seemed to weigh up every word before he spoke himself. "Okay. What are you going to do about it?"

"I know what I want to say but I'm not sure how to go about it," Leonora told him. "I'm terrified of starting off on the wrong foot, and then having Edward walk out on me before we get the chance to talk properly." A look of anguish crossed her face at the thought. "If that happens, our good relationship could be damaged forever. Edward is very deep and he could feel so hurt that he might distance himself from me and Diana and Jonathan."

"I understand what you're saying," Daniel said softly.

"So it's important that you approach the subject in a gentle, caring manner." He paused for a moment. "If we were to rehearse something it might make it easier."

"What exactly do you mean by *rehearsing*?"

"If we work out the exact words that you start off with – words which express the fact that you love and care about him and want to help. Then hopefully Edward will take his cue from there and start talking himself."

Leonora's brow furrowed. "But what if he tells me that he wants to be with Christopher Hennessey no matter what?"

"Then you have to accept it and keep loving and supporting him."

Leonora shook her head. "I don't know if I can do that."

"But you must," Daniel said.

There had been a few moments' silence and Leonora briefly wondered if she was seeking advice from the wrong person. Daniel Levy seemed very accepting of the homosexual relationship that she found so repellent. Would she have been better going to someone who would have advised her to take a firmer stance? At the end of the day, she reckoned, if the relationship continued, then that is exactly the reaction Edward would face from the vast majority of people he encountered.

"How do you think Andrew would have handled this situation?" Daniel asked her softly now.

Leonora flinched at the mention of her dead husband's name. "I have no idea," she faltered. "Thankfully, we never came up against anything like this . . . I don't think either of us could have envisaged facing such a predicament."

"I think I know how he would have reacted," Daniel said. "I think he would have initially been defensive and very protective of Edward's reputation – just as you are now. But after he had time to think about it, I'm sure he would have come back with a more open attitude and have been willing to look at things in a different way."

"What makes you think that?" Leonora asked.

"Because I know that Andrew had a very sensitive, understanding side to him. I know that he was very capable of seeing things from another person's point of view."

Leonora's face tightened. "I think you are talking about the professional side of Andrew," she said quietly. "I am talking about the Andrew I knew as a husband and a father."

Daniel nodded his head. "Of course," he agreed, "and I'm not trying to suggest that I knew him in the way that you did." He paused, searching for the right words. "But I did know the personal side of him to some extent. I'm not saying that he confided in me completely but he did talk over some issues that gave me some insight into the depth of character that he had."

Leonora felt a small pang of alarm now. Had Andrew discussed intimate details of their marriage with the man she was now sitting opposite? Did Daniel Levy know more about her than she realised? Did he know details about the raw wound that she still carried around inside her? The wound that refused to heal. The wound that had never let her truly grieve for her husband.

The thought made her want to lift her handbag and coat and flee from the bar – far away from here and far away from him.

Daniel Levy's hand came across the table now to

catch hers. "Leonora," he said gently, "whatever you think of me, I want you to know that I hold you in the very highest regard – and I promise that you can trust me. This situation with Edward is a very delicate one. For your sake and Edward's – and for the friendship I had with Andrew – I want to help you."

Tears suddenly sprung into Leonora's eyes, and as she reached for her handbag to search for a hanky, she knew they were too obvious to hide. "Oh dear God!" she said, lifting a corner of the hanky to discreetly rub at her eyes.

Daniel gave her a few moments to compose herself. "I think it will help if you start off apologising to Edward," he said quietly.

"For what?" Leonora whispered.

"For exaggerating your heart problems . . ."

There was a small silence.

"That will give you the opening to explain why you did it. You can then go on to tell him how you rang and he came onto the phone presuming your call was from his friend Christopher – and explain that the details he gave could only lead to one possible conclusion."

Leonora's tears dried as she listened and they rehearsed exactly what she would say. By the time they had gone over the scenario twice, the curtain call came for the concert.

At the end of the night Daniel had left Leonora, asking her to ring and let him know how things had gone.

But the week had come and gone without her finding a suitable moment to discuss anything personal. Or so she tried to tell herself. In her heart she knew she was avoiding the issue.

Glenmore House was much busier than usual as Leonora

had managed to get a local woman, Mrs Burke, to come to help Mrs O'Shea. Mrs Burke was pleasant enough and willing to do anything she was asked, but Leonora found her a bit too inquisitive, and on several occasions came across her scrutinising family photographs and opening cupboards that she had no business opening. Mrs O'Shea wasn't too impressed with her helper either, feeling she was altogether too familiar. Several times during the week it crossed Leonora's mind how very silly and immature Rose Barry had been to refuse the position in the house and the chance of a good education. Instinctively she knew that the housekeeper and the young girl would have got on very well, and in a strange way she was disappointed for herself as she felt Rose might have filled a small gap in her own life.

The days went past and suddenly Leonora realised that she was running out of time. Then the day of Christopher's arrival dawned and a determined Leonora asked Edward if he would come out into the garden to help her to pin up a trailing rose bush which had blown down in the wind.

Edward was in a jovial mood but, knowing him so well, Leonora could tell that he was trying to appear more relaxed than he actually was. But there was a light in his eye that hadn't been there since he had come back home.

They walked out into the garden, pausing to look at the vegetable patch to see how the cabbages and cauliflowers were doing, and then they stopped again at the strawberry patch to check how the crop was coming on.

"I'd say they're ready to pick now," Edward told her. "If you like I'll pick a bowl when we're finished this little job and we can have them later in the evening." He gave a beaming smile. "Strawberries and fresh cream is a big favourite of

Christopher's. He used to love having them when he came here for weekends from school in the summer."

Leonora's chest tightened as she thought of all the weekends that the two boys had spent in Glenmore House together when they were teenagers, all the hours they spent up in Edward's room supposedly playing *Monopoly* and chess. God knows what they had been getting up to. The thought made a shiver run through her and Edward noticed.

"Are you cold?" he asked, concern in his voice.

"Not really," Leonora said, struggling to smile at him.

"How are you feeling these days?" he asked, as they walked towards the walled part of the garden where the rambling roses were growing. "I know that you're probably putting on a brave face but most of the time you just seem like your old self." He put his arm through hers. "I have to keep reminding myself that you're not actually very well."

Leonora immediately took her cue. "Can we sit down for a few minutes, Edward?" she said, motioning towards the old sturdy bench that she and Andrew used to sit on. "I need to talk to you . . ."

They sat and then, when they were settled, she took a deep breath and started.

"I have a very serious confession to make and I only hope you can find it in your heart to forgive me."

Edward looked startled and then alarmed. "What is it?"

"I'm not seriously ill, Edward. The doctor thinks I have angina but it's not as serious as I've made out – and I don't need an operation."

There was a silence which Leonora suddenly found herself filling.

"I am so sorry for deceiving you but it was done with

the best of intentions. I really needed you to come home to Ireland."

"But why did you lie?" Edward sounded bewildered rather than angry. "Why didn't you just tell me that you wanted me to come home for a while?"

"Because you wouldn't have come for no good reason and I couldn't have expected you to."

Edward stared at her now. "But why did you need me so badly?"

Leonora felt stuck for a few moments – not sure how to continue. Then, she remembered what Daniel and she had rehearsed. She reached over and took her son's hands in hers. "Edward," she said in a shaky voice, "I wanted you to come home because I knew you were in trouble. I knew what was going on between you and Christopher . . ."

Edward's face immediately darkened. "What are you talking about?" he said, his hands now rigid in hers. "What do you mean about me and Christopher?"

Leonora's face started to crumple. "Oh Edward, I know about your relationship – your very close relationship! I phoned you very late one night and before I had a chance to speak you came on the line, presuming I was Christopher . . . and I heard everything you thought you were saying to him."

Edward's face was stony now. He pulled his hands away from his mother and then stood up – several feet away from her. "I don't know what you heard – or think you heard, but it's not something I'm prepared to discuss. The friendship between myself and Christopher is completely private."

Leonora felt her throat and chest tighten. "Edward,"

she said, her voice trembling now, "I would not have interfered, except for the fact that I was very concerned about you for months before this phone call, and so were Diana and Jonathan. We all felt worried. Your phone calls had dwindled away, and whenever anyone spoke to you, they noticed there was a big change."

"Have you discussed this with Diana and Jonathan?" His voice was low and strained.

"No . . . no. I wouldn't dream of discussing this with them without having spoken to you." Then, when she saw the frightened, defensive look in his eyes she remembered Daniel's advice again. "Edward, I love you very, very much. We all love you and only want to help you. When I heard you that night on the phone, in such utter misery, I felt I had to do something, *anything*, to get you away from the situation."

His threw his hands up in the air now. "But you don't understand!" His voice was loud now, bordering on a shout. "Nobody understands!"

"I do understand, Edward," Leonora said, her voice firmer now. "I know that you are very unhappy because you're separated from Christopher – by distance and by the circumstances of his wife and family – and I want to help you in any way I can."

Edward started to laugh now, a hollow kind of laugh that didn't reach his eyes. "Help me? You thought that by bringing me back to a country where I can't even get a decent business up and running was helping me?"

"You were so unhappy, Edward. I heard everything you said on the phone – and I felt that you needed to get away to think things over." Her voice dropped now.

"And you needed to give Christopher and his wife time on their own."

Edward stared at his mother. "You had no right to interfere! What you heard was not your business. If I'd wanted you to know, I would have told you. It is much too complicated and sensitive to involve other people."

"I'm sorry you feel like that but I truly did it out of love and concern for you. I did it to help you." She halted. "And I'll continue to help you, Edward – if you'll allow me – to find the path that will lead you to happiness and peace of mind. Whatever that path is – even if it means you and Christopher making some sort of life together – I'll be there behind you."

"I don't need anyone's help," Edward said quietly and firmly.

Leonora nodded her head. "Whether you want my help or not," she told him, "you will always have my love."

* * *

Leonora did not phone Daniel Levy after the pale and grim-looking Edward left for the airport. There was nothing to say. All the careful rehearsals they had gone through had come to nothing and all Daniel's theories about the situation had come to nothing.

Edward had clammed up and their relationship was now at its lowest point ever. And Leonora now felt that her 'bull in a china-shop' approach had quite possibly caused irreparable damage not only to her relationship with Edward but to the relationship he had with Jonathan and Diana as well.

Around five o'clock that evening when Leonora was

expecting Edward to arrive with his guest, he phoned instead to say that they had decided to book into a hotel in the city centre instead.

"I didn't want you worrying," Edward said in a strained voice.

"Thank you for letting me know," Leonora replied. "I hope you both have a nice evening."

She asked no questions and she did not mention the meal that she and Mrs O'Shea had cooked, nor did she mention the bowl of strawberries that she had picked for Christopher Hennessey. She had quietly phoned Terry to tell her the meal was cancelled but when her artist friend began to gently probe as to the reason, she found herself saying she hadn't time to chat and would ring back soon.

When Daniel Levy phoned later that night to check how things had gone and how Leonora was, she asked Mrs O'Shea to tell him that she had gone to bed with a slight headache and would contact him when she felt better. She hadn't the heart or the energy to tell him that all the planning and rehearsing had failed quite miserably.

The thing she had feared most – an estrangement from Edward – had now happened

*   *   *

It was the following evening when Edward's car pulled into the drive at Glenmore House. Leonora was around the side of the house, mindlessly deadheading roses. Anything that required more serious concentration was out of the question, as her head and stomach were out of sorts with all the anxiety. She had slept very badly, going over and over the row with Edward, wondering where she should have said something different.

Daniel had phoned twice already today and she had instructed Mrs O'Shea to tell him that she wasn't at home. Mrs O'Shea had raised her eyebrows in disapproval and then tutted.

"Don't look at me like that, Lizzie," she had told the housekeeper. "He has expected me to work some kind of magic with the situation over Edward and I just can't do it."

Lizzie had put her hand on Leonora's arm. "Edward and Christopher are the same boys that you used to love taking swimming and horse-riding," she reminded her gently. "If you can just remember that. People don't change that much – they're still the same underneath it all."

Then, just as Leonora was mulling over her sensible advice and beginning to feel a tiny bit better, the housekeeper added, "I have to remind myself of that constantly when I'm thinking about our Willie. He was a lovely young lad and as decent as you'll find. Then look what happened to him."

"Yes, thank you, Mrs O'Shea," Leonora had said briskly, feeling no consolation whatsoever to have her son compared with the Scotswoman's drunken, volatile brother.

When she heard the car tyres crunching on the grave outside the main entrance, Leonora took a deep breath, laid her gardening basket and secateurs down, and walked around the side of the building. She had no idea whether to expect Edward on his own or with his friend.

Edward stepped out of the car and gave her a wave and then Christopher Hennessey emerged from the passenger seat. As Leonora caught the reassuring glance that passed between her son and the tall, fair-headed, athletic-looking Christopher, she knew immediately that the relationship was stronger than ever.

She wondered if Edward had come home to patch things up or whether he had merely come to pack his things and disappear out of her life forever. The thought of it was too painful to bear.

Leonora went towards them, her heart lurching, trying to muster up something that looked like a smile of welcome.

"Mrs Bentley!" Christopher said, his tanned face lighting up when he saw her. "It's lovely to see you!" He went to greet her with an outstretched hand but when they got closer the handshake developed into a hug and a kiss on the cheek. "You look wonderful," he told her. "You haven't changed a bit since I last saw you."

Leonora was thrown off her guard with his effusive welcome. "You look exceptionally well yourself, Christopher," she said quite truthfully. "How was your journey over?"

"Great," he told her. "Some drama with a bit of turbulence as we were touching down in Dublin but nothing the pilot couldn't handle."

She looked over at Edward who was fiddling with his car keys, looking slightly awkward. When their eyes met she saw a look of pure vulnerability in his eyes and a wave of protectiveness shot through her. She went over to him and gave him a kiss on the cheek and a hug and then put her arm through his. His whole demeanour was stiff and defensive but Leonora made herself act as though everything was perfectly normal.

"Are you ready to eat?" she asked in a hearty voice. "Mrs O'Shea has a lovely beef casserole ready to warm up in the oven." Then, without waiting for an answer she said, "Come inside now and we'll have some drinks."

Mrs O'Shea gave both men an effusive welcome then rushed on down to the kitchen to put the finishing touches to the casserole she had made from the piece of beef she had cooked the day before. She was delighted that all the lovely food she had cooked for the cancelled meal could now be transformed into something equally as delicious. She absolutely abhorred waste and there was nothing she liked better than the challenge of making plain meat and vegetables into something else. She would sauté the cold boiled potatoes, make a nice white sauce for the cooked cauliflower and broccoli and add another glass of red wine to the simmering beef dish. With the help of some tiny new boiled potatoes and freshly picked peas, the meal would be even better than the one she had cooked the night before.

Leonora guided the men into the drawing-room where they both sat down on the sofa, then she went over to the drinks cabinet. "Whiskey, brandy, port or wine?" she asked. Then she thought. "Or perhaps I could make us all a nice cool Martini?"

Edward looked at his mother, his face anxious and grave. "Could we have a talk first?" he asked. "Before we all get too settled, Christopher and I think it might be best to sort a few things out."

Leonora's heart was thudding now as she came to sit in the chair next to the sofa.

"We've talked long and hard, Mother," Edward started, "and we've come to the decision that no matter what happens – and no matter what other people think – we want to be together." He reached over and took Christopher's hand now and squeezed it.

Leonora felt her chest tighten as she saw the evidence of their feelings before her eyes. She looked from one to the other, unable to find the words to react to the declaration.

Sensing her difficulty with the situation, Christopher slid his hand out of Edward's grasp. "Mrs Bentley," he said in a low voice, "I know this is a very difficult thing for people to accept – especially a parent. We don't want to hurt or embarrass anyone and in many ways it is the far easier route to pretend we're just two ordinary professional men. But the fact is we're not. We fall into a small minority group. It's not a group either of us would choose to belong to but we have no option. Please believe me – we've fought against it ourselves." He gave a deep sigh now. "As you know, in my attempts to live a normal life, I actually got married and I'm the father of a child."

Leonora eventually found her voice again. "That's a very big thing to walk away from, Christopher."

"And I haven't done it lightly," he said. "I tried and tried to make it work . . ."

Edward intervened now. "The decision about Christopher's marriage has been taken out of his hands. Theresa has left him."

Leonora looked at Christopher. "When did this happen?"

"She decided to come back home to her family in Galway. We actually travelled over together with the baby."

"And how are things between you?" Leonora asked.

"Much better than I could ever have hoped for. It turned out that she married me on the rebound from a broken romance, and really . . ." he cleared his throat, "in her eyes I didn't compare to the previous fellow. She said she knew from the day we got married that it was the wrong thing to have done. Looking back, I suppose we were both just pretending – trying to replace what we truly wanted with something else."

"How very sad," Leonora said, both saddened and relieved at the news. "Especially for your little daughter."

"I absolutely adore her," Christopher said, "and I've promised to send money every month to help with her upbringing. Theresa has also said that I can see her any time that I'm over here, and when she's old enough she can come out to America or wherever I am."

"That's very, very civil of her," Leonora said. She halted for a moment. "Do you mind me asking if Theresa knows of the very close friendship between you and Edward?"

"I think so. She hasn't asked outright about us but she has referred to it in a roundabout way. I think she prefers not to know any details of our relationship, so that she doesn't have the awkwardness of explaining it to the rest of the family. She's just going to say that it was an amicable split and that she hated living in America away from her family – which is true – and that I didn't want to give up my career out there."

"Well, her attitude must have certainly helped," Leonora said. She had many questions that she wanted to ask – like whether they would stay in Ireland or go back to America – but she felt perhaps it wasn't the right time. It would all come out in the fullness of time.

"There's no doubt about it," Christopher agreed, "it has lifted a huge burden off me. I don't know if I would ever have got the courage up to walk out. Theresa is a wonderful woman and she knew that we both deserved to be happy with whoever made us happy."

"Christopher has been very loyal," Edward said, "and he was prepared to give up our friendship forever if it meant that his marriage might have worked."

Leonora suddenly felt a great clarity about the situation. "But it wouldn't have worked – and it wouldn't have been the right thing," she said quietly. "If you don't love Theresa the way a husband should – and if you never can."

"That's what I realised some time ago," Christopher said, "but it's a very difficult thing to come to terms with. I know now I could never have those feelings for Theresa – or any other woman . . ." He looked over at Edward. "Yet for us it's the most natural thing in the world. There's no effort in it – there's nothing to work at – it just feels right."

Edward closed his eyes and nodded. "Being with Christopher is the only thing that will make me happy. I know it's not what you or my father would have wanted for me – but it's the way that's right for me."

And as she looked at the two men – so obviously meant to be with each other – Leonora suddenly knew without a doubt that it was the right thing.

So be it, she told herself.

She gave them both a beaming smile. "What did we decide about the Martinis?"

* * *

After dinner when Christopher was unpacking in his room, Edward came to his mother and put his arms around her. "Thank you," he told her, "for being so understanding and open-minded about this situation." Then, when she went to speak, he moved back and held his hands up. "I'm not expecting you to embrace our relationship or to say you approve or anything like that. I know it's difficult and will continue to be difficult at times for all of us."

"Oh, Edward . . ." Leonora said, tears coming into her eyes. "I just worry about you – how hard things might be at times, the way other people might treat you."

"We'll deal with it," Edward said firmly. He paused. "I also want to say I'm sorry about the way I acted and spoke to you yesterday – you didn't deserve it. I was just afraid of everything – meeting Christopher again, you finding out – everything was going around in my head and I just couldn't cope. You're a wonderful mother and you've always been there for me, all my life. Both you and Daddy."

Leonora's heart lurched at the mention of Andrew's name.

"But the thing with Christopher and me was the only thing I kept from you. I honestly hoped it would go away – that we would grow out of it. But of course we haven't."

"I can see that . . ." Leonora gave a little sigh. "If many normal couples felt the way about each other, the way you two do – marriages would be so much happier."

"Well," Edward grinned, "you know what you're talking about. That's exactly the kind of marriage you and my father had. You must still miss him terribly . . ."

"Yes. I miss the way we were for so many years. I just wish it could have lasted for much longer."

They chatted about more practical things then and Edward told Leonora that if she didn't mind he was going to go back to America with Christopher the following week.

"We both know that we can't live as a couple here," Edward said quietly. "In certain areas in New York, no one will bat an eyelid at our relationship. We will be able to mix with other similar couples." He gave a little shrug. "Of course we will have to be discreet at work and that sort of thing, but we're not the flamboyant types who will be flaunting our lifestyle. We just want to go back and get our business and our lives back on track."

"You'll be working together again?" Leonora asked.

"Yes," Edward said, his beaming smile giving away his obvious delight. "Hennessey and Bentley Architects, will be back in business again."

* * *

Leonora organised another small dinner party for Edward and Christopher's departure the following week. She invited Terry again and this time she invited Daniel Levy. Mrs O'Shea pushed the boat out and did a full Italian meal which she knew Edward loved. She had studied her *Francesco's Kitchen* recipe book and decided she would do *Bella Rosina Eggs* to start with – it was simple enough with boiled eggs, mayonnaise and chopped parsley – then a large dish of lasagne for the main course, followed by a traditional Italian trifle.

On the evening, Daniel appeared with a fine bottle of wine and a beautiful bouquet of flowers. He leaned in close after giving Leonora a small, careful peck on the cheek and said, "I am so pleased that things have worked out for Edward and his friend – and for you."

She brought him into the privacy of the drawing-room where they were all due to have drinks before the meal. "He doesn't know that you know about his situation," she said, suddenly worried that it could be blurted out during the meal.

Daniel touched his finger to his lips. "I will treat him exactly the same way I've always treated him." Then he said. "If you find it difficult at times, Leonora, just remember that Edward bringing Christopher is the same as when Diana brought James or Jonathan brought Emily. You would be wary of invading their privacy or making assumptions about things. Really, it's not that different."

Leonora clasped her hands together. "I can't bear the thought of them sharing a bed together . . ."

"And how do you feel when you think of Diana and James in bed together?"

Leonora stopped for a moment to think. "Quite uncomfortable . . ." she admitted.

Daniel smiled. "Exactly. It really is not that different when you think about it."

Leonora was delighted that the dinner went off exceptionally well, with the vibrant, bejewelled Terry entertaining everyone with lots of outrageous stories from her travelling days. She had also thanked Edward profusely for work he had done on the plans for the extension to her cottage.

"It's wonderful," she told him. "I'll be able to expand my art classes now and hang bigger canvases on the walls." She then made a sweeping gesture with her arm towards Leonora, her rows of bangles clinking as she did so.

"While I have such an appreciative audience, I would like to make an important announcement about this much-in-demand lady!"

Everyone looked at Leonora expectantly, while she looked totally bemused.

"I received a letter this morning," Terry stated, "from people in Donegal asking if I could get in touch with the artist, Leonora Bentley, to commission a set of *six* paintings for their restaurant! They had been visiting friends and saw her lovely work on the wall and demanded a contact address."

Leonora's hand flew to her mouth. "No!" she said. "You must be joking."

"No joke," Terry told her. "I have the letter with me." She bent to the floor to rummage in her large suede patchwork bag and came up with the envelope.

Leonora sat in utter shock as the letter was passed around the table.

"Well done, Mother!" Edward said, his voice full of pride. "You certainly kept us all in the dark about your talents." He looked at the others. "She had me convinced that her paintings were just childish daubing – I can hardly believe this."

"Edward," Terry said now, "you must encourage your mother to use one of the empty rooms in this huge house as a studio."

Leonora shook her head. "Now, Terry – that is taking things a little too seriously."

The artist gave a high tinkling laugh, showing evidence of a little too much wine. "This, Leonora," she said, waving the envelope high in the air, "is only the start! The best is yet to come. Next year we will have a joint exhibition together."

Daniel raised his glass now. "To Leonora!" he said, looking directly at her. "And may she have many more successes in life!"

Leonora looked back at him and smiled – and then she saw the warmth and appreciation in his dark brown eyes – and something else.

Something she was still so afraid of.

She shifted her gaze to look at the others around the table – at the happy, laughing faces. So many unexpectedly good things seemed to have happened recently – Diana's baby, the situation with Edward being resolved and now this amazing news about her art.

Only a few months ago she felt that her life was in the final phase – that all she had to look forward to was loneliness and old age.

Was it was possible that her life had taken a totally different direction from the one she expected? Was it possible that she could be entering an entirely new, adventurous phase?

Chapter 45

After the landlord left, Hannah wandered around the small two-bedroom house that would be her home in Galway for the next year while she completed her college course.

She had pleaded for the single room on account of the fact that she had never shared a room with anyone else in her life before and said she really didn't think she could sleep if she had to share. The landlord had shrugged and said he didn't care who went into what room, as long as he got the rent money every month.

Hannah knew that she would probably have to face the wrath of the other two students she would be sharing with over her *fait accompli* but after a summer with all the bitchiness amongst the female staff in Slattery's hotel she was well used to conflict. She would simply ride it out, saying that the landlord had made the decision.

She mounted the stairs now to her bedroom to unpack and sort out all her things. By the time the other girls arrived that afternoon, she would have her own room looking as though she had lived in it for ages.

It was a fraction bigger than the room in the hotel but the good-sized window that looked out onto the small street gave it a feeling of light and airiness and certainly made all the upheaval of moving across the city worthwhile.

The room, albeit small, gave Hannah a great sense of freedom in more ways than one. For a start, it got her away from the constant bickering of the hotel staff and the watchful eyes of Mr and Mrs Slattery. And it got her away from the possessiveness of her younger cousin.

When she had started her mild flirtation with Paul, she had never for a minute imagined that he would take things so seriously and become totally obsessed with her the way he had. He was no longer the cheery, light-hearted lad she enjoyed being with, and had somehow changed into this possessive, jealous lad she hardly recognised.

At the beginning he had been grand, happy for them to be part of the staff group going to pubs and dances all together when they had the same night off. But things had gradually started to change. Paul had started to change. He began to check the staff rotas and became obsessive about Hannah and him having the same days and nights off. Everywhere she went, he wanted to go with her.

He had no longer trusted her to go to the pub if there were any of the other male staff going. He was convinced that the other barmen and the porter all had their eye on her. And when she agreed that she would only go out with the female staff – the ones that she was still on speaking terms with – that still wasn't enough.

The stories that he would hear the next morning about lads buying her drinks or walking her back to the hotel upset him, and she would have to deal with him in floods of tears, begging her not to go to dances without him.

"But, Paul," she had tried to reason with him, "you know we can never be proper boyfriend and girlfriend. I told you that from the very beginning when we started messing around with each other. We promised that we would keep it light and easy and not make it into any big deal."

"I'm not," Paul had said unconvincingly. "I'm only looking out for you. I don't want you going off with lads that are only out for one thing. You deserve better than that."

"But I'm not going off with anyone," Hannah had said innocently. Chance would be a fine thing, she had thought to herself. What lad's going to look at me with you constantly giving everyone the evil eye?

The summer months had passed with Hannah trying to keep Paul's attentions to a level where no one would notice that they had a closer relationship than was acceptable for cousins. But it had become increasingly difficult with Paul coming to her bedroom most nights and refusing to leave. He had now admitted that he was in love with her and "didn't give a shite whether people thought it was right or wrong".

"It feels right from where I'm standing," Paul had said, "and if our consciences are clear about it, then I don't give a damn about anyone else."

The problem was Hannah didn't feel the same.

Paul had become a millstone around her neck in the same way that Simon Connelly had become. She suspected that he grilled the other staff for information and, knowing that they would think it odd that two cousins had such a peculiarly close relationship, she had concocted what she hoped was a convincing story. She had told them how her parents and Paul's parents were really, really strict, and if word got back about her having anything to do with men, she would be brought straight home.

"Paul is only looking out for me," she had explained, "because they only let me move to Galway because they knew the Slatterys and Paul would be keeping an eye on me." She had given a little anguished smile. "Paul knows how much my college course and being independent means to me, and he doesn't want me getting dragged back up to Tullamore before I even start."

The staff she explained this to had all nodded their heads as though they understood – and really Hannah didn't care a jot whether they did understand or not – she just wanted them to ignore Paul's odd behaviour which was getting out of hand.

Everything about the way Paul was acting was irritating. If she'd had even the slightest notion that her mad, carefree young cousin would turn into this jealous, emotional wreck she would have run a mile from him when he suggested getting her a job in the hotel along with him.

So far, she had been able to keep their physical relationship to petting – which she knew was still wrong – but lately Paul had become obsessed with them having just one "proper" night together to have as a memory for the rest of his life.

"Don't be ridiculous," Hannah had told him. "We're cousins – we're related. How can we have full sex together?"

"Nobody will ever know," he had pleaded. "I've never had sex with anyone and I want you to be the first girl." He had looked deeply into Hannah's big blue eyes. "And I want it to be *me* that you sleep with for the first time." He had taken her hands in his. "If we can do it just once, I'll be able to look back on it and be happy."

"I think it's entirely mad! And it shows what a young, stupid boy you are to even think of it! What if I was to get pregnant, Paul? What would happen then?"

The fear of such a dreadful thing happening had quietened down his affections for a while but Hannah knew that his feelings were only stifled and hadn't gone away.

Then, just a week ago – one night when he had far too much to drink – Paul had completely broken down, and confessed to her that he was madly in love with her. But the thing that had totally frightened Hannah the most was when he suggested that they could actually run away together – to England or to America – where no one would know they were related. And where they could live as husband and wife together. He said they could both get away from their parents and families who didn't give a damn about them anyway.

"I'll always love you and look after you," he had told her, tears streaming down his face. "And no one will ever come between us."

Hannah had really given out to him on that occasion and told him that he had gone completely mad altogether and that she would be going straight back home to Offaly if he didn't stop.

Then he had started crying – *really* crying. Sobbing and talking to himself. Crying so loudly that Sinéad the chambermaid had gone up to Joe Slattery and said that something was going on in Paul Barry's room and that someone better do something about it.

Joe had come down to Paul's room and demanded to be let in, but after warning her cousin that she was going back to Offaly if he didn't shut up, Hannah had gone out to the corridor to talk to their employer. She then had to concoct yet another big story about Paul having got drunk because he was upset over a girl that he'd met at the dancing in Galway who had rejected him.

"He's mad about her," Hannah had whispered to Joe in the dimly-lit corridor, "but she's told him that she doesn't want to see him again."

Joe had shaken his head and not looked entirely convinced. "I've never heard him going on about any other girl apart from yourself," he said. And then he had uttered the words that made Hannah's blood run cold. "I don't like to say it but Mary feels he has an unhealthy interest in *you* ... that he's a changed lad since you came to work here. His mind's not on his job or anything."

"No, no," Hannah told the hotel owner. "It's just that we've both had a few family problems and he feels I'm the only one that he can rely on and talk to ..."

"What about his sister Rose? They always got on well together. I'm sure if she knew how strange he was acting she'd want him to go back home. I'm sure she'd be able to talk sense into him."

Somehow, Hannah had been able to convince the hotelkeeper that there was nothing untoward in Paul's feelings for her. She had told him how horrified she was to even contemplate such a weird thing. That she would rather go straight back home and forget her college course if it was the truth. That she would want to put miles and miles between them.

"I'm sure it's this girl that he likes," she insisted. "When he's sober in the morning, I'll have a strong word with him and tell him he's going to lose his job if he doesn't pull himself together."

"That's exactly what he needs," Joe had agreed. "And if he gets back to his old self, then we'll say nothing about tonight. He's a decent lad and anybody can make a mistake where girls are concerned. And I'll make sure I give him a warning about drinking too much." He'd rolled his eyes. "They all go through it when they leave home for the first time. Ah, sure, I did the very same meself."

Hannah had heaved a sigh of relief when Joe Slattery went back upstairs. The only saving grace was that Mary Slattery had gone to her ailing mother's house that night and wasn't there. She wouldn't have been so easily convinced and would have insisted on seeing Paul and speaking to him herself.

Early the next morning when Paul had sobered up Hannah had really laid everything on the line. Then, she had pulled out her ace card – the one that had worked on her father – and told him that if people ever found out what had gone on between them that she would kill herself.

"For Jesus' sake, Hannah!" he had said, his eyes wide with shock. "Don't be saying things like that!"

"From now on," she had warned him, "we are back to being just normal cousins. No more talk about us running away together or any nonsense like that, do you understand?"

Paul had nodded, looking shamefaced at all the trouble he had caused.

"I made a mistake giving in to you earlier on," she had said. "And I shouldn't have led you on that time about giving you a kiss if I could buy you a shirt. It was stupid of me to say it but I didn't know it would go any further." She had paused to let the point sink in that he was the one who had instigated it all. "I never imagined it would lead to all this mess . . . and I don't want you to get into any more trouble with the Slatterys or have to tell your mother and father that you won't leave me alone." She reminded him of his father's reaction to him drinking. "Can you imagine what he'd have to say if he heard about the carry-on of you last night?" Then she had finished by saying, "From now on, I keep to my room and you keep to yours. Okay?"

And thankfully Paul had agreed and kept to his promise. Hannah had held her breath for the first few days, then when she saw that he had taken her at her word, she kept her head down and got on with her work.

After Joe Slattery's reaction to the incident, Hannah knew that all the staff must have their suspicions about her and Paul but no one had actually confronted them. Not even Mrs Slattery. So Hannah had made sure that she gave no one any reason to fall out with her. The last thing she needed was a row where Paul would jump in and get involved, and then it would give anyone who had a grudge against her the chance to throw accusations at them.

Since that disastrous night, she had crossed off every day on the calendar from then until it was time to leave the hotel and start at college.

In the early weeks of working as a chambermaid, Hannah had hoped she might keep the job on at weekends when she went to college but she now knew this wasn't an option. She had to leave the hotel and leave Paul behind her – in the same way she had left Simon behind in Offaly.

* * *

Hannah's new housemates – Josie and Nora Tierney – turned out to be two sisters from somewhere in County Cork who were on the same course as her. And she was delighted that her fears about them arguing over the single bed were unfounded as they were used to sharing a room and preferred it. Although both girls were small and slim like Hannah, they were rather plain and, coming from a small country village, they were impressed with their new glamorous housemate who seemed much wiser in the ways of the world

After a few nights of weighing the girls up, Hannah decided that they could be very useful friends to her. Josie was very clever with figures and money which was very handy since they had to learn bookkeeping which Hannah hated and found very difficult. Nora, whilst clever enough, was also a great sewer who had brought her machine up to Galway with her. Hannah knew if she played her cards right, the two girls would not only help her with college work but would make her cheap, fashionable clothes.

Towards the end of her first month, Hannah was delighted with the way things were going with her typing, shorthand and general secretarial work. However, despite Josie's help, she was struggling with the accountancy classes. It was the subject she dreaded most and the elderly woman who taught the class made it seem very complicated.

Then, towards the end of October, the elderly accounts lecturer went off on sick leave to have a serious operation, and a new one came in her place. And from the moment the tall, blond-haired, good-looking Robert Ryan walked into the classroom, Hannah knew another chapter in her life was due to start.

Chapter 46

Rose woke up and as she lay staring into the semi-darkness the picture that wouldn't leave her mind came flooding back. It was two days since she had gone down to the Guards' Barracks on an errand and walked around to the back door to find her mother and Guard McGuire standing by the cooker, locked in a passionate embrace.

They hadn't heard her and she had silently retraced her steps back outside the building. She had stood there for a good ten minutes until she heard them laughing and chatting again, and then she had come back to the door and knocked loudly before walking in.

They had just acted as if everything was perfectly normal and Rose had found herself acting as if everything was perfectly normal too.

Since then, the scene she witnessed had haunted her.

Her upset at the awful incident had obviously shown in her demeanour because her mother and father and grandmother had all asked her if she was okay. She had just told them that for some unknown reason she was feeling a bit washed-out and they had left her alone.

But this morning Rose decided that she couldn't lie in bed allowing the thoughts to torture her any more. It was only when she sat up that she realised her grandmother wasn't in the bedroom. She looked at her watch, quickly got out of bed and then padded across the cold stone floor to get her slippers and lift her dressing-gown from the hook on the back of the door. She shivered as she got dressed, the winter chill sweeping under the door. She was glad her two sisters were in the room next door now, because the slightest noise woke them in the morning and she wasn't in the mood for their chirpy chatter so early.

Her mother and father weren't likely to be up and about for a while yet since it was a Saturday morning, so she hoped she might get a chance to talk to her granny before anyone interrupted them. There was no one else that she could discuss the situation with. She felt if she didn't unburden herself soon that her head might just explode with all the thoughts that were rattling around inside.

Rose was glad to feel the welcoming warmth of the range as she opened the kitchen door. She was also suddenly aware of the comforting, safe feeling of knowing that her granny would be there – making sure that the fire in the range was hot enough for cooking the breakfast, that the kettle was boiled, and that any other preparations necessary to start the day off were done. Martha's main purpose, especially on a cold, wintry day, was to see that family life would tick on as comfortably as possible.

That feeling was more precious than ever to Rose as she recently felt that a lot of the things in her life that were once solid and dependable seemed to be crumbling away.

Martha Barry was sitting at the kitchen table in her

nightdress and dressing-gown, and with her rosary beads in her hand. She turned when her granddaughter came into the room and gave her a warm smile, dropping the beads into her lap.

"You're up early, girleen. Is anything the matter?"

"Do you want me to give you a few more minutes to finish saying your prayers, Granny?"

"Not at all! I've had plenty of time to say any prayers I need to say."

Rose came to stand beside her at the table. "You're up very early this morning. Were you not able to sleep? Were you not feeling too good?"

"Ah, sure I'm grand enough, Rose. What else would you expect at my age? It's only my legs as usual and I find it easier to breathe when I'm sitting up straight." She looked over at the range. "There's tea made in the pot a short while ago, although you might want to add a bit of boiling water just to freshen it."

"Will you have another mug yourself?"

"Ah, go on – I might as well."

Rose poured both mugs and then brought them to the table. Then, after checking that the door out into the hallway was closed tightly, she came back to the table. "Granny," she said in as low a voice as her grandmother's hearing would allow, "I need to talk to you."

"Go on . . ." The old lady indicated the chair next to her.

Rose sat down. "It's about Mammy . . . but I don't want you to think bad of her . . . and I don't want you to go saying anything to her or to Daddy."

"Rose, my girl, I learned a long time ago not to go poking my nose into anything that's not my business."

She lifted her mug up. "And as far as your mother's concerned, you know I think the world of her."

Rose's face was a picture of anguish. "Mammy doesn't know I know – but I've not been able to sleep since it happened . . ."

"Get it out, Rose," her granny said, her face unusually dark and serious.

Rose took a deep breath that almost hurt her chest. Then it all came out in a rush. "I went down to the barracks to drop off a loaf of bread and I walked in on her and Guard McGuire and they had their arms around each other and were kissing . . ." She put her head in her hands. "I can't believe it – I can't believe my mother would do such a terrible thing!"

"Now, now, Rose," the old lady said in calm, soothing voice, "it mightn't be as bad as it looked . . ."

"But, Granny, it definitely *is* as bad as it looked – in fact it's a whole lot worse." Rose's voice started to crack now and her eyes were wide and anguished. "I saw them before – back a few months ago – down at the barracks again. I saw Guard McGuire touching Mammy's face and they were looking into each other's eyes." She wiped a tear away with the back of her hand. "I'm really worried . . . I don't know what to do. What if Daddy finds out?"

Martha Barry reached forward now and clasped her grand-daughter's hands. "Now, girleen, you need to calm down. You're getting too worked up about it all."

Rose stared at her grandmother. "But aren't you shocked? Don't you think my mother's a really terrible woman for what she's done?"

"But we don't know that she's done anything that

bad," Martha said in a hushed voice. She squeezed Rose's hands reassuringly. "For all we know it might be nothing more than a nice friendship. I know Guard McGuire and he's a very nice, very decent man."

Rose shook her head vehemently. "No, he's not! Not after this, he's not. How can he be decent when he's had his arms around my mother, kissing her? He's a married man and she's a married woman. It's a sin – a mortal sin!"

Martha took a shuddering deep breath. "Rose, life isn't as black and white as we think it is, and there could be all sorts of reasons why they're both looking for a bit of comfort in each other."

"But it's wrong, Granny – isn't it?" Rose persisted. "They're both married!"

The old woman closed her eyes for a moment and then nodded. "Yes, of course it's wrong – but I don't think Guard McGuire has an easy time with his wife and you know as well as I do that there's times when your father can be a very difficult man. Now, I'm not saying that he's not a good man – he's my son and I love him dearly." She raised her eyebrows. "But he can be very hard-hearted when he has a mind to. Look at the way he went against Paul, just because of a stupid, youthful mistake. Your mother tried to talk him around – and I tried myself – but he can be as stubborn when he sets his mind to it."

"I know he's awkward. Don't forget that he turned on me as well that time. But Daddy's moods are just the way he is – what Mammy is up to with the Guard is far, far worse!"

Martha Barry looked her granddaughter straight in the eye and then prodded her finger on the table. "You need to listen to me, Rose – and listen well. We both know that whatever friendship your mother and Guard McGuire have is stupid and wrong – but it doesn't make them bad people. I've known Frank McGuire since he was a young lad – long before he became a guard – and he's a soft-hearted, decent man. Your mother has been a hard-working woman all her life and she's had very little time or money for herself, and she's never complained. In my opinion, they've both been having a bit of a rough time at home and have turned to each other for a bit of comfort. I would bet my life on it that it's not gone any more serious than that. Where would they have the time or the place to go together? They both have families to be with and places to be at certain times."

Rose went to speak again – to say that they were obviously meeting up in the Guards' Barracks when they knew there was nobody else around – but her granny held her hand up to silence her.

"Now, I do agree with you that it can't go on. Of course it can't. Something has got to be done before it does become a very serious matter." Martha took another long deep breath, then pressed her hand tightly to her chest.

"Are you all right, Granny?"

"I'm grand. I'm only thinking . . ." Then, after a few moments, she leaned over and put her hand on her granddaughter's shoulder. "You're going to have to be very grown-up about all this, Rose, because a lot of what happens is going to be down to you."

Rose's eyes narrowed. "What do you mean, Granny?"

"I've thought about it, love, and there's no other way out of it. You're going to have to speak to your mother and tell her what you saw. You've got to warn her that she needs to call a halt to whatever is going on between herself and Frank McGuire."

"But she won't listen to me," Rose argued. "She'll go mad!"

"She will listen to you," Martha said with some certainty. "After she simmers down a bit, she'll give plenty of thought to what you have to say."

Rose shrugged. "I think it might be better if you spoke to her."

"That would put her in a much worse position. If she thinks I know, it will be at the back of her mind that you told me first, and she would always be wondering if I might tell your father."

Rose pondered on this for a moment. "But I've never spoken to my mother about anything like that before . . . I don't know if I could even broach it."

"You'll have to, Rose," her grandmother said firmly. "I know it's hard for you but you're a grown woman now, and these are the kind of things we all have to face at some time. You have to do it for the sake of the whole family."

A pounding feeling came into Rose's head and she closed her eyes.

"You might not believe this, Rose – but your mother will be grateful to you for doing this," Martha went on softly. "She's caught up in the bit of attention and affection that she's getting from somebody else and she thinks it will go unnoticed. She doesn't think that she's causing anybody any harm."

"It sounds almost as though you're on her side, Granny, and not on Daddy's."

"It's not a question of sides, Rose. It's about human nature. Something you'll know all about one day because it hits us in all shapes and forms." She squeezed Rose's hand again. "Now, you know what has to be done – so forget about it for the time being and have your tea and a bit of nice fresh bread and butter. It'll keep you going until the big breakfast is cooked later."

Rose did as she was told and her granny cleverly changed the subject until they were chatting about how many hours Rose would be working down in Purcell's over the Christmas and New Year period.

"When you have a few days off now, it would do you no harm to take a trip out to Galway and stay with Hannah. A break away from the house would do you the world of good." She nodded towards the hallway door. "Once you've said your piece to your mother, a couple of days away would give her time to think about it."

"But you know what Hannah's like, Granny. I don't think I could stick a few days with her."

"Well, as I told you when you read that last letter out, I think it sounds as though the girl has changed – like she's grown up a bit. Her letter was full of her college and all her studying and that kind of thing."

"I suppose I could think about it," Rose said, giving a little shrug. "It would be nice to see Paul again. He's only been home for the odd visit since he left."

"He was very quiet when he was home a few weeks ago," her granny remembered. "And it didn't sound as though he was seeing too much of Hannah since she left the hotel. Ah, I suppose that's the way things go."

Just as Rose had finished her breakfast, Martha Barry got up from the table to walk towards the back door and the outside toilet.

"You look very stiff this morning, Granny," Rose said, looking concerned.

Martha nodded and smiled. "Old age, girleen," she said, her voice breathless with the effort of getting up, "it's only old age."

As they walked slowly outside into the freezing winter morning, it crossed Rose's mind that she still hadn't told her granny or her mother about Leonora Bentley's offer.

She didn't know how her mother would react – or if she would even take it in. Rose had felt from the summer that her mother often seemed very distracted and, after seeing her with Guard McGuire, she now knew the reason.

Rose left her grandmother at the door of the toilet, then walked to the stone wall at the back of the house and waited to walk the old woman back inside. It was a bitterly cold morning and the sharp sea air made her catch her breath as she stood looking out over the greenish-grey water.

She felt surprisingly lighter having unburdened herself to her granny. And when she thought about it, the suggestion of her going to Galway for a few days to leave her mother thinking things over was a very good one. It meant that she wouldn't have to be around to see her mother's angry face for having dared to accuse her of such a terrible thing.

A short while later Martha Barry came out of the little wooden hut. She went a few steps and then, leaning heavily on her walking stick, paused to look around her.

Rose waved at her but the old lady didn't react.

"I'm still here, Granny!" she called to her.

She gathered her dressing-gown around her against the chill wind and ran towards her grandmother. As she got closer, Rose immediately knew that something was wrong. Martha Barry seemed to be just staring into space – a vacant look in her eyes.

"Granny?" Rose called again and then, as she saw the walking stick begin to wobble, she knew the old lady was going to fall back. She lunged forward and caught her in both arms.

Martha's eyes had now gone far back in her head and she wasn't hearing anything. Her whole body now slumped into a heavy weight in Rose's arms. Rose sank to her knees.

"Mammy!" Rose roared. "Daddy! Come quick!!" She couldn't leave her granny lying on the freezing damp ground and she was trying to hold the old woman up until she got help to carry her into the house.

Rose knelt there on the ground holding her granny for several minutes before anyone heard her cries for help.

By the time that her father appeared at the door, the exhausted Rose knew it was too late.

Martha Barry had died in her arms.

Chapter 47

Paul received the phone call about his grandmother on the Saturday afternoon. His mother had gone down to the Guards' Barracks with a list of names and contact numbers to let relatives and family friends know the sad news.

Paul's immediate reaction was very mixed. He was shocked and saddened when he heard his granny had died but this was secondary to the feeling of delight that he now had a very bona-fide reason to contact Hannah. His mother had asked him to go out and break the sad news to his cousin.

He had gone several weeks now without seeing her because Hannah had made it very clear that she did not have time for him or any other friends at the moment – apart from the two strange sisters from Cork that she shared the house with. He had gone around to the house on numerous occasions after she had moved but he found his cousin cold and distant. Any time he actually got inside the house, her housemates were there like two little terriers listening to every word and watching his every move.

It was only when Joe Slattery took him to the side and told him that if he didn't buck up he would be out of a job – and without a reference – that he had pulled himself together.

"I don't care about your personal life," Joe told him, "but I can't have a barman who's not paying attention to his customers and who's giving change for a feckin' pound when he was only given ten shillings!" He'd wagged a warning finger. "Now, you're lucky that I know your family and all belonging to you – or you would be gone out of that door long ago." He'd glanced over his shoulder to check his wife wasn't around. "And you're very lucky herself hasn't got wind of your latest mistakes, because she told me a fortnight ago I'd have to get rid of you. And I know well she won't give you a reference if we have to let you go. Where would you be then?" Then, seeing the dazed, confused look on the boy's face he had softened a little. "I know well what's wrong with you . . ."

Paul had looked up at him, ready to deny whatever was said. He knew that whatever chance he had of Hannah and him being friends again, it would be gone if she knew he had admitted to their unusually close relationship.

"Anyway," Joe said now. "You need to sort yourself out." He had lowered his voice. "And if I were you, I'd give women a feckin' wide berth for a while until you've copped yourself on a bit. That lady had you dangling on a string and no doubt about it."

Scared and embarrassed, Paul had taken the talk to heart and for the last few weeks had certainly 'copped himself on'. He had made sure he paid full attention to everything at work and he had made sure that Mr and Mrs

Slattery noticed it. In fact, he had become so absorbed in his work that he found he was forgetting to think about Hannah. In the last week or so she had become something that he only thought about in any great depth when he was in bed. The rest of the time he was too busy making a good impression at work and trying to re-establish friendships amongst the staff that had been badly neglected when his cousin had taken up all his attention.

He had also filled one of his empty weekends off by taking a rare trip back home and he was more than grateful now that he'd done it, otherwise he would have no recent memories of his grandmother. The weekend had gone better than he expected and he and his father had actually had a decent conversation about Paul's work in the hotel and what it was like to live in the city. His mother had baked a cake.

* * *

The doorbell went and Hannah and Robert Ryan pulled away from each other. It rang again.

"It will be old Mrs Murray from the house opposite with the key," Hannah suddenly remembered. "She's going out to visit somebody in the hospital this afternoon and she asked me if I would let the cat out."

"As long as you don't let the cat out of the bag about us," Robert said, deliberately making his educated Dublin accent broader and slapping her playfully on the behind.

"Don't worry about that," Hannah laughed. "She'd have me dragged down to the priest if she got wind of the fact I had a man in the house. Especially one as gorgeous as you!"

After quickly pulling on a cardigan and her pyjama bottoms, Hannah came rushing downstairs to answer the door. She opened it just wide enough to take the key off the neighbour without her noticing that she wasn't fully dressed.

The smile on her face faded when she saw her cousin standing on the doorstep. "Paul!" she said, completely caught off guard. "Are you not working today?"

"No. I need to talk to you." He put his foot up on the small step, prepared to walk in, but Hannah didn't open the door any wider. He looked up at her, his face dark and his brow furrowed. "I've come down to tell you some bad news."

Hannah stifled a sigh. Paul had used every excuse under the sun recently to come to see her. She had hoped after the last, very frosty reception that he had got the message. But apparently he had not.

"What do you want?" she asked. "I'm just going into the bath now so I haven't much time to chat."

"I'm sorry to take up your precious time," he told her, his face tight with anger now, "but I thought you might like to know that Granny dropped dead this morning."

"Oh, my God!" she said, her hands coming up to her mouth.

Paul, seeing that she had let her guard down, moved forward so that she had no option but to open the door wider to let him in.

"I was asked to let you know straight away," he told her, walking into the small living area that led on into the kitchen.

He sat down in an armchair and then put his head in his hands.

Hannah came over to stand in front of him with her arms folded. "What happened?" she asked in a flat voice. "Had she been sick before it happened – or did she just die in her sleep?"

Paul lifted his head and looked directly at her. "She actually died in Rose's arms," he said, his voice accusing, almost as though it was Hannah's fault.

"Oh, my God! Do you know when the funeral is?"

Paul shrugged. "Monday or Tuesday, no doubt." He raised his eyebrows. "I take it you'll find the time to come out for it?"

"Of course I will," Hannah said. Her eyes flickered upwards as she heard a noise. Paul followed her gaze towards the staircase.

"Have you somebody in?" he asked.

Hannah nodded, a red flush now stealing over her chest and neck. "The girls are there."

A pained expression came on his face and he shook his head. "You're never on your own these days and I'm beginning to feel it's deliberate. I don't know what you've been saying about me to those two monkeys you share the house with but one of these days I'm going to tell the pair of them to feck off out of it!"

"Shush!" Hannah told him, looking more agitated now. "Josie and Nora are nice girls. They don't mean any harm."

"Nice girls?" he scoffed. "They would drive you up the wall the way they go on – they're like a pair of chattering chimps." There was a small awkward silence. "Look, Hannah, I didn't come here to argue with you. I've never wanted that." He looked into her eyes. "I've always thought the world of you and I don't want us falling out – not at a time like this. I'm heartbroken about my granny dying . . . and I know you were fond of her too."

Hannah nodded her head and swallowed hard. She was desperate to get rid of Paul but he had come to see her with a very valid reason and it was difficult to just throw him out.

"When are you thinking of going out to Kilnagree?" she asked, tightening her folded arms even more.

"This afternoon. The Slatterys have told me to take the time off from today until after the funeral."

"And are you going to stay home for that long?"

"I might as well. I'll be needed out at the house. There will be a lot of things to be done. I thought you might like to travel out with me." He looked around the room. "It's not as if you have anything to stop you coming. It's a lot easier to get time off a college course than work."

Hannah bit her lip. "It's just that I have exams . . ."

"They'll expect you there. You're part of the family."

"But not on your granny's side," Hannah reminded him. "I'll definitely come for the removal to church and for the funeral . . ."

Paul stood up now. "So you're not coming out to Kilnagree with me today?" he said, his voice rising.

There was a noticeable shake in Hannah's hand as it came up to her mouth now. "I have exams the week after next and I need to study . . ."

"You'll have plenty of time to study when the funeral is all over! You should be out at the house to show support for the family. My mother and father have always been good to you and my granny has cooked you hundreds of breakfasts over the years."

538

"I thought the world of her but I'm sure it will be fine if I come out for the removal and the funeral. My mother and father will probably be down then."

He shook his head. "I wouldn't have believed," he said, his voice louder again, "how quickly somebody could turn. It's well seeing where your loyalties lie these days and it's certainly not with people who have been very good to you."

"That's not fair," she told him, her voice rising despite herself. "I've always been very grateful –"

"Hannah?" a male voice called down the stairs. "Is everything all right?"

Everything suddenly froze.

Paul's eyes darted from Hannah to the staircase and then he stood transfixed as a tall blond man in his late twenties came down the stairs, dressed only in trousers, and in bare feet.

"Hannah?" Robert said, his eyebrows raised in question.

She turned towards him, her face dark and serious. "It's all right," she told him. "This is my cousin, Paul." She looked at Paul. "This is Robert Ryan – he's a friend of mine – he's one of the lecturers from college."

Robert came toward him with his hand outstretched. "Pleased to meet you, Paul."

Paul looked at the half-dressed, handsome, smooth-sounding Dubliner and immediately knew that this was where Hannah's affections and attentions were now being directed. An older, obviously educated fella who no doubt had plenty of money. A fella who didn't know that only a few weeks ago Hannah was all over the cousin he was now being casually introduced to.

Paul deliberately turned to the side, ignoring Robert's offer of a handshake.

Hannah rushed in to try to diffuse the awkward situation. "Paul was good enough to come out to tell me that there's been a death in the family – his granny dropped dead this morning. His family have all been very good to me over the years and I'll obviously be going out for the removal and the funeral."

Robert's gaze moved from one to the other, completely baffled by the obvious tension. "I'm sorry to hear about your loss," he said to Paul.

Paul moved towards the door now. "My granny dying is obviously more of a loss to some than it is to others." He glanced back at Hannah. "I'll be seeing you – if you can find the time in your busy college diary."

Chapter 48

Still shocked from the dramatic and unexpected death of Martha, the grieving Barry family had taken refuge in the familiar routine of the funeral rituals leading up to the main event on the Tuesday.

On the Monday morning Paul had walked down to Purcell's bar to order the crates of beer and two bottles of whiskey and sherry that the waking procedure would require. Rose had gone in the opposite direction, down to the church hall with Veronica and Eileen to borrow their large white tablecloths and some glasses for drinks.

"I'm taking a walk down to the barracks to fill a box with spare teapots, cups and saucers and some big plates for sandwiches," Kathleen Barry told her husband. "We don't know how many will come back to the house for tea and sandwiches for the removal tonight and after the funeral, and we don't want to be short of delph. The sergeant says that one of the guards will bring it back up in the car for me and take it back when we're finished."

Stephen nodded towards the closed coffin in the corner of the room "Wouldn't she have enjoyed being here helping with the making of the tea and the bite to eat? She was always in her element when she was cooking and feeding people."

It was often the custom to leave the coffin open to allow viewing of the dead body but the family decided that it would be kinder on the younger girls to have the lid closed. Kathleen felt it was better that they were left with a picture in their minds of their granny when she was alive, as opposed to the shrouded, waxen lifeless figure that now reposed in the polished wooden box.

Kathleen put her hand on her husband's shoulder. "In a way she is still with us," she said softly. "Martha will always be with us."

"This will be a different house after she's gone," Stephen sighed. "Everything will be changed." He looked around the kitchen. "It's already changed. There's a big part of the place gone." He shook his head. "Ah, anyway, the whole world's changed too quickly in a short time. The children are growing up too fast and you don't know how they're going to turn out." He sucked his breath in now. "Look at Paul – look at the way things went there. I never thought he'd turn into a complete *amadán*!"

"We've got good children," Kathleen cut in now. "Rose has never given us an ounce of trouble, Veronica and Eileen are doing fine at school, and Paul is a grown man, a working man, out earning his own living and making his own way in the world."

She lifted her coat and scarf now, not wanting to hear all her husband's litany of complaints about the family. It was all he seemed to do lately. And now that the calming influence of Martha Barry was gone, he seemed to be sinking into total despondency.

"I won't be long," she told him. "Rose and Paul will be back any minute, so will you all manage any people paying their respects until I come back?"

Stephen inclined his head, a weary look on his face. "Most of them won't come until tonight." He looked up at the clock. "The brothers will be here shortly and we'll go down to see the priest about the final arrangements."

"I'll give Sheila a ring from the Guards' Barrack and find out what time they're arriving, and I think they'll probably pick Hannah up in Galway on their way out. The three of them can have Paul's room and he'll sleep in with the girls on the floor."

Stephen shrugged as though the arrangements were nothing to do with him.

A knock came on the kitchen door now and Kathleen went to open it. It was a neighbour from a few houses down the road.

He gave the usual greeting that was offered on the occasion of a death in the family. "I'm sorry for your troubles," he started, respectfully taking his cap off. "I wondered if I might have a few words with Stephen about the grave?"

Kathleen brought him in and waited while he gave his condolences to Stephen and then went over to say a few prayers at Martha's coffin. Then she left the two men to discuss the details of the grave-digging.

Death was a time that drew rural Irish families together and one of the many customs around the burial was that the local men would organise and then dig the grave for their neighbours. It was a job that was done with great respect, each family knowing that the time would come soon enough when they might be calling on a neighbour to do the same sad task for them.

Kathleen was glad to get out of the house and away from the sombre atmosphere. It was a bright but cold December day and she walked at a brisk pace, knowing that there would be plenty of work back at the house on her return

Already she was feeling the loss of the quiet but cheery Martha – who was much more than just a mother-in-law to her. Over the years, the old lady had been as true a friend as the relationship could allow and she wondered now how different their lives would all be without her.

*　*　*

Rose walked back towards the house, two heavy bags full of white linen tablecloths in either hand. Her two younger sisters walked beside her, both carefully carrying boxes with various-sized glasses in them.

Veronica stopped for a moment to hitch the box higher up in her arms, using her knee.

"Are you okay?" Rose checked. Her voice was flat and weary and her heart much heavier than anything they were carrying.

"It's better now," Veronica replied. The box was bulky and awkward but she didn't want to complain, because she was grateful to be involved in the funeral proceedings as it made her feel more grown-up.

Rose walked along, answering her sisters' questions in a rote fashion. Although her heart was broken to have lost her beloved grandmother, she was grateful for the practical things which had to be done which made things a little more bearable.

Her anger and confusion over the incident with her mother was now overshadowed by the sadness of her great loss. How life could ever return to normal in their white-washed cottage, she could not imagine.

Paul had been more upset than Rose could have imagined and when they were on their own he had completely broken down in her arms. This had never happened before and, as she was holding him she was sharply reminded of having held her grandmother in her arms as the old woman took her last breath.

When Rose got back to the house she put the tablecloths down on her mother's bed as instructed and the glasses in the kitchen. Paul came in just ten minutes behind her and Rose made a pot of tea. She was just going to pour it when a knock came to the door and when she opened it two short, heavily-made brothers that Paul had gone to school with were standing on the step. They handed Rose a loaf of brown bread that their mother had baked, and a fruit loaf. They came in and paid their respects and Rose poured them a cup of tea and sliced up the fruit loaf.

The lads were slightly awkward – not quite sure what to say under the sad circumstances – and after a few minutes the chat moved onto the latest local GAA match.

"Will you have sugar?" Rose asked the bigger of the lads and, when he turned to answer her, his hand caught the white ceramic jug that Martha Barry had brought to the house many years before. He moved quickly to catch it – but wasn't deft enough – and the jug went crashing onto the stone floor. The lad was full of apologies and immediately offered to buy a new jug.

"Don't worry," Rose told him, with a reassuring smile,

"it's only an old one we've had for years." But inside she felt another little bit of her granny had been taken away.

She quietly cleared up the mess and, after making sure the lads had enough to eat, she told Paul she was walking down to meet her mother. It had dawned on her that the jug was the only one they had in the house and her mother would be mortified if she had to put a milk bottle out on the table. She would have to go quickly down to the barracks on the bike now and hopefully catch her mother before she left to borrow a decent-sized jug until they had the time and the money to buy another one.

"I'll only be gone a short while," she told her brother. "If you need help with anything, the girls are down in their bedroom reading."

She put on her heavy dark winter coat and a warm red knitted scarf and set off for the barracks.

* * *

A short while earlier, when Kathleen Barry had reached the Guards' Barracks, she noticed that there were two bicycles parked outside. One she recognised as Frank McGuire's but the other was one she had never seen before – and she was surprised to notice that it was a lady's cycle.

She went around the back and had already stepped through the door when she realised that the visitor was the tall, thin, pinch-nosed Mrs McGuire. She was taken aback when she saw her because it was rare that any of the guards' wives came near the barracks but she quickly recovered and pinned a cheery smile on her face.

"Hello, Mrs McGuire," she said, taking her headscarf

off. "It's not often we see you down here. It's a very cold day out there, isn't it?"

There was no response from the Guard's wife, although he himself rushed in to say, "It is indeed a cold day, Mrs Barry."

Kathleen started to take her coat off, expecting to receive some words of condolence on the family's loss from the visitor but there was none forthcoming. With a growing feeling of unease, she hung her coat on the back of the chair and then glanced over at the guard and then at his wife. Something in Frank McGuire's face immediately alerted her that all was not well.

Kathleen felt her stomach starting to churn and then, to break the silence, she said, "I hope I'm not disturbing ye both but I have a few things to pack that Sergeant Doherty said I could borrow for the funeral."

The stony-faced woman walked over to Kathleen now, her eyes narrowed and her arms folded. "By the sounds of it," Alice McGuire said, standing almost six inches above the housekeeper. "I think you've already done too much disturbing."

Kathleen's heart lurched.

"Now, Alice –" the Guard started to say.

"Be quiet, you!" his wife ordered. She looked back at Kathleen now. "I know this mightn't be a good time for you with all that's going on in your house – but since I have the rare opportunity, I want to tell you that people are talking."

"Talking about what?" Kathleen said, her face now drained to white.

Alice McGuire thumbed in the direction of the equally stricken-looking guard. "About the way you've been carrying on with my man. It's been reported back to me by another guard's wife that you two have been seen looking very cosy together down in this barracks!"

"Well, you've been told lies!" Kathleen said, her heart pounding against her ribs. "I've never been what you call 'cosy' with any of the guards, and I certainly wouldn't risk my job or my marriage carrying on with your husband or any other man." She looked over at the Guard. "Isn't that right?"

He shrugged. "That's what I've been telling her. Whoever started this rumour is only causing mischief."

Alice McGuire didn't look convinced. "Well, isn't it highly coincidental now that Frank was down here on his own today and you just happened to have turned up?"

"Well, that's exactly what it is – a coincidence." Kathleen looked and sounded rightly indignant because she'd had no idea the Guard would be there on that occasion. Then tears began to prick her eyes. "Whatever rumours you have heard, Mrs McGuire, they are nothing but vicious lies. I'm only down here during the daytime when I'm working and I'd like to know where I'm supposed to have the time or the opportunity to get up to anything even if I wanted to – which I don't."

Alice McGuire paused for a few moments, digesting that piece of information. "Well," she said, "there's no smoke without fire and, whatever you two say, there's enough going on to make people talk."

"I've already told you that there's nothing going on, Alice," Frank McGuire said. "It's all a pack of lies."

"Well, I wonder what Sergeant Doherty would have to say about these lies?" Mrs McGuire said. "Maybe he needs to sort all this out and, if there were any lies told, deal with the person."

The thought of having Sergeant Doherty's wrath down on her suddenly overwhelmed Kathleen and the tears she had been fighting started to flow. "Dear God!" she said, moving backwards to lean against the old pine cupboard. "If Stephen gets to hear about these terrible rumours, I don't know what he'll do." She took a deep breath, trying to steady herself. "He's in a bad enough state trying to cope with his mother dying . . ." She put her head down now and her whole body started to shake with wracking sobs.

Mrs McGuire suddenly looked alarmed. The woman standing opposite her did not look at all like the Jezebel she thought she was going to encounter. And when she considered everything that they had said, it didn't sound as though anything could really have gone on. Well, not that serious anyway.

"Frank knows I'm not the type to go causing trouble in a family – especially one that's just had a bereavement," she said now. "But you have to see it from my point of view – how it sounded to hear that my husband was getting too friendly with another woman."

Kathleen nodded her head. "Of course," she said, dabbing her eyes with a hanky. "I would feel the very same myself."

"Well, I suppose we could leave it at that . . . if there's no truth in it, then there's no point in us making things worse by dragging other innocent people into it."

Kathleen felt weak with relief.

* * *

Rose had parked her bicycle beside the other two that were already there. She'd walked around the back of the building and come to a halt at the door that led into the barracks, reluctant to open the door in case she witnessed a similar scene to the last occasion. Then, when she heard the voices, she felt a little wave of relief wash over her. There were obviously a few people around. She'd lifted her hand to knock on the door when the voices suddenly rose to shouts and made her freeze.

She stood listening and recognised her mother's voice and Guard McGuire's voice, and then she heard another woman's voice that she wasn't sure of. By the heated exchanges she immediately knew that there was some kind of argument going on, but the door was heavy and the walls were thick, making it hard to distinguish exactly what was being said.

Rose had moved a few feet away from the door, unsure what to do, wondering whether she should stay there until her mother came out and pretend she had just arrived. She stood for about five minutes and then she heard the door opening and Guard and Mrs McGuire came out together, talking in low, serious voices. They stopped in their tracks when they saw her.

"Hello, Rose," the Guard said, "your mother is inside."

"Hello," Rose replied, suddenly putting two and two together. Her mother and the Guard's wife had obviously been arguing and it must have been to do with what was going on between her mother and the Guard. A wave of shame and anger washed over her at the thought of her mother causing all this serious trouble.

Mrs McGuire looked at the girl and her eyes

narrowed. "Did your mother know you were coming down here?" she suddenly asked.

Rose halted for a few moments before answering, because something told her that whatever she said might make a difference to whatever they had been arguing about inside. At worst, it could cause trouble for the whole family.

"We're sorting out the things for the funeral," Rose said, carefully evading the question, "and my mother asked me to give her a hand."

"And did she ask you to come down to the barracks this afternoon?"

"I couldn't come down with her because I had to go to the church hall," Rose said, "so I said I would follow her down. I often come down here to help out."

The Guard's wife looked mollified by Rose's answers, thinking that there couldn't be many opportunities for any underhand business if Kathleen Barry's daughter was in and out of the barracks all the time.

When the Guard went off on his bike in one direction and his wife in the opposite, Rose took a deep breath. She was going to let her mother know that she knew. She gave a brief tap and then marched in to see her mother sitting at the kitchen table with a hanky held to her eyes.

She looked up. "Oh, Rose," she said, her voice weak and quivering, "I've made a big mistake and an awful fool of myself . . ." She put her head in her hands now and started to cry again.

As she looked at her devastated mother, all the anger and indignation she felt suddenly changed into something else. Exactly what – she didn't really know. It was some kind of mixture of pity and sadness – and total confusion.

"I've not done anything really, really bad," her mother said, "but I've been awful stupid." She motioned to Rose with her hand to sit beside her. "I don't know if you're old enough to understand this, Rose," she said, wiping the tears away with the back of her hand, "but I'm going to tell you anyway . . . because I've nobody else to talk to. I would have talked about this to your granny – even though she's my mother-in-law – but she's not there any more."

Rose felt a rush of grief now and the feeling of confusion intensified.

Kathleen sniffed and shook her head. "You see, I got friendly – I suppose, in a way, I got *too* friendly with Guard McGuire."

"I know," Rose said quietly. "I saw you."

Her mother's head jerked up. "You saw me . . . what?"

"I saw you kissing him last week. I came down here last week and the kitchen door was open and I saw you both." She paused. "You were so wrapped up in each other that you never even noticed me."

Kathleen's eyes were large with shock and her hands came to cover her mouth. "Oh, dear God!" she whispered. "How could I have been so stupid?" She sat like a statue for a few moments and then she suddenly moved and grabbed Rose's hand. "That was a far as it went – it was only ever a kiss – and only a few times. He's just a nice, kind man whose wife is very hard on him."

Rose stiffened as the sound of her mother's excuses. "It's still wrong," she told her. "You're both married. If Daddy found out . . ."

"Oh, Rose," her mother said, shaking her head. "Don't say that! And you don't need to tell me – I know how wrong it is. You probably won't understand this because you're only a young girl – but there are times when I feel very lonely. Especially since Paul went away – and the way it all happened over that stupid row at Easter. Your father is so bull-headed that he won't forgive him and he definitely hasn't forgotten. Nothing Paul does will ever be right, no matter how hard he tries." She gave a little shrug, her eyes still damp with tears. "I know I have you and the girls still at home but there are times when you need an older person who cares about what you're thinking and what you are feeling. Somebody to tell you to put your feet up after a hard day at work and walking backwards and forwards in the rain and the cold. Most of the time I'm so busy I don't have the time to think about feeling sorry for myself – but every so often it hits me. For the last while your father doesn't even seem to notice I'm there half the time. I don't know what it's going to be like now your granny's gone." She looked at Rose. "That's how I came to get a small bit too close to Frank. He's a nice man and you can talk to him."

"Granny knew," Rose said in a flat voice.

Kathleen's face darkened. "How on earth did Granny hear about it when she hardly went out of the door?" Her face crumpled now. "Has there really been talk about us? That's what Mrs McGuire said – that's what the row was about before you came in."

"I guessed that," Rose said. She took a deep breath. "I've never heard any talk and nobody has ever hinted it to me."

"She said it was another guard's wife that told her – she never said any names." She halted for a minute, her breath still anxious and rapid. "But how did your granny get to hear if there was no talk?"

"It was me that told Granny – we were talking about it just a few minutes before she died."

"Oh, no . . . no!"

Rose suddenly felt a rush of compassion for her mother and she immediately knew what her granny would have wanted her to say and do. She reached across the table and gripped her mother's hand. "It's okay, Mammy. Granny didn't have a bad word to say about you. All the things you've just been saying now, she said the very same things. She understood. She said she knew how difficult Daddy was at times – even though he was her own son – and she said how hard you worked and got nothing for yourself." She squeezed her mother's hand tightly now. "Granny liked Guard McGuire too, and she said he wasn't a bad man either . . . but she was worried for you both. She said it had to be stopped."

"Oh, Rose! It'll be stopped all right," she sobbed. "There was never much to it apart from a few kisses – all we ever really did was chat. What a terrible mess I've made of things!"

"It'll be all right," Rose heard herself say.

"But I'm terrified your father will get to hear if Mrs McGuire did."

"If there was any talk, it was just between the two guards' wives. As long as you both keep yourselves to yourselves, it'll all be forgotten."

Ten minutes later, when Sergeant Doherty came in the back door, Kathleen was still sobbing. He looked at the two women and then he took his official Guard's hat off and held it to his chest. "I'm very sorry for your trouble, Kathleen and Rose. Mrs Barry was a fine woman . . . if there's anything at all we can do to help."

"Thank you," Rose said. She squeezed her mother's hand. "We're just sorting out a few things and then we'll be gone." She suddenly remembered the jug and her heart lurched. Oh, Granny, she thought, what am I going to do without you? What are we all going to do without you?

Stephen Barry was right – things would never be the same again.

* * *

Rose walked back with her mother, wheeling the bike which was laden with as much as the basket and the handlebars could carry in the way of cutlery, dish-towels and a decent-sized jug. Kathleen had now composed herself and all the way back she talked about how determined she was to put the mistake she had made behind her.

Rose also had a great sense of relief that the matter that had troubled her so much had been more or less resolved. And she knew she had her grandmother to thank for it. It was as if on that very last morning, Martha Barry had passed on a tiny bit of her wisdom to Rose, which had given her enough insight to make some sense of her mother's action. The old woman had quietly demonstrated a great understanding of human nature and all its weaknesses – and, most of all, had shown how important it is to be able to forgive.

Later in the afternoon, as she was pouring milk into yet another cup of tea for the string of mourners, it suddenly struck Rose that she had mistakenly reassured her mother about the fact that nobody had been gossiping about her and Guard McGuire.

Her mind had gone back to Michael Murphy and the

wedding over in Gort – and then she remembered the incident in the ladies' toilets when she had overheard two women saying something about her mother. Someone, somewhere, had obviously heard the gossip through the Guards' wives. Bad news did indeed travel fast – but thank God she hadn't known it at the time.

But with her new, mature understanding of the situation, Rose could now comfort herself that things like that were a nine-day wonder. If her mother and Guard McGuire kept their distance from each other, as they had promised, any gossip would eventually die down.

It would be someone else's turn next, Rose thought ruefully.

There were always the illegitimate babies and the couples rushing to get married to be talked about in whispers, the bank-teller caught embezzling money from the till, and the sudden deaths – to mention but a few topics – that would soak up the interest of the rural communities.

* * *

On the morning of the funeral, the family and extended family made their way – walking, cycling or driving – to the church. Then, when Stephen Barry and his family were all settled in the first two pews, the mourners they hadn't already seen made their way to the front to offer their condolences.

Rose recognised the majority of people who came in a long stream along the front row, shaking hands with each of the family members. Although she tried hard to acknowledge each person when they came to her, inevitably at times it became one big blur.

Then Diana Tracey came to take Rose's hand in hers and say how very sorry she was for the family's loss. Rose acknowledged her with a quiet "Thank you", and then James Tracey came along and gave his commiserations as well. Seeing Diana Tracey – even in the midst of her sorrow – Rose was reminded of Leonora Bentley's job offer, and it suddenly hit her how much things had changed in her life since she had last seen the older woman.

As the last of the mourners came forward now, Rose glanced up and saw a tall, very well-dressed man coming towards them. It was only when he stopped to shake her hand that she realised it was Liam O'Connor.

"I'm very sorry for your troubles, Rose," he said, bending low so she could hear him. "I was home for the weekend and I heard about your grandmother."

Rose looked up at him and saw the look of genuine sincerity in his eyes. "Thanks, Liam," she said quietly. "It was good of you to come." He continued to shake hands with the rows of mourners and when Rose lifted her head to look a few moments later, he was gone.

When they all filed out of the church behind the coffin, Rose noticed Liam standing over by the wall talking to James and Diana Tracey. He was dressed in a well-made dark suit, with an impeccable white shirt and a black tie, and carrying a dark overcoat, and it struck Rose how comfortable and confident he looked talking with the professional couple.

Rose hoped he wouldn't try to speak to her again today as she couldn't be sure how her sombre-faced father might react.

But Rose needn't have worried. The last glimpse she

got of her old admirer was when she saw him at the back of the silent, respectful crowd as they lowered Martha Barry into her grave. He had obviously taken Rose's last rejection to heart and had kept his distance as she had asked the last time they spoke to each other down at the pub.

* * *

As Rose lay in bed that night, reflecting on all the painful things that occurred in her life recently, she realised that she hadn't thought of Michael Murphy for days. Not even once. She had been so busy with everything else in her life that she hadn't had the time to brood over him.

And even more surprising, she found it hard to conjure up a picture of him in her mind. He now seemed like a dim, shadowy figure she once knew. And now that she had felt *real* pain and loss, she realised that what she had felt after Michael Murphy's departure was a kind of loneliness – the loss of a childish dream.

When she thought about him now she felt nothing.

She realised that her feelings for him had been those of a young naive girl.

With all the growing up she had been forced to do in the last few days, Rose could see that quite clearly now.

Chapter 49

Hannah was elated.

She hung up the phone in the public telephone box in the centre of Galway and, with a barely concealed smile on her face, walked as quickly back to the house as her high heels and tight skirt would allow.

Josie and Nora were sitting at the small table studying.

"Guess what?" she told them, bursting with the good news.

"You've bought a new lipstick?" Nora ventured.

"Nope," Hannah said, flopping in a chair beside them. She lifted a hand to brush away a strand of her blonde hair. "Something much, much bigger."

"Go on," Josie urged. "Tell us."

"I've just been on the phone to Daddy and guess what he's going to buy me if I come home for Christmas?"

The girls looked at her with clueless expressions on their faces.

"A car! He said he's going to buy me a car to bring back after the holidays. We'll be able to go for runs here and there at the weekends."

"You'll be able to come to Cork with us for a weekend!" Nora said, clapping her hands together in delight.

"Indeed I will," Hannah said, beaming at them. She had no intention of going to a remote village in County Cork for the weekend with the two boring sisters but the car was a handy carrot to dangle in front of them. She would be able to take them on the odd drive out to Ennis or even to Connemara and keep them on her side. Recently, things had become a little strained in the house as the two girls weren't over-enamoured by Rose's romance with Robert Ryan. They liked the lecturer well enough but they didn't like being part of Rose's grubby little secret as relationships between lecturers and students were banned and everything had to be kept very hush-hush.

And while the girls liked having such a glamorous friend and housemate, they had been very taken aback the first time that Hannah didn't come home all night. She had given them some cock and bull story about meeting up with a friend from Slattery's Hotel and staying the night in one of the staff rooms, but they knew perfectly well that she had stayed the night with Robert Ryan in his flat down by Spanish Arch.

Since then, Hannah had stayed out regularly and not even bothered to make up any excuses and it made the sisters feel used and taken advantage of.

Hannah, having grown more astute since leaving home, knew that she had a bit of ground to make up to keep them on her side, and she knew that the car would help her to do just that.

* * *

Christmas back in Tullamore went much better than Hannah could ever have envisaged. Her mother was much calmer and easier than the family had ever known her and even Hannah's brothers had commented on this. Hannah presumed that her father had had a very strong word with her mother when she told him after Martha Barry's funeral that she had no intention of coming home for Christmas. She had the option of staying in her little house on her own or even going to Cork with her two housemates.

Bill Martin must have thought long and hard about the situation and decided that a very big, very generous offer was needed to bring his daughter home – and the car was the ideal solution. He knew that it would give Hannah another skill to add to her growing accomplishments and it would give her a bit of independence when she was at home. The other thing that struck him was that it would give Sheila Martin something to brag about to her friends at church. Very few families in Tullamore had cars and even fewer could afford to pay for cars for their daughters. Bill Martin knew that his wife would be delighted sitting in beside the pretty, well-dressed Hannah, and watching the attention she and the car would get driving up and down the town.

The first day Hannah arrived home was spent going around looking at cars, the second day actually choosing one from a garage in Athlone – a five-year-old, green Morris Minor with a pull-down black roof – then going to the bank to sort out the cash.

Hannah felt a huge thrill of excitement sitting in the passenger seat as her father drove the little car back from

Athlone to Tullamore. He had promised that he would take her out every day in the car for lessons, so that by the time the holiday was over she would be able to drive back down to Galway on her own.

On the second evening she was back at home, Simon and Ursula came out for a visit and to see Hannah's new car. As the group circled around the car in Martins' yard, taking in every detail about the Morris Minor, Hannah wondered how on earth she had ever got romantically involved with the pompous, petty-minded Simon.

While she had been away at college, she had occasionally thought back to her first love affair and thought that the smartly dressed bank clerk, Simon Connolly, had given her a good education in matters of sex. But when she looked at him now in his staid tweed suit and heard him moaning about the children and his demanding mother-in-law, she could see quite plainly that he was an old-fashioned, boring, selfish man. And when she compared him to the gorgeous, intelligent, casually dressed Robert Ryan, she could see not one attractive attribute that Simon possessed.

When Simon offered to take Hannah out for driving lessons, she quietly demurred, knowing exactly what he was hoping for. When they had a few minutes on their own, she told him that recently her conscience had bothered her greatly about their illicit affair.

"There's a little church at the end of our street in Galway that I go to a lot," she said, "and I've been lighting candles and praying for forgiveness for the mistakes that you and me made earlier."

"You're kidding me now!" Simon had said with some

disbelief. Hannah had never given him the impression that God and religion – or the fear of it – ever entered her pretty blonde head.

"No, I'm not. What we did was really wrong, but I was only a young schoolgirl and I didn't really understand."

"Didn't understand?" Simon repeated, his eyes wide with shock. Then, as he looked at the innocent-faced Hannah, a feeling of alarm swelled up inside him. What if she was to repeat this to anyone else? What if she was to confess it to a priest and he advised her to tell her mother or even the Guards?

"Ah, sure you were always grown up for your age," Simon said, brushing her concern aside, but her words had touched a raw nerve. "But maybe you're right . . . we should put it all in the past. I might think about lighting a few candles myself . . ."

Hannah saw little of Simon over the holidays and knew that she would never have to worry about his attentions again. She spent every spare minute practising her driving with either her father or brothers – and keeping well out of her mother's way.

By the time everyone was out in the yard and waving her off as she headed for Galway in her little green, soft-topped car, Hannah felt that her trip back home over Christmas had been well worth her while.

As Hannah drove down the long road from Ballinasloe to Galway, she realised that she'd never had such a good Christmas at home. The only thing that had spoiled it was missing Robert with his funny sense of humour and his dancing eyes.

It wouldn't have made any difference if she had stayed in Galway because he had been going back up to Dublin for Christmas.

"I'll miss you," she had told him when she got off the train at Tullamore, leaving him to carry on to Dublin.

"You'll be too busy out and about to miss me," he said, grinning. "I know perfectly well you'll be at all the local dances and driving around in the new car that your daddy's buying you."

"If I learn how to drive it quickly maybe I could drive up to Dublin to see you? I could even stay the night."

"At my parents' house?" Robert had laughed and shaken his head. "Not a chance. The place will be like bedlam. My brother and his wife and the kids are coming over from London." He had grabbed her knee playfully. "And you know we're not supposed to be letting anybody know about us – I could lose my job."

"They don't need to know that I'm one of your students or how we've met. It's dead easy. We can just say that I work in an office in Galway and you met me at a dance."

Robert raised his eyebrows, pretending to be shocked. "Lies come very easy to your lips, Miss Martin."

"It's only white lies," Hannah said, sticking her tongue out at him. "If we can't stay at your family's house, maybe we could go into a bed and breakfast for the night."

"It's better that we don't meet up," he said. "We'll both go our separate ways for the Christmas holidays and make the best of it." Before she had a chance to argue further, Robert had taken his face in her hands and kissed her on the lips. "You are absolutely gorgeous," he told her, "and I'll count the days until we are back in Galway together."

And it was those words that had kept Hannah going all over Christmas, and she too had counted the days until she was back in Galway, looking into his lovely dark eyes again.

Chapter 50

Christmas and New Year passed almost unnoticed in the Barrys' cottage.

There was little or no celebration. There was no writing of Christmas cards, no secret, excited wrapping of presents and no great preparations for the Christmas meal. While Rose had no interest in the festivities herself, she felt sorry for her younger sisters.

"Shouldn't we buy them something from Santy?" she asked her mother. "They're very young and they won't really understand about mourning."

"It's your father," her mother had said. "He said that the only celebrations in the house this year will be religious ones. I asked him if we could buy them a doll each or maybe a game but he said they're old enough to understand what death means. He won't budge on it."

At the last minute, Stephen conceded just a little and agreed that the girls could have a book each and some drawing books and coloured pencils to keep them occupied over the cold, dark nights.

Paul hadn't come home for Christmas this year,

mainly because he was working St Stephen's Day and there would be no transport back to the hotel. He could probably have got around that but when he realised that there would be no celebrations in the house whatsoever, he decided that having Christmas dinner with the Slatterys and other members of staff who couldn't travel home either, was a better option.

He had given up all hope of seeing Hannah over Christmas, as she told him that she was going back up to Tullamore for the festive period, as her father had promised her a little car if she came home.

At first Paul had been surprised at her turnabout regarding Tullamore, as she had always professed that she was never going back – but then he realised that it was yet another example of Hannah's inconsistencies. She would go whatever way the wind blew. She would put up with her mother for a week or two if it meant she got a car out of it.

At the end of the day, Hannah would always suit herself.

Rose found the whole festive period the most depressing she had ever experienced. She had very little work in Purcell's pub as all the family were around and they didn't need any extra help, so she spent most of her time at home. She missed her grandmother terribly, and was acutely aware of the silences in the house that the cheery old lady had filled.

As she observed her father's tight-set jaw on Christmas Day when they all sat around the table, Rose understood why her mother had strayed that little bit off the marital path. God knows what would have happened if Mrs McGuire had decided to tell her father about the rumours. Her mother had been terrified of that happening but it looked as though the guard's wife had decided to let the matter drop.

Guard McGuire had caught her mother for a few minutes one morning when there was no one around and said that he was thinking of putting in for a transfer to another barracks. He said they both might find it easier to forget their friendship if they weren't seeing each other practically every day – and he felt his wife might be more trusting if she didn't have to think of them being together any more.

Kathleen had told Rose all this, saying that she would feel really guilty if Frank McGuire had to move away because of her.

"I'd leave myself," she had told Rose, "if I could find as good a position anywhere else. But sure, there's nothing here. There's not even a decent job for a young clever girl like yourself."

* * *

It was a Sunday in the second week of January when the heavily- pregnant Diana Tracey came to speak to Rose as they came out of ten o'clock Mass.

"I was hoping I would catch you," Diana said, giving her a warm, friendly smile.

Rose immediately wondered if the vet's wife was going to mention Leonora Bentley's offer of work in Dublin, and she was completely taken aback when Diana offered her another job.

"I wondered if you would be interested in coming to work for me in the house?" she asked. "The baby is due in a few weeks and I'm beginning to find it hard to manage the house and the dogs and everything, and I'll definitely need help when the baby arrives."

Rose didn't need to think about the unexpected offer. Apart from having time on her hands, she could definitely do with the money. "That would be grand," she said eagerly. "I'm not working much at the moment and I don't need to be at home so much any more." She didn't explain that it was because her granny had died – there was no need. Everyone knew everyone else's situation in the village.

"If you're free, come down to the house tomorrow morning and we can chat about it," Diana said. She raised her eyebrows and pulled a little face. "I don't know how my mother will take it – I know she had high hopes of you working for her in Glenmore House. But I told her you were a homebody at heart and that nothing would ever drag you away from Kilnagree."

Later, Rose had walked down to Cathy's and told her about the housekeeping job at Diana Tracey's.

"But that's just brilliant!" Cathy had said, delighted for her friend. "It's exactly what you're looking for. It means that you can still stay at home like you've always wanted." She had paused thoughtfully. "That Bentley family must really like you – it's amazing that both the mother and the daughter have offered you jobs." She shook her head. "And then offering to put you through college, I've never heard of anyone being given a chance like that before." She'd given a low whistle. "You'd only have to offer me that once and I'd be gone like a shot." Then seeing Rose's face tighten a little, she'd rushed on saying, "But you have to do what suits you, Rose. You're not the ambitious type or anything like that. Even though you were the cleverest in the class, you've always been content to stay at home doing the cooking and the cleaning. And it's nice for the rest of us who might go away, to know that there will always be somebody like you at home to give us all the news."

For some reason Rose felt very put out by this speech of Cathy's but she concealed her feelings.

The girls had sat chatting for a while and then Cathy said, "Did you hear any more from the fella in America?"

"He sent me a nice sympathy card – it arrived last week," Rose said, giving a wry little smile. "He must have heard about Granny from one of the hundreds of people he writes to."

"Oh, he would have been genuine enough," Cathy said, not wanting Rose to feel embarrassed about him all over again. "If he'd still been living here, he would have been at the funeral." Then she suddenly remembered. "Did you see Liam O'Connor at it?"

Rose inclined her head. "He came up to sympathise with us."

"I hardly knew him," Cathy went on, her voice high with surprise. "He was so well-dressed he looked like one of the gentry. Apart from the fancy suit, he had a lovely dark hat and winter coat. And did you see his black van?"

Rose shook her head. "No, I only saw him standing in the churchyard – and he was chatting with the Traceys."

"He's fairly moving up in the world," Cathy said, sounding like a much older woman. "Kilnagree will be too small for the likes of Liam now – and fair play to him."

Kathleen Barry had been equally effusive about Diana Tracey's suggestion. "It's a heaven-sent opportunity for

570

you," she had said. "More regular hours than working in the pub and you might even get the chance to travel with them." Her eyes had lit up. "I've heard about families like the Traceys taking their housekeepers and children's nannies on holiday with them. They're the kind to go travelling to England and further abroad – you never know what kind of opportunities it might give you. They'll no doubt have more children and they'll want to keep you on." She closed her eyes for a moment, lost in thought. "Just imagine it, Rose – travelling here and there, and all you would have to do is mind the children and the oul' dogs for them. Sure, isn't that all you've been doing since you left school – and they'll pay you well for it."

Rose was weighing up all the practicalities. "How will you manage without me at home during the holidays when Eileen and Veronica are off school?"

"Ah, sure they can mind themselves now. Won't Veronica be going to the big school over in Gort soon and Eileen won't be long following behind her. They've grown up a lot recently and they're more than capable of making a cup of tea or putting on the potatoes. Don't be minding about them – they're well able to look after themselves."

"Are you sure?"

"They'll be grand. You're not going to miss a chance like that."

As she had been explaining to her mother all about the housekeeping job with Diana Tracey, it dawned on Rose that she'd never got around to telling her mother or her grandmother about the almost unbelievable offer that Leonora Bentley had made to her when they met down at the shore. The time had never been right – and if she were really truthful, she hadn't looked for the right time. She hadn't wanted anyone forcing her to go to Dublin while there had still been hope for her and Michael Murphy.

That night Rose lay in bed, tossing and turning and going over things in her mind. If her granny had been alive she would have got up and made them both a cup of tea, and she would have chatted her worries out and listened to the old lady's advice.

But her granny wasn't there and her mother had enough on her plate, so Rose had no option but to work things out on her own. In one way she was pleased with the job offer but, as she eventually started to doze off, there was a niggling little voice at the back of her head telling her that maybe it wasn't quite right.

* * *

The following morning when Rose woke up everything suddenly seemed very clear to her. As she opened her bedroom curtains to look out at a white landscape completely covered in a fine layer of snow, she knew that she wasn't going to take Diana Tracey's job.

And she knew exactly what she *was* going to do.

"Can you believe we have snow? You're going to have to wrap up well, and be very careful cycling down." Her mother was already up and about and had got the range going. There were two kettles boiling on the hob – an ordinary-sized one for tea and a bigger one for filling the basin to wash in. "I knew you'd want to have a strip-wash this morning for going down to Mrs Tracey's."

After a cup of tea and a boiled egg and toast, Rose got washed in the privacy of her own bedroom and dressed in her smart black skirt and the good lilac blouse that Leonora had bought her. Her mother helped her to put her hair up in a tidy chignon, and then Rose finished off with a light touch of make-up and a spray of her *Chanel No 5* perfume.

"You look lovely," Kathleen Barry said. "You look as good as any of the women in the magazines."

Rose had laughed and, as she studied herself in the wardrobe mirror, she knew that her mother had got a little bit carried away. She didn't look like a model – that was more Hannah's style – but she knew that she looked well enough.

* * *

Diana Tracey brought a pot of coffee and some lovely warm scones into the cosy sitting-room. "Gosh," she suddenly said as she put the tray down on the table, "I should have checked. Are you okay with coffee? It's proper ground stuff – but I've made it with boiled milk so that it's not too strong."

"Grand," Rose said, her cheeks flushing a little. She had never had real coffee -- in fact she'd only ever had the bottled kind on rare occasions – but she suddenly felt eager to try it.

But she knew she wouldn't be relaxed enough to drink the coffee or eat a bite until she had got something off her chest.

"Mrs Tracey . . ." she started.

"Diana," the vet's wife said, smiling at her. "You make me feel ancient calling me that. If you're going to be working with me, you'll have to get used to it."

"Well, about that, I wanted to ask you something – well, put a suggestion to you . . ."

A small frown came on Diana Tracey's face. "Go on."

"I wondered how you would feel if there was someone a bit older and more experienced than me available for the job?"

"Don't *you* want it?" Diana's voice was high with surprise.

"I think it's a great offer but if you don't think it's being too forward of me – I wondered if you might consider my mother instead?"

"But your mother is the housekeeper for the Guards, isn't she?"

Rose nodded. "But I think your job might be more suitable for her. She's looking for something with a bit of variety – she's been doing the same thing for years. She's a great cook and she's great at washing and ironing and everything like that."

Diana's eyes narrowed in thought. "Well, yes," she said, nodding, "a mature woman like your mother would be very suitable." She paused. "But what about *you*? If your mother takes this one, that means only one of you will have work."

Rose felt a little rush of excitement. "Well, I wondered if the position at your mother's house in Dublin is still available?"

"Ah . . ." Diana said, smiling broadly now. "There's only one way to find out." She pointed to the phone on the small round table by the armchair. "If you dial, I'll call out the number of Glenmore House to you now."

Chapter 51

Mrs O'Shea had been very difficult for the last few days since she heard the news that she was to have a helper in the house. "I hope this girl is nothing like that Mrs Burke you brought in when I had the bad arm." She took a dishcloth she had been bleaching in the sink, rinsed it under the tap and then proceeded to wring it out vigorously.

Leonora, who was reading the morning paper, had stifled a sigh of annoyance. "No, Mrs O'Shea," she had said, trying to keep her patience. "Rose Barry is very different from Mrs Burke."

The housekeeper now shook the damp cloth out, making a loud noise like a bird flapping its wings. "That one nearly drove me mad. She asked questions non-stop and she was poking her nose into everything. And she wasn't the best at hoovering – I had to keep following her around, picking up bits after her."

"Yes, Mrs O'Shea," Leonora said, folding her paper over. She would have to go into the drawing-room to get any peace to read.

"What time did you say the young girl gets in? I've a few things to do to get her room ready yet. Thank God it's a lovely sunny day – I'll be able to get this bit of hand-washing out on the line." Mrs O'Shea had been sorting out Diana's old room upstairs for the new member of staff. Diana would need one of the bigger rooms when she came on her next visit as she would need space for a baby's crib and all the accoutrements.

Mrs O'Shea had washed and ironed all the bedding, cleaned the two arched windows and hoovered and polished everywhere. When that was all done, she had then cleared any bits and pieces of Diana's that were left in the wardrobe and chest of drawers.

"I've said I'll meet her at Heuston Station around three o'clock," Leonora said, as she vanished out of the kitchen door with her paper under her arm and her coffee mug in her hand.

Later on, after Leonora had picked up her car keys for the journey to Dublin and sorted out some mail she wanted to post en route, she paused to check her diary. She had a feeling there was something marked down for the afternoon.

"Oh, Mrs O'Shea, the young fellow who is working on the furniture might call out with the small table for the hall. He said it would either be today or tomorrow."

"Is that the nice cheery young lad that fixed the cabinet with the funny legs in the bathroom?" the house-keeper enquired.

"It is," Leonora said. "If you wouldn't mind asking him to look at the panelling in the hall. He said he would look at it around the end of January when he knew he had a full week to devote to it. You can tell him to leave the bill for the table and I'll sort it out."

* * *

When Rose stepped off the Galway train carrying her suitcase, Leonora was there waiting for her. The cream Mercedes was parked just outside the station and, as she slid into the cream leather seat, Rose felt that both the train journey and now the drive in the car down to Lucan were all exciting indications of the new life she was about to start.

When the car turned in the drive of Glenmore House and drove up through the rolling, perfectly kept lawns, Rose caught her breath. It was much, much bigger and grander than she had imagined and she said as much to her new employer.

"It is a big rambling house," Leonora agreed, "although we only use certain rooms on a daily basis which keeps down the work. But we do have a lot of visitors and that's why I need someone to help Mrs O'Shea. She's getting on a bit and it's really getting a bit much for one person." She gave a little laugh. "Not that Mrs O'Shea would agree with that – she still thinks she's as capable of doing it all as she ever was." She smiled at Rose and raised her eyebrows. "I won't say anything more until you meet her. No description would do her justice."

There was a small black van outside the house when Leonora pulled up. "Leave your case," she said, getting out of the car. "Tommy Murray, the gardener, is around the back of the house, working on the greenhouse. He'll be happy to lift it in for you."

Rose felt her heart quicken as she followed Leonora

up the steps, through the big heavy door and into Glenmore House. She took in all the lovely old furniture and the paintings and the tall vases of flowers as she went along, wondering what it would be like to wake up in this huge house every day.

"I'll take you in to meet Mrs O'Shea first," Leonora said. "The kitchen is at the bottom of this corridor. You'll probably be ready for a cup of tea and something to eat."

Rose wasn't actually that hungry, as her mother had packed a small bag with sandwiches and slices of fruitcake and apple tart. In fact she had so much food that she ended up sharing it with a woman and a little boy who had travelled up to Dublin with her.

As they came towards the kitchen door, Rose could hear voices chatting and laughing and she slowed up a little, suddenly feeling self-conscious.

"Here we are," Leonora said, looking back at her and smiling encouragingly. "You can smell Mrs O'Shea's lovely baking before you reach the kitchen."

Rose turned in the door now to see the housekeeper sitting at the table, drinking tea opposite a tall, dark-haired young man in casual work-clothes.

"Mrs O'Shea," Leonora said, "I'd like you to meet Rose Barry."

When Rose walked into the big airy kitchen she saw a small, thin, sparrow-like woman in a black dress and a white apron.

Then the young man stood up from the table and Rose thought she must be imagining things as she found herself face to face with Liam O'Connor.

* * *

Later, when Rose had gone upstairs in her bright, sun-filled bedroom to unpack, Mrs O'Shea turned to her employer. "Who would have believed it?" she said, shaking her head.

"Believed what?" Leonora said distractedly, rifling through a pile of envelopes that had arrived while she was out collecting Rose. She picked out one with an American postmark and started to open it.

"That Liam and the young girl would know each other. They both come from Kilnagree!"

"Of course," Leonora said, sliding the fine sheets of airmail paper out from the envelope. "I should have thought about that and mentioned it to Rose. It was actually James who recommended him – don't you remember – when we were last down?"

"I'd forgotten. I'd mentioned to him that there was a young girl starting work at the house today," Mrs O'Shea rattled on, "but of course I never made the connection."

"Rose," Leonora cut in. "Her name is Rose." She hoped that the Scotswoman wasn't going to start going odd on the girl, as she was wont to do with anyone she took a dislike to.

"Aye, well, you'll have to give me a bit of time," the housekeeper said sniffily. "I'm still getting used to the name." She paused, then she started to laugh. "When I think of the look on both their faces when they saw each other. I don't know who got the biggest shock!"

Leonora was only half-listening to the housekeeper's musings as she read down the first page of Edward's letter.

"Well, it wasn't until we were sitting here chatting

with her that I discovered they knew each other really well. In fact they went to school together, although Liam's a couple of years older. She must be decent enough because he had nothing but the height of praise for her and her family."

Leonora looked perplexed for a moment. "Well, of course she's *decent*, Mrs O'Shea – you surely don't think I would knowingly employ someone who wasn't?"

"It's still nice to hear an outside opinion. You can't be too careful who you bring into the house – or Diana's house for that matter. Rose tells me that her mother is getting on great working for her."

"I'm delighted," Leonora said, starting on the second page of her letter.

Mrs O'Shea stood up from the table now and started to gather up the mugs and plates. "She was saying that her mother had taken down every one of those old Nottingham lace curtains in the house and given them a good bleaching. I'm looking forward to seeing them when we go down for the christening for I noticed they were looking a bit on the grey side when I was last there." She went over to the sink. "I believe the young girl lost her granny just before Christmas? She must have been very fond of her – she had tears in her eyes just talking about the poor old soul . . ."

Leonora smiled to herself. In spite of Lizzie O'Shea's guardedness, it sounded very much as though Rose and the housekeeper would hit it off well.

Leonora went back to finish off reading her letter while Mrs O'Shea got on with the washing up. She had a smile on her face when she came to the last paragraph.

All was working out back in New York for Edward and Christopher. They were in the process of looking for a house together and they had also taken on a new office in the area they were hoping to move to.

Leonora couldn't remember when she'd had such a cheery, upbeat letter from Edward. A weight had been lifted off her shoulders. She suddenly realised that she could stop worrying about her elder son – he now had Christopher Hennessey to look after him and care for him. If he was ill or if anything went seriously wrong in his life she knew that Christopher would immediately get in touch. It was the same way that Diana and James operated, and Jonathan and Emily. Edward was no longer solely her concern. She had never imagined that there could be such a positive side to his relationship.

A tap came on the kitchen door and Liam O'Connor came in. "I've had a look at the panelling," he told Leonora, "and I think it should polish up well. It will probably take a full week's work." He hesitated for a moment. "If you don't mind me commenting – I noticed that there's a piece of one of the carvings damaged down behind the main door –"

"Oh, it's been like that for years," Leonora said. "In fact I think it was like that when I first moved in here. I'm so used to it I hardly notice it now."

"Would you like me to take a mould of it and see if I can make a new piece? I did work like that in one of the offices in the Four Courts in town recently. It doesn't look too intricate and I can easily stain and polish it to make it fit in with the rest."

Leonora's eyebrows were raised in admiration. "Really?"

Liam nodded. "I'll bring the materials for the mould

when I come back to start on the panelling next week and then I'll work on the carvings back in my place in Dublin and bring it out when it's finished."

"Wonderful!"

"It could take a few weeks, or even longer, because I've a lot on at the moment," he warned her. "Like the antique furniture, I only get the chance do it in my own time in the evenings and weekends."

"There's absolutely no rush. I've waited all these years – a few more weeks or months isn't going to matter!"

"I'll head off now," he said, giving a little salute to Mrs O'Shea.

"Cheerio, Liam," the housekeeper said, "I'll look forward to seeing you next week, and I'll make sure and have some of that ginger shortbread that you liked."

"Don't be going to any trouble for me," he said, smiling warmly. "I'll quite happily eat anything that you bake. It's better than anything that can be bought in a shop."

Mrs O'Shea beamed with pleasure. "Well, let's just say that it's certainly fresher and a lot cheaper than anything you would buy in a shop."

Liam looked at Leonora now. "Do you mind if I call up to Rose to say goodbye?"

"Oh, please do. She's in the first bedroom at the turn of the stairs."

* * *

When Rose heard the knock she glanced anxiously around the room, hoping it looked tidy enough for her new employer, then she crossed the thickly carpeted floor to let her in.

For the second time that afternoon, Rose was shocked to find herself staring into Liam O'Connor's eyes. She had gone upstairs earlier on in a kind of a strange daze, feeling that everything about Glenmore House was unreal. The size of the place, the anticipation of meeting new people, and then – seeing him there.

"I'm off now," he told her, "and I thought I'd just wish you well in your new job before I go."

"Thanks, Liam," she said, her voice a little stiff and awkward. Seeing him now reminded her of the row they had the last time they spoke properly down outside the pub at home. She was reminded of every word he had said to her about Michael Murphy and it made her feel very foolish. She wondered if he was thinking the same thing.

"Who would believe the pair of us would end up working in Dublin? And meeting up in the very same place," he said in an incredulous voice. "You could have knocked me down when I saw you downstairs." Liam laughed now and shook his head. "I didn't know you knew the Traceys and Mrs Bentley so well – and I never would have believed in a month of Sundays that you would end up moving away from Kilnagree."

Rose couldn't tell whether he was laughing at her or with her. "Well," she said, starting to blush, "things change and sometimes that makes you look at things differently."

The humour drained from his face. "It does," he said, "and I suppose things have changed a whole lot back at home now that your grandmother has gone?"

"Yes . . . indeed they have."

GERALDINE O'NEILL

"I'm sorry, Rose. I could tell it was very hard on you at the funeral."

"It was good of you to come."

"Well, I was actually back home for the weekend, so the timing was grand." He shook his head. "That sounded bad . . . I don't mean it was grand your granny died."

Rose gave a weak smile. "I know what you meant."

Then suddenly, they both seemed to run out of things to say.

Liam gestured with his thumb towards the stairs. "I'd better go – I've a pile of work waiting for me in Dublin . . ."

As he turned to go, Rose suddenly got a strange feeling of loss – as if the only familiar thing in this big new, imposing world was walking away from her. Even if he was the last lad from Kilnagree that she would have wanted to see. She moved a few steps behind him. "Liam . . ." she said in a low voice, "how do you find living in Dublin? Have you found it easy to settle?"

He looked back, smiling again. "It's grand. I love it. I've made lots of friends – some Dubliners and some from all parts of Ireland. The dancehalls are great and the picture houses and I've joined a local hurley team. Between work and all the other things that are on the go, I never have a spare minute."

She nodded her head. "That's good to hear." He had obviously found his feet and was no doubt the centre of attention again as he had been in Kilnagree. He'd always been a good mixer and a good sportsman.

Liam raised his hand in a friendly salute "I'll be seeing you. And the best of luck in the new job."

After he had gone Rose went back into her room, closed the door behind her and went to sit on the bed. She looked around the room with its high, decorated ceiling and tall windows dressed with floral pelmets and tied-back curtains, and then she looked at the double bed with the lovely pink counterpane and matching pink pillow-slips. It was the biggest bedroom she had ever been in and yet the Scottish housekeeper had told her it was one of the smaller double rooms.

She knew this room had been Diana Tracey's, but there was nothing around the room now to indicate that anyone in particular had been there. It was just a nice, big bright room, and it was now Rose Barry's bedroom.

A totally blank canvas for her new life.

Chapter 52

The following day, Leonora decided to leave Rose on her own for a few hours with Mrs O'Shea and head down to Terry Cassidy's. She was going to start on one of her paintings today and was armed with a sketchbook with a few vague outlines, plus her trusty tin jug and a few other bits and pieces that might give her inspiration. It was a sunny day with a light breeze, which the housekeeper decreed was perfect for washing the downstairs windows.

"I'll do all the ones I can reach without standing on anything," she told her employer, "and Rose can do the higher-up ones. After that we'll give the kitchen cupboards a good clean out."

Terry was already in the studio working on an abstract floral painting on a really big canvas. She was dressed in a large pair of men's denim dungarees with the bottoms rolled up and she had her hennaed hair completely covered with a green polka-dot scarf. "Be careful," she warned Leonora, "I went a bit mad earlier and I think there are splashes of paint on the tables and floors. I haven't had time to stop and clean up yet."

"It's okay! I have my old fisherman's smock on and I

may well add a few splashes of my own." She smiled to herself, knowing it was most unlikely that she would ever let herself go enough to paint in the dramatic ways that Terry did. Whilst the artist would think nothing of using a large piece of natural sponge to give a dappled effect, or on other occasions flick paint from the end of the brush to create a speckled effect, Leonora stuck to her basic sketches which were then painted over in oils.

"So how are all at your end?" Terry asked. "Any more news on the baby front?"

As she set out her paints and still life pieces, Leonora brought her up to date on Diana's pregnancy, then filled her in on the news that came in the letter from Edward.

"Wonderful," Terry said. "They're such lovely boys. I really enjoyed the night with them at Glenmore House." She dipped her fingertips in a purple mix of paint, and then stretched up to the top of the canvas to sweep the colour into a colourfully cloudy sky. Then she stepped back to get a good view of it. "Have you heard from the dashing Mr Levy since then?"

"He's phoned a few times," Leonora said, squeezing a tube of white oil paint onto her palette.

Terry looked over at her. "And have you rung him at all?"

"No. There's no need to phone him. He knows how the situation worked out with Edward and Christopher. There's no point in ringing for time-wasting chit-chat."

"You know he's in love with you, Leonora?"

Leonora looked at the artist and gave a bemused smile. "I think we're both a bit too old for that sort of thing – don't you?"

"No, I don't. I think he's a lovely man and you make a lovely couple."

"But we're *not* a couple," Leonora pointed out. She directed her gaze at all the items she had laid out on the table. She moved the mottled tin jug to one side and then picked up a bunch of pale blue and purple dried hydrangea blooms and stuck them in it. "Daniel was just a good friend of Andrew's."

Terry put her head to the side, a thoughtful expression on her face. "If that's the case then there's something about the pair of you that doesn't quite add up. He acts as though he is very comfortable with you – and yet you are very cool with him. He acts as though he knows you much better than you're actually admitting to."

Leonora was rummaging about in her art box now, not lifting her head. "That's one of the things that annoy me about him – Daniel is too familiar and too presumptuous. It must be something to do with his work. I suppose psychiatrists are used to ferreting around in people's lives."

Terry suddenly clicked her fingers. "I've got it!" she said, as though she had found the answer to something "It's as if he's waiting – patiently waiting."

"Waiting for what?"

"I'm not quite sure." She shrugged. "Maybe waiting for you to come to your senses and realise that the pair of you belong together?"

"I'm afraid that's utter nonsense," Leonora said, her voice tense now. "And it's not going to happen. I realise now that I was lucky being able to trust one man for many years in my marriage – but I had to learn to my cost that nothing lasts. People change and you can never get things back on the same track."

Terry realised that she had touched a raw nerve. "I'm sorry, Leonora. I don't mean to poke my nose into your business . . . I was just trying to give a friendly opinion."

"And I appreciate it." Leonora gave a smile which didn't reach her eyes. "At least when I'm on my own, I know what I'm up to." She looked over at the multi-coloured artist. "Being single, you must understand that, Terry. There's a safety and a certainty when you don't have to rely on anyone else. It may be lonely but it is *safe*."

Terry moved her paint-splashed hand to push an escaped strand of red hair back under her scarf. "I suppose it is." She looked at the petite, ash-blonde woman across the room from her and gave a low, longing sigh. "But even now – even at this stage in my life – there's not a single day I don't wish for the right man to come along and sweep me up in his arms, and tell me that he wants to look after me. And even now I still wish I had someone special that I could share things with – my art successes, when I try out a new recipe . . . someone to share my bed at night. Somehow, I feel it's never going to happen for me." She rolled her eyes. "I suppose I've grown a bit odd in my ways over the years. Being on your own makes you do that. You are lucky to have the choice, Leonora – I wish someone like Daniel Levy was in love with me."

"I can't deny that I haven't enjoyed his company," Leonora admitted, "and at one point I did let him get very close to me." She closed her eyes against the memory. "Much, much too close . . ."

"And did he do something wrong?"

"Not at all. I loved every minute of his company, I loved doing all the things you've just described, but then I became afraid . . ." Tears began to blur her eyes. "You see, I trusted Andrew completely and he let me down. He let me down so very badly. Then, before we had a chance to repair any of the damage, he suddenly died – and I was left with all the unanswered questions. Not knowing what had been genuine and what had been false. Quite simply, Terry, I can't take the risk of being hurt again."

Chapter 53

Hannah's period was ten days late. It was rarely late. If she was pregnant – which she was fairly certain she was – she knew that she had nothing to worry about. Robert Ryan would take care of everything for her. They had been going out a few months but already Hannah could tell he was the right one to settle down with. He had a good job, he had a nice little house and she knew that once her father got over the shock – once he saw the type of person that Robert was – he would help them out financially too.

At first the idea had been frightening but the more she thought about it, the more appealing the idea of a baby had become. She'd had enough of different lads now, and she knew her looks would always get her most fellas she fancied. But she had learned from her flings with Simon and Paul and a variety of short-lived romances, that the important thing was to have the right kind of man. She wanted a nice life with somebody she could look up to and not feel embarrassed with. She wanted a life like the couple in the hotel who had given her the ten-shilling tip.

Robert Ryan was that perfect man. But she knew from the way he went on about settling down that he didn't envisage doing that for a while. He had only taken on the accounts lecturing post until the sick woman he had replaced came back. At the moment it didn't look as if she would return for a while, so the job might run on until the summer. After that, Robert warned Hannah that there was a chance he might have to move to Dublin or Cork for work. He had even mentioned the possibility of moving over to London. Hannah couldn't contemplate the thought of being without the handsome, clever Robert.

But the baby would ensure they would be together no matter what.

* * *

The following Friday Hannah had a half-day from college. Josie and Nora had gone off on a coach home to Cork for the weekend. They had been a bit off with Hannah because they had begged her to come with them – so that all three could have that promised weekend away in Hannah's car – but she told them she had to visit her aunt and uncle in Kilnagree that weekend.

Nora's brows had come down. "Is that Paul's family? The weird cousin from the hotel?"

Hannah had nodded, wishing the two sisters would go and get a life of their own, instead of wanting to do everything with her. "Paul's grand now," she told the girls. "He's got himself a nice girlfriend, somebody that works at the hotel with him – so he's not bothering me any more."

The girls had brought their bags to college and gone straight to the bus-station, and Hannah went off in a different direction to pick up some steaks and onions, a fancy pudding and a bottle of wine for a special meal she had planned with Robert that night. Then she went home, tidied things up for a bit and then went out for the appointment she had made with her doctor.

The appointment she had told no one about.

* * *

When they had finished eating and were sitting in front of the fire with a glass of sweet Italian wine in their hands, Hannah quietly told Robert her news.

Robert was stunned. "What are we going to do? We can't have a baby – we have no money, we only have rented rooms and I don't even have a permanent job!"

"We'll work something out," Hannah said confidently. "Other people manage. Besides, the baby won't come until after I've finished the college course, so I'll be able to go out to work or maybe even do typing work at home. I could buy a little typewriter like Josie's and you could ask around for any of the lecturers who need work typed up."

Robert was very quiet and distant all weekend. On the Saturday morning he made excuses about going to the library to look up reference sections on some sort of Economic History lecture he had to give to one of the other classes he taught. On the Sunday he said he had to go back to his own place as he had to prepare work for an inspection the college was having the following week.

Hannah had been smiling and understanding. She

couldn't have expected him to react any other way. It was a shock – but she had no doubts that Robert would get over it.

Instead of worrying, she had walked around the shops in Galway on Saturday looking at baby clothes and baby prams, and then she had gone to a wool shop to buy some white wool to knit a little pair of bootees. She knew that Diana Tracey's baby was due soon and she thought that it would be nice to knit a small baby present for her.

It would give her practice for knitting for her and Robert's baby.

When she met Paul and his new girlfriend last week, he had told her that his mother was working for Mrs Tracey now. Hannah knew that it would give her a good excuse to go back to the imposing white house down by the sea. It was just the sort of place she could imagine herself and Robert and their children living in.

The Traceys were professional people like Robert and when she gave them a gift for the baby they might well decide to invite her and Robert over for a meal. Hannah thought that since Diana and she had so much in common, like music and fashion, that the vet's wife would probably think that their babies would make good friends too.

Chapter 54

Rose went out into the hallway to pick up the mail that had just been delivered. She walked back towards the kitchen, checking the envelopes as she did so. She had her hair tied up neatly and was dressed in a plain black skirt and a blue turtle-neck sweater, with the little pearl brooch that the Slatterys had given her. Leonora and Mrs O'Shea had discussed what Rose should wear for work and they both agreed that her job wasn't the same as the housekeeper's as she would be doing things like going out to the shops or the post-office, taking Leonora's books to the library and that kind of thing – the sorts of chores that Mrs O'Shea was finding too much for her now. They decided that a smart skirt and jumper or blouse would be fine, unless she was helping with the garden or heavy cleaning jobs.

Rose was delighted to be able to wear her own nice clothes most of the time, as it meant she always looked decent when she walked into Lucan town.

"You've a pile there this morning," Mrs O'Shea commented. "Anything for ourselves?"

"There's one for you," Rose said, smiling at the elderly house-keeper, "and it has a Glasgow postmark."

Mrs O'Shea pulled a face. "Not likely to be anything good," she said, taking the envelope from her. She checked the handwriting. "Our Monica, you'd know her spidery scrawl anywhere."

"I've two – one from home and a big brown one," said Rose. She looked at Mrs O'Shea. "Is Mrs Bentley coming down soon or do you think I should take her mail upstairs to her?"

The housekeeper glanced at the clock. It was just gone nine o'clock. "I'd leave her lying on a wee bit longer. She was late getting in last night. Some concert or other in the middle of Dublin and I think she said they were going on to somebody's house after it."

"It sounds lovely," Rose said wistfully.

She would love to go to Dublin to a concert or a play, but there was no opportunity for anything like that yet. She had been working for a few months in Glenmore House and, even though she was really enjoying it, she hadn't really made any friends. Apart from girls she had begun chatting to after Mass, the only young person her own age that she'd spoken to on a regular basis was Liam O'Connor. But that didn't count really because he didn't come to see her as a friend – they only saw each other when he was back and forward doing work for Mrs Bentley.

There was also a young, studious-looking man who worked in the library who had asked Rose to go for a drink, but apart from feeling he wasn't really her type she didn't want to mention going out with lads to Mrs Bentley just yet.

Mrs O'Shea raised her eyebrows. "She was with that

arty crowd again – they're always going off somewhere these days."

"Oh, you mean Terry Cassidy? She's a lovely person – very funny."

"I don't know about funny," Mrs O'Shea said, opening her envelope. "Very *odd* would be more like it." She paused. "Although I shouldn't really criticise her. In her own way she's the finest. And she's brought her ladyship out of herself no end this year. She's back to her old self."

Rose smiled at Mrs O'Shea using the term 'her ladyship', because she knew the housekeeper thought the world of Mrs Bentley and, although it sounded like a derogatory title, it was more of an endearment than anything else.

They both began to read their letters, Mrs O'Shea slowly following every word of hers with her finger.

Rose's letter was full of news from Kilnagree. The big brown envelope contained all the forms and information for a teacher-training course in Dublin that Leonora had suggested.

Rose stared out of the kitchen window for a few moments, considering the situation. College in Dublin would be the answer to everything, she reckoned. She would get the chance to meet other girls her own age and maybe get some kind of a social life.

She looked over now to tell the housekeeper about the forms, only to see that the Scotswoman had tears streaming down her face.

"Mrs O'Shea! What's the matter?"

"Och, it's just a wee bit of bad news, hen." The housekeeper searched in her apron pocket for a hanky to dab at her eyes. "It's our Willie – he had some kind of a turn – and they've only given him a week at the most to live." She lifted the envelope with a shaky hand. "This was posted last Thursday . . ."

Leonora came downstairs as Rose was making a cup of tea to try to comfort the housekeeper. The Scotswoman made a gesture to her not to say anything, which Rose instinctively ignored.

After saying good morning, she said to her employer, "Mrs O'Shea's had a bit of bad news from Scotland . . ."

"Lizzie, what's the matter?"

"It's just our Willie again . . ."

The housekeeper went on to explain and then Leonora told her to go and phone someone in Glasgow who could tell her more up-to-date news.

When she came off the phone, Mrs O'Shea was clearly upset. "Och, he's finished," she said, trying to sound matter of fact. "They said he's not eating or drinking . . . it could be any time now."

"You have to go over immediately," Leonora stated. "If you don't, it might be too late."

"Sure, how can I just up and go? How can I go at such short notice?"

Leonora stared at her for a few moments, and then she said, "We'll all go. I'll bring you over in the car to Glasgow and Rose can come along and read the map and help me navigate our way around. I'm sure there's a boat goes overnight to Scotland. I'll phone and book it right now."

Both Rose and Mrs O'Shea looked at her in shock.

"No . . . you can't do that," Mrs O'Shea said. "How can you come over to Glasgow?"

"Easily," Leonora told her. "We'll book into a hotel for a few nights. You won't need to worry about us."

The housekeeper's face crumpled. "But I'll have to stay for the funeral . . . what would you do to fill your time?"

"We'll keep ourselves busy. I'm sure we'll find plenty to do in Scotland."

* * *

By the time they were on their way up to Dublin Port, in spite of the tragic circumstances, Rose began to feel a growing a sense of excitement. She had never done anything like this in her life before and the fact that Mrs Bentley had immediately asked her to go with them – had thought she was a suitable companion – had made her feel better about herself than she'd ever felt before. And she felt strangely proud of the fact that they were setting off on this spur of the moment, unplanned journey on their own, without depending on a man to organise it for them.

As they drove along in the comfortable Mercedes, Rose suddenly realised that everyone had been right – her granny, her mother, even Liam O'Connor. She had been settling for too little back in Kilnagree. She realised that the future she had been dreaming about with Michael Murphy, had been totally dependent on *his* achievements and she had only pictured herself in a traditional, supporting role. She had never imagined that her future might lie in her own hands. Now, she could see quite clearly that she had been selling herself short – that   she was capable of doing a lot more than she had imagined.

But it had taken Leonora Bentley to make her see it.

* * *

In the morning, Rose studied the map carefully and was able to navigate them out from the port in Glasgow to the hospital where Mrs O'Shea's brother was.

Most of the time they were quiet as they drove along but occasionally they chatted about the scenery and debated about signposts. At one point Mrs O'Shea suddenly remembered about the cabinet that was due to be dropped off at Glenmore.

"It's okay, Lizzie," Leonora told her. "I left a message at Liam's office to let him know that we'd be gone. He'll deliver it next week." She paused. "By the way, I saw Liam at the concert the other night."

Rose's ears pricked up. Surely Liam O'Connor wasn't at the sort of concert that Mrs Bentley went to?

"Oh," Mrs O'Shea said, "and what was he doing there?"

"He was there for the concert, of course," Leonora said, "and he was with a very attractive-looking girl and another older couple. He came over to talk to me and I have to say he looked very well – I've only ever seen him in his work clothes, but he looked very impressive in a smart suit and tie. He's a very clever young man – I'd say he'll go far."

Rose sat silently as they discussed Liam now, pretending to concentrate on looking at the map. It felt very strange to hear him being spoken about in such a way. Who would have believed that someone she would have gone to school with would end up going to concerts in Dublin?

The housekeeper grew quieter and quieter the nearer they got to the hospital her brother was in, and she was silent by the time they drew up in the hospital car park. Rose went into the reception desk and checked where they should be, and then they took the house-keeper along a series of corridors and up a lift to find the ward where her brother lay dying, flanked by several of his close family.

Leonora and Rose left her with her family and went off into the hospital canteen to get something to eat. Every so often, Rose went back through the hospital corridors to check how things were going, until eventually she knew she wouldn't have to check any more. Willie had lingered on long enough for Mrs O'Shea to come and sit with him for a few hours, then he had died with his sister holding his hand.

* * *

After settling Mrs O'Shea in with relations for the four days leading up to the funeral, Leonora and Rose went off in search of a hotel in the city centre. Terry Cassidy had recommended the one by the Central Station, so Leonora booked two single rooms for them. They spent the next few days visiting art galleries and museums in Glasgow. On one of the days they took a drive out to Loch Lomond and on another they caught the train to Edinburgh.

Rose had never seen such a beautiful place as Edinburgh, and was mesmerised by the beautiful Princess Street Gardens and the famous flower clock. Leonora took notes on the layout of the flower beds for her own garden, and the names of any plants and shrubs which caught her eye. They wandered up to the castle, stopping to look at the old houses as they went. They had lunch in a café on the Royal Mile and went to look at the Greyfriars Bobby statue, then they spent the afternoon in the big art gallery.

"Rose," Leonora said, when they sat back in the train heading for Glasgow again, "I have enjoyed your company immensely and I'm very grateful to you for coming with me."

"I've had a great time," Rose said, her eyes shining. "I don't mean to be disrespectful to Mrs O'Shea's brother, and I know it wasn't meant to be a holiday, but I have really enjoyed it."

"And so have I," Leonora said, smiling warmly at her. "It will give you an idea of how to find your way around cities, although I'm sure you'll find Dublin easier than either Glasgow or Edinburgh. Have you decided which course you're going to apply for yet?"

"Probably teaching. I think it's something I would really enjoy." She paused. "I'll make sure I work hard at my studies and at Glenmore House. I feel bad about you paying all that money . . . and I want you to know that I'm very, very grateful."

"I know you are, dear," Leonora told her. "But I can afford it and I feel that it is money well spent. You have fitted in so well at Glenmore House with me and Mrs O'Shea. You've given us both a new lease of life, you know. "

"Have I?"

"Yes. I don't feel so bad going out the odd night, now that I know Lizzie has you for company. After her accident I've become very aware of her age and I feel with you around she's willing to take a back seat at times." She paused for a moment. "I know we're probably not much company for you but you have a whole new life at college to look forward to and you'll make lots of new young friends."

Rose looked out of the train window now at the rolling Scottish hills. "I think my new life has already started," she said, smiling.

Chapter 55

On the day that Leonora's car was due to make its way out to the port in Glasgow for the return to Ireland, Terry Cassidy heard a car pulling up on the gravel outside her small cottage and went to the window to investigate. It was a shiny black Rover. When she saw the tall, distinguished man get out, she immediately recognised the striking silver hair. It was Daniel Levy. She smiled to herself and went out to greet him.

"I hope you don't mind me calling unannounced," he told her, "but I was up at Glenmore House and found it all closed up. I remembered your invitation to come and have a look at your art studio, so I thought it was a perfect opportunity."

"Come in, come in," said Terry, with a wave of her bejewelled hand. She was wearing a flowing red and yellow beaded top with bell-shaped sleeves. "We'll have a coffee first and then I'll show you around."

They went into the sitting-room and, like Leonora on her first visit, Daniel was captivated and intrigued by all the art work dotted all around the room.

"They've all gone to Scotland," Terry told him, as she brought out the cups of coffee and a plate of little colourfully iced cakes. "Mrs O'Shea's brother had only hours to live and they were planning on staying for the funeral."

Daniel made a small whistling sound. "Poor Lizzie! She's really had it bad recently."

"She really has." Terry handed him a cake on a small plate. "Rose went with them. You've met her, haven't you? A lovely young girl from County Clare."

"I met her briefly and Mrs O'Shea was singing her praises. Great worker apparently and a very clever girl." He gave a little sigh. "I haven't been out to Glenmore House much recently. There doesn't seem any point in going."

"But you're good friends with Leonora – surely you wouldn't stop visiting?"

"It can be awkward," Daniel stated, not sure whether he should say any more. Then he thought about the lovely evening he had in Glenmore House with Terry and Edward and Christopher. Leonora must have thought her open-minded and trustworthy enough to invite her. He decided to take a chance. "You know there's a history between Leonora and me?"

Terry nodded. "I can see there's definitely *something* between you . . ." She took a bite out of a pink cake.

"She is adamant that she doesn't want any kind of a romantic relationship and at times she's flatly refused my friendship. I've persevered – I've hoped that she might come around but lately I'm beginning to think I'm wasting my time." He raised his eyebrows. "And maybe I should just give in and respect her wishes . . ."

Terry dusted down a few crumbs from her colourful

top. "Don't give in just yet," she advised him, "because I think she's struggling against the fear of being hurt – rather than rejecting you."

"Do you think so? I find the whole situation very confusing. There was a time when we were very close . . . I don't know what I did wrong."

"I'm sure you did nothing wrong. In my opinion, if Leonora could let herself go enough to trust any man – it would be you."

"But why is she so fearful? She had a long and happy marriage and Andrew adored her . . ." He paused, remembering back to the conversations he'd had with Andrew in the last year of his life. "I know they had a bit of a blip . . . but I thought they had sorted it all out. Maybe I got that wrong?"

"Well," said Terry, "maybe you did . . ."

Chapter 56

Kathleen Barry was amazed to see her niece standing on the doorstep of Diana Tracey's house at nine o'clock on a Friday morning.

"Hannah! Is everything alright?"

"Yes, yes, but I'm in a bit of a rush," Hannah said, her eyes darting around in a distracted manner.

A very heavily-pregnant Diana Tracey came to the door. "Hello, Hannah," she said, "it's lovely to see you. Are you coming in to have a chat with your aunt? I think Kathleen has just made a pot of tea."

"No . . . no . . . thanks for asking, but I'm in a rush. I'm going up to Dublin and I just called for Rose's address. I have a car now and I'm driving up there."

Diana looked at her, sensing that something was wrong. "If you come in for a few minutes, then I'll draw you a little map which will take you right to Glenmore House."

"Would you be able to draw me another map for how to get to Dundrum? I've another friend out there who I might call out to see."

"Certainly. Would you like to ring Rose now? They're usually up and about early in Glenmore House."

"No," Hannah said, in a strangely flat voice. "I'm not sure when I'll be calling out – or if I'll even have time. It's just in case . . ."

A short while later Hannah came out of the house, holding the maps tightly in her hand. She jumped into the car and, after giving a little wave, quickly drove off.

Kathleen thought it most strange that her niece had not lingered for a minute more than was necessary inside the big house she adored. Hannah hadn't even seemed to be aware that she was in the house – nor had she even given any of the expected pleasant greetings to a woman due a baby in a matter of weeks.

It was very obvious that Hannah had much more pressing things on her mind.

* * *

Rose came cycling up the drive of Glenmore House and found herself smiling when she saw Liam O'Connor's black van parked outside. When she went inside, carrying a bag of Leonora's library books, she could hear Mrs O'Shea and Liam chatting down in the kitchen.

As she walked along the corridor, she halted to admire the cabinet that Liam had just brought back – a very intricately carved walnut piece, with fancy scrolled legs. All the other items had been returned to Glenmore House in perfect condition and the wood panelling and carving in the hall was now back to its former glory. Liam O'Connor would have no need to call out at the house any more.

Rose knew that she was going to miss seeing him. She

had got used to their chats every week or so and they had swapped any news they got in their letters from Kilnagree. Liam was also very cheery and kind towards the old Scottish housekeeper and that had made Rose warm further to him. But however relaxed Liam was in Glenmore House, Rose felt that the memory of the row they had about Michael Murphy down at Slattery's was still etched in both their memories.

"I've been hearing all about your trip to Scotland," Liam said when she came to sit at the kitchen table beside them.

"It was beautiful," Rose said, her eyes shining at the memory.

"Scotland is on my list of places to visit," Liam said. "I was over in London for a weekend earlier in the month and it was an eye-opener. Amazing!"

"You're fairly getting around," Mrs O'Shea told him. "I hear you were at a fancy concert in Dublin recently."

"Sure, you can't go anywhere in Ireland without being seen," Liam said, laughing. "We were in The Shelbourne Hotel for a meal before the concert and we met one of our biggest customers in there! You think Dublin is big enough to get lost in and then you turn a corner and you meet someone you know."

Rose caught her breath at the mention of The Shelbourne – everyone knew it was one of the fanciest and most expensive hotels in Ireland. Where had Liam O'Connor got the money and the confidence to go to such a place?

"I believe you were all dressed up to the nines in your suit and everything," Mrs O'Shea said, "looking like a right toff! And I believe you had a very glamorous young lady along with you?" There was a definite question in the housekeeper's tone and she sipped her tea, hopeful of more information.

A slight flush of embarrassment came to his face. "Ah, you have to make a bit of an oul' effort every now and again," he said, evading the point. "You can't be going to these places and not look right." He winked over at Rose. "Isn't that right, Miss Barry?"

Rose smiled back, thinking how very clever Liam O'Connor was to give not one thing away. He was obviously moving up very quickly in the world – and mixing in circles that could only be imagined back in Kilnagree.

* * *

As soon as she heard that her daughter had gone into hospital, Leonora lifted the bag she had ready and waiting and headed off in the car for Kilnagree, leaving Mrs O'Shea and Rose to hold the fort at Glenmore House.

Later that evening she rang to say that Diana had had a baby girl and that both she and the new arrival were doing well.

"She'll be delighted to have a baby granddaughter," Lizzie O'Shea told Rose, as they sat by the fire in the drawing room, Leonora having offered them the comfort of the room while she was away.

Mrs O'Shea examined the sewn-up Aran cardigan for which she was now knitting the button band. "I don't know what I'm doing finishing this off," she sighed. "It was supposed to be for our Willie, God rest his soul. If I hadn't been so far on, I would have ripped it all out and knitted something else with the wool."

"You can always give it to somebody else," Rose ventured.

"Aye, I suppose I can." Her brow furrowed in thought, then her face suddenly brightened. "Do you know who it might fit? Liam! The very fella! I can just picture him in it – can you?"

Rose looked at the bulky, shapeless garment. "Yes," she said, trying not to smile," it would look perfect on him."

Just then the bell sounded.

"I'll get it," Rose said, jumping up.

Mrs O'Shea looked at the clock on the mantelpiece. "Who could that be at this time of night?"

Rose was halfway down the hallway when the doorbell rang again – and then again. She halted when she got close to the door, not sure what to expect, and then she took a deep breath and opened it.

There, soaked to the skin and shivering, was her cousin Hannah.

"Thank God!" Hannah said, throwing herself into the startled Rose's arms.

Rose was dumbfounded. "Hannah, what's wrong?"

"Rose," Hannah sobbed. "I need your help . . . I'm in terrible trouble!"

Rose guided her cousin inside the house and closed the door. By this time, the housekeeper was coming down the hallway towards them

"It's all right, Mrs O'Shea," Rose said, over her shoulder. Even as she was saying it, she knew it was *not* all right. "It's my cousin, Hannah."

Mrs O'Shea came to look at the damp, bedraggled visitor. "Bring the girl in to the fire, Rose. I'll make some hot cocoa."

Then she went off to the kitchen, while Rose took Hannah's wet coat and shoes and went to find her a warm cardigan and a pair of slippers.

"So, Hannah, what is it?" Rose asked when she returned and seated herself next to her cousin.

"I was going to write and tell you," Hannah said "but I was waiting until I knew the date of the wedding first."

"What wedding?"

"Mine . . ." Hannah looked up to see her cousin with her mouth open in shock. "I've been courting this lovely man down in Galway – he's a college lecturer. But something has happened. He went home to his family in Dublin – in Dundrum – on Wednesday, and I haven't seen or heard from him since."

Rose looked at the bedraggled blonde-haired girl with mascara streaking down her face and wondered what on earth had possessed her to come to Glenmore House of all places.

Hannah wiped a tear away with the back of her hand. "I drove up to Dublin yesterday – up to his family's house – but they say they haven't seen him either."

"Maybe he's gone back down to Galway," Rose suggested. She wondered now if this was all a big fantasy thing that Hannah had made up – that she had blown out of all proportion. How on earth could she be getting married to someone she'd just met?

Hannah shook her head. "No . . . I phoned the college and they said he'd finished working there on Wednesday. The woman he was replacing came back."

"Maybe he had to go somewhere to sort out work or something like that," Rose suggested, totally confused by the whole situation. "Why didn't you just wait in Galway to hear from him?"

"Because . . ." Hannah said, tears running down her cheeks now, "because I'm afraid he might not come back . . . I think he's scared of the responsibility."

"I still don't understand . . ."

"Are you pregnant, hen? Is that why he's run off?" came Mrs O'Shea's voice from the door.

Startled, the girls turned to see her advancing, tray in hands.

Rose looked at Hannah now, expecting her to be outraged. Instead, she had her blonde head in her hands. There was an ominous silence.

"Are you expecting a baby, Hannah?" Rose asked softly.

Hannah slowly nodded her head. "I found out last week."

Rose felt her head reeling. Hannah had caused some trouble before but this was the worst possible news she could have brought.

Mrs O'Shea brought the tray over to the table. "Have a wee sandwich now, hen," she said kindly to Hannah. "You'll feel much better after eating."

"But I need to find him," Hannah said, starting to cry again. "I need to know what's going on."

Mrs O'Shea looked at Rose. "I think a nice warm bath and then a decent night's sleep would do her the world of good," she said in a low voice. "What do you think? She could share your double bed for the night and it would save us having to make up another one at this hour."

A feeling of resentment washed over Rose. Once again, Hannah had come pushing into her life where she wasn't wanted. Pushing into Glenmore House. It was the same way that she had pushed into Diana Tracey's house. Whatever Rose had, Hannah always seemed to want a part of.

Then she chided herself for her selfish thoughts.

"Of course, Mrs O'Shea," she said. "That's a good idea."

* * *

Hannah wasn't a lot better in the morning. She had slept badly and had dark rings around her eyes. She had also been sick before her breakfast and then again afterwards. She was very quiet but in a distracted sort of way. Every time Rose or Mrs O'Shea started a conversation with her, she kept losing track of what was being said and drifting off into her own thoughts.

"That girl isn't fit to go anywhere," the housekeeper told Rose when they were clearing up the kitchen and Hannah was back up in bed again. "And the weather doesn't look a whole lot better today." She nodded towards the window which was streaked with raindrops.

"Well, she can't stay here. She's going to have to go back to Galway or back to my Auntie Sheila's in Tullamore." She paused. "They have a phone – do you think I should give them a ring?"

Mrs O'Shea sucked in her breath. "I think she has to make that decision – she's a grown woman. I don't think it's our place to go phoning her mother." She paused. "I think she needs to get hold of the father of her child

613

before she goes any further. If he's a college lecturer, you'd think he would be decent enough to stand by her. She is a lovely looking little thing."

"What can we do?" Rose looked really anxious now. "Mrs Bentley will go mad at me when she comes back . . ."

"Don't be worrying. I'll explain it all to her."

Rose suddenly felt as though it was her grandmother talking – giving her advice. "You're very good, Mrs O'Shea."

The housekeeper raised her eyebrows and smiled. "And you were very good to me accompanying me to Glasgow."

Hannah came downstairs again in the early afternoon, still pale, but looking a little bit brighter.

"I want to go back into Dublin to see if Robert's arrived yet," she told Rose when they were in the kitchen on their own.

"But you're not fit to go anywhere," Rose told her. She took a deep breath. "If you want my opinion, Hannah, I think you would be wise to go home to your mother and father."

Hannah stared at Rose for a few seconds and then she let out a sort of low wailing noise. "Noooooooooo!" she said, her eyes closed and her head shaking vigorously from side to side. "I can't tell my mother – she'll kill me! She'll kill me for this."

Rose felt really alarmed. "Stop it, Hannah!" she said, putting her hand on Hannah's arm to calm her down.

But it didn't work. Instead, Hannah wrapped her arms around herself and started rocking back and forth.

"Don't tell Mammy!" she wailed. "Don't let Mammy and Daddy know! I can't tell them until I have Robert along with me!"

Mrs O'Shea, who was cleaning the downstairs bathroom, came rushing along the hallway when she heard the noise. "What's happened? What's wrong with her?"

Rose explained and then they both sat on either side of Hannah, Mrs O'Shea talking to her and gently rubbing her back until she calmed down again.

"There's no need to tell anybody anything yet," the housekeeper said. "Just give yourself time to think it all through."

"I've got to find Robert," Hannah said, her voice stronger now and full of determination. "I've come all the way up to Dublin to find him and I know when I talk to him that everything will be all right. He could be out at his parents' house now. I told them I'd come back again today."

"I'll come with you," Rose said, standing up. "We'll go and get ready now."

"You'll have a bowl of my home-made soup and some bread before you leave. It'll help to keep you going," Mrs O'Shea said.

Hannah went out to the car to get a bag with some spare clothes and Rose walked out with her, holding an umbrella over them both.

Then, as they were walking back into the house, a car engine sounded in the distance. Rose paused for a moment and then saw the familiar black van coming up the drive.

"It's Liam O'Connor," she said, wondering what had brought him out this morning.

"I'll go on and get dressed," Hannah said, as though Rose had never spoken, and then she went inside.

The van pulled up beside Hannah's car and Liam got out.

"Hi, Rose," he said, coming towards her with a cheery

smile. "Mrs O'Shea phoned and asked me to call out when I was next around here, so I thought I'd take a run out when I was quiet. I believe she has some kind of a surprise for me. Have you any idea what it is?"

Rose remembered the conversation about the Aran cardigan from last night. She managed a weak smile. "Whatever she gives you, Liam, make sure you look delighted because she's put a lot of work in it."

As they walked along the hallway she told him that Hannah was up visiting from Galway and had stayed the night.

"I suppose you were out dancing or out on the town?" he said, grinning at her. "I can't imagine Hannah being the type to sit in."

"She didn't arrive until quite late last night . . . and actually, she's not too well . . ."

As soon as she saw Liam, Mrs O'Shea went rushing to the airing cupboard to get the Aran cardigan for him. She insisted that he try it on in front of herself and Rose and, like a good sport, he pulled it on and buttoned it up without a shred of embarrassment.

Rose looked at him and wondered if he would say anything about the length of the sleeves or the fact that there was a strange bulge in the seam at the side.

"Perfect!" he said, looking down at himself. "Absolutely perfect. I'll keep it for special occasions at the weekends."

"Now go down the hallway to the bathroom at the bottom and look at yourself in the full-length mirror," Mrs O'Shea told him. "Rose will show you where it is. I want you to be sure that you like it – I don't want you taking it for the sake of it."

Rose led the way down the hallway and when they got into the bathroom, Rose opened a tall cupboard to reveal a long slim mirror. Then Liam went to stand in front of it.

Rose watched him as stared at himself wearing the Aran cardigan with its slightly too long sleeves and the funny bulge. He pushed the sleeves up to make then fit better, and then he smoothed his hand down the side as if that would magically remove the bulge. A bubble of laughter came up into her throat which she swallowed back. Then another one came.

"How do you think it looks?" Liam said, turning to her.

Rose had both hands over her mouth now as she struggled not to laugh.

"Are you laughing?" he asked incredulously. "Are you laughing at Mrs O'Shea's *geansaí*?" He deliberately used the old Irish word for the jumper which made it sound even funnier.

Rose closed her eyes and then it all became too much. She went into a full belly laugh. "Oh, I'm sorry . . ." she spluttered, her whole body shaking.

Liam went back in front of the mirror now and pulled the sleeves right down over his hands. "I suppose they are a bit long looking," he said, smiling at her.

Rose had her hand to her throat now as she struggled for control. "It's the bulge at the side . . ."

"It's bliddey awful, isn't it?" he said, shaking his head. "What am I going to say?"

His comical expression made Rose laugh even harder.

"Don't you dare come into the kitchen with me now,"

Liam warned her, "or I'm likely to start laughing as well, and then we'll both be in trouble with Mrs O'Shea."

"Oh, don't!" Rose said. She sat on the edge of the bath, taking deep breaths and then she looked up at him and they both started laughing again.

Then Liam stepped forward and took her hands to pull her to her feet. The next moment she was in his arms and their eyes met and the laughter suddenly changed into something else.

They stared at each other for a few seconds and then Liam gently took her face in his hands and brushed her lips very lightly with his. Rose felt a sudden wave of physical longing washing over her. A feeling much stronger than the one she had felt with Michael Murphy.

When he could see she wasn't resisting, his confidence soared and his arms tightened around her and he kissed her again – properly this time. And they stood locked in each other's arms, kissing and swaying together.

The kissing eventually stopped and Rose moved her head to lay it against Liam's shoulder. Then, when she felt the roughness of the Aran wool against her cheek, the picture of the long sleeves and the strange little bulge came into her mind and she started to laugh again.

Liam held her at arm's length and looked at her with a bemused smile. "I hope my kissing you wasn't that funny?"

Rose looked into his eyes. "No . . . but the *geansaí* is a different matter!"

He held her close again, stroking her thick dark hair – and then a thought came into her mind.

"Liam . . . I'm not sure if we should be doing this . . . don't you have a girlfriend?"

"You mean the girl at the concert?"

Rose pulled away to look at him. "Yes. Are you still going out with her?"

He shook his head. "No, and I never really was. Helen is my boss's niece and she often helps out in the office. Fergal had tickets for the concert and he asked me if I'd make up the fourth place. I have to admit she had a bit of an eye for me but I put her straight. She knows I'm not interested." He hesitated. "The only girl I'm interested in – and have ever been interested in – is you, Rose." He put his hand under her chin now and tilted her face so that he could look in her eyes. "Is there a chance you could have changed your mind about me?"

Rose looked back at him. "Yes, there is."

His eyes lit up with hope. "Can we go out together soon? Whenever you like . . . we can take it easy, see how things go?"

Rose nodded. "As you say – we can see how it goes." Although she would have loved to have just stayed there in that small space, being kissed and held in his strong, muscular arms, she knew that there was a much more pressing situation in the house.

"Liam," she said now, "can I really trust you?"

He looked at her quizzically. "Rose . . . surely you know I wouldn't do anything to hurt you? I've waited all this time to have a chance with you – and I don't need to be told that I'm only second best. But I'm willing to wait and see if that might change."

"I didn't mean about *us*. I meant could I trust you not to say anything about a very delicate situation with

Hannah? She's come to the house because she's in serious trouble."

"Rose, anything like that goes without saying. I'm not going to go talking about Hannah or you to anyone. I never have – not even that business with Paul – I never said any more about it."

Rose bit her lip. "Oh, Liam . . . I wasn't fair to you then and you were so good. My father blamed you and it wasn't your fault. I should have faced up to him and explained it more, but . . ." She looked at him and she could see the painful memories of her rejection and the comparisons with Michael Murphy were still very raw for him. She stood up on her tip-toes now and kissed him full on the lips. "For your information, Liam O'Connor, you're *not* second best. Michael Murphy was only a daft, childhood dream. It wasn't real. I never knew him at all and I realised that months ago."

"Really?" he said, and there was definite hope in his voice.

"Really. At this moment in time – and as a grown-up woman – you're honestly my very first choice . . ."

For a moment she thought she saw a glint of a tear in his eyes but he moved to pull her close to him and she wasn't sure if she'd imagined it.

Rose went quickly on then to fill him in on Hannah's situation, and – just like the time when Paul had behaved foolishly – Liam just nodded his head and calmly weighed up the situation.

"I'll drive you both up to Dublin," he told her. "I don't like you being stuck with her on your own the way she sounds and I think it would be safer for you both to have a man around going into a strange place."

"Oh, Liam, you don't know what a great relief that would be!" She paused. "But there's one thing you'll have to do first . . ."

"What?" he asked.

"You're going to have to go up to Mrs O'Shea now and tell her how wonderful you think the *geansaí* is!"

Leaving Liam to deal with that, Rose went upstairs to call Hannah.

She found her cousin posing in front of the mirror, wearing Josie's black-coloured pencil skirt and Rose's favourite lilac blouse with Rose's good black patent stilettos. She had a wide black belt on which pulled the whole outfit together.

As Rose looked at her, she suddenly saw a desperate girl in front of her, who had been deserted by the father of her baby. A girl who felt she couldn't rely on her own mother or family to help her. A girl who had no one else to turn to except a cousin who didn't even like her.

How much worse could her situation be?

The exasperation that she always felt with her cousin seemed to seep away and Rose suddenly saw Hannah as a desperately sad and needy girl. She went over and put her arms around her. "Don't worry," she had told her. "Things will work out one way or another."

Chapter 57

When they reached Robert Ryan's house in Dundrum, Liam parked the green Morris Minor a bit further up the road and turned to Hannah.

"What do you want to do?" he asked.

Hannah took a deep breath. "I'm going to have to see his parents and find out if they've heard anything from him since yesterday." She bit her lip. "And I think I'm going to have to tell them about the baby, otherwise they won't understand. They'll think I'm just some sort of highly-strung, immature girl chasing him all over the place."

Rose thought that the way she had just described herself was exactly how Hannah was, and she wondered if her cousin had any notion of how she actually appeared.

Rose moved into the front seat beside Liam and they both watched as Hannah walked over, in Rose's good high heels, to the semi-detached house and knocked on the door. Then they saw the door open and Hannah take a dainty step inside.

They sat in the car for nearly half an hour, wondering

what was going on in the house. Every so often, Liam leaned over and gave Rose an encouraging kiss on the forehead or reassuringly squeezed her hand. At other times she found herself leaning her head on his shoulder, thinking that everything in the world suddenly seemed safer and more manageable by his side.

Eventually the door of the house opened and to their astonishment Hannah came walking out hand-in-hand with a tall, handsome man who was definitely a few years older than herself. They came across the road toward the car, Hannah smiling and chatting and looking much more like her old self.

Liam rolled the window down and casually leaned his elbow out as though it was a perfectly ordinary situation.

"This is Robert," Hannah said, beaming from ear to ear. "And this is my cousin Rose and a friend of hers from Clare."

Robert leaned in the car now and shook hands with both of them and Rose caught a whiff of whiskey off his breath as he greeted them.

"Sorry about all this mix-up," he said, rolling his eyes as though it was somehow funny, "but I had a bit of business to sort out the other side of Dublin . . . had to meet a few friends and I didn't know Hannah was looking for me."

"He was planning to go back to Galway today," Hannah cut in. "Weren't you?"

Robert nodded. "Anyway, everything is sorted now . . ."

Hannah gave a little giggle. "We're getting married next month! Robert's family know and it's all arranged.

He has a job to start up in Dublin after Easter and we're going to rent a place up here."

Rose immediately wondered about Hannah's course but thought it was best to say nothing at this point. "Well, congratulations!" she said instead. Privately, she was horrified at the quickness of everything, and the way that Hannah had changed from being in the depths of despair to the elated bride-to-be. And she wasn't too sure how happy Robert genuinely was. At the moment he just seemed like a man in a bit of a daze.

But, she thought, men were always mad about Hannah and maybe he might feel lucky being the one to actually catch her.

"And, not that I even need to ask you," Hannah said, leaning into the car to Rose, "but you'll be my chief bridesmaid, won't you? Robert's brother is going to be the best man." She gave a little squeal of excitement. "And my housemate Josie and her sister Nora will be the other bridesmaids, and Nora will be making all the dresses!" She squeezed Robert's arm. "I've got it all worked out – I've even picked out the pattern for the wedding dress I want!"

"Amn't I the lucky man?" Robert said, rolling his eyes again and smiling. But he pulled Hannah in close to him and kissed her affectionately on top of her curly head, and Rose suddenly thought that it just might work out after all.

Chapter 58

Leonora walked around the garden, still in her dressing-gown and pyjamas, with a cup of tea in her hand. Her blonde, bobbed hair had been given a brief brush and her face was devoid of anything but the moisturising cream she automatically put on after washing her face and brushing her teeth.

Her gaze moved across the newly cut lawn to the flower-beds and the roses climbing up the wall and then across to the tidy rows of vegetables. Then, her eye caught an old cream, chipped enamel bucket that Tommy Murray had been using to transport the vegetables in and her mind began to tick over. She could picture the bucket filled to the top with carrots and purple onions and maybe the leafy green tops of celery sticking out. Then she pictured it again overflowing with huge pink peony roses, and the thought of the contrast between the chipped enamel and the beautiful delicate flowers made her smile.

Terry would be thrilled.

Leonora now had the basis of her eleventh and twelfth paintings. She only had another thirteen to work out and she would have the twenty-five paintings that she needed for the joint art exhibition that the artist had planned for them both in September.

At the beginning Leonora had been terrified at the enormity of coming up with the ideas and then producing twenty-five paintings, but Terry had quietly encouraged her, telling her to make near copies of the paintings she had already sold and then work on variations on the same theme. And it had worked. The ideas were now coming thick and fast. So much so, Leonora felt she was almost becoming obsessed by it. She often woke in the morning thinking of ideas and she would find herself suddenly studying a very mundane object that would transform itself in her head into something quite different.

But, she told herself, thinking of all these wonderful artistic things kept her from dwelling on all the other things that had tortured her. And it was much better going to bed at night and falling asleep in bed with an art history book in her hand rather than an empty whiskey glass.

Of course she still thought of Edward and Christopher and worried about them, and she constantly found herself of the phone to Diana checking that the baby – Annabelle – was sleeping and feeding as well as she should be, and that Diana was getting enough rest. Although she knew that she certainly was this week, because not only did she have Kathleen Barry there on hand but this week and next she had the good company of Mrs O'Shea.

Leonora had dropped Lizzie and Rose off at the station in Dublin a few days ago, and James Tracey had picked them up in Galway. Already Diana had informed her that the housekeeper and Mrs Barry were now the greatest of friends and the elderly Scotswoman had even walked up to the small white-washed cottage and had spent an evening with the Barrys. Seemingly, she and Rose's father had got on very well together, both sympathetic and understanding of the other's recent bereavement.

And, Diana had confirmed, her mother had been perfectly correct about her suspicions of the growing friendship between Rose and Liam O'Connor. And Lizzie O'Shea had even managed to convince Stephen Barry that she had found Liam O'Connor a thoroughly decent character, and hopefully had sown the seeds for acceptance of him as a suitable boyfriend for his daughter.

The big surprise over the few days had been hearing about Hannah's impending marriage and the reason behind it, but Diana said she was sure that the pretty, ambitious Hannah might benefit from a bit of responsibility. She might learn – as the vet's wife herself had learned – that babies teach you how to give unreservedly instead of always taking.

All in all, Leonora thought as she walked back towards the kitchen, things had not worked out too badly. Things were busier in Glenmore House than they had ever been. With Rose there now and Terry Cassidy calling practically on a daily basis, the house seemed almost as busy as it had been when there was a whole family.

Once again, Terry had been right – in this case about the art studio. After a long discussion on the phone to Edward in America, she had prowled around all the rooms in the big rambling house until she eventually settled the large, light-filled room upstairs that had once been Andrew's office. A room she hardly ever went into.

Tommy Murray and Liam O'Connor had emptied it in less than a half an hour. In a matter of days the whole thing had been set up as a studio and Leonora now worked at whatever time of the day or night it suited her. And if she woke at three o'clock in the morning and couldn't get back to sleep, she reached for the paintbrush instead of a bottle.

Leonora was just walking in the kitchen door when she heard a voice calling from the side of the house. Tommy Murray, coming to the house early to do the fencing at the back, she thought. But when she turned back she recognised the unmistakable, silver head of Daniel Levy coming towards her. Leonora felt her face flush and her hand came up to pull her dressing-gown tightly across her chest.

"Daniel . . ." Her voice was slightly stiff and cool and her brow creased. "What brings you here at this hour of the morning?"

He looked directly at her. "Because, Leonora, I heard you were here on your own."

"And why would that matter to you?"

"Because," he said, "I wanted to speak to you about a very personal matter and I didn't want us interrupted."

Leonora took a deep breath and pulled herself up to her full height. "I don't think we have anything personal left to talk about – anything we haven't said before."

"Ah, but we have," He held his hand out, indicating that they should go inside.

"Would you like a cup of tea?" Leonora asked him.

"Not until later," he said.

Leonora pulled out a chair at the old pine table.

"Okay. Sit down and let's get it over . . . let's have the usual row."

Daniel sat down in the chair opposite her. "I don't want to row with you," he said, his voice slightly hurt. "And I didn't come to talk to you about us . . . I came to talk about Andrew."

Leonora's face stiffened.

"I think I have some information that might just make a difference to how you feel about him. Information that had been confidential but, now that Andrew is gone, I feel it's information that should be shared."

Leonora's heart began to flutter in anxiety. She tried to put on a brave face. "But why have you decided to give me this information now?"

Daniel had been expecting this question and had checked it was okay to tell Leonora. "Because I was speaking to your friend, Terry, and from the gist of the conversation I had with her – and from the conversations I had with Andrew – I know that you have some unresolved difficulties that I might be able you with."

Lenora's eyes widened in shock. "How dare you be so presumptuous!" she said in a voice that bordered on a shout. "And how dare Terry Cassidy betray my confidence and our friendship!" She stood up now, her fingertips resting on the table and her whole body shaking. "I want you to leave my house *now*, Daniel."

"Terry is a true friend and she told me because of her concern for you."

"I feel betrayed," Leonora said, "by my husband and now by my friend."

"Andrew loved you, Leonora," he said quietly. "He

629

never stopped loving you. The relationship that he had with his client was a misjudgement – an aberration on his part – but he never reciprocated her feelings. And he never slept with her."

Leonora froze. For hundreds of nights she had lain in bed imagining that very scene. Andrew and another woman naked together, making love together. Doing the thing that was so special to her and him.

Was it possible that he hadn't broken their trust in that one special area?

Was there a chance that the nightmares might be over?

She sat back down. "How do you know?" she whispered.

"Because he told me." Daniel leaned his elbows on the table. "He had no need to lie to me – he knew that every word he told me was confidential. And up until this very moment, it has remained confidential."

Leonora looked in his eyes. "What is the truth then?"

"I'm not going to delude you, Leonora. It was obviously a lapse and an error of judgement on Andrew's part that he became in any way involved with that woman – but it was not the serious betrayal that you thought it was."

"But she phoned Glenmore House," Leonora said, her voice now high again with emotion. "She phoned and she told me that she and Andrew were in love, and when I confronted him he admitted to me that he had become involved and had been going out with her. He admitted that he found her attractive ..." Leonora put her head in her hands now. "And of course he did – she was a very striking, elegant and younger woman."

"But she wasn't *you*, Leonora," Daniel told her softly, "and although Andrew was tempted, he did *not* have sexual relations with her. I know that for a fact. He told me that he had been foolish by being flattered by her attentions – and he had enjoyed a couple of dinners out with her – but that was it. That was as far as it went. On the last occasion that they met up, she had paid for meal to celebrate the fact that her sessions with Andrew had come to an end. It was the last time he would have seen her. When he discovered that she had booked a room for them in a hotel, he realised that he had got into very dangerous waters with her and immediately pulled back. But of course it was too late. She was humiliated and the next morning she phoned you and then lodged her complaint with the Medical Board. And, as you know, the complaint was not upheld. Andrew was thoroughly investigated and nothing untoward was found."

"But it was still a slur on his character. Still a slur on his professional reputation," she argued. "And worst of all – as far as *I* am concerned – a slur on our marriage. He ruined everything that we had held precious."

Daniel nodded his head now. "I know it must have been hard –"

"Been *hard*?" she repeated in a high incredulous voice. "That's an understatement if I ever heard one. It's the worst thing that has ever happened to me. He dropped a bomb on our marriage – on our family. How I ever kept that to myself without the children finding out I will never know. There are times when the effort nearly killed me. And all the while he went around with the injured look of a dog that had been kicked." She halted to catch her breath. "The stupid, stupid man . . . he must have known that by letting this woman too close to him he was leaving himself wide open to speculation – to accusations." Her voice was strained now. "And surely – and this is the unforgivable part – he must have known that by giving her attention – whatever kind of attention it was – he was betraying me?"

Daniel nodded. "He was devastated by the situation and he was devastated at his own stupidity. But that's all it was, Leonora. He loved you dearly – beyond measure. He sat in my office on several occasions and broke down in tears. The woman was absolutely nothing. He was just a man who felt flattered. A bit of middle-aged vanity. When you measure it against all those long and happy years of marriage, it was almost insignificant. If he had been in any other profession, no one could have commented on it. It would have merely been seen as a man enjoying a few hours' company in a restaurant with an attractive woman. A man who went happily home to his beautiful, intelligent wife and children and never gave the situation a thought."

"But why didn't he *tell* me nothing had happened between them?" wailed Lenora.

"Did he try?" asked Daniel quietly.

"Yes, of course he did but . . ." Leonora fell silent. Yes, he had told her. But she hadn't believed him.

Daniel stood up. "I'm going to leave you now, Leonora. Because I think you need time on your own to think all this over." He halted. "But I would ask you one thing – please don't take your feelings out on Terry Cassidy. She is a genuine, decent woman who thinks most highly of you and was only concerned for you."

Lenora looked up at him with tear-filled eyes. "I don't know how to react to any of this . . ."

"Take your time and ring me if there's anything I can do to help." Then he said, "You are a very special woman, Leonora. Andrew was lucky to have you and he knew that. He loved you to the very end."

* * *

It took Leonora two long days and nights to digest and make sense of everything that Daniel Levy had told her. Gradually, all the defences and the walls she had built up against her husband began to crumble and dissolve. Finally, she was left with the realisation that Andrew had paid a very high price for his small foolish mistake. The vanity that had made him feel flattered had cost him all the happiness he could have had for the remainder of his days.

Perhaps if she had tried to understand and tried to forgive him, things would have been different. Perhaps if she had enough trust in him to believe him when he said he had not slept with the other woman . . . perhaps then he wouldn't have had his heart attack.

And that thought had overwhelmed Leonora to the extent that she cried for three solid hours.

But at the end of it all, she had had to come to terms with the fact that Andrew had brought it all on himself. If he had kept his mind on his work at all times and his heart solely on his wife and family, none of it would have happened.

It was hard not to blame herself but she knew that it would not help things one iota now.

And as the days went past, she began to see that it was beginning to feel better – a whole lot better.

She still felt guilt and regret for her part in it all but she could now grieve for Andrew as the loving and decent husband she had believed him to be for all those years

The ice was beginning to melt.

She could almost feel her heart opening up again.

Chapter 59

Hannah was quietly married in Tullamore Church on a sunny Friday morning in May, when – her mother hoped – most people would be busy working and not take any notice.

A month or so before, Robert Ryan had accompanied Hannah down to the family farmhouse in Offaly and had asked for her hand in marriage. Hannah had been quietly confident with her handsome husband-to-be by her side and had given them a good account of all his professional qualifications.

After her parents had got over the shock and disappointment of her pregnancy, her mother had begun to feel a sense of relief at the knowledge that someone else would now be responsible for her highly-strung daughter. The fact Robert Ryan was a college lecturer had also helped to soften the blow and, in the longer term, would be something to brag about locally. Hannah had also surprised the family by doing very well at college and only a few weeks after the wedding she would be finished her course. Sheila Martin was further relieved when she heard that Hannah and Robert planned to move to Dublin – far enough away so that she and the baby wouldn't be annoying them in Tullamore too often.

Any reservations that Robert had about being responsible for a wife and child were eased when Bill Martin presented the couple with a substantial amount of money to go towards their new home. Things suddenly seemed a lot more manageable to him – he had a new job to start in Dublin and a bride who everyone said looked the spitting image of Marilyn Monroe.

Robert Ryan began to think that he hadn't done too badly after all.

There was a small crowd at the wedding, just close family on both sides and Hannah's two good friends, Josie and Nora. Rose was her bridesmaid as Hannah had planned but her mother had quickly disabused her daughter of the idea of a big wedding. There would be no other bridesmaids and no fancy white wedding dress. Sheila Martin said it was hypocritical and would only draw attention and criticism on themselves.

Instead, the bride's mother had taken Rose and Hannah for a day up to Dublin, to do the only thing mother and daughter had ever enjoyed together – shopping. Hannah had picked a cream lace dress and a matching jacket edged with a touch of blue, and Sheila and Hannah had picked a plainer blue dress and jacket for Rose which co-ordinated with the bride but would not overshadow her.

At first Hannah had been disappointed not to have the white wedding she had always imagined – the gorgeous dress and veil – and all the attention that would accompany it.

But she had the husband she wanted – the clever, handsome Robert – and soon she would have their beautiful baby.

And she knew that there would always be occasions for her to shine later.

Since she was bridesmaid, Rose was invited to bring a partner. She thought it over carefully and then asked Mrs Bentley if she could have the Easter week off to visit her parents. Leonora had agreed.

Rose found Mrs Bentley had changed over the last month or so. She seemed somehow lighter in herself, almost younger. One afternoon recently, Rose had actually caught her singing along with the radio as she sat in front of her easel painting a picture for her new granddaughter's bedroom.

"Don't say I told you," Mrs O'Shea had whispered to Rose, "but I think it might be to do with Daniel Levy. I heard her on the phone and they're going off out to some posh 'do' together next week." The Scotswoman had put her hands together as though praying. "You never know where it could lead to."

Leonora Bentley hadn't been the only one who seemed to have changed.

Rose had been nervous about seeking her father's permission to ask Liam O'Connor to the wedding. He might not be so easily approved. He wouldn't be Michael Murphy.

"You know I've always had reservations about that O'Connor lad," Stephen Barry said, "and it would have to be him that you're asking me about . . ." He thought for a few moments and then he looked over at his wife. "But I suppose everybody can make mistakes . . ."

"Indeed we can," Kathleen said quietly, "and we can all learn from them – whatever age we are." She looked directly at Rose now and gave her an encouraging smile.

"I have to admit that your granny spoke very highly of that lad," Stephen said now, "and so did Mrs O'Shea – and she's had plenty dealings with him in Dublin. And I'd say Mrs O'Shea's not a woman who would be easily fooled." He shook his head. "Neither her nor your granny."

Rose's heart had lifted. It was still much too early to see where things might lead with her and Liam. But it was going in the right direction.

* * *

As she stood on the steps of the church now, self-consciously posing for a wedding photograph with the bride and groom and the best man, Rose thought how much things had changed in the last year. Some good and some bad.

The biggest things had been losing her granny and then leaving Clare.

Both things had previously been unimaginable but now she realised they were part and parcel of life.

Then, as the cameras clicked and flashed, she caught sight of Liam standing to the side, chatting to Paul and her father. He turned his head to look at her and their eyes met. He winked encouragingly at her and smiled, and Rose felt a warm glow.

Unlike Hannah, she wasn't comfortable standing in the spotlight and Liam instinctively understood that.

As he somehow seemed to understand many things about her.

In the last few weeks she had spent all her days off with him, seeing the sights in Dublin, and they had spent evenings at the pictures, eating out or having a drink together in the nicer city pubs.

They had talked and talked – as they always did so very easily together. They had talked about coming home for a weekend together to Kilnagree where they could go for walks down by the shore and visit each other's families. They had even talked about going to Mass together on the Sunday, so that people would know that they were officially a couple.

And Rose had told Liam that whatever happened in the future – however far they travelled – she would always want to come back home to her family and her friends.

She would always come back to Kilnagree
She would always come back to Clare.

The End

In Conversation with

GERALDINE O'NEILL

Has writing always been an important part of your life?

Yes. As far back as I can remember I have always loved both reading and writing. When I was a young girl reading *Bunty* magazine, I was so impatient for the next edition that I used to write my own 'follow-up' episodes to the stories, imagining what would happen next.

I won a couple of small prizes for writing stories at primary school which encouraged me. At secondary school, I loved writing essays and short stories or book reviews.

I learned to type at school which has come in very handy, as I now type my books straight into the computer.

Tell us about your writing process. Where do you write? When? Are you a planner or a "ride-the-wave" writer?

I tend to do a mixture of both. When I start the book the main characters are already formed in my head and I usually have the opening scene planned. I also have a general idea of where the story will go and how it will end.

Then I start writing. As I go along new characters emerge, and I find both they and the main characters do and say things I don't expect – which can take the story off in a completely different direction to what I envisaged!

I usually find myself going along with these unplanned adventures as they often make the most memorable scenes in the book. It is the difference between consciously planned writing and the unconscious creative mind taking over.

I find the mixture of these approaches produces the best work for me.

Since your first novel Tara Flynn was published in 2002, how has your life changed?

In some ways my life has changed a lot – in other ways it hasn't changed at all.

The main changes are in time-scheduling as I now have to make time for my writing commitments and (try to!) meet deadlines etc. Before I was published, I just wrote when I felt like it.

My spare time is now more writing-orientated. I have given courses on writing in Ireland, UK and abroad and I'm often asked to speak to groups, give readings of my work at library events etc. I also have more contact with my agent, publishers and other writers.

My personal life hasn't really changed. My family has always been my main priority, and I see all my old friends as regularly as I did before I was published. I still teach in the local primary school although I recently took a two-year career break to write full-time.

I am lucky to have two careers that I love, and I find they compliment each other.

A lot of your other books are also set in rural Ireland in the 1950's/1960's, the Tara trilogy, A Different Kind of Dream and Aisling Gayle. The Grace Girls was set in 50's Scotland. Why is this period so appealing to you, do you think?

I think it appeals to me because it's a period that had a very strong visual element. I loved researching the clothes, the hair-dos, the music, transport etc. *The Grace Girls* gave me great scope with two sisters close in age, getting dressed and made up to go out to parties or on dates. I also discovered information about the infamous 'lacquer-bug' which gave great cause for concern amongst the ladies who kept their hair piled up and well-sprayed from week to week!

I think women enjoyed being feminine without feeling too pressurised and made weekend rituals of curling their hair, pressing their clothes, checking if their shoes needed to be heeled etc. They weren't expected to appear with a new outfit every week with the latest bags and shoes.

I feel many of today's women must be exhausted keeping up with regular waxing, fake tans, hair extensions, eyelash extensions, facials, false nails etc.

I've had treatments done for special occasions, and know how time-consuming not to mention expensive it must be to do it every weekend.

Do you have a favourite character in Leaving Clare?

I enjoyed writing about my main character, Rose Barry – a lovely, family-oriented, fairly naïve girl – who was typical of her time.

I also enjoyed writing about Hannah, whose behaviour was more outrageous than most girls in the 50's and I never quite knew what she was going to do next. Some characters tend to take on a life of their own and Hannah was definitely one of them!

I also enjoyed writing about the attractive, mature Leonora as her character has a lot of depth and life-experience. It was great to be able to show how people can change their attitude and direction in life at any age. It also gave me a different angle to explore a more privileged character's attitudes to class, family, close relationships, religion and sexuality. I also loved writing about her gardening and art work as they are both hobbies I have an interest in.

Going to the local dance is an important part of Leaving Clare. The setting of the Ballroom of Romance era is very atmospheric in the novel – why so, do you think?

The Ballroom of Romance era has always fascinated me, and I've enjoyed writing dance-hall scenes in many of my books. There's a great feeling of fun and glamour about the time – but there's a lot of innocence as well.

I've spoken to numerous women from Ireland, Scotland and England who talk glowingly about their dance-hall days. It was a place where they could enjoy themselves on the dance floor, and there was always the chance they might meet their future husband.

Incidentally, both my parents and my husband's parents met in 50's dance halls

I was too young for The Ballroom of Romance era, but I loved the discos of the early 70's where boys asked girls to dance, and there was always a race to pick partners for the 'slow dances' which were reminiscent of a waltz. Apparently that sort of dancing is no longer in fashion with teenagers and, if that's the case, I think young girls today are definitely missing out!

What character & scene was most difficult to write?

I think the intimate scenes between Hannah and her love interests (suffice to say there were a few –

I don't want to spoil the story for readers!). I find these sorts of scenes always take longer as I need to choose my words very carefully. I don't want to offend my readers by using language which will shock or make them feel uncomfortable.

Equally, I don't want to avoid describing love scenes to the extent that readers don't actually know if anything has happened! I avoid obvious clichés or repeating the same safe scenes over again. I try to come to each of these scenes with a fresh eye and realistic language that reflects the two people involved.

Living in the Midlands of Ireland, do you think this has influenced your writing?

I think all the places I have lived and visited have definitely influenced my writing. It's much easier to visualise and describe places you know well. Familiarity with a place – the scenery, the towns and villages and the mixture of people in it – give a much more authentic feel to writing.

The main setting in *Leaving Clare* is naturally County Clare, with other chapters set in Tullamore in County Offaly and the Lucan area of Dublin.

The *Tara Flynn* books and *A Different Kind of Dream* are all set around the Offaly area where my mother's family are from and where my husband and I have lived since 1991. *The Grace Girls* is set in Lanarkshire, Scotland, where I grew up.

Who are your favourite authors and favourite novels and why?

All time favourites would be *The Prince of Tides* by Pat Conroy, John Mortimer's *Rumpole of the Bailey*, and anything by Alan Bennett.

I like these writers because they have a real eye for detail and personal idiosyncrasies. They know what makes people tick, and they also make you laugh.

I also enjoy books by Anita Shreve, Joanna Trollope, and I loved *The Bridges of Madison County*. I also enjoyed Irish author John Boyne's *The Boy in the Striped Pyjamas*.

I read a huge variety of books by different authors, as I'm in a book circle with twelve other members. We take turns at picking a book and then everyone reads it and we meet up every month to discuss it over wine and food – it's interesting and very sociable. It also opens your mind to books you wouldn't normally read. In most cases I've enjoyed something about the book. Occasionally I've read books and abandoned them halfway if they are not to my taste – as others have done with mine. Literature is like music or art – everyone is entitled to their opinion. Life is too short to plough through a book you don't enjoy!

Tell us a bit about your next book?

I'm currently working on two books. One is set between rural Ireland and Newcastle-upon-Tyne (where I went to college!) in the 50's and 60's.

The story opens as Lucy Wilde is putting the final stitches in her wedding dress when jealousy and betrayal strike. In the aftermath, she finds herself on a journey to begin a whole new life in a big, bustling city. Along the way she meets people who help her discover strengths and talents she didn't know she possessed. She uses these talents to build a different, very successful life to replace the dreams she left behind in Ireland. As Lucy's business career moves onwards and upwards, she steadfastly refuses to trust in love again. But when fate brings unexpected wealth and new social standing in Newcastle's business world, she discovers it's very hard to avoid male attention.

The other book is a complete departure from my usual books as it is a hard-hitting, contemporary, 'woman in jeopardy' type of book about a reclusive author now living in New York. As the story unfolds, the layers are peeled back in her life to reveal a dark tragedy which overshadows all the relationships in her new life.

I'm enjoying writing both books, although I'll be focussing on my 50's book for the next few months as it is due in for summer.

If you enjoyed *Leaving Clare*, don't miss out on
Tara's Destiny,
also published by Poolbeg.

Here is a sneak preview of Chapter one . . .

TARA'S DESTINY

Geraldine O'Neill

Chapter 1

BALLYGRACE, OCTOBER 1965

Tara opened the bedroom curtains of the big bay window. After looking at the grey October sky for a few moments, she let her gaze wander down into the garden of Ballygrace House. Everything was still and calm this morning, but the evidence of the previous weekend's storm was obvious.

She had spoken to her father on the phone several times before she and William, her young brother-in-law, had set off from Stockport for the boat journey to Ireland yesterday morning. William was on half-term from school in London, and Tara was taking a long overdue week off from running her small hotel.

'The worst of the weather is over now,' her father had informed her in the last call, 'so ye should have a reasonable journey across. Now, don't be drivin' too fast through Wales, and take it easy on those oul' winding roads down from Dublin. They're not like the English roads; they can be greasy and treacherous at this time of

652

the year. And make sure you have your spare tyre well pumped up.'

Tara had raised her eyes to the heavens and listened patiently to her father's advice about cars and driving and roads – which Shay Flynn actually knew nothing about. But she listened because she knew he meant well, that he was trying to advise her in the way that Gabriel, her husband, would have done. But Gabriel had been dead for over three years now, and although she still missed him every single day, Tara had learned to look out for herself when it came to practical matters.

'Don't worry, I'll be careful,' she had said.

She looked down now at the bigger fallen branches that Shay had dragged into a damp pile, where they were waiting until they had dried sufficiently to be sawed into manageable logs. Then, they would be carried in a wheelbarrow into one of the outbuildings to dry out completely, and used later for fuel on the house fires.

Her gaze moved further back to the fence which bordered the garden, and the field behind where two lively children's ponies had once run. One for Gabriel and one for his sister, Madeleine.

But that was a long time ago. The field was now let to a neighbouring farmer for grazing sheep. As far as Tara could see, the once-sturdy fence had been damaged by the high winds in at least two places. The elderly farmer had obviously done a patch-up job on the fence with branches and bits of wood, but it would have to be done properly.

Tara would have to organise somebody to do the work, and she would have to do it *today*, otherwise her father would be doing it himself. If it hadn't been for the constant rain over the last few days, he would have been out to start on the job already.

No matter how many times Tara told him to get a local handyman in to do any extra work – or to give him a hand – Shay always ended up doing the job by himself or with Mick, his brother. But the fact was, they were getting too old for heavy work. Both men were now in their sixties, and while Tara's uncle Mick was prepared to listen to his wife, Kitty, about what he was still capable of doing – or not – her father certainly wasn't. Tara's stepmother, Tessie, could warn him until she was blue in the face, but it made no difference.

Tara stared out of the window for a few minutes, a thoughtful look on her face, then she walked back across the bedroom to put her warm velvet dressing-gown over her pyjamas, and went downstairs.

As she laid the kitchen table for breakfast, Tara heard a noise from upstairs. She smiled. It was a sure sign that William Fitzgerald was growing up, when she was awake and moving before him in the mornings.

When he was younger – on their trips over to Ireland or when William came to Stockport – he would have been waiting for her and Gabriel in the kitchen or dining-room. But he was now exhibiting all the traits of a normal, growing teenager – eating more and sleeping longer.

The first thing Tara had done when she came downstairs was switch on the radio, then rake out the range and get it fired up again. Ella Keating, the local woman who helped out in Ballygrace House, had set the fires in the other rooms, ready to be lit, and she had left bacon, sausages and black-

and-white pudding in the fridge. Ella had also offered to come and cook the breakfast, but Tara had told her not to rush up early every morning. It was good for her and William to do things for themselves. She heated up a griddle pan and started cooking.

In truth, although she was grateful for help around the big, old rambling house, Tara was happy to have some time there on her own. She often sat in the cosy kitchen, remembering the days and nights she and Gabriel had spent in the house during their short marriage, and her mind would wander further back, to when she came to Ballygrace House as a young girl and Madeleine Fitzgerald's best friend.

The sausages, bacon and pudding were soon cooked, and she put them in a dish to keep warm in the oven.

'Something smells good,' William said, coming into the warm kitchen. He ran his hand over a clump of dark hair that was sticking up at the back of his head.

As Tara turned to look at him, she was suddenly startled to noticed he was wearing Gabriel's old blue tartan dressing-gown. Why she should have been surprised she didn't really know, because she had loaned it to William the last time he was here and it must have remained hanging in the spare room wardrobe.

Flustered, she went back to the slices of soda bread that were now frying in the pan alongside two eggs. 'There's tea in the pot,' she told him, 'or orange juice in the white jug.'

'Great,' William said, reaching first for a small glass and then to the centre of the round table for the jug of juice. After pouring his drink, he lifted the white paper napkin that was at his place and spread it over his lap. 'These are useful things, Tara,' he said, running his hands across the square of stiff tissue. 'I suppose you can just throw them away after using them. My mother still has the old-fashioned kind that have to go to the laundry every week to be washed and starched.'

Tara turned the eggs in the pan, then glanced over her shoulder at him. 'We have lots of linen napkins, too,' she told him, 'but it's easier to use the disposable ones when there's only the two of us here.' She gave a little shrug. 'It's the same as us eating in the kitchen; it's easier than waiting for the fire in the dining-room to warm the place up and then having to carry all the food through.'

'I think it's nicer eating in here,' William told her. 'It's more cosy and relaxed. We always eat in the dining-room at home – breakfast, lunch and dinner.' He looked around the kitchen now. 'Being here feels like being on holiday.'

'I'm glad you enjoy it,' Tara said, smiling warmly at him. 'I love coming back to Ballygrace House, too, and it's lovely having company.' She stopped. 'But you're lucky that you have such a nice stepfather. Harry is very good at going to rugby and cricket matches with you, and taking you and your mother out for drives or up to the West End for the theatre and that kind of thing.' She checked that the eggs and bread were fully cooked, then moved the frying pan to the edge of the range, away from the strongest heat.

'Oh, Harry is very good to me,' William quickly agreed. He took a drink of his orange juice. 'It's just that everything is more relaxing here in Ireland . . . I don't have to think about schoolwork or anything like that.'

Tara was glad now that she had offered to bring the boy with her. It killed two birds with one stone, giving her the chance to check on Ballygrace House and see William at the same time. The only drawback was the time of year, with the late October mornings and evenings becoming darker and longer. It was not the best time to have a holiday. But, Tara wryly told herself, beggars can't be choosers. She had to take the time off from the hotel when it was convenient for the business and not for her own personal life. She knew when she bought the Cale Green Hotel in Stockport that she would have to commit all her time to it for the first few years.

'I can't promise anything very exciting this week,' Tara said now, as she lifted the dish from the oven, and began dividing the sausages, bacon and black-and-white pudding between two plates. 'I've got to do a few jobs around the house, and have to organize work to be done outside before the winter sets in.'

'I was looking out of the upstairs hall window earlier, and I noticed that the fence at the back of the garden is broken.' William started to laugh. 'Could you imagine what would happen if all the sheep escaped from the field?'

Tara felt a sudden stab of annoyance. It was the sort of thing she dreaded might actually happen.

'They would demolish the whole garden!' William went on, with a childish gleefulness. He shook his head. 'I can just picture Shay running about and swearing his head off as he tried to herd them back into the field.'

'I'm afraid I don't find that very funny, William,' Tara said, a touch snappily. 'It just adds to the list of things I need to have done around the house.' Then, seeing the chastened look on the boy's face, she softened her tone. 'With the hotel and everything, I feel as if I'm neglecting Ballygrace House. I'll have to try to get as much done as I can this week. Next year I'll try to spend a bit more time here.'

'Maybe I could help you with some jobs?' William ventured. 'Last time I helped Shay mend the door of the turf-shed.'

Tara slid the eggs and fried bread on to the plates. 'That's kind of you, William, but there's been quite a bit of storm damage around the house. I'm going to have get proper workmen in.'

William raised his eyebrows and smiled. 'Shay won't like that.'

'I don't think it's fair to leave all the work to him,' she said, trying not to sound irritated again, 'and I'm going to have a chat with him about it later today.'

Jim Reeves was singing 'I Love You Because' on the radio, and Tara hummed along to it as she brought the hot plates to the table. 'Do you like this song?' she said, trying to move to a more lighthearted subject.

'Not really, but my mother does,' William said. 'Harry bought the record for her last birthday. Do you like it?'

Tara put a plate down in front of William and one at her own place. 'I suppose I do,' she said, 'I've never really thought about it.'

William lifted his knife and fork and started to cut up a sausage. 'What's your favourite group?' he chattered. 'I think I like Herman's Hermits and the Beatles the best.'

He suddenly laughed. 'I suppose you like the Bachelors because they're Irish?'

Tara's shook her head and laughed, too. 'To be honest,' she told him, 'I haven't got a clue about music at the moment. I'm a bit out of date compared to a teenager like you. Sometimes I hear a song and I like it, but I don't know who sings it, and then I get the groups all mixed up.' She reached for the teapot and poured herself a cup, then poured William one, too.

'Don't you listen to the radio?' he asked incredulously. 'Or watch *Top of the Pops* on television?' He popped a piece of sausage into his mouth, then pierced the yolk of his egg with his fork.

'I'm so busy at work that I never have the radio on, and when I'm at home I'm usually in the dining-room catching up on the hotel accounts, or occasionally reading or playing the piano.' She gave a little sigh. 'I never really get the chance to watch television, either. I don't think I've ever seen *Top of the Pops*, although I have heard about it.'

'You are very out of date, Tara,' William told her with a grin. 'You'll have to get more with it or you're going to be left behind with all the oldies like my mother and Harry – or even Shay!' He was giggling now, so much so that he almost choked on his mouthful of food, and tears started streaming down his cheeks.

'I didn't think I was *that* funny,' Tara said, rolling her eyes and laughing with him in spite of herself. 'I suppose I'm going to have to get *you* to bring me up to date. The next time you're in Stockport or I'm down in London, we'll sit down together and watch this *Top of the Pops*.'

William nodded, wiping his damp eyes with his napkin. 'Have you ever thought of getting a television here, Tara?' he asked now.

She shook her head. 'There would be no point,' she said. 'I wouldn't have the time to watch it. Sure, I hardly have the time to read the newspaper when I'm here.'

'Shay was delighted when he got it in last year, wasn't he?' William said. 'He said it was about time everyone in Ireland came out of the Dark Ages and got the telly.' He took a bite of soda bread and chewed it thoughtfully. 'I remember him saying that Ballygrace was in a better spot for the BBC than Tullamore, and that you should get a television here as you'd get a great reception.'

Tara shook her head. 'If I paid heed to every suggestion that my father made,' she told him now, 'I'd be running around like a headless chicken.'

Another song came on the radio and William said, 'Now, Tara, that group is called the Kinks and the song is called "You Really Got Me"'.

'OK,' Tara said. 'Let's stop chattering now and get on with eating our breakfast while we're listening to it.' She lifted her teacup and took a sip from it, glad of the excuse to have a few minutes' peace from her young brother-in-law's entertaining – but constant – chatter.

Later, as they were clearing the table, William suddenly stopped in his tracks, pointed at the huge kitchen dresser and yelled, 'A mouse! A mouse has just run under the cupboard!'

Tara closed her eyes and took a deep breath. She'd have to go out today and buy new mousetraps and poison, otherwise Ballygrace House would soon be completely over-run. She wasn't one of those women who screamed and ran at the sight of a mouse – it was part and parcel of living in the country.

But it was another thing to feel guilty about. She knew she was neglecting the beautiful old house that she loved. And it was one more thing to add to her ever-growing list.

•—◆—•

If you enjoyed this chapter from

Tara's Destiny by Geraldine O'Neill

why not order the full book online
@ www.poolbeg.com
and enjoy a 10% discount on all
Poolbeg books

See page 662 for details.

•—◆—•

POOLBEG WISHES TO

THANK YOU

for buying a Poolbeg book.
As a loyal customer we will give you
10% OFF (and free postage*)
on any book bought on our website
www.poolbeg.com

Select the book(s) you wish to buy
and click to checkout.

Then click on the 'Add a Coupon' button
(located under 'Checkout') and enter
this coupon code

 USMWR15173

(Not valid with any other offer!)

WHY NOT JOIN OUR MAILING LIST
@ www.poolbeg.com and get some
fantastic offers on Poolbeg books

*See website for details